Caught Sleeping

The Senator's Wife Series Book II

JEN LYON

Caught Sleeping: Book Two of The Senator's Wife Series

First Print Edition

Copyright © 2023 Jen Lyon

ISBN: 979-8-9877320-3-8 (paperback)

Published by Doss About Publishing

Edited by Jesseca Wegener

Cover design by Chelsea Keene

To the women of the USWNT,
Thank you for your continued courage and commitment in
the fight for equality.
LFG!

caught sleeping: idiom
1. The state of being unprepared for something that happens, and perhaps losing an advantage as a result

Chapter One

"Tell me, how long did you think you'd get away with it, sleeping with my wife?"

Carlton Cleveland leaned back in the excessively padded executive chair, his smug smile framed by the thickness of his jowls. His drawl reeked of smoke and sarcasm, the disdain in his gaze abrasive against Alex's skin.

"I'm—I'm sorry?" Alex heard the quiver in her voice, the feeling of the room floating around her.

"You're sorry?" The man plopped heavy elbows on the smooth surface of the varnished oak desktop, his eyes darkening as his tone shifted toward anger. "You're sorry, you don't understand the question? Or you're sorry for sleeping with her?"

Alex opened and closed her mouth, but no sound came out.

"Which is it, Miss Grey?"

"Senator Cleveland, I—"

"That's President *Cleveland, you little twit!" He slammed his hands against the oak. "And I have irrefutable evidence you've been fucking my wife!"*

Alex woke with a start, the pounding of the senator's fleshy palms against the flat of his desk still ringing in her head.

Senator. It was still *Senator* Cleveland. He wasn't president. Alex wasn't standing in the Oval Office. And the bullying southern politician wasn't accusing her of sleeping with his wife.

Though, she *was* sleeping with his wife. But that was beside the point.

Drawing a steadying breath, she let it out slowly, trying to exhale the uneasy feeling of the dream. It was early morning, a faint glow of light casting the shadows around her into nebulous form.

Alex sat up, forcing the remainder of her grogginess aside, and took a mental note of her surroundings.

December. San Francisco. Catharine's bed.

With thousands of miles travelled and the dozens of hotel room ceilings she'd woken to over the course of the last eight months, it always took a second to remember where she was, and what challenges her day would bring.

In the case of this morning, the only sensation greeting her was relief. She'd flown into San Francisco on a red-eye from New York City, where she'd had a layover during her journey home from Madrid. There'd been a series of friendlies against Germany, England, and Spain, and the States had come out with two wins and a draw. A solid way to close the year for the US Women's National Team.

Now, in late December, her offseason could begin. Which would consist of three weeks, instead of the three months she was accustomed to in the years prior to having begun her international career. A price she'd be willing to pay tenfold over, time and again.

In a whirlwind of eleven short months, Alex had made an appearance in every international match since the SheBelieves Cup the previous February. She'd netted four goals by the time the CONCACAF W Championship started in late summer—the tournament that served as the World Cup Qualifier for the following year—and earned her first start in the third group stage match against Mexico, in which she'd come one crossbar shy of scoring a hat-trick. By the time the winter European tour rolled around, she'd found herself a consistent fixture on every Starting XI, and closed the season with seventeen caps and eleven international goals. Stats she'd once only dreamed of. A year she'd never imagined possible.

And, if nothing went wrong—if she stayed fit, healthy, kept her head about her—she was par for the course to make the twenty-three woman roster heading to the World Cup in England in seven months. Isabelle Atwood—the senior squad manager—had told her as much on the flight home.

"I'd wager to say, in your current form, you're climbing toward the pinnacle year in your career. I'm glad I took a chance on you, Grey." It was the most rewarding thing Izzy Atwood had ever said to her. The closest thing to a compliment on her successes she would probably ever garner from the impenetrable ice queen. Enough to make Alex grin like an idiot when she settled into her seat beside Erin Halsey for the remainder of the flight across the Atlantic.

"You look like you just joined the mile high club," the goalkeeper had razzed her, her thick brows knit in mock skepticism. "Kind of gross, since the only other person I saw heading to the toilets was Monica."

"You don't think she's my type?" Alex had returned, before sticking her tongue out at her friend, unwilling to allow thoughts of Monica Ashby to ruin her high. The rivalry between them had become almost legendary, heightened by the mid-season trade that had brought the Bluebells defender to the roster of Sirens FC. And, as if the forced proximity of playing with her on both club and country hadn't been hellish enough, things had been made significantly more awkward by the unexpected, somewhat creepy fact that Monica arrived in Oakland somehow dating Caleb Anderson.

But those thoughts had been here nor there on the remainder of her flights back to San Francisco. Even Monica Ashby wasn't enough to ruin her soaring exuberance at Atwood's compliment or the burgeoning euphoria that always reared its head with the knowledge she would soon see Catharine.

Rubbing the heels of her palms against her eyes, Alex blinked at the rising sun glistening through the wall of glass facing the waterfront. The bed was empty beside her, the duvet drawn over the plush Egyptian cotton, the pillow without a single wrinkle, as if no one had slept there at all.

She tried to swallow her disappointment. She'd known Catharine had to work early. Alex hadn't been expected to fly in until late morning. But when the red-eye had come available and Alex had ducked into the cab after landing at SFO at oh-dark-thirty, she'd made a last minute decision to tell the driver to take her to the Marina District, instead of crossing the Bay Bridge to her Oakland apartment. She hadn't seen Catharine in over two months—what felt like an eternity, given the tender duration of their relationship.

Reminiscent on the flight from JFK, she'd recounted exactly how many times they'd seen one another since the SheBelieves Cup at the beginning of the year.

Six. Six brief, bittersweet, stolen moments. Never longer than two nights in a row. Never without the plague of indiscretion that trailed behind them.

Never without the threat of Carlton looming and the shadow of HEG ebbing over Alex's shoulder. But now they would have three weeks together—Christmas, New Year's, Alex's twenty-eighth birthday. Three weeks in which neither of them had to step on a plane or leave the city—off to another state, another country, another match, another political rally.

Catharine still had to work—she would not have been Catharine without her business calls and legal briefings, her midnight teleconferences and sunrise meetings at the top of Bridgeview Tower. Yet somehow, whenever they were together, she still managed to make Alex feel like she was the only thing that mattered—that the rest of life was irrelevant—the multimillion dollar business transactions, her husband's presidential campaign, the high stakes world she lived in. She made the minutes, the hours, the short days they spent together seem real, tangible, something to hold onto. It gave Alex hope during the long absences apart. Alleviated the doubts that inevitably slipped into her mind. Dimmed the uncertainties of their future together.

As if her thoughts had manifesting qualities, Catharine appeared in the threshold to the suite, one paper to-go cup and one porcelain mug in hand.

Surprised, Alex sat up against the headboard, drawing her knees to her chin. "I thought you'd left already."

"Without saying goodbye?" Dressed in a sharply tailored three-button blazer and pencil skirt, Alex watched Catharine cross the room, wondering how she could manage to look so stunning before seven in the morning. It was one of those enigmatic superpowers only a woman like Catharine Cleveland could possess. By contrast, Alex was sure she looked like a zombie that had crossed eight time zones in eleven days, had turf rash covering both elbows and the left side of her jaw, bags under her eyes that rivaled Jack Skellington, and tussled bedhead that divulged the embarrassing reality that, despite arriving at the waterfront townhouse unannounced at two in the morning, disturbing Catharine from her own coveted sleep, she'd hardly made it through dropping her bag in the hall and pulling off her tennis shoes before collapsing onto the bed, dead to the world. Not the long-absent reunion she'd planned when deciding to forgo her own apartment.

"Did you sleep well?" she continued in Alex's silence, pressing the steaming porcelain mug into Alex's hand and taking a seat on the edge of the bed.

There were times Alex still felt shy in her presence. Awed by the awakening reality that this woman was really hers. By the liberties it granted her. The intimacies it afforded.

"I'm sorry I woke you last night."

"Are you daft?" Catharine admonished with a smile. "I loved waking beside you this morning. I always hope you'll choose to come here, whenever there is an option. I'm only sorry I allowed Nicole to schedule a seven a.m. meeting. If I'd known you'd be in early, I would have postponed." She reached a hand to brush back a loose strand of hair that fell across Alex's face, her fingers lingering against her cheek. "I was hoping we could get dinner this evening? Before your party?"

Her party. Alex had forgotten. Tonight was the Christmas party for Sirens FC, organized by their coach, Rodney Collins, and hosted by HEG. It was going to be held in downtown San Francisco at *Town Hall*, one of the swanky restaurants a few blocks from the waterfront. Not far from Catharine's office in Bridgeview Tower.

"Where were you thinking?" Alex cursed herself internally for the question. As if her answer hung in the balance of what restaurant Catharine chose. As if she wouldn't have dined with her at the back deli with the C rating inside the fish market if that's where she wanted to go.

"*House of Salt*?"

The answer surprised Alex. *House of Salt* was one of the restaurants Catharine frequented for business, within throwing distance of Bridgeview Tower. A place everyone would know Catharine, offering no anonymity or discretion. It had become an unspoken rule between them, the clandestine nature of their relationship. Paramount to the success of Catharine's pending divorce from Carlton and Alex's continued endorsement with HEG. Though, lately, Alex had convinced herself she'd be okay with ending the latter. The endorsement income was significant and had been life changing the previous year. Her relationship with HEG had opened the door for her transfer to the Sirens, caught the attention of the National Team, and, without doubt, been the spark that lit the flame to rekindle her stagnant career. But now, it was just money. And if a cut to her bank account was all she suffered in order to live an open life with Catharine, she would have given it up without a second thought.

But there was more to it than HEG. More than just Alex.

With Carlton's presidential campaign well underway, the primaries getting ready to kick off in a matter of months, it had become more important than ever for her and Catharine to keep their relationship private. Under wraps. If Catharine broke her agreement to stand beside her husband throughout the duration of the election—if she was the cause of any sort of upset in his campaign—all hell would break loose over the negotiation of their separation. And, as far as campaign upsets went, Alex didn't imagine there would be a much greater upset than the breaking news revealing one of the GOP's presidential candidates' wives was having an affair. With a woman.

The disaster it would cause for Catharine—for her company—for her life —was on a leviathan scale. A scale Alex didn't want to be the one to tip.

So *House of Salt* was unexpected. Not only because of Catharine's frequent patronage of the restaurant, but because there had been reason to believe Carlton had been having Catharine followed at times. Suspecting something.

Alex worried the suggestion of the restaurant was an extension of an olive branch. That Catharine had sensed her downheartedness over the last couple months at the hurdles of their complicated affair. They didn't dwell on the challenges—they had such little time together it seemed senseless to waste conversation on obstacles that could not presently be changed—but Alex knew Catharine could read her like an open book. And wanted to make her happy.

How ironic it was to find herself on the flip side of the relationship she'd shared with Caleb. With him, he had always been the one dissatisfied, wanting more. And now, Alex found the tables turned, where she was the one who craved more from Catharine. More than what they had.

But she didn't want Catharine to feel that pressure. To make decisions at odds with her careful nature in order to try and please Alex. No matter how much she wanted a place in Catharine's world. At her side. To have her join her as her plus-one at the Christmas party. To have her come to her games. To simply live a life together where it didn't matter what restaurant they chose.

"I told Amelia I'd go with her to that autograph signing at Soccer Pro in Berkley." She offered her an easy way out.

Catharine seemed undeterred. "Isn't that over early afternoon?"

"I—yes, I guess it probably is."

"Come with me to dinner, Alex." She shifted on the edge of the bed, drawing one of her stockinged legs up underneath her, her fingers trailing across Alex's shin. "I want to spend time with you before Nathalie arrives. Just the two of us."

Alex had also forgotten about Nathalie. She was flying in tomorrow to spend a few days—or weeks, depending on her schedule. Her show had closed over the fall and she'd been auditioning nonstop through the winter months. Another time, Alex would have been glad to see her. She'd come to like her. They texted off and on. Nathalie had even come to one of her games in New Jersey and they'd had lunch once during a long layover Alex spent in NYC. But for these three weeks that she was home, she wanted Catharine to herself. As selfish as that made her.

But as much as her thoughts wanted to dwell on Nathalie and the impending likeliness of finding herself a third wheel, she quickly found it impossible to think of anything other than the fingers that had abandoned her shin, journeying past her knee, along the long bone of her thigh.

"Are you trying to seduce me into saying yes?" she teased, though the words came out with a quiver, belying her attempted indifference to the touch.

Catharine's smile was sly, the gaze she cast at Alex taking full advantage of the length of her long lashes and the cerulean blue of her eyes. "If that's what it takes to get you to say yes."

Not that it was ever far from her mind, but Alex had temporarily forgotten the hold Catharine could command over her with the simplest of touches, the most mundane of words. She sat motionless, transfixed as Catharine leaned forward, her lips suspended a breath from her own, the fingers that had been at her thigh skirting to the hem of the t-shirt she'd fallen asleep in—the one she'd been wearing since boarding a plane in Madrid. Not really the sexiest of attire.

"Well?" inquired Catharine, her palms cool against the skin at the small of Alex's back, her smile flickering at the hitched breath she was forced to take.

"You know I never tell you no." The whisper was all Alex could manage, feeling Catharine's lips graze hers, the words spoken into her mouth. But as she reached for Catharine's face, to slide a hand to the back of her neck, to draw her in, Catharine sat upright, extracting herself from Alex's grasp.

"I can't be late." The refusal would have been upsetting if the words hadn't been laced with Catharine's own disappointment, her eyes holding Alex's with an apologetic smile.

"No." Alex shook her head, still trying to find her breath. "We wouldn't want to keep the export chairman of China waiting, would we?"

It came out harsher than Alex intended and Catharine winced, rueful. "The Russian Ministry of Commerce, I'm afraid." She started to stand, then sat again, looking back at Alex. "I'll make it up to you."

Alex realized she'd hurt her feelings, stung her with her sarcasm. "It's fine, really—"

"It's not. You flew fifty-eight hundred miles to get here and I can't even stay long enough to have a cup of tea. When we haven't even seen each other in sixty-seven days."

Despite Catharine's seriousness, Alex couldn't help but smile, trying to decide between teasing that it wasn't tea she wanted, or marveling at the fact that she knew exactly how many days it was since they'd last been together.

She decided on neither, and went with coy instead. "Well, you've convinced me to dinner, Mrs. Cleveland. I guess we should see where it leads from there."

"Be careful what you ask for, Miss Grey. I can be very persuasive." She reached forward, touching a finger to Alex's lips, and for a fleeting second Alex could see it cross her mind to stay, to forgo her responsibilities, her sense of accountability and obligation. And simply knowing she held that power, that capability to change her mind, to stay her, to keep her here, washed the disappointment of the morning away. Gave Alex a sense of comfort. Of contentment.

"I'm counting on it." Alex caught the finger against her lips and gave the palm a kiss, before swinging her legs over the side of the bed and rising to her feet. She picked up the to-go cup that had been set on the nightstand and held it out to Catharine. "Don't keep the Russians waiting. You don't want to singlehandedly be responsible for starting World War III."

"Wouldn't Carlton love that," Catharine muttered, accepting the cup while leaning in to offer Alex a chaste kiss on her mouth. "Six o'clock?"

"Yes. Six." Alex returned, but the mention of Carlton had flashed Alex back to the discomfort of her dream, the threat in the senator's voice. She'd forgotten about it until now.

Mistaking her grimace, Catharine reached to squeeze her hand. "I don't deserve you. I don't know why you put up with me."

Because I love you was the answer, but Alex didn't dare to say it. Not here. Not like this. It seemed too heavy a thing to lay on her. Too much for the morning. Instead she just gave a nonchalant shrug with an arch of her brow. "Tonight you'll have to remind me."

Chapter Two

The elongated shadow of Bridgeview Tower cast a noir atmosphere across the entrance to *House of Salt*, the handsome century-old brick building nestled in stark contrast to the towering high-rises sprouting up around it.

Catharine loved the ornateness of the building, reminiscent of the old bootlegging warehouses during the Prohibition, with its exposed beam ceiling and open floor plan, the original wood plank flooring magnificently refurbished to its original shine. It was the character of the structure that had drawn her to the building in the first place. The history within its walls.

The gatekeeper—a brawny, jovial Samoan named Hemi who had been with the restaurant since its opening day—greeted Catharine with a wink from his twinkling eyes as he threw open the glass doors and called over his shoulder, "Mrs. Cleveland," before gallantly stepping aside to hold the door for her and Alex.

"Merry Christmas, Mrs. Cleveland," he smiled, broad dimples displaying in the center of his rotund cheeks. "Would you prefer your usual table or drinks at the bar?"

"Table, thank you, Hemi."

"Today's special is, of course, the Hammersley Oysters paired with shrimp and pork agnolotti. Though on this blustery night, perhaps the British Baldy Ribeye might be a more suitable selection." He recited the drink pairings he felt would go well with each dish as he lead them to Catharine's habitual table centered in one of the floor-to-ceiling windows overlooking Mission Street.

"Auchentoshan single-malt scotch—neat—for me, Hemi," Catharine cut off his chatter as he pulled out her chair, knowing well the amicable host had a love of his own voice and would continue to no end if given the opportunity. At least it meant he'd paid no attention to Alex, who'd developed a hint of reticence since they'd stepped through the door. She'd asked again if they should go somewhere further from Catharine's office, less known, less conspicuous, but Catharine had waved her off. She hated the restrictions she'd been forced to place on their relationship. The rules. The furtiveness. The duplicity. She wanted to alleviate some of the tension that had surfaced. Reassure Alex it wouldn't be this way forever.

"There's an excellent Aquadeco," she suggested to Alex before Hemi could begin to serenade her with the wine list. "Or a house brewed kombucha—"

"A gin and water, please," Alex said to the host, drawing a subtle arch of Catharine's eyebrows. When Hemi had at last departed, Alex gave a dismissive shrug. "It's offseason. Besides, I'm going to need something stronger than mineral water to get me through this party."

"I'll count myself lucky you didn't say you needed it to get through dinner," Catharine teased, nudging the toe of her high heel against Alex's ankle under the cover of the table.

Alex's lips turned in the subtlety of a playful smile, her eyes catching Catharine's, some of the rigidity leaving her shoulders. "I'll suffer through somehow."

Deciding on an appetizer of oysters and opting to split the sea bass, they fell into silence as the hordes of last minute Christmas shoppers weaved past the street front window, shoulders hunched against the wind sweeping up from the bay. It was the first meal they'd had together outside of a hotel restaurant and it felt as liberating as it was perilous—out to dinner, like any other couple.

Only, it wasn't like any other couple, and they both knew it. No matter the pretense.

At length, Catharine settled back in her chair and picked up her tumbler, pausing with the glass a few inches from her lips. "I was thinking—after Christmas—maybe we could take a trip down the coast for a few days? Perhaps to Southern California?" She regarded Alex over the rim of her scotch, trying to gauge the guarded reaction.

"Would that be prudent?"

Catharine hated the sensibility of the question. That Alex would even have to ask it. She pressed her lips together, feeling the permanent souvenir of the scar along the inside of her lip that Carlton had left her the night of the gala. The reminder of why the question was sagacious, even if she didn't want to admit it.

She'd meant it, this morning, when she'd wondered aloud why Alex continued to put up with her. Eleven months they'd been covertly building this fragile relationship that hung between them—nearly a year—and in all that time Catharine had been able to give her almost nothing.

She tried to remind herself the secrecy wasn't only for herself. That it was necessary for Alex, too. Neither of their professional lives could handle a public acknowledgement of their partnership in the current climate. But she'd also begun to realize Alex would have been willing to risk her relationship with HEG if it meant they could live their life together out in the open. But Alex was young and held an innocence to the understanding of how harsh the world could be, and how easily a life could be turned upside down by the court of public opinion.

It wasn't that she felt Alex wouldn't be able to handle it—she was tougher and braver than Catharine had ever been, or probably ever would be —but she didn't want her to have to. Not now. Not with Carlton and his campaign. Not with the rising tide of her blossoming National Team career. The World Cup. The publicity and fame that would follow. She didn't want to see her hurt. But at the same time, she knew Alex needed more from her —more than what they had. And admittedly, the feeling was mutual. Catharine wanted more than stolen nights in clandestine hotels. More than texts and late night conversations. There had to be a balance. An in between.

But was it prudent, as Alex asked? Probably not. But she couldn't find it in herself to care. She wanted Alex. Time with her. Away from everything. Everyone.

She shrugged, ignoring the question. "We could stop in Monterey. Morro Bay. Santa Barbara. Spend New Year's in San Diego."

"You would have time for that?" Alex couldn't hide the smile in her voice, the optimism of the idea. Just as quickly, the smile faded. "What about Nathalie?"

"What about her?" Catharine raised a single eyebrow. "She loves the coast. She'll enjoy the trip, no doubt." She tried to maintain her look of nonchalance, of disregard, but as Alex's face fell she immediately regretted her jest and shook her head, reaching beneath the table to touch Alex's knee. "*Alex.* I'm only teasing. Nat's a big girl. She'll be more than happy to entertain herself in the city. Jules is in town. I want you all to myself—for whatever few days we can afford."

Alex's relief was palpable, her eyes brightening with her smile, but the look was lost as quickly as it had come and Alex's body went rigid as her gaze darted beyond Catharine, the anxious quiver of a breath catching in her throat.

Reflexively, Catharine withdrew her hand, sitting up straighter as a voice —familiar, yet unplaceable in the blink of time it took for Catharine to turn and identify the speaker—descended over their table.

"Well, popular place tonight."

The voice she may not have known in the instant, but the face was no stranger. Smug, handsome, imperious, Caleb Anderson looked down at them from his towering height, a perplexed smile tugging at the corner of his lips.

"Can't say I expected to see you here, A." His eyes drifted to Catharine, analyzing her behind his pale gray gaze, before flicking back to Alex. "Last I knew you didn't care for haute cuisine."

A girl stood beside him, an inch or two taller than Alex, with a sporting physique and athletic posture Catharine had come to recognize went hand-in-hand with the athletes in Alex's field. Unlike Alex, however, her face was caked beneath layers of makeup and the provocativeness of her mini skirt left little to the imagination when it came to displaying what assets she had.

"Hello, Mr. Anderson," Catharine intervened when it became clear Alex was lost for a reply. "A pleasure, as always."

"Likewise, Mrs. Cleveland. What a surprise. We appear to have a knack for running into one another in the most unlikely of places. And with Miss Grey, of all people. I had not realized you two remained in contact."

"What are you doing here, Caleb?" There was an accusatory tone Alex left unchecked as she finally found her voice, her hazel eyes narrowed with suspicion.

"Treating the lovely Miss Ashby to dinner." His entire demeanor exuded a wisenheimer air Catharine found obnoxiously well-suited to the arrogant young braggart. With languid calculation, he draped an arm around the waist of his date, who was glaring at Alex with ill-concealed contempt. "Monica is blessed with an impeccably educated palette and I've assured her this restaurant serves the finest tête de veau in the city."

Catharine suspected the hostile twit at his side couldn't begin to comprehend what tête de veau was, let alone enjoy it.

A beat of silence resumed as Alex said nothing, leaving Catharine to maintain the conversation.

"I must concur, there is no finer French cuisine in the city. Perhaps none better this side of the Atlantic, if one were to trust Jay Rayner of the *Observer*." She kept her tone even, her smile polite. The ostentation in the boy's cavalier manner and lofty tone was galling, but she was loathe to allow him to see her annoyance. He knew exactly what game he was playing, but Catharine knew it better. She had married the master of insolence. This cheeky boy had nothing on Carlton.

"It's so peculiar we should run into you here, Mrs. Cleveland," Caleb went on without any attempt to conceal his smirk. "It was just the day before yesterday that I happened upon an editorial piece about you in *The Guardian*. And suddenly here you are."

"And here I am." Catharine's tone flattened, awaiting his next move. *The Guardian* was one of Britain's more liberal papers. The editorials had not taken a kindly view toward Carlton and his campaign, which meant, in turn, *she* would be thrown out for fodder by the publication—Carlton's collateral damage. Never mind all the good they had written about her over the years... her fundraisers, her charitable contributions, her work in the humanities. She had been reduced to nothing more than the armpiece of the knob running for the US presidency.

"It was a fascinating essay, really. Titled *The Senator's Wife*. Have you read it?"

Catharine could feel her pulse quicken and had to mindfully still her fingers from drumming the edge of the table. Wherever he was going with this, she did not like it. It was not an article she'd been made aware of— Nicole must have missed it—but based on the pomposity of his smile, there was no doubt it was less than flattering.

Raising her scotch to her lips, she shrugged through a nonchalance she did not feel. "I don't make a habit of reading opinion pieces, Mr. Anderson. If I care for fiction, I'll turn to Atwood or Angelou."

"Understandable, Mrs. Cleveland. No doubt with your husband entering the primaries it is hard to find time for anything outside of his campaign." He paused, tilting his head in such a manner that his slyness only heightened, accentuating his despicability to an entirely new level, if that was even possible. "No matter what the editorial suggested."

He waited, dangling the bait, jiggling the lure, but Catharine refused to bite. She would not give him the satisfaction.

Undaunted, he continued. "It seems the author felt reason to believe the devout Mrs. Cleveland was perhaps estranged from her esteemed husband, hypothesizing an escalated sense of turmoil on the horizon of the fabled Cleveland Kingdom." The pale slate of his eyes flickered beneath the string of accent lights, watching her with all the intentness of a bird of prey waiting on its quarry.

Maintaining her impassivity, Catharine gave him nothing, hoping he could not read beneath her cool exterior to see where his well-aimed arrows had found their mark. Whatever he thought he knew—whatever *The Guardian* suggested—it was all just speculation. She had to remind herself of that.

"Deceptive thing, editorials. Giving voice to those who believe they hold compelling insight on subjects they know nothing about." She set down her scotch with a steady hand, holding his gaze without wavering. He was only grasping at straws. Whatever implications hummed behind his innuendoes were nothing more than blind supposition. Gambling without a trump card, hoping for her to reveal her hand. A foolish boy at a foolish game.

"As you said, Mrs. Cleveland," he allowed, his close-lipped smirk reappearing, "nothing more than an opinion piece. An entertaining work of fiction."

"C'est la vie, Mr. Anderson. I have been plagued with media my entire life—it simply comes with the territory. My father always said 'there is what is written, there is what is wrought, and there is what is right.' And it is up to us to decide what to believe."

"A wise man," Caleb conceded with affected politeness.

Beside him the bottle blonde shifted restlessly, lost by the conversation. Her gaze had swayed from shooting daggers at Alex—who'd remained silent through the exchange—to covertly attempting to size up Catharine beneath the length of her glue on lashes.

"I'm sorry," Catharine turned her attention toward the girl, taking the opportunity to redirect the dialogue, "you didn't introduce your friend. I'm Catharine." She held out a hand, which was met with only the limpest of handshakes, the dark eyes averting to the fleur-de-lis centerpiece in the middle of the table.

"Monica," she muttered, her former animosity transitioning to insecurity under the scrutiny of Catharine's gaze. "I play soccer with Alex."

"Oh, come on, babe," Caleb laughed, settling his arm over her shoulders, "don't be so humble. Monica was one of the most noteworthy trades over the offseason. With her stats, her lustrous international career, the Sirens were lucky to have been able to afford her."

"I'm sure that was quite a financial strain for Mr. Hargrove," Catharine subdued an eye-roll, before at once regretting her pettiness, grateful neither the girl nor Caleb appeared to comprehend her jab. Regardless her growing dislike of Monica, and outright disdain for Caleb, it was unnecessary to ridicule the appallingly low salaries allotted women in professional sports. But there was something about Caleb Anderson that rubbed Catharine the wrong way—always had. Beyond his blatant disregard for Alex. The embarrassment he'd caused her. The hurt he'd left behind.

As Caleb droned on about Monica's accolades, Catharine flashed a glance across the table and caught Alex's eye. There'd been no mention Caleb was dating one of her teammates. It had been months since his name had come up at all. She couldn't help but wonder if it hurt Alex, to see him with someone new. Someone with whom she clearly shared a history of animosity.

But there was no hurt in the hazel eyes. Only a hint of apprehension; the fear they'd been found out, intermixed with an uncommon glint of hostility Catharine hadn't seen in her before. Whatever it was between her and Monica reached beyond the simple annoyance of the girl dating her ex.

Tuning back into Caleb's soliloquy of Monica's 'invaluable contributions' to the Sirens defensive line, Catharine cut him short, finished with his interruption and clear attempt to get beneath Alex's skin. "Well, I imagine you must be heading to the same Christmas party Miss Grey was just telling me about. No doubt you'll want to get on with your dinner." She tapped the table with finality, a blatant signal to send them on their way.

The boy did not take the hint.

"We are," he drawled in that same low, drawn out Southern twang Carlton resorted to while plodding along on his high horse, "but only for a brief appearance. Miss Ashby and I are celebrating our six month anniversary and I have a surprise evening planned for us." He squeezed her shoulders, his arm hung over her like property, and took a lengthy glance at Alex. She may have been over him, but it was obvious the sentiment wasn't mutual.

"Just think, Monica," Alex broke her silence, returning Caleb's stare with no hesitation, "maybe you, too, can be the involuntary star of your own viral video."

Feathers ruffling like a goaded guinea hen, Monica parted her heavily glossed lips to snarl a reply, but Caleb beat her to it, simpering behind a flash of injury. "Oh, come, A! Surely we're past that by now. Let bygones be bygones and all that, right?"

Alex gave no reply.

"Enjoy your dinner, Mr. Anderson." Catharine motioned in the direction of Hemi, who'd paused several feet away throughout the exchange, waiting to lead the couple to their table. "You wouldn't want to miss your reservation."

"Oh, we will," Caleb assured her, the snideness in his tone elevating, "but there's no rush. A good friend of mine, Mr. Bontemps, owns the place. The reservations are fully booked months in advance, but he was kind enough to get me in last minute. He's a big fan of Miss Ashby, you see." Again, the smirking smile touched what otherwise would have been his handsome face, and he paused to take a sweeping glance around. "You can't beat the menu or the ambiance."

"Indeed, you can't," Catharine acquiesced, raising her scotch to her lips to hide her own smile. The boy was finally departing, and she knew it was best to let him go, but the sheer imperiousness of his demeanor got the better of her, and she couldn't help herself when he'd at last turned to follow Hemi.

"And *manages* the place, I think you mean," she called out as if it were an afterthought, staying his steps.

"I'm sorry?" He raised one of his blonde eyebrows in query.

"Mr. Bontemps. He *manages* the restaurant. *I* own it. Well, it and the building it resides in. So I'm always delighted to hear when it meets a patron's expectations." Catharine lifted a hand to call Hemi, who at once rushed to her side.

"Please upgrade Mr. Anderson to window seating," she smiled politely at Caleb, "it is his six month anniversary, after all."

When they had gone, Catharine collected herself with a slow breath, before exhaling and looking at Alex, who remained quiet, staring out the window.

"Not, perhaps, the romantic dinner I had planned," she laughed, trying to make light of the encounter. She didn't care about the boy—or his arrogant exchange—he'd proven himself too self-absorbed to put two and two together about her and Alex. It was the mention of the article that unsettled her. That it had run to print without her being tipped off. *The Guardian* had never been her enemy in the past.

Carlton's staff didn't follow the UK media as closely as the stateside papers, but they'd stumble across it eventually. She would need to address it before that happened. To know what was in it and if there was anything damning or just typical tabloid-selling nonsense. She'd meant what she said to Caleb—she didn't make a habit of reading editorials about herself or her company. People would write what they would write and there was little one could do about it.

But in this case she needed to know the content. Carlton would lose his mind if it was something that would paint his perfect family name in an unattractive light.

"I'm sorry. I had no idea—"

"Don't be ridiculous, Alex. Of course you didn't. It's no matter. He's a pompous arse, nothing more."

"Do you think—?"

"No. He is far too conceited to see past his own ego. Put it from your mind. The only thing I'm sorry about is that you have to go and suffer more of that this evening."

Alex didn't laugh. "I'm used to it. He's been flaunting Monica for months."

"Does it bother you?"

At that Alex's eyebrows shot up, fine lines appearing at the corners of her eyes. "*Him*? With Monica? God, far from it. They deserve each other. I'm just relieved he has someone else to obsess over." She paused, then smiled. "Do you really own this building? Or were you just messing with him?"

"I own it."

Alex shook her head, amused. "Of course you do."

"What does that mean?" It wasn't the response she'd expected.

"I just shouldn't be surprised. You hadn't mentioned it. It just—sometimes it makes me realize how many things I really don't know about you."

"Well," Catharine tilted her head, her voice low and gaze unblinking, regarding Alex with a knowing smile, "stick around a while. You can learn anything you want to know about me. I think you'll find I'm a lot more predictable than you seem to think."

"Is that so?" The green flecks in Alex's eyes glittered in the flickering flame of the candle tucked amongst the centerpiece of lilies. "Tell me something, then. Something I don't know."

Catharine thought a moment. "I have only two steadfast rules for investing."

"Ah," said Alex, her disappointment at the answer evident, assuming Catharine had missed the coyness of her exchange. "And what would those be?"

"One," Catharine freed a foot from its high heel, bringing her stockinged toe up along the inside of Alex's calf, eliciting an unsteady intake of breath across the table, "I only invest in things I enjoy. Things that bring me happiness." She maintained a straight face, drawing her foot up higher, along the inside of Alex's thigh, beneath the hem of her cocktail dress. "And two, my investments must hold promise of a future. They must be something I believe in."

"Why do I get the feeling we're no longer talking about real estate?" Alex had attempted Catharine's same nonchalance, but fallen short, her hand slipping beneath the tablecloth to intercept Catharine's foot, a smile dancing at the corners of her lips as she held the ankle captive.

"Oh, are we not?" Catharine teased, and Alex shook her head, amused.

"I don't know how you do it."

"Hmm?" Catharine waited for her to continue.

"Just—take everything in stride the way you do. Never let things get to you. Remind me in one moment you're this... this... formidable, titanic force—unreachable, one would think—and in the next moment all you have me thinking about is how soon I can get home with you, find myself alone with you."

"I like that word, coming from you."

The mischievousness of Alex's smile spread, her thumb moving to Catharine's ankle. "Which word?" she trailed her fingers along the smoothness of the stocking, continuing up her calf. "*Alone?*"

"That one goes without saying, but no: *home.*" It was exactly what Alex's presence in her life had given her. A breath of life to something less than lived.

The flush already present on Alex's cheeks deepened, her eyes averting to the table, but then she surprised Catharine by looking back up, maintaining the fledgling confidence she'd begun to show. "Let me get this party over with—and then, I believe you made me a promise this morning… one I intend to hold you to." She smiled, reluctantly releasing her leg from her hold, and sat back in her chair. "Home. Alone."

Chapter Three

"You can't continue to ignore me, A."

Alex recoiled at the familiar moniker as Caleb leaned over her shoulder, seizing the opportunity to corner her while she had stepped into the hall leading from the patio to the main bar. She'd kept herself tucked safely between Amelia and Halsey since arriving at the party, aware Caleb would be unwilling to approach her with the Australian at her side. There was no room for doubt as to Amelia's distaste of him, ever since their altercation at her birthday the previous year. For the little good sense Caleb possessed, trying not to piss off Amelia Walker appeared to have actually fallen on his radar.

But Alex's phone had buzzed twice with an unknown number—no message left—and when a third attempt was made she'd finally abandoned the patio table to find a quieter place to answer the call.

Pointlessly, it had turned out, as a high-pitched screech of a teenage voice had squealed "she answered!!" when Alex said hello. Another case of her phone number being leaked on Tumblr—the third time in seven months. Something she expected had to do with Monica Ashby, yet was unable to prove.

Annoyed, she'd shoved her phone back in her purse, distracted by thoughts of having to stop at Verizon in the middle of the holiday week leading up to Christmas, and not noticed Caleb approach.

"Go back to your date, Caleb." She didn't bother to look up, instead occupying herself with fishing out an unnecessary tube of chapstick from the bottom of her purse. Anything to keep from giving him the indication she was open to a conversation.

"I'm worried about you," he tried again, leaning so close she could feel the heat radiating off his body—smell his habitual woody cologne, a scent that made her stomach turn. She hated the proximity of him. The intimacy of his nicknames and sense of familiarity.

His breath, sour with bourbon, was damp against her cheek. "You've been keeping some strange company lately. You know folks are bound to talk."

The chapstick slipped from her fingers, clattering against the brightly polished concrete floor, as her pulse slammed a chaotic rhythm at the base of her throat. She didn't bend to pick it up.

Catharine had been wrong. He had suspected something.

"Fortunately you don't have to worry about the company I am keeping any longer," she snapped, grateful for the anger that hid the quiver of her tone. "Now get out of my way."

He unfolded a strong arm across the threshold, barring her exit. Alex could feel sweat prick at her temples. He, of all people, was not who she wanted sleuthing around.

"What is it you want, Caleb? Who I associate with has nothing to do with you. She's a friend and we met for dinner. Now leave me alone."

The derisiveness of his laugh slipped beneath her skin, pricking at her every nerve.

"You think I'm talking about the senator's wife? Who cares about that jet-setting bitch and her la-di-da attitude? You know who I'm talking about. And it looks bad!"

Alex finally looked up at him, trying to decipher if he was playing games. The fact that he dismissed the mention of Catharine so easily threw her off guard, and now—despite wanting nothing more than to get away from him—she was intrigued about where the conversation was going.

"I have no clue what you're talking about."

"Oh come on, A. Nescience isn't your style."

"That's a big word for you, Caleb." All her pent up animosity over the past year was boiling over. The things he'd put her through. The embarrassment. The way he'd used her. "Say what you have to say or get out of my way."

"You know who I'm talking about," he repeated, glancing over his shoulder to make certain they were alone. "Your Aussie pal."

"*Walker*?" Alex was incredulous, unable to curb her laugh. Her friendship with Amelia was the least of her concerns. "You don't like that I hang out with Walker? As in—our team captain? The reigning MVP of the league? One of the greatest midfielders to ever play the game? *That* Aussie? Wow," she shook her head, bewildered, "you're really stretching it this time. That's bold, even for you."

"I'm not talking about her talent as a player, A. How good she is on the field doesn't matter. Anyone with half a brain can see that she's—she's—"

A slow dawning realization washed over Alex like the raising of a veil. She finally understood what he was saying. Where he was going with his tirade. Her eyes widened, her mouth twisting into an angry, disbelieving smile. "She's…?" She wanted to hear him say it. To force his bigotry out loud.

"Jesus, Alex! She's a queer! A dyke! And none too subtle about it! If you aren't careful—"

"Half the women in this game are gay, Caleb. Pull your head out of your ass and look around!" She turned away, suddenly worried she'd said too much. That he might take it as a confession—an admission of her own. She bent to swipe up her dropped chapstick, stuffing it in her purse, not daring to look at him for fear he'd see something he should not. "This conversation is over."

He continued to block the hall. "HEG's not happy with her. I have it from a reliable source—"

"A reliable source?" Alex knew she should duck under his arm, walk away, engage with him no further, but she couldn't bring herself to do it. To let him say his piece and get away with it, unscathed. "Who? Your invidious snot of a girlfriend? Oh please. Monica only wishes she were half the player Amelia Walker was in grade school—"

"A *reliable source*, Alex! There's talk her contract won't be extended another year, no matter what kind of results she puts out on the field! They already plan to drop her from *Kickstar*. She's too—you know! Not the representation they want for the brand…"

"Monica's spewing garbage in your ear, Caleb, and making you look like a fool. HEG knew exactly what they were getting with Amelia Walker and she's never made any pretenses to appear otherwise." She had to look away, stinging herself with her own words. Amelia wasn't a coward. Not like she was. Cashing checks based off an image built entirely on a lie. If *Kickstar* was going to drop anyone's endorsement, it should be hers. "You need to just worry about you, okay? I can take care of myself."

"Walker, Halsey, Sawyer. They all have one thing in common, A—you don't want it to reflect poorly on you—"

"No, *you* don't want it to reflect poorly on me—"

"Because I care about you, Alex! Listen to me! We worked—*you* worked," he corrected himself, somewhat contrite, "too hard to throw it all away."

"I don't even know what to say to that."

Because there was so much to say to it. She wanted to tell him to fuck off. It was none of his business who she hung out with. Who she loved. Who her friends loved. What lifestyle they led. She wanted to tell him Amelia and Halsey and Sawyer were the best things that ever happened to her—because of them, she felt normal, far from the freak her aunt and uncle would have had her believe she was, if they ever knew... Even if she wasn't ready to live out in the open, even if the only person she'd actually come out to was Sawyer, it was still her friends who carried her through. Even if they didn't know it.

But she would say none of that to him. Not now. Not ever. He didn't deserve her confidence. He didn't deserve her truth. Instead, she shook her head and forced herself to look him in the eye. "Sawyer and Halsey have been my friends for years. You never had a problem with them before."

"It's different with Walker. You can't be that oblivious to it."

"And you can't be stupid enough to think I care what you have to say."

"Jesus!" Caleb slapped his palm against the wall. "Maybe you can throw everything we had together away in the blink of an eye, but I'll always care about you, and be looking out for you. I'm just saying—watch the company you keep. You're not invincible, A. No matter how much you think you are."

Alex ducked under his arm—she had to get away from him before she said something she truly regretted—but then stopped at the end of the hall. "You know, Caleb—I'd rather have friends like them—in my corner, supporting me, lifting me up—than..." Her voice faltered. There was so much she wanted to say. So many bitter, pent-up feelings she'd suppressed. But as angry as she was, she wasn't cruel.

"Than *what*, Alex?" He prodded, unwilling to let it go. "You'd rather hang out with your horde of carpet munchers than *what?*"

Her mouth opened and snapped shut again. A whirl of insults flew to her tongue, but none of them suited how she felt. The hurt, the outrage, the fact that he could still break her heart, even now. After all that had passed.

She stared at him, trying to see the boy she'd once loved. The boy who'd spent countless hours each week, year after year, on uneven, dew laden fields, tending goal as she perfected her shots, playing 1v1 as she strengthened her style. The boy who'd had words of encouragement every time she fell short of her goals and high fives of victory when things came together. The boy who had never missed a game. Who drove her to and from practice until she got her driver's license, who waited in the rain, the heat, through the early morning trainings and late moonlit runs. The boy she would have done anything for. The best friend she ever had.

But whoever that boy had been was gone. He no longer existed.

"Every one of them has my best interest at heart. All those years I thought you were in it for us—and I could never see the only person you were looking out for was you. *Your* dreams. *Your* goals. No one else's." She held the slate of his gray stare, unfazed by the hurt that shot across his face, followed quickly by anger. "I let you control me. Suck the joy out of what I loved most. Force me to do things I never wanted. Not anymore, Caleb. You'll find plenty of girls that are okay with that. But it won't be me."

Calmly, she turned on her heel and shouldered through the door, welcoming the blast of warmth from the overhead heaters and miserable refrain of *Funky, Funky Christmas* by New Kids on the Block, made only worse by a handful of her drunken teammates shouting the lyrics from the bar. She refused to give Caleb a single moment more of her attention. To listen to any more of his excuses.

Or to think too much about what he'd said…

She fielded her way back to the table where Amelia was sitting with Halsey and her plus one at the furthest corner of the patio.

Were people really talking about who she hung out with? Did people really think she and Amelia… She forced her attention to the table. Caleb had just been blowing smoke. Trying to get under her skin.

"I'm heading out!" she yelled over the droning bass of the boyband carol. "I've had all the celebrating I can handle for one night."

"What? Already!" Halsey's freckled cheeks, pale from the Northern California winter, were flushed with alcohol, her six foot frame unfolded in a mess of lazy angles. Beside her, her date, a platinum-haired midfielder from Stanford, snuck a glance at Alex beneath the brim of her 49ers hat, before quickly averting her attention to the label of her beer. "Starstruck," Amelia had teased Alex the first time they'd met the girl after the Sirens/ Warriors championship match a couple months earlier. "Erin better watch out—she's no *Alex Grey*." Alex had rolled her eyes at the time, but now she thought Amelia may not have been too far off the mark.

Still lounging in her chair, Halsey draped an arm around the blonde and motioned toward Amelia who was fishing lime seeds out of her vodka tonic with the tail of a prawn. "Don't leave us to the mercy of this one! I don't think I can stand listening to her gripe about not being able to surf on Christmas morning for another moment longer."

Amelia pitched the vodka-soaked shrimp tail at Halsey, almost landing it in her mouth. "Belt up, will you? We'd have to hire a horse and sleigh to go caroling in whatever backwoods sticks you come from."

Halsey flashed her the bird and Amelia flicked her thumb off her top teeth before the pair of toddlers turned their attention back to Alex.

"You just barely got here," Halsey complained, sliding a sweating beer bottle in Alex's direction. "Sit. Have a drink. Big brother's not watching you tonight. Hell, half the HEG reps are sloshed inside the bar."

Amelia arched one of her full brows, a smug smile on her face. "Oh, I think *Hollywood*," she loved the humiliating nickname when it was available to embarrass Alex in public, "has plans that don't include us tonight, Erin." She winked at Alex, who only glared back at her in unconcealed annoyance.

"Oh, you have plans?" Amelia's teasing innuendo sailed over Halsey's head.

Bless Erin's callow heart. She was the number one rated goalkeeper in the world, but her cylinders weren't always firing at the same speed as the conversation.

Thankfully.

"I haven't been home more than a few nights in a row for almost a year, so forgive me if all I want to do is drag on some sweatpants, settle in with a cup of tea, and binge watch all five seasons of *Damages* before preseason begins."

"Bullshit," Amelia coughed into her hand, "I doubt there are any pants involved in your immediate future."

Alex seared the Australian with a glare Halsey didn't notice.

"*Damages?*" Halsey's date risked a glance at Alex, fiddling with her blonde bangs.

"Yeah—Glenn Close?"

The girl stared at her blankly.

Amelia was momentarily shaken off her teasing. "*Fatal Attraction?* The boiling rabbit…?"

No recognition. Amelia rolled her eyes and looked at Halsey. "Mate—educate your girl."

"Sure thing, grandma." The keeper side-eyed her date with a wry smile and the two burst into tipsy laughter as Halsey hauled herself to her feet and swiped up their empty bottles. "Another round?"

When she'd slugged Alex in the shoulder farewell and sauntered to the bar with the blonde on her arm, Amelia planted her elbows on the table and fixed Alex with her emerald stare. "So… staying in the city tonight?"

Catharine wasn't a subject between them. For all of Amelia's teasing, she never pressed Alex on the topic, and beyond her playful jests intended to never let Alex forget she'd sized her up at the Hope Gala, she left her personal life alone. It was just one of the million attributes that had solidified the hard-nosed midfielder as one of her closest friends.

Alex gave a noncommittal shrug. "Probably."

Another roll of the keen green eyes.

Across the bar Monica's high-pitched squeal of laughter cut through the melody of *Jingle Bell Rock*, drawing the attention of half the patio. She had drawn the short crop of her blouse up just high enough to reveal the scarlet lace of her bra, and was leaning backward over the bar top as the bartender placed a jello shot on her abdomen. Alex watched as Caleb bent to take the body shot, his eyes flashing over to where she sat, before tipping back the shooter.

"You know that's all a show for you," Amelia said, watching the scene with disgust. "He's got a gutful of piss. Aren't you glad you're not the one who has to take him home tonight? Festy."

"You have no idea."

Amelia laughed, making a gagging sound, and slung an arm around her shoulders and Alex suddenly hated herself for feeling self-conscious—for her thoughts flying to what Caleb had said—her *horde of carpet munchers.* How dare he make her feel uncomfortable, shamefaced around her best friends—women she loved, who loved her in return. What a complete and utter bastard he was.

She could still feel his eyes on her after she'd turned away from the little scene at the bar, Monica having risen to grind against him to a miserably whiny rendition of *Santa Baby*.

Without giving him the satisfaction of a return glance, Alex ruffled Amelia's shock of blonde hair, kissed her on the cheek—to the Aussie's surprise and potential disgust—and snatched up her purse to head for the door.

Chapter Four

Catharine stabbed the call end button and dropped her mobile onto the settee, her husband's languid drawl still ringing in her ears. The call had been too entirely pleasant, too amicable, his acquiescence to their agreement too easily gained. *Merry Christmas, my dear*, he'd closed the conversation, and though the words had tinted of his habitual sneer, it wasn't the *go to hell* she'd anticipated.

This close to their negotiation deadline, she'd expected him to ghost her. She'd imagined a week of being sent straight to voicemail, forcing her to eventually track down his assistant, Matthew—home for the holidays in Michigan—and threaten him that if he didn't flush Carlton out of whatever hinterland hole he'd crawled into, she'd take out a full page ad in *The Wall Street Journal* announcing their pending divorce.

Instead, he'd answered with a congenial *Catharine, I meant to call you earlier*, acknowledged that he'd been tardy in reviewing the settlement offer she'd sent over a few weeks prior, and promised to have it signed and returned before the end of the week. There had been no attempt to stall her —to delay the inevitable. They'd agreed, early last spring, to have all the paperwork in order, a settlement agreed upon, ready to file, by the first of the year. That way, wherever his campaign ended, be it the primaries, less than sixty days away, or—God help her—the general election, there would be no further postponement to proceed with the divorce.

All things she'd predicted a colossal battle over to get him to comply.

He hadn't even been drunk. It was near midnight in South Carolina, the hour in which his siren's song gravitated him toward a bottle of single malt and an irascibility that would filter into a raging petulance by the following morning. But tonight there had been no slur to his voice, no stilted cadence in his tone.

Something was amiss. But she didn't dare question the geniality, instead deciding to hang onto a thread of hope that perhaps he really meant to follow through with his promises, to let her go uncontested, and was simply basking in his levity due to the incomprehensible good luck he'd experienced on his campaign trail. His ratings were up—she couldn't begin to comprehend why—his position looked propitious going into the primaries, and there was the horrifying possibility beginning to loom that he might actually secure the GOP nomination, taking his bid for the presidency all the way to the November election.

It was unfathomable. Inconceivable.

And starting to look like a plausible nightmare.

But none of that was here nor there. Tonight, she could do nothing more than take him at face value—and wait for him to show his cards.

Flipping open her MacBook, she took another glance at the time—just after nine—and phoned Nicole. The woman answered on the first ring. Amongst her innumerable attributes, it was one of the things Catharine appreciated most—she was always available. If Catharine was working, Nicole was working.

"I was thinking about what Volkov said this morning," she began, clicking through her notes from earlier in the day.

A half an hour later, engrossed in her phone call, Catharine glanced up from her screen and stifled a gasp. Alex stood in the center of the room, still dressed from her party, her purse and heels in hand, watching her with an amused smile on her lips. She must have come in through the garage entrance, silent on the stairs.

"Hey," Catharine mouthed, smiling, holding her mobile to the side. "I didn't hear you come in."

"I didn't want to interrupt you." Alex shrugged out of her coat and laid it on the coffee table before crossing to sit beside her.

"I wish you would," Catharine whispered, gesturing at her computer with a grimace. "Debrief of Russia." She tapped the mute button on her phone, Nicole's voice still recounting the numbers Catharine had asked her to relay. She should be paying attention, but calculations of the Russian ruble didn't hold the same interest they had a few moments ago. "How was the party?"

"Lacking the presence of the only person I want to see tonight."

"Is that so?" Catharine ran her thumb across Alex's lower lip, so acutely aware of her nearness she contemplated disconnecting her call, feigning a broken line. But she'd been the one to ask Nicole to run the numbers, and had woken her attorney, Gordon Liebermann, home in New York, to connect a three-way conference in the middle of the night.

"I've missed you," she said instead, reluctantly returning to her mobile, her eyes still on Alex, who had the beginnings of an arched smile lingering as Catharine tried to regain the conversation.

Nicole, ever focused, finished the tallying, giving no indication of noticing Catharine's waning attention, and continued with her notes. "Gordon, if I understand correctly, you still maintain an in-person signing won't be necessary?" she asked, filling the silence when Catharine did not immediately respond.

The attorney's tired voice grumbled the affirmative.

Catharine disagreed. "Unnecessary, maybe, but custom dictates—" Her thoughts faltered as Alex leaned over, brushing her hair aside to kiss the side of her neck. She took a quick breath, starting again. "Custom dictates —" Dictates what? The ending of her sentence faded.

"We'll gain better leverage by maintaining our distance in this instance. We need not to appear overeager."

In the back of her mind she knew she had an intelligent argument to make to the contrary—something about a show of presence to prevent a home field advantage—but her capacity for an apt rebuttal had fled as Alex ran her lips from her ear, down her neck, making her way across her collarbone in an agonizingly slow procession.

"Overeager," she parroted the word—a habit she detested in others—and closed her eyes, aware only of the smile she could feel on Alex's lips as the woman dared her to admonish her—to chastise her for the interruption.

A scolding Catharine had no intent to make. Alex's occupation she had no wish to disrupt.

But, still, *Russia*.

"If we sign remotely—"

Alex's hands slipped beneath her tank top, raising the hem, her mouth moving from her clavicle, across her breasts, trailing down her abdomen. "We'll look weak," she managed, certain the only thing weak was her resolve to finish this phone call.

Fingers worked at the drawstring at her waist and Catharine closed her eyes, tipping her head back toward the ceiling. She needed to focus, yet when Alex bade her lift her hips, that she might slip her lounging trousers to the floor, she was not hesitant to comply.

"If you're set against a virtual notarization, I'll need some time to make arrangements." Gordon was talking, his voice droning in his thick east coast accent, but Catharine had difficulty processing his words. "There's the logistical hardship of an entry permit, of course, and…"

At some point Alex had knelt to the floor in front of her and removed her computer from her lap, while Catharine's mind had become entirely incapable of functioning, beyond the awareness of the immediate engagement of Alex's intentions—unrelenting, insistent.

Nicole was talking, and Gordon again. Alex—her hands. Slow. Deliberate. Teasing. Catharine gripped the back of the settee.

And then there was silence.

She realized they were waiting on her reply.

"I—" She tried to catch her breath with only mild success. Where would she want to meet Volkov? She thought that may have been the question.

"Ust-Luga."

"Ma'am?" Nicole's voice, full of concern. "Are you all right?"

Shit. Ust-Luga was on the opposite side of the country. "I'm sorry, I meant Novo—Novoro—"

"Novorossiysk," Nicole came to her aid.

"Yes." Catharine pressed her forearm against her forehead, trying to focus. Trying to breathe. Trying not to arch her back, to pull Alex forward, to end the misery of her dallying.

"Look, let's just go with your recommendation, Gordon. Sign remotely."

"Are you certain?" He was stunned at her about-face. She was not one to relent—at least not without a fight. But Russia and Volkov and the billion dollar export contract with the Novorossiysk sea port was the furthest thing from her mind. The act of simply exhaling without a shuddered breath had become a task almost too difficult to grasp.

A fleeting realization that the glass wall facing the boulevard remained transparent, the electronic tint unactivated, gave her a moment of pause. But the second story of the townhouse wasn't visible from street level. One would have to be out on the docks—possibly even on the water—to see through the windows.

Nicole was asking about timing.

And Alex's mouth had changed course from its unhurried exploration, shifting gears to an assertiveness that erased all intelligent comprehension.

"I'll need to look at my calendar." She smothered a laugh, her voice distorted, the words a waterfall of letters no longer making sense. "Wednesday. How about? Morning?" Her free hand found its way to the back of Alex's neck, her fingers running up into her hair as she tried to find some semblance of composure to close the conversation.

"Wednesday is Christmas Day, ma'am." Nicole was hesitant. "But if that's the day that works—"

"No!" Catharine lost her battle with suppressing her laughter, no doubt startling both her assistant and attorney on the other end of the line. But she couldn't find it in her to care. Alex's present endeavor held her full attention, leaving no room for anything else. "No… of course it is. Christmas, I mean." Eyes still shut, her breathing shallow, she relented her hold on Alex's hair, reaching over to slap the top of her MacBook closed before shoving it to the floor. "Let's all—a couple days, let's take them off. Nothing's immediately pressing. We'll work out details on Thursday."

"Yes, Mrs. Cleveland. Thank you." Twelve years with Catharine had given Nicole the judiciousness not to question her authority, no matter the absurdity of the circumstance.

Gordon, on the other hand, was less accepting. "Sure… let's table the signing of the most substantial contract of the year." He huffed and cleared his throat with deliberate disapproval.

"Merry Christmas," was all Catharine could summon before fumbling to end the call, all thoughts of contracts and WorldCargo and the conversation with Carlton disappearing.

"Alex."

She needed to ask her to wait. To allow her to rise, to close the blinds, to shut them behind the safety of their asylum of shuttered windows and locked doors. To keep them safe. To follow her own rules. But she couldn't. She couldn't do anything beyond respond to the physical need of drawing her closer. Of lifting her legs up over her shoulders, crossing her ankles behind her neck, pressing her heels into the flat of her back. Giving in to the urgency that overcame her. Superseding her temptation to draw the sensation out. Surrendering herself to the feeling of falling. Of floating. Of losing her foothold of self-command.

Unable to endure it any longer, she rocked forward, her body shuddering, and found purchase of her hands in Alex's hair. Her thoughts stilled as she pressed her face against the back of her head, forcing herself to let go. Yielding to the testament that no matter how hard she tried, there were things beyond her control.

Long after midnight, Catharine stretched out in the Adirondack chair on the third story balcony of her master bedroom, breathing in the mist from the bay. The masts of the boats docked in the marina bobbed up and down in a rhythmic cadence as mild swells rolled in from the sea. The night had grown foggy, the temperature warming under the mantle of cloud cover, leaving only a gentle crispness in the air that cooled her cheeks.

Alex sat squeezed in beside her, the chair unaccommodating for two, but neither gave mind to the snugness of the fit. They were sated, wrapped in each other's arms, with only a throw blanket for cover.

A comfortable silence had fallen between them, both lost to the privy of their thoughts.

On another day, Catharine would not have allowed them to sit so close together, to risk being exposed as they were to the boulevard. But it was late, the city quiet, the fog concealing, and she craved the nearness of Alex. The familiarity of her body. Her warmth. Her scent. The slow echo of her heartbeat she could feel against her cheek. She wanted the night to linger, endless and unchanging, for the sun to keep to its slumber beneath the flat of the horizon.

For in that protected moment, that shrouded sanctuary, she could feel the promise of their future. The way it might one day be. The life they could live. The love they could share. But with the rising of the sun, the safety slipped away, and the precarious reality of their present took its place.

Chapter Five

Her apartment smelled musty, reminiscent of an unused storage closet of a high school locker room. Alex skipped the light switch, leaving the door open to allow the early morning sunlight into the hall. She was in a hurry. Nathalie had promised to make breakfast—classic French crepes she'd insisted were her family's Christmas Eve Morning tradition—and though the woman was a late riser, Alex didn't want her or Catharine to be waiting on her.

When she'd left before dawn she only told Catharine she was going for a run. She hadn't mentioned her trip to Oakland to retrieve the Christmas present she'd ordered that had finally arrived in the mail. Not after Catharine had made her promise not to get her anything. That the only thing she wanted for the holidays was to spend them with her.

A stack of envelopes was piled on the kitchen table, dropped there by Amelia who'd been keeping tabs on her mailbox, but she'd flown home to Melbourne the night before where she would spend two weeks with her family before preseason began. And even though Alex had hardly seen her since she'd been home from Europe, she still felt her absence acutely, knowing she was so far away.

A large manila envelope stamped *do not bend* in red ink was on top of the pile. Alex grabbed it and slipped her fingers beneath the seal, shaking out the single sheet of heavy artist paper onto the table. It was a watercolor, intricately detailed, of a small sailboat cruising beneath an old stone bridge. In the cockpit were two figures, both silhouetted in shadow, a woman and a child—the woman's hand on the girl's shoulder.

When Catharine talked about sailing, she spoke little of her ocean crossings or exotic trips in the turquoise waters of distant islands. Nothing of the tall ship excursions. The capes she had rounded. Even her classic ketch, docked in Yacht Harbor across from her townhouse, was seldom mentioned. It was her life growing up on the Thames she spoke about. The sailing dinghies she had crewed with her mother. The early morning races along the bends of Henley-on-Thames. Of the few photos she kept in her house, the one Alex felt Catharine loved most was a photo from her childhood. A photo of she and her mother.

The photo was old, discolored, water damaged and torn around the edges, tucked into a simple silver frame. Alex had considered sneaking it out to have it restored, but she'd worried too much about the possibility of something happening to it in the process. Instead, she'd snapped a photo of it, and found an artist to recreate the image in the style of Dürer, Catharine's favorite painter.

By the dim light shining in from the hall, Alex thought it was perfect. Exactly what she'd been hoping for. The only gift she could think to give to the woman who had everything.

Before she could slip the painting back into the envelope, the door to her apartment swung shut, immersing the room in darkness. It startled Alex, the velocity with which it had slammed. Feeling her way around the table, she started for the light switch, but froze midstep when the silence was interrupted by footsteps, the sound of breathing that wasn't hers.

Facing a moment of terror, Alex hesitated, uncertain if she should try and hide, or grab for something to protect herself, but before a conclusion could be reached, the lights came on and she found herself staring at two figures standing in her kitchen threshold.

"Easy, lady," the nasal voice of a northeasterner warned as Alex sidestepped toward her kitchen counter, prepared to dive for a knife, but her progress was stilted as her eyes fell on the second figure, standing behind the speaker, his face obscured in shadow.

"What—" The word came out an indistinguishable whoosh of air, Alex's mouth going completely dry as her heart found its way through her ribcage and into her throat. Even as poorly illuminated as he was, she would have known the man anywhere. "What are you doing here?" she managed, still frozen in place.

A new form of fear spread from head to toe, leaving her weak and unsteady on her feet. No longer was she concerned with basic survival. The presence of the man in front of her brought a completely different terror—one she didn't know how to face.

"I hope you'll forgive the intrusion, Miss Grey." The Southern drawl was barbed with sarcasm as Senator Carlton Cleveland stepped into the light. "I realize I may have given you a fright, but I assure you, I mean you no harm." With a jerk of his chin he sent his companion toward the front door, the exchange of a nonverbal agreement passing between them.

The retreating figure was not a man Alex knew, his face not one she could have picked out of a crowd, but his hat—a worn Braves cap, the old school A in cursive—she'd seen it before. Months ago in New York. The weekend she had gone with Catharine to see Nathalie's show. The first time Catharine had grown paranoid Carlton was having her followed.

"Have a seat, Miss Grey." Carlton drew her attention back to him, motioning toward her kitchen table.

Alex didn't move. Didn't breathe. She could hardly think.

Carlton Cleveland was here—in *her* apartment. The man running for President of the United States. Catharine's husband.

Which meant only one thing.

"I—" she had to say something. *Do* something. "You have no right to be here, Mr. Cleveland. You must leave." It was the most idiotic, ridiculous statement that had ever fallen out of her mouth. Yet it was the only thing she could bring herself to say.

"I don't believe you are in a position to be telling me what I do—and do not—have a right to, Miss Grey. Recent history would indicate you yourself are a little hazy when it comes to crossing lines of what is—and *isn't*—yours."

"Get out, Mr. Cleveland," she tried again, this time finding her voice in earnest, a rush of anger setting in place. No matter who he was, what he wanted, the intrusion was uncalled for.

"That's *Senator* Cleveland to you, my dear." His words rolled out like an acerbic molasses, coating the air between them. "*President* Cleveland, in the future. A fact you will do well to remember."

It was her dream relived, the nightmare unfolding.

"Only if this country has lost its mind."

"Sit down, Miss Grey." The mock cordiality vanished as the senator emphasized his command with a pound of his fist against her doorjamb.

Alex's thoughts flew to Catharine's blackened eyes, the scar along the inside of her lower lip. She took a shuddered breath, telling herself he could not hurt her. The walls of her apartment were paper thin, her Uber driver still waiting in the parking lot. There were too many witnesses. He had come only to scare her.

A successful endeavor so far.

"Sit down," he repeated, dragging a chair out from the table. "There are a few things we should talk about."

Alex felt like the walls of her cramped kitchen were shifting, closing in around them. His proximity, the fury radiating beneath his temperate exterior, stole the air from the room, sending an unnerving chill creeping along the nape of her neck.

"I have nothing to say to you." The defiance was pointless. Senator Carlton Cleveland would not be standing in her kitchen, risking breaking and entering, without the certainty of the upper hand. She needed to know what he knew. Only then could she decide what to do about it.

"You will," his smile was cold and calculating, "but for now, I'm content to do the talking." He settled himself at the table and shoved the chair opposite across the floor with the toe of his Oxford. "Now, *sit*."

He couldn't hurt her. She repeated the mantra as she sank into the seat.

So he knew about her and Catharine... she could handle this.

"I don't need to tell you why I'm here." His eyes flicked to the table, catching sight of the watercolor, sending his snide mouth into a tight smile. Alex reached for the painting, but Carlton was surprisingly quick, snagging the paper between his fleshy fingertips.

"How romantic," he crooned, dragging his thumb across the silhouette of the little girl. "What a thoughtful gift, Miss Grey. No doubt my wife would have loved it."

Alex kept her silence, sweat pricking at her temples, her palms growing slick.

Carlton chuckled, a hollow, empty sound that made his jowls twitch above the collar of his suit, before letting the paper slip back to the table.

"So," he dropped heavy elbows onto the artwork, steepling his hands before him. "It would seem we have a little situation."

Across the kitchen the fridge hummed and the faucet dripped its slow, incessant cadence. There was a honk from the parking lot—her Uber driver was growing impatient—and the sound of water running through the pipes of the ceiling as a toilet flushed in another apartment.

Alex heard little of it. She was supposed to be back in the Marina District. Back in the townhouse with its endless unfolding beauty, the warmth of its cheerfulness, the murmur of the kettle boiling, the seagulls crying the song of the bay.

Back to whispered good mornings. A hand that found hers beneath the breakfast table. Lips that turned a smile every time their eyes met. Allusive glances that brought a flush to her cheeks, reminding Alex of every part of her she'd kissed.

Back to Catharine.

This could not be happening. This could be no more than the repeating of a nightmare.

Only this time she knew there would be no jolting awakening to save her. No relief in the dismissal of a dream.

"You are young, Miss Grey, and perhaps naive. No doubt you fancy yourself in love—if, uh, that's the sort of sentiment a person of your… unnatural tendencies… can believe." He stared at her beneath his drooping brow, his judgment palpable through the thickness of his drawl. "And I can't say that I blame you, truth be told. My wife is an alluring woman. I could see how she would be a Circe—to someone like you."

Someone like you. The proverbial punch. An outcast. A deviant. The Southern Baptist's "one of them." *Them* being anyone different than they were.

"You have no proof."

He smiled. "I was hoping we could get that out of the way." Reaching into his lapel he drew out his phone, flicking open an app and sliding it across the table. "I'll give you a moment to review those, then we can continue."

Mechanically, Alex picked up the device, already knowing what she would find. The man in the ball cap. Catharine's paranoia. Carlton's certainty as he sat there with his smug, repulsive smile.

The first photo was of her and Catharine in Colorado, entering the Four Seasons Resort. Malcolm in the background. Alex felt the nerves in her fingers tingle, grateful her hands didn't shake. The dinner in Vail—had been last February, almost a year earlier. She swiped to the next photo. New York

—the theatre. The first place Catharine had grown uneasy, pointing out the man in the hat. The next image was Catharine in Tennessee, sitting in the stands, the SheBelieves Cup banner in the distance. Alex felt the tang of bile as she continued to scroll. There was a photo of her and Catharine in Monterrey inside a hotel restaurant—the only game Catharine had attended since her first match with the US team. She had been followed everywhere. For all this time.

She quit scrolling and dropped the phone. "These don't mean anything. We're friends."

"Please continue, Miss Grey."

"I don't need to. What do you want?"

Again, he smiled. "For you to finish the photos—and then we'll talk shop."

Alex didn't move, so Carlton reached across the table and continued scrolling for her. "Here—this was a personal favorite. The old and the new."

She glanced down to see a photo of them at *House of Salt*, Caleb and Monica standing beside the table, just a few days earlier.

Carlton chuckled again. "I thought I'd hit the jackpot when these were texted to me. Finally, my cautious, callous wife let down her guard." He swiped through a series of photos showing just the hint of Catharine's bare foot touching Alex's ankle beneath the table. "Seemed like more than friends. Little did I know…" His smile grew, his fingers scrolling faster, all while Alex tried to convince her stomach not to lose its contents. "Here we are. The holy grail." He flipped the phone around to face him, stared at the screen, shook his head with the continued simpering of a smile, and placed it back in Alex's hands. "Do you do that with all of your friends?"

The chill that had skated along Alex's spine suddenly turned to ice, the frozen feeling expanding, snapping, as if her entire body might crack. She couldn't look away. She and Catharine in the living room the night after her Christmas party, the photo grainy from magnification, taken at great distance. Yet still, their faces legible. Their relationship unquestionable.

After a spell of silence in which the dripping of the sink drove Alex to near lunacy, Carlton reached to take his phone, slipping it back into his pocket. "Miss Grey, my wife is not a reasonable woman. She never has been. But you, on the other hand, seem like a reasonable girl."

"If you think I care about being threatened, you're going to be thoroughly disappointed, Mr. Cleveland," Alex spoke with far more confidence than she felt, though she also knew she wasn't bluffing. Whatever he threatened her with—exposure, ruination of her contracts, even the decimation of her career—whatever it was, she would face it. She'd known, since the first moment she'd allowed herself to fall in love with Catharine Cleveland, what risks were at stake. What the outcome might be. But she was in love with Catharine—loved her more than anything else in her life. The rest of it could crumble—everything she'd worked for—she would let it go, to keep Catharine.

"Oh, but I don't," Carlton tipped his heavy frame back in the chair, his dark eyes shining some pleasure of his own keeping. It was not the response she'd expected and his amusement grew as her uncertainty prevailed. There was a perverseness to his enjoyment that raised gooseflesh along her forearms. "I don't think you care about any of that. That fact's been established. It took some time to figure you out, Miss Grey, but let me reassure you—I never go to war without doing my homework. You are young enough, and, if you'll forgive me—stupid enough—not to care about your reputation. All those years of sacrifice to get where you are… I do believe you would be willing to throw it all away. But," he took a moment to pause for dramatic effect, hooking his hands behind his head in leisure, "what I do think you care about is my wife."

Her face betrayed her as soon as the words were out of his mouth. The wave of bile crested, threatening as he watched her, his smile steady, knowing he'd struck a chord.

This couldn't be happening.

"With that being said, I think there are a few things I should explain you may not know about Mrs. Cleveland, Alex. I may call you Alex, yes?" He drawled, complacent. "We are past formalities, I imagine. The line gets a bit fuzzy when you're talking to someone who's been fucking your wife."

The déjà vu of her dream paralyzed her.

He leaned forward, splaying his fingers across the painting, and looked at her with sudden interest. "Is that what you call it, even? Fucking? Can two women fuck? I've always wondered how you get that done. Without, you know…" He laughed, distracted by his topic. "And with Catharine, of all people. I was dumb enough in my youth to think that marrying a beautiful woman meant they'd be insatiable in the sack. Wanton. Lascivious. How wrong I was—it's true what they say about the English—even at twenty my darling wife was a frigid, impermeable corpse to fuck. It would be easier to suck a golf ball through a garden hose than get a willing blow job from that bitch." His lips curled in derision. "All those times, enjoying it even more, just knowing how much she hated it."

Alex swallowed, trying to shut out every word from his abhorrent, despicable mouth.

"You all right, Alex? You look a little green around the gills. Would you rather not discuss how I've fucked my wife all these years? No exchanging notes? Giving tips?" His fingers drummed the watercolor. "Vulgarity not your style? Funny—you wouldn't know it from those photos." When Alex didn't respond he continued. "I digress. We could talk about tupping the impervious Mrs. Cleveland all day, but neither of us have time for that. So let's cut to the chase, shall we?" His jaw worked back and forth in a motion that reminded Alex of a contemplative cow chewing cud. "You're going to stop seeing my wife. Immediately. Permanently."

"Why would I do that?" Alex forced her voice into something more than a whisper. "She is divorcing you."

"Ah, yes—that." His brow furrowed, leaving half a dozen deeply etched lines across his forehead. "We have a complicated arrangement, she and I. Far past your comprehension, with stakes higher than you could ever imagine. I know you fancy yourself important, child, and I am sorry to be the one to break it to you, but in the scheme of things you are absolutely nothing. Do you know exactly what is at stake here, Alex?" For once he appeared genuinely interested in her answer.

"Your presidency."

"My presidency." He snorted a laugh. "That goes without saying. But you don't care about that. Why should you? My presidential election is the least of your concerns. Brooks Corp., however—that should be more interesting to you."

"You think I care about Catharine's business?" For the first time it was Alex who laughed, a touch of her former anger beginning to resurface. "That's what this is about?"

"No." The glint never left his eyes. "I don't think you care about her business or her money. As I said, it took a while to figure you out—you poor, besotted, romantic fool. That's not what I meant." He spoke plainly now, his drawl receding, his words casual, as if he were explaining the very basics of arithmetic to a child. "But I do think Catharine cares about it. Perhaps not enough to avoid the risk of losing it over you—she's clearly quite taken with you, Miss Grey, and, I won't lie, I can't blame her. The first time I saw you, soaking wet in my foyer, I thought you looked like a satisfying lay. I'll commend her there—but again, I divagate. As I mentioned, she is not a reasonable woman, my wife—which is why I am having this conversation with you, instead of her."

"I have no control over the decisions she makes. Whatever risks she chooses to take are her own accord."

"You sound so very Catharine right there. She's rubbing off on you. But you're quite right. Which is why you'll be the one to end this sordid little affair so it does not become a choice she has to make."

"You've wasted your time, Mr. Cleveland. Now, if you'll excuse me—" She began to rise.

"Do you know how many people are employed by my wife?"

She remained half standing. "No. A lot."

"A lot," he mimicked her. "Over fifty-thousand-a-lot. That's just World-Cargo. Do you understand what type of industry we are talking about, Alex? Any idea what kind of money?"

"No! And I don't care," she stood, tipping the chair over behind her. "Get out of my apartment!"

"More than twenty billion dollars in revenue. But you can't comprehend those numbers."

"You're right. I can't," Alex slapped her palms against the table, wanting nothing more than to overturn it, to fling it in his face.

"Do you have any idea of the seismic disaster it would be for a corporation like that to fold overnight?"

Alex stared at him, trying to figure out his angle.

"You realize we live in the twenty-first century where being gay is not a crime, right?"

"To our Holy Father's disappointment—as a girl born to a devote Baptist and raised by a preacher and Sunday school teacher, I am sure you are well aware your heavenly transgressions."

"You needn't concern yourself with my soul, Mr. Cleveland. That's between me and God to figure out."

"Amen," clapped the senator emphatically, before returning to business. "Are you aware of the affair my wife had with Nathalie Comtois before we were married?"

Alex gave a noncommittal shrug.

"Good. Then perhaps you will also be aware of the accord my wife made with her father when she assumed command of his company?"

Alex didn't respond.

"Ah, I see. Maybe not. Well, to be concise: Catharine made a promise— and I will tell you, for all of our differences, I have to hand it to her—she doesn't take her promises lightly, as I'm sure you've found. Well, she promised her father no shame would be brought to their family, including Brooks Corp. and by shame, well, you can put two and two together, Miss Grey." He gave a dismissive flip of his hand. "She's done a good job at it, I'll give her credit. She's a formidable business woman. Tougher than I ever anticipated. Smarter, too." He laughed, as if it were a shocking revelation. "And up until you came along we seemed to have gotten through okay. She had her business. I had my politics. None was worse for wear. But it seems you can take the girl away from the sin, but you just can't take the sin out of the girl—"

"If you don't leave, I'll—," Alex took a step toward the hallway, but Carlton shot out a hand that caught her with a strength she'd not given him credit for, shoving her toward her chair still lying on its side.

"You will know when I am finished," he snarled, "now sit."

There was something just cold enough, just angry enough, to encourage Alex to comply. She righted her chair, and sat, resigning herself to listen to the rest of what he would say.

"Colonel Brooks had enough foresight to position a safeguard, just in case his daughter's good judgment floundered. Now I imagine you think she owns the corporation, but do you know what a minority shareholder is, Alex?" He didn't wait for an answer. "It's basically a pawn. A nonentity. A *stooge*, we like to call them in politics—because they are worthless— insects with no power, no voice."

Alex listened, not looking at him.

"So as you have it, Mrs. Cleveland may run Brooks Corp. She may have built it to what it is, controlled it for over twenty years, made all of the decisions and sacrifices. Spilled her blood, so to speak. It's been her life work, her legacy, and one she has right to be proud of. But when it comes down to it, she is nothing. Her father holds the control, and she knows it. And I promise you, if the Colonel thought, for just one moment, that she had broken her vow... he is not a man to be trifled with. Not a man to be made a fool. I give you my word, it is no idle threat to say he would dissolve their empire in the blink of an eye. There is a reason she made the decision to leave Ms. Comtois without ever looking back. It may hurt to hear it, Miss Grey, but you are no different."

Alex stared at the backsplash over the electric burner, thinking about the day Catharine showed up at her apartment to invite her to the symphony. It seemed a lifetime ago. What would have happened if she'd let Catharine leave that day, instead of stopping her on the doorstep? Where would they both be now?

Carlton's fist rattled the table, jumping Alex out of her reverie. "Do you hear me, girl?!"

"Yes."

"Are you so selfish to not understand the magnitude of this? The consequences? The number of people who would be unemployed? The number of companies that would collapse—the domino effect of lives it would destroy!" His voice had risen, all veneer of his southern charm discarded, his veins bulging beneath the heavy ticking of his jaw. "This may all be a game to you—a good time—but I assure you there are folks who feel otherwise! Your friend, Amelia Walker, for example."

At last Alex looked at him head on. "What does she have to do with any of this?"

"I had a bit of research done on her father, Mr. Walker. It seems he is a man who has battled with mental illness... questioned his self-worth. A better WorldCargo employee than he has been an investing businessman. At nearly a million dollars in bad debt, your friend Amelia has been sending her earnings home to keep the family afloat. If he were to lose his job—a career that has been his entire life—how do you think he would respond?" Carlton raised his unkempt brows. "People turn to dark places in their loss, Alex. Dreadful places. And the Walkers are just one family. One story.

There are tens of thousands of others just like them. So I will ask you, Miss Grey: is it worth it?"

It felt impossible to gather her thoughts. To understand everything he'd said. Why hadn't Catharine mentioned her father still held control over her company? That he could cripple it at his leisure. Why would she have taken the risk—let Alex take part in the peril unwittingly?

To answer Carlton's question: no…it wasn't worth it. It wasn't worth the lives that could be destroyed. Most especially Catharine's.

Tears threatened out of nowhere and she bit the soft flesh of her cheek to drive them away. She refused to cry in front of this man. To let him see he'd won.

"I have no control over Catharine. She will do what she will do. I'm sure you're aware of that."

"I see." His composure regained, he collected himself into the slow drawling Southern politician once more. "There is one last thing I will mention. And do not think I am making light, my dear. I do not play at this game. If, by some chance, the aforementioned consequences of your impending actions are not enough to steer you in the right direction, I'll have you know this: my wife is not invincible. You yourself were privy to her most recent near-death catastrophe. She's known for her solo outings on the sea. Even the most experienced of hands fall prey to Mother Nature—to the turning of the tides. Are we clear, Miss Grey, on what I am saying?"

The previous sickness flooded back over her, made her feel lightheaded, her pulse weak. Of all his threats, it was this last one she believed the most. "What is it you want me to do?"

"Call it off. Simple as that."

"It isn't as simple as that," Alex brought the back of her hand to wipe at her eyes, aware her voice was trembling. "Catharine will want to know why. If I tell her—"

"You will *never* tell her, do you understand?" He lunged to his feet, dragging her up by the collar of her sweatshirt, nearly pulling her across the table. "Are we clear, girl? You will *never* breathe a word of this conversation to anyone." Her dropped his hold, allowing her to stumble backward.

"She's not going to believe I just walked away. She knows—" Again Alex swiped at her eyes, furious to realize her cheeks were wet. "She knows I love her." The words were nothing more than a smothered sob. Words she had never said aloud before. The last words she wanted to admit, standing here, in front of him.

"Then your story better be convincing." He regarded her coldly, unaffected by the wave of emotions Alex was drowning in as she tried to keep her head above the surface. "You clearly excel at making people believe you are something you are not—I think Hargrove Entertainment Group would agree, don't you? You'll think of something." He straightened the lapels of his suit and smoothed out invisible wrinkles, pausing to pick up the painting still on the table.

"I should mention, Miss Grey," he kept his attention on the canvas, holding it up for inspection, "you need to handle this problem today. Not tonight. Not tomorrow. *Today.* And if you do as I tell you, I give you my word no mention of this will reach Colonel Brooks. Those photos will go somewhere they will never be seen. Your career will remain intact. Perhaps Miss Walker's work visa will even continue to be valid in the United States." He added this last part as an after thought, though Alex knew it was far from a casual remark. It was a reminder of his reach, his power. The enormity of his control. "She would have liked this, you know," he said absently, folding the canvas in half, then in half again. "She always loved that photo. It's the only one she has of her mother." He tore the sheet in several strips and dropped the pieces on the table, several watercolored fragments fluttering to the floor. "I think we have a tacit understanding that Mr. Jones—my colleague you met earlier—will be keeping tabs on your progress? Just so we are on the same page." He backed into the hall. "Merry Christmas, Alex." And then he was gone, the front door clicking shut behind him, sealing the silence of the room.

Alex stood for a moment, staring at the torn parchment, before allowing herself to sink to the floor, her body trembling with the release of endorphins, her emotions catapulting between relief and fury.

She wanted to scream. To pummel her fists into the tile of the counter. To shatter the dishes in the sink. But she didn't have the strength to rise. Instead she knelt on the floor, sobbing until she choked, her forehead pressed to the cold linoleum, suffocating in her tears. In her anguish she pounded the heel of her palm against the floor until a pain shot up her wrist, spasming to her elbow, but she didn't care.

Dropping onto her side, she drew her knees to her chest, and cried until the world faded away.

Chapter Six

Catharine overturned the ceramic cup in her lap lunging for her mobile.

"Alex!" She couldn't curb the admonishment in her voice, despite the sheer relief that left her nearly breathless. She'd imagined the worst over the last six hours, every strike of her grandfather's clock leading her thoughts to darker and more upsetting places. "Where are you? What's happened?"

"I'm sorry."

The relief was short-lived, Catharine's heart instantly sinking. There was something raw, something desolate to Alex's tone that stoked her anxiety anew. She sounded far away, as if she were speaking from the inside of a tunnel.

"Where are you?" she tried again, dread clinging in the air like the contents of her toppled cup of tea.

Alex cleared her throat and in the background there was the mumble of an announcement over an intercom, but she couldn't make out the words.

"I'm so sorry." A lengthy pause ensued in which Catharine could hear the sniffling gasps of unchecked tears as her own panic boiled over.

"Tell me where you are." She tried to level her voice, to stay calm. Whatever it was, she would fix it. "I'll come get you."

"I have to go to South Carolina." Alex released a noisy exhale, trying to ward off a sob.

Across the room Nathalie had risen from the settee, alarmed, but Catharine held up a finger to silence her.

"Has something happened to your aunt or uncle?"

"No. No. They're fine. I'm fine. I mean—" she hesitated, the monotone announcement of the intercom interrupting in the background. "They're mostly fine. My—my aunt called. She needs some help—at home—she needs me to come home for a little while."

It was the first time Catharine had ever known Alex to lie to her. The stuttered words, the halting breaths, her inability to answer a simple question. She stood, kicking aside her cup that had landed on the ground, and walked to the balcony. She needed air.

"When?"

"Now. Today."

Her panic surged. "Alex, what is going on? Talk to me." She leaned over the glass railing and stared out at the water. The bay was filled with sailors and windsurfers enjoying the beauty of the mild Christmas Eve afternoon. They had planned to take her ketch, *L'lune Alouette*, out for an evening sail. To watch the sun set behind the Golden Gate from the water.

Her inquiry was met with silence.

"Please." She found it hard to breathe. "Whatever it is—talk to me. I can help. We'll make it right." The problem was, she had no idea what she needed to make right. No idea as to what could possibly have gone wrong. "It's Christmas Eve," she said at last, as if that would make any difference.

"I know." The hoarseness of Alex's voice was catching, as if her tears had started afresh. "I'm sorry, Catharine. I am. I—I'll call you when I get there, I promise."

"Alex, stop. Please don't hang up." Catharine clung to her phone, feeling as if this conversation, this moment, was the fraying fiber of her lifeline. If she hung up, something would be severed. And she didn't even know why.

"I have to go. I have to catch my plane."

"Then let me go with you to Carolina! Alex, please! Talk to me. Please don't shut me out. Let me help. Whatever it is, let me fix it."

There was a stifled laugh that sounded more like a sob. "You think you can fix anything." She sniffed, drawing a grating inhalation, and when she spoke again her voice had calmed. "I need a week or two, Catharine. I'll call you tonight when I land. Please—just… give me a little time."

"I'm begging you, Alex—tell me what's wrong." She cupped her hand over her free ear, as if hearing better might help her understand. "Come home. Let's talk. If you need to go to Carolina we could go together in the morning. I can help if you'll let me."

Another announcement carried across the airport terminal in the background, drowning out the final suffocating sob. "Catharine, I—" she seemed on the verge to say something else, then changed her mind. "I have to go. I'm truly sorry."

There was silence on the end of the line, and for a long second Catharine thought she had hung up, but then Alex's voice returned, little more than a whisper. "Please... please don't come for me. I'll call you tonight. Or tomorrow, if I get in too late. Just—please don't come." And then the call was disconnected and Catharine was left standing on her balcony, feeling as if she'd been blindsided by a train.

"What was that?" Nathalie's hand startled her on her arm.

Catharine watched a windsurfer sail dangerously close to a cargo ship before darting across the wake the freighter left behind. "I don't know. She said she had to go back to South Carolina."

"Today?" Nathalie dropped her hip against the railing. "Right now?"

"Yes."

"Why?"

"I don't know, Nat!" Catharine snapped, brushing past her into the living room and tossing her mobile on the coffee table. "I don't know anything." She felt hollow, her anger misplaced at her friend's questions while the thread that held her life together began to unfurl at a blistering pace.

"Should you fly out there? It's not like her at all—"

"She asked me not to," Catharine cut her off, uncertain if it was hurt or fear that sharpened her tone. "She said she'd call when she lands." She turned to her friend, looking for answers Nathalie could not give. "I'm sure everything will be fine."

A sentiment neither of them shared. But Catharine could think of nothing else to say as she waited for the inevitable hammer to fall.

Chapter Seven

Two days after her twenty-eighth birthday, Alex boarded a plane back to California. It was a Friday afternoon, with the Sirens preseason training camp beginning Monday. She'd been gone a little over two weeks and couldn't put off her return any longer.

She'd spent the first three days with her aunt and uncle. After showing up Christmas morning on their doorstep—a little hung over from her pity party at the Charlotte airport hotel the evening before—she'd not started the unexpected visit off with a great impression.

Her aunt hadn't even settled down to the cup of Dunkin' Donuts house brew Alex had arrived with—her peace offering for the intrusion—before commenting on her pallor, her reclusiveness, her red-rimmed eyes.

"You don't look well, Alexandra. *Commifornia* has not lured you into needles and booze, I hope. I understand their governor has made illegal substances available in public restrooms in order to push his Marxist agenda."

Alex hadn't had the energy to find her previous gentle method of redirecting her aunt's misguided obsession with QAnon conspiracy news. Her nerves on end, exhausted from her own despair, she'd instead stood from the table, told her aunt to remove her tinfoil hat, and taken the stairs two-by-two to her old bedroom, which had been reappropriated to her aunt's knitting room before Alex had even finished her last load to her dorm at Clemson her freshman year.

Several hours later, after making her dreaded call to Catharine—a less than sixty second conversation that consisted of her repeating a rehearsed excuse of coming to help her aunt, and needing to take a week or two for herself, with interspersed apologies for the short notice—she stood in the familiar living room of the three-bedroom derelict home she'd grown up in and apologized to her aunt for her rude behavior. Her uncle had stood by the crumbling fireplace, arms folded across his concave chest, shaking his head in disapproval.

"I don't like it, Alex." At least he'd always had the courtesy to call her by her given name. "You show up here, unannounced, looking like someone we hardly recognize, and treat your aunt like she's one of your soccer club friends—as if that behavior will be tolerated in this house. All this fame and fortune has changed you."

Staring at the shag carpet—original from the seventies—Alex had mumbled her apology a third time, while idly wondering what they'd been doing with the regular intervals of money she'd sent for her uncle's project of "home repair." Nothing was changed. The home was still slowly slipping into neglect, though she had noted a new Audi in the driveway and the flash of pearl stud earrings beneath her aunt's tightly permed auburn hair.

After a begrudging *apology accepted*, her aunt had suggested to Alex she quit playing "that game," come back to Carolina, settle down and make use of her college degree to begin a real career.

"Not that there's probably much use for a woman in Agricultural Engineering," she'd continued over dinner, without Alex bothering to correct that she'd majored in Architectural Engineering. "Maybe best to get married, start a family—let him take over the breadwinning. No more selling yourself for commercials like a common Hollywood strumpet. Milly Ross said she'd seen one of your ads on TV." Her aunt tsked. "Remember *Proverbs*, Alexandra, and what the good Lord says about vanity: *Charm is deceptive, and beauty is fleeting; but a woman who fears the Lord is to be praised.*" Yet before a full minute had passed, her uncle had asked if Alex would "lend a bit more" to get the state of the house under control. "Your father would be pleased knowing your dedication to the family."

She'd tried her best to make herself useful. To be the dutiful niece. But by the third day she couldn't take the confining detention of Carlisle, South Carolina a moment longer. The suffocating nearness of the life she'd once lived. The place she'd grown up. The people who had held her down. Not while she was hurting as much as she was. Not when her every waking thought was on Catharine. On California. On where she was supposed to be. *Who* she was supposed to be. Who she *was*.

She woke early, thanked her aunt and uncle for their "hospitality," slipped an envelope containing a check into her uncle's outstretched hand, and bid her farewells. "You'll miss church tomorrow," was all her uncle had commented, his focus on tearing open the envelope to count the zeroes.

After, she'd Ubered to the coast, booked a hotel on the water, and spent the following two weeks riding a rollercoaster of emotion—split between running on the sand, sobbing beneath the pier, and wanting to call Catharine; to tell her everything. To let her fix it all.

But this wasn't fixable. For all of Catharine's power, fortune, determination, and resolve, this was one thing she could not repair. Of all the things Carlton had said to Alex, there was one that stood out above the rest. Catharine was not a reasonable woman. She would not allow herself to be blackmailed or told what to do. She was not the girl her father had bullied into submission anymore. If she knew what had happened, she would meet Carlton's challenge head on. And Alex was afraid Catharine would rather watch her world burn than allow Carlton any semblance of control for a single second longer. To be told what she was and wasn't allowed to do. Who she was and wasn't allowed to love.

Alex couldn't let her risk that. She couldn't let her destroy everything she'd built—everything she was. Not for Alex. Not for anyone.

New Year's Eve was spent closed inside her hotel room with the curtains drawn. Trying not to imagine the trip she and Catharine were meant to be on. The California coastline. Trying not to think of the hurt Catharine would be going through on the opposite side of the country. Hurt she had caused and been unable to take away.

Her birthday came and went, Alex dragging herself for a run in the morning—running until she could run no further—and spending the afternoon sitting on the floor of her ensuite's luxury shower, waiting for the hot water to go cold. A feat that took over two hours, leaving her skin pruned and mind blank.

She'd considered calling Sawyer. Her apartment was less than an hour away. She could tell her everything, beg for advice, get it off her chest. But she already knew what Sawyer would say. *Go to the police. Send him to jail for breaking and entering. Expose him to the world.*

It was impossible to explain what kind of man he was. What he was capable of doing.

So Alex spent the remaining days alone. Until there was no time left. Until she was forced to go home.

To face Catharine. To do what must be done.

When she opened the door to her apartment she found the lights on and Amelia perched on her kitchen bar, browsing a copy of *Women's Health*. The Australian's smug grin was on the cover, her wild blonde hair perfectly unkempt, a soccer ball tucked under one tattooed arm and the NWSL Most Valuable Player trophy clutched under the other. Proof of her total domination of the American league since the moment she'd arrived a year earlier.

Tossing the magazine onto the table, she slid from the counter and tugged open Alex's fridge. "I chucked out all the spoiled stuff—smelled like a rubbish bin when I came in here." She paused, glancing up at Alex, taking in her startled expression. After the Carlton incident, Alex had found herself jumpy about returning to her apartment, and hadn't reacted well to walking into the unexpected company. "You all right, mate?"

Alex tried to swallow down her moment of fear. "Yeah. What are you doing here?" The question came out harsher than she meant it. Amelia spent as much time in her apartment as she did in her own. It should have been no surprise to find her waiting for her after they'd both been gone for so long.

"Honestly?" Amelia shut the fridge, but not before Alex saw she'd restocked it with all Alex's favorite foods. A simple gesture of her friendship. Of the generosity that lay behind her callous exterior. "I wanted to catch you before you skipped out on me again. You've been a cryptic bastard in your texts. What's going on?"

Alex forgot about her fear and the food. After discovering she'd been followed… photographed… for months on end, Amelia's appearance in her apartment suddenly felt violating. Her privacy compromised. She didn't want to have this conversation. She wanted to be alone.

"I told you. It was a family thing." She remained standing in the threshold—the same one Carlton Cleveland had occupied two weeks before—and motioned toward the door. "I'm sorry, but—I'm tired. I'm not up for company tonight."

"That's fine," Amelia gave an apathetic tilt of her head. "I'll leave you alone. Just after you tell me what's going on."

"Nothing. It was personal, like I said."

"Right." Amelia made no move to leave. "At first I thought you meant personal as in *personal*—like the kind of personal that involves moonlit yachting and feeding each other grapes and that gagworthy bilge—and then I got the sense it was a fair bit different than that. Don't placate me, Grey. What's the story here?"

Terrified Amelia would catch a glimpse beneath her surface, Alex's panic redirected itself to anger. Throwing her bag down the hall, she spun back to the doorway and jabbed a finger toward Amelia. "I don't owe you an explanation! I don't owe you anything! It was personal—it's handled, I'm back in time for camp, and that's all you need to know!" She slammed her hand against the doorjamb, and then yelped, the frame catching her directly on the spot already tender from where she'd pounded the floor after Carlton's visit. A burst of pain travelled from her fingertips to her elbow as her vision flashed white from the excruciation. This was different than the soreness of the last two weeks. This was not a bit of swelling, a potential bruise.

"Fuck!" She doubled over, clutching it protectively against her stomach. "Fuck!" The first expletive was for the pain. The second was for her embarrassment.

Amelia was immediately at her side. "Grey." Calloused fingers touched her wrist before she flung them away.

"Just get out, Amelia! Don't touch me!" Tears—tears she had thought ran dry in Carolina—tears of fury, anguish, hurt and desperation, slipped down her cheeks before she could wipe them away. "Leave me alone. Please."

Amelia was quiet a moment, standing beside her, before a tentative hand was set on her shoulder. "I don't know what you're going through, Grey, and you don't have to tell me. You're right. It's not my business. But whatever it is—you're not going through it alone. You can't get rid of me that easy." There was a gentleness to her voice Alex had never heard from her before. A sincerity entirely separate from her regular sarcastic tone. She crossed to the door as Alex turned a cold shoulder, stopping in the threshold. "I'll give you some time—but you know I'm just one floor down."

Two hours later Alex found herself in the Marina District, numb from cold and the half bottle of ibuprofen she'd swallowed trying to get the pain in her wrist under control. One-handed she worked her phone out of her pocket and checked the time. She'd texted Catharine before leaving her apartment. Told her she was back in California and asked if they could meet. She had to get this over with. One more minute of dreading it and she felt like she'd lose her mind.

Arriving early, Alex wandered along the grass of Marina Green until she saw *L'lune Alouette* come in from the bay. Catharine had been out on the water, but told her they could meet at the docks. A clear indication she already suspected what was to come. Any other time they would have met in the comfort of Catharine's home.

Unable to wait for the hour to roll around, she started for the Marina entrance. It hurt too much to stand there on the boulevard, across from the townhouse, knowing she might never set foot in it again.

Her hand on the handle of the gate leading to Yacht Marina's gangway, her text tone chimed. She paused, pulling it out to glance at the screen.

An unknown number.

—what r u doing alex? we had an agreement

Alex scanned her surroundings. The temperature was near freezing, the wind bitter, and there weren't many people around. A few yacht club members furling sails. A couple joggers on the trail. None who looked suspicious. No eyes turned her way. The constant crawling of her skin that lingered, ever present, for the last couple weeks amplified in intensity. The nausea resurfaced, never entirely going away.

They were still watching her. Following her. Tracking her every move.

—Breaking it off. Like I was told to do.

The fingers of her right hand shook as she typed, still cradling her left arm against her chest. Hitting send, she glanced around. He was there, somewhere.

The response was immediate.

—be smart alex
—Fuck you!

She crammed her phone in her pocket and started through the gate, but paused on the platform to pull it back out. As angry as she was, she was even more afraid of what Carlton's watchdog would do if he thought she meant to confess everything to Catharine.

—I haven't said a word. And I won't. Now leave me alone.

There was a swift response, but she left it unread, flipping the phone to silent and heading down the gangway.

Chapter Eight

"Will you come sit?"

Alex stood half a dozen feet away at the end of the dock, her arms folded across her chest. Her expression was vacant, her face pale, her eyes never lifting to look at Catharine.

"No. I can't stay." She shifted her weight from foot to foot, uncomfortable from more than the cold. There was a defensiveness about her Catharine had never seen before.

Bending to finish organizing her dock lines, Catharine said nothing. She'd known whatever this was—whatever had happened—had changed everything. Alex had said she needed some time—but from the moment Catharine answered the call on Christmas Eve, she knew *time* would change nothing.

She completed the final cleat hitch, stepping back onto the deck of *L'lune Alouette*, and straightened, wiping the salt on her rain trousers, wishing inanely she'd been wearing anything other than the coveralls meant to keep out the winter sea. It didn't matter what she was wearing. It wouldn't change the conversation. It wouldn't change the outcome.

She resigned herself to get on with it. To finish whatever this was.

"Are you going to tell me what is going on, Alex?" She knew she could make the conversation easier. All she had to do is ask if it was over. Tell her, after whatever fabrication fumbled from Alex's mouth, that it was okay; she understood. That this was best, for both of them.

But she refused. She wasn't willing to make this easier. Not this time. Nothing about this was easy. She was owed an explanation. She had given Alex every part of herself. Been entirely open and honest. So whatever she'd done to be shut out—to have it end this way— wasn't right. Wasn't fair. And she'd be damned if she made it easy.

"I just can't do this anymore, Catharine." The hoarse voice was bereft of emotion, her hazel eyes, dark beneath the cloud cover, fixed across the bay.

"This?"

"This." Alex nodded. "You and I."

"Do I get to ask why?" Catharine wavered between wanting to jump to the dock and slap Alex—slap her from her torpor, bring her back to life—or fold her in her arms and hold her, to tell her everything would be all right. But she did neither.

Alex took a deep breath, centering herself, and at last met Catharine's eyes. "I need to focus on myself. On my career. I promised myself I would never let anything get between me and the game. I have worked my entire life to get here and I can't risk it anymore." The words sounded scripted and rehearsed, something she had worked through a thousand times.

Catharine felt feverish beneath her heavy rain gear, her cheeks flaring.

"And you decided all of this on Christmas Eve? With no warning? No discussion? You just went for a run and decided it was time to end it? Then bolted away to Carolina to figure out how to tell me?" It all came out angrier, more bitter than she'd meant it, but she didn't believe Alex, and wanted the truth. Even if she had to goad her into admitting it.

"Please." For the first time Alex's voice wavered. "Don't."

"Don't what?" Catharine snapped the dangling halyard taut, busying her hands with drawing the line through the block. Her anger grew deeper, more authentic than before. "You want me to tell you it's fine? That it's no big deal, Alex? We had our fun, let's shake hands and walk away? Or maybe you want me to say we can still be friends? Catch up from time to time?"

The bitterness that permeated her laugh was surprising, even to her. A fury was waxing inside her, threatening to explode with words she could never take back. Taking a shaky breath, she turned her back to Alex, trying to collect herself, to compose her thoughts.

"Tell me someone threatened you, Alex."

There was a long silence. "Catharine." Alex's voice was gentle, without the robotic quality it had held since she'd arrived. It was enough to almost make Catharine look back. To give her hope. But before she could turn, Alex spoke again. "No one threatened me. No one knows about us. Not even my friends. What I told you is the truth. When I left that morning, I realized…" Behind her Catharine could hear the unsteady breath, the threat of tears once more. "I realized I'd grown to want too much. I'd started to think I didn't care what happened in my career. Soccer became secondary. I would have given it all up if it meant I could have a life with you. And that's not what I want." From the hitch in her breath, Catharine knew her struggle with tears had been lost. But she couldn't bring herself to look at her. To console her as she once would have.

For two weeks she'd convinced herself someone was forcing Alex's hand. HEG had caught wind of their affair, or Caleb, or that girl, Monica, had figured them out. She'd considered that Carlton may have gotten suspicious and sent one of his puppets to scare her off. Or even that Alex had simply grown cold feet through the publicity of Carlton's presidential campaign—and become overwhelmed. It had never actually dawned on her that this was something Alex could really want. That the decision had been hers, and hers alone.

"I never wanted to take your career from you. I never wanted anything but for you to succeed." Catharine's breath grew shallower with every exhalation. She felt blindsided, knocked off kilter by a backhanded, vicious blow.

"I know."

"So it's easier for you to just…walk away? To just…end it?"

"You think this is easy?" Alex's voice was quiet, but her resentment was real. "There is nothing *easy* about this! It's just what is right!"

"For who?!" Catharine whirled to face her, nearly slipping on the damp surface of the deck, having to grab a lifeline to keep her balance. "Did you ever think about me? How I would feel?" There was a tightening in her throat, her vision growing blurry from the stubborn tears that caught at the back of her eyes. She shook her head, the two of them at last holding each other's gaze. "I love you, Alex," she managed, the admission nothing more than a whisper. "I love you."

They were three words she had never strung together, not once in her life, to anyone. But she meant them now. She would have begged—pleaded on hand and knee, implored Alex to reconsider—if she had thought it would have made the slightest difference. She would have humiliated herself, offered anything and everything, if it would have had even a remote chance of changing her mind.

But she could see that it wouldn't. The decision had been made. The outcome was final. She'd known it since that first phone call seventeen days earlier. She'd just refused to believe it. She'd refused to give up the best thing that had ever happened to her without a fight.

But you couldn't fight for something that was already lost when there was nothing left to win.

Alex turned her face away, shutting Catharine out for the last time. All that was left to say had been said.

A surge of despair flooded her, filling the well of loneliness she hadn't known since Alex had come into her life. Unable to breathe, unable to think, she sank back against her mast, letting her body slip to the deck, her head between her knees, and wrapped her arms around her, feeling as if she needed to physically hold herself together. She would have traded anything in her power to simply disappear, to find a place where she could fall apart, hidden from the world.

"Catharine."

Squeezing her eyes shut, she ignored the tears that escaped. She would not allow herself to look. Because she knew if she looked once more she would forget herself and beg. And she couldn't. Her pride—her dignity— was all she had left.

"Alex, please go."

For a time there was silence, a long hesitation, before she finally heard the slow, soft steps leave the way they'd come. And when she finally dared to open her eyes the sun was low and Alex was gone. And she was more alone than she'd ever been.

Chapter Nine

Alex could do nothing but watch as Monica Ashby's poor clearance fell like a gift at the right foot of the Tyrants midfielder. Surrounded by acres of space, Bethany Hayes—the Penn State grad acquired by the DC team in the first round of the draft—leapt on the opportunity to leave a mark during the first professional start of her career. With only four minutes of regular time remaining in the first half, the twenty-one year old rookie laced a rocket into the back of the net, bringing the score to two-nil.

The crowd of Sirens fans booed with shouts of *offsides*, but Alex knew the sideline ref had made the right call when her flag stayed down.

They were playing like shit. The second of three preseason games, the Sirens were disjointed, half their players newly acquired through trades over the offseason. They looked nothing like the team of the previous year that had surprised the entire league by making it into the Championship finals. A loss of 2-1 to the Portland Warriors, but still an unheard of accomplishment for an expansion team. The Tyrants, on the other hand, looked to be in midseason form, cohesive and communicative on the pitch.

"No worries!" Amelia hollered, adjusting the captain's armband slipping down her sweat soaked elbow as she jogged to the center circle to reset. "Chin up." But Alex could tell she'd have a lot more to say as soon as they hit the lockers.

Five minutes of added time went up on the fourth official's board and the play was back at it. The Sirens were gassed and the Tyrants smelling blood, seeking a third goal before the whistle.

Legs burning, Alex received a cross from Molly Rodrigues, finding herself with a clean run down the middle, and sprinted toward the box. She'd shaken loose of the center back who'd jostled her around all evening, and had sighted her shot just as her legs were clipped out from underneath her. Darting face first into the turf, Alex waited for the foul to be whistled, but no call came. The Tyrants keeper scooped up the ball and sent it back toward center.

"Bullshit!" Alex cussed, slamming the heel of her hand into the grass, before immediately regretting it. She'd only had her cast off a week and the healing bones still gave her trouble. She couldn't afford another injury. Not after she'd been left off the US roster for the fractured metacarpals.

Though she knew a broken hand had meant nothing to the National Team coach, Izzy Atwood. Plenty of players played with upper extremity injuries. It was her mediocrity over the eight weeks of preseason club training that had left her home while the National Team kicked off the year with the SheBelieves Cup. Atwood had just used the injury as a gentler letdown when discussing Alex's absence from the roster with the media.

To Alex, she had been more direct.

"We'll reassess in the spring. There's not much time left before summer, but if you really want this, I'm sure you'll have things sorted, Grey." Atwood didn't have to spell it out. There was only one camp left before the final decisions would be made for the World Cup roster. And in Alex's present condition—broken bones aside—she hadn't made the cut.

Shoving herself up from the grass, Alex hustled back into play. The National Team coaching staff would be reviewing tape, even if it was just a preseason game.

Another few turnovers and Alex found herself in position to challenge Angela Covey—the defender who had given her trouble all night—just outside the eighteen. A half a head taller and twenty pounds heavier, Angela grappled shoulder-to-shoulder with Alex, before snaking her arm around her and pulling her to the ground by her hair, their legs entangled and ball pinned between them. The short blast of the whistle sounded. Breathless, Alex rolled to the side, struggling to her knees to quickly resume play, certain she'd earned a free kick with the challenge. Instead, to her disbelief, she found the ref pointing the other direction, the foul awarded to the Tyrants.

Livid, Alex launched to her feet. "You've got to be kidding me!" She glanced toward the defender, still writhing around on the grass, her face clutched in her hands. "I didn't touch her!" She took a step in the ref's direction, her frustration of the match blazing.

"Simmer down, eleven." The ref didn't look at her.

"She pulled my fucking hair!" Alex stood in the way of the free kick, still challenging the official.

"This is your warning."

Amelia had jogged over, eyeing Alex, who was unwilling to disengage. "Grey—"

"You're fucking blind."

"Captain, get your player under control, or I will."

"The only thing you should be doing is awarding her an Oscar for her performance." Alex jerked her shoulder away from the hand Amelia set on her. "This is total bullshit."

Without a word the referee went to her pocket and withdrew a yellow card, holding it in Alex's direction.

"For what?!" Alex would have lunged forward, all common sense vanishing, if Amelia hadn't had the back of her jersey in a vice grip, dragging her aside.

The crowd booed the booking, jeering the ref as Alex shook herself free of Amelia's hold.

"What is bloody wrong with you?" Amelia hissed in passing as the free kick was taken and she ran down the field.

For the last minute of the half, Alex couldn't focus. She'd only received three yellow cards in her entire professional career. Never once had she sworn at an official, no matter the call. But she couldn't shake the anger building inside of her. The frustration that had been lingering, day in and day out, for months on end.

Her off-the-pitch emotions were affecting her play. They had been since the first day of preseason training. The lowness that she felt, the emptiness, beginning with Catharine and waxing with the National Team cut, were somersaulting her psyche.

Nothing about her was a hundred percent. Not mentally. Not physically. And her game was telling.

The whistle blew twice to conclude the half and Alex started for the tunnel.

"Grey." It was Rodney Collins, the Sirens head coach. "How are we?"

Given that her first inclination was to snark a response at his use of the royal "we," her answer probably should have been anything other than "I'm good, Rod, I promise." But it was what came out and it was the story she was sticking to as they headed for the lockers.

"You don't look like you out there."

"I'm sorry. I—there were a lot of bad calls. I guess I just got tired of it."

"Hmm," he nodded, noncommittal. Unlike Izzy Atwood, Rod Collins was anything but direct. "How's the hand?"

"Good as new," she lied, opening and closing it as if to prove its function, despite the swelling that lingered around her knuckles.

"Excellent. No more bar fights," he teased, trying to lighten the mood, but the quip fell flat given her uncalled for display of non-professionalism on the field a few minutes prior.

Alex's smile was strained. The injury was what was known as a Boxer's Fracture, or Scrapper's Break, because it was a common injury from punching something with a closed fist. She'd said it came from a fall while running and nobody had questioned her, though she knew it was likely little believed. But it wasn't like she could admit it had started by pounding the floor of her apartment when her lover's husband—who happened to be running for president—dropped in to blackmail her into breaking off her affair with his estranged wife. In this case, the lie seemed respectfully qualified.

The dressing room was quiet with an undercurrent of tension running between the players. Collins did his best to rile up morale and Amelia cussed at them with a few expletives only an Aussie could conjure, and then they were due back on the field.

Deftly avoiding their captain, Alex hustled into position, feeling Amelia's anger permeating as she trotted out behind her.

"Get it together, Alex," was all she found time to say before the whistle blew and the kickoff for the second half was underway.

Get it together. She repeated the phrase over and over, trying to clear her head. *Focus. Breathe. Respond, don't react.* She could do this.

And then in the seventy-fifth minute Alex found herself jockeyed off a fifty-fifty ball and clipped the ankle of her opponent, who flopped to the ground. An overreaction from the defender, selling the foul to the ref, who didn't hesitate a second to blow her whistle and award the Tyrants the free kick.

Alex felt her focus slipping once again, her anger taking its place. There was no card, thank God—just a verbal warning from the ref, which Alex brushed off in annoyance—and the play resumed. Two more turnovers and a mishandled ball by the Tyrants allowed a brilliant header from Molly Rodrigues, putting the Sirens on the board. And then two minutes later, Amelia leveled the score.

"Let's go, let's go, let's go!" Amelia shrugged off her celebrating teammates and clapped her hands together, encouraging the squad. With several minutes left on the clock, there was still a chance to close the night with a win.

Feeling her inadequacies, and the little impact she'd made in the game, Alex forced her tired legs to find another gear. Rodney hadn't chosen to sub her out, despite sitting on a yellow, which meant he still expected something of her. Was still counting on her to deliver. To do something. Anything.

A corner earned by Alex's fellow forward, Jess Combs, brought a stoppage time goalscoring opportunity for the Sirens. Settling in the crowded box to await the ball, Alex grappled with her opponents for position. The emotions were high, the game on the line for both teams, and the Tyrants had called their full squad in to defend.

Amelia took the corner, lofting the ball into the six, and Alex left the ground with half a dozen others to try and get her head on target. In an attempt of gaining superior aerial advantage, Alex miscalculated her leap and swung her arms with too much velocity, driving them out behind her. She felt the immediate connection with bone on bone, her elbow making contact with what felt like a face, and then the unavoidable collision of her body with another.

Coming down in a heap, twisted at an awkward angle, something snapped beneath her, and a scream of pain pierced through the chanting crowd, pounding drums, and shouts from players who'd continued contending for the ball.

It was the rookie midfielder, Bethany Hayes, who Alex rolled off of, the young woman curling into a fetal position and screaming into the grass.

"Hey," Alex reached for the girl's heaving shoulder, "are you okay?" A question to an answer she already knew. She'd felt the snap, heard the crack, and knew that scream. It wasn't the cry of seeking the ref's attention.

It was the wail of devastation, one part pain, two parts terror at the prospect of a season ending injury.

Shoved away by the Tyrants goalkeeper, who dropped to her knees and waved medical over, Alex pushed herself to her feet, feeling dazed. The ref was running at her, digging in her pocket, her whistle dangling from her lips. She withdrew a card and it took Alex a moment to comprehend the situation—she was already riding on a yellow—a second yellow equaled a red, meaning ejection from the game. But no yellow was produced—the official had jumped immediately to red.

A straight red. The same instant result as two yellows, but with different long term consequences.

"I—" Alex didn't even know who she was trying to talk to—who to appeal to. The injury had been unintentional. There had been no malicious intent. No matter her frustrations, her competitive nature, Alex had never intentionally harmed another player in her entire career. She was conscientious. Respectful. She'd never played dirty—especially toward a young player just starting her breakout career.

"I'm sorry," she tried to kneel beside Bethany, but the ref was pointing to the sidelines and her teammates were shouting and it became impossible to focus at all.

As she headed off the pitch, Jill Thompson—a winger traded from the Bluebells to the Sirens—was in the official's face, yelling an angry protest, questioning the card. "For what reason?" she demanded, her blonde ponytail swinging wildly beneath her headband as she fended off Amelia, who tried to hook her arm and draw her away. Jill was a longtime captain for the National Team, with over two-hundred international caps, and was entirely unafraid to show her displeasure at a bad call.

"Captain," again the ref was looking to Amelia to get her team under control.

Alex took a seat on the bench before a hand touched her shoulder. It was Lynn Armstrong, the assistant coach, gesturing toward the tunnel. "Alex, you can't stay here."

In the chaos of the moment, Alex had forgotten a red card meant you had to leave the area completely. Ejected players weren't permitted near the pitch or technical area. And then there would be a suspension—how many games, she didn't know. But given the straight red, the punishment would be more severe.

Before walking into the tunnel, she glanced back toward the field, where the medical staff was still working on Bethany Hayes. They'd brought out a stretcher. The girl was still lying on her back, her hands covering her face.

"Are you fucking trying to throw it all away, Grey?" A hand grabbed Alex's arm as she hurried toward the private exit, anxious to get into the crisp Oakland air. Amelia's dimly lit face was damp with perspiration, her pale cheeks crimson with rage. She was barefoot, warmups pulled on, a pair of socks in her hand, clearly having skipped her post-game ritual to find Alex before she'd managed to leave the stadium. "Because if that's what you want, right now you're doing a bloody fine job of it!"

"Leave me alone." Alex tugged her arm from her grip. She'd changed and slipped out of the lockers before the final whistle had blown. She wasn't sure what the protocol was for a red card—no doubt she was meant to wait for a dressing down from the coaching staff—but she hadn't wanted to wait around. The team was owed an apology. So were Rod and Lynn. She'd screwed up and let everyone down. Hurt a girl who—depending on the gravity of the injury—might not play again. But she couldn't deal with it tonight. She couldn't bring herself to care. About anything.

Whatever consequences were headed her way, she'd deal with in the morning.

The tunnel was silent, both teams still in the dressing rooms, with only the security guard smoking outside the exit door. Uncomfortable under the scrutiny of Amelia's stare, Alex stared at her friend's bare feet.

"How's Hayes?"

"Pretty busted up, mate." Amelia shook her head. She'd been Alex's crutch the last eight weeks, her proverbial shoulder to cry on. She never asked what happened with Catharine and Alex had never offered. But she'd kept Alex going through what had threatened to be the crippling of her career.

Trudging through the lowest of lows, Alex would have resigned herself to self-pity and loathing had it not been for Amelia's tough love and a grating sarcasm she suspected coated more sympathy than the pragmatic Australian was ever willing to let on. But she wasn't a sugarcoater, and was entirely unafraid to call Alex out when she felt she was wrong. And tonight, she'd been wrong.

"It was an accident."

"You played like a fucking muppet. The whole night. You're so busy feeling sorry for yourself you can't even see the enormous chip on your shoulder you're carrying around. You think everyone's out to get you."

"I didn't mean to hurt her!" Alex annunciated every staccato word, her temper brewing. "I was trying to win the ball."

"You spit the dummy at the ref! You may as well have put a target on your back for that official. You're so busy trying to prove yourself you made a terrible judgment call. And it's all because whatever you're dealing with—whatever bullshit you've got going on in your personal life—has given you some bizarrely skewed sense of self-worth. But now it's leaking onto the pitch and tonight someone else paid the price for your recklessness."

"Oh, quit with the psychoanalyzing, Amelia—"

"I get that you're hurting, mate—and I think you think you don't care if this all falls apart. But I know that's a load of horse shit. You're better than that." She gestured toward the lockers. "Now get your arse back in there to talk to Collins. He's the one who's going to have to appeal to the review board to contest the call."

"He saw what happened. I don't have anything to say. It wasn't intentional—"

"That ref booked you for violent conduct, Alex! Get a bloody grip! That's three games—maybe more!" Her fingers pressed into Alex's forearm. "This isn't a joke! You stole that girl's season over a worthless preseason match!"

Alex yanked herself away so hard she nearly tripped backward over her untied laces. *Violent conduct!* Two words no athlete ever wanted to hear thrown their way.

"I'd trade her places if I could." Alex backed toward the door. Amelia was right. She'd been trying too hard. Needing to matter too much. She had to apologize.

But she couldn't face Collins right now. If she did she would do something even more self-destructive—like hand in her resignation. And she knew, deep beneath her current sinking despair, she didn't want that. If she didn't have this game, she would have nothing.

"Tell me what the outcome is."

"Alex—!"

Pulling the hood of her sweatshirt over her head, Alex pushed her way out the door.

Chapter Ten

Russia Officials Railroad WorldCargo Expansion in Port Kaliningrad in Response to Presidential Candidate Cleveland's Platform On Tariff Taxes and the War Against European Exportation: Is Turmoil Brewing in the Cleveland Empire Amidst British Heiress and American Presidential Hopeful?

Catharine threw the Washington Post onto her desk and tapped the speaker button on her office phone harder than intended, sending the receiver clattering across her keyboard.

"Carlton?" She picked up the handset and set it back in its cradle, uncertain if she'd lost the call.

"Well?!" His accusation reverberated through the speaker.

"Well, what?" Tipping back in her chair she closed her eyes. This was the fifth call from him this week she'd taken along these lines.

"*Turmoil*? Presidential *Hopeful*? What is this garbage, Catharine? Who have you been talking to?"

"Oh for God's sake, Carlton—I can't silence all your critics for you every time something goes to print!" How this latest headline had become her fault was beyond her. She was the one dealing with a half billion dollar stalemate with the Russian commerce officials due to her husband's imprudent remarks against the European trade market. If anyone should be livid it should be her. Not to mention the belittlement of referring to her as the *heiress* of WorldCargo. As if she had done nothing more than inherit the transportation giant while sitting back on her thumbs enjoying the revenue.

The media had not been kind to Carlton or the platforms he ran on—his campaign fueled by archaic policies that transgressed the morals of even the most conservative members of his party and stomped the ideology of the progressive thinkers, as he promised to reinstate the country to the *good old days*—whatever those had been. But the South and a scattering of midwestern states had latched onto the concept, interpreting the deceptive jargon to mean less government control. A sentiment Catharine found ironic, considering as a senator her husband had written some of the most governmentally intrusive bills the state of South Carolina had ever seen.

"They get this crap from somewhere, Catharine! Your press agents aren't doing their job! First the whole debacle with *The Guardian*, and last week *The Times*—now this! Your name shouldn't be coming up in my campaign, God damnit!"

"Amen!" Catharine did not have the patience for him today. "There is nothing I would prefer more than my name being distanced from your war mongering platform!"

"*War mongering*!?" he roared and Catharine considered disconnecting the call. Their fragile agreement was treading on dangerous grounds. Unsubstantiated rumors were amuck about the impending demise of their relationship, and every day she grew closer to penning a release for her PR to publish—confirming the speculation to be true.

But she didn't. She'd made it this far. Through the dog-and-pony show cross country campaign trail, the townhalls, the debates. And last month the South Carolina primary where Carlton had somehow skated to the top, clearing his path to the National Convention in July. Never in her wildest dreams had she imagined he'd make it out of the spring. But she'd given her word, and as long as he held up to his end of the bargain, she would stick to their agreement—all the way to November, if needs be.

His rant continued and Catharine turned her attention to sorting emails.

After a minute or so, the voice of her secretary came over the intercom. "Miss Comtois to see you, ma'am."

Catharine muted Carlton's line. "Send her in."

Nathalie hesitated in the doorway when she heard Carlton's voice on the speaker.

"He can't hear us," she waved a dismissive hand. "What did you find?"

Nathalie was distracted by the call. "He hasn't noticed you aren't engaging?"

"Trust me, he prefers to hold both sides of the conversation."

"Can I pop on the line? Tell him about your latest investment?" Nathalie arched a subtle grin.

"I take it you found something you liked?" Catharine tugged the *Washington Post* from beneath the hip Nathalie had rested on her desk, smoothing out the crease in annoyance. She didn't know why she cared. It was just going in the bin.

"You know, you could have an extra chair in here—at least put on a front of welcomeness toward your guests."

"I don't entertain guests in my office," Catharine dumped the article in the recycling. "The last thing I want them to feel is welcome."

Before Nathalie could quip back, Catharine held a finger to her lips and unmuted the call, cutting Carlton off mid-sentence. He'd gone off about a dip in polls he attributed to her continued business with Singapore, but she'd failed to connect his bizarre theory of how the two were related.

Nor did she care.

"I have a meeting, Carlton," she said brusquely, "I have to go."

"Catharine, did you even hear—"

She ended the call with a tap of her fingertip, reveling in the silence that ensued. Twenty-two hundred miles away and he could still find a way to make her life a living hell.

"Do you really need a chair?"

Nathalie's umber eyes narrowed. "No wonder the papers call you formidable. If this is how you treat me, I can't imagine how you'd treat someone you don't like."

"Who said I liked you?" A smile infiltrated Catharine's voice. "Anyhow—I'm busy—what did you find?"

Nathalie steepled her fingers, pressing them against her lips, her eyes shining. Catharine hadn't seen her this excited about a project since they were young.

Two weeks ago, following another disappointing email from her agent indicating no upcoming auditions in sight, Catharine had suggested a different approach to lift Nathalie's stagnate career. A theatre company. A selfish suggestion, on one hand—it would keep Nathalie local, in the city, instead of traveling across the globe. But it also offered a stability and element of control—a performance space she could make her own. And to Catharine's benefit, Union Square, in the heart of San Francisco's theatre district, was prime location to some of the best real estate investments in the state.

"There's a building on Castro not far from 18th. It's not on the market yet, but it's supposedly going to be listed soon."

"Make an offer. Don't let them list it." Catharine's fingers drummed the side of her desk. "Seal the deal before they have any other interest."

"Don't you want to think about it? This all fell into fruition very quickly."

"Would it make a good theatre?"

"Yes."

"Do you like the location?"

"It's perfect."

"Then what is it you want me to think about?" Catharine tilted back in her chair to regard her long time friend. "I trust your judgment. I believe it will be a good career move for you and a solid investment for me. I don't see what else there is to consider."

Nathalie pushed off the desk and made a casual loop around the room, stopping in front of the wall of glass facing north over the bay.

"I guess some people might inquire about the price? The condition? The cost of renovation? You know, all those things that go along with purchasing century-old real estate in the middle of the most expensive city in the country." She turned back to Catharine. "Does any of that interest you?"

"No." Catharine was blunt. "Not really. Is the price fair?"

"Tony felt it could be attained at market value. Maybe less."

"Offer five percent above the going rate. Cash. A fourteen day escrow."

"Cate, that would be like—"

"Give them twenty-four hours to accept or tell them we'll move on."

"N'importe quoi!" Nathalie threw her hands up in exasperation. "Fine. I'll have Tony draw up a proposal and run the numbers and see if it all makes sense."

"Good." Catharine went back to her emails.

"I also found an apartment." This time Nathalie was more tentative, watching Catharine for a reaction. This was not something they had talked about.

"Oh." Catharine stared at her open spreadsheet, trying to feign indifference. "I didn't know you were looking."

"You know I can't stay with you forever." She circled back around to the desk. "It's nearby, less than a mile away in Pacific Heights."

"Not forever, but you know you can stay with me as long as you'd like. There's no rush—"

"I know, Cate." Her voice was gentle as she cut her off. "But I need to establish my life here. I need to get back on track and create a space to work in. And," she flicked her a wry smile, "I want to leave my dishes in the sink and fold my laundry on the kitchen table. Maybe drop a bath towel on the floor from time to time."

"Hmm," mused Catharine, "with habits like that it's surprising they even let people like you live alone."

Nathalie tutted with mock indignation. "There's also that leggy ballerina —you know, the one Jules introduced us to after La Sylphide? Let's just say I've been waiting for you to go out of town... give a little detailed exploration to find out if she's really a blonde—"

"I'm sorry, how soon did you say you could sign the lease?"

"Ferme-la!" Nathalie laughed, casting her a scornful gaze.

Catharine forced herself to smile. She'd known, with the prospect of the theatre, Nathalie would begin looking for a place of her own. She'd stayed with her since Christmas, dedicating her days to a personal crusade to keep Catharine company, intent on not allowing her to feel the sting of being alone. Trying to keep her mind off Alex. Off the depression knocking at her door. But it wasn't Nathalie's job to make up for all that was missing in Catharine's life. And she knew she had to let her go.

In tune to Catharine's thoughts, Nathalie tentatively broached a subject she knew was taboo.

"I read an article about Alex this morning. It was in the sports section of the *Chronicle*. Did you know she was cut from the US team?"

Catharine did know. Several weeks earlier she'd found herself googling Alex's name, despite her better judgment. She was still looking for answers, even as the months passed, grappling to understand what had led to the disintegration of their relationship. The weight of not knowing—of being caught so unaware—had taken a heavy toll. There had been no sense of closure, making it impossible to put the matter to rest. And she despised the weakness in herself she'd uncovered given how affected she still was.

"Why would I know that?" Her tone was sharp, her focus returning to her computer.

"It sounds like she's had a rocky start to the year."

Do I look like I damn well care? Was what Catharine wanted to say. Instead, she shrugged.

"That's unfortunate."

"I guess she also broke her wrist."

Hand. She'd read she'd broken three bones in her hand.

"No doubt she's fully recovered. Bones don't take long to heal."

"Ah." Nathalie pressed down on her stapler, her idle hands plucking up the discharged scrap of metal. "So you're keeping tabs if you know the injury is old."

"She was favoring the hand when we spoke on the dock. I can put two and two together without having to comb the sports section of the papers, Nat." It was at least a partial truth.

"I see," Nathalie singsonged, treading further along dangerous ground. "It was mentioned she was expelled from a game last week. Something about a card and a foul."

"Whatever that means." Catharine grew more irritable, knowing she did know what it meant. *Red card. Yellow card. Penalty kicks. Free kicks. Corner kicks. Throw-ins. Headers. Half-turn.* All terms she'd become familiar with over the last year. She thought about the night of the gala, teasing Alex in the Fairmont that she'd have to learn what a red card meant. The two of them talking about their future together—where it might lead. The night Catharine first knew—while standing on the sweeping staircase of the City Hall urging her peers to demonstrate their noblesse oblige—that she was in love with the Carolina girl. The night Carlton had destroyed everything, planting the seeds for the slippery decline of their relationship before it had hardly had a chance to grow.

She tidied papers on her desk that needed no tidying, refusing to engage further in the conversation.

"I guess she hurt another player—broke a girl's leg. It said she'd been fined and given a three game suspension. She'll miss the season opener for her team."

"I wasn't aware you'd become the world's most dedicated football fan," Catharine flashed her eyes to Nathalie's, holding her gaze with a challenge. Daring her to say one more word.

"I'm not." On rare occasion the woman had the ability to maintain the patience of Job. "I'm just a fan of seeing you happy, Cate. And you're not happy."

"I'm even less happy talking about it."

"Then why not reach out to her? How can you just let it go—"

Unreasonably incensed, Catharine flew to her feet. "Just let it go?!" She slammed her palms against her desk, marring the surface with the band of her wedding ring, upsetting the phone from its cradle. She knew her outburst was far too dramatic than suited the situation, but continued unabated, anyhow. "You think I just *let it go*, Nathalie? Tossed it aside?! You weren't there! I know you want to think there is some great conspiracy afoot behind all this, but you're just bloody wrong! She decided she had to make a choice between me and her career and she chose her career. And you know what? It's understandable! Let's not pretend I didn't make the exact same decision twenty-five years ago!" Catharine yanked at the ring on her finger, trying to pry it from her hand, but the band had bent and grown stuck behind her knuckle. A fitting metaphor for the damnable marriage she couldn't seem to quite shuck off. "So I'm hardly in a position to condemn her for it! I guess what goes around comes around—and karma finally caught up with me!"

In the ensuing silence the upturned receiver started to chime a busy signal, the irritating sound a flash point to the pinnacle of Catharine's tantrum. Unable to stop herself, she flung her arm across the surface of her desk, sending the phone and keyboard and stack of papers she'd been reviewing soaring to the floor.

"I'm done talking about this!"

Stunned by the outburst, both women stood on either side of the desk, neither knowing what to say. Catharine couldn't remember the last time she'd lost her temper with Nathalie. Never, perhaps. At least not like this.

"I'm sorry, Nat." She bent to collect the unfortunate items of her misplaced anger as Nathalie retrieved the phone. "I know you're trying to help. I just don't want to talk about it anymore. I need you to let it go." She fiddled with her wedding band, turning the ring round and round in its lopsided circle, unable to meet Nathalie's eyes. "I have a conference with my legal team about this Russia debacle. Can we get dinner tonight and finish talking about your apartment? I promise to be in a more proper frame of mind." She looked up. "Forgive me?"

For once Nathalie offered no biting words of sarcasm, no teasing wit to set the situation right. She only looked at Catharine for a long moment, before reaching forward to squeeze her hand and then left without a word.

Chapter Eleven

Alex woke to the strumming guitar riff of Billie Joe Armstrong rocking his way through *Manic Monday*. Groggy, head pounding, it took her a moment to source the sound. There was a familiarity to the tune in her half lucid state, yet it was so adverse to the dream she'd been lost in—swimming futilely toward a boat floating out to sea—she had trouble placing the significance behind it.

Then it struck her.

Rodney Collins. His ringtone.

She lurched forward, flailing for her nightstand, but instead found herself faceplanting onto the economy carpet of her living room floor, dragging an empty bottle of Grey Goose with her. She was still dressed, one tennis shoe on, her phone blaring its punk-rock anthem beside her.

While her brain struggled to catch up with her body's jolting wakefulness, she temporarily forgot the chain of events that had led to the splitting headache now assaulting her.

"Rod?" Her cotton-mouth and disoriented tone belied her level of consciousness.

"Good morning." The lack of cheerfulness in his tone indicated the morning was about to be anything but good. "It's a no go on the appeal. The three game suspension stands. Along with a thousand dollar fine to the club."

Alex blinked herself into focus, still sitting on the floor. *Three games.* Which meant, with one game already served—she'd sat out the final preseason game against the Salt Lake Panthers the night before—she'd miss the regular season opener in Florida this coming weekend, and the South Carolina match at her former home stadium the week after. A disastrous way to start the season, and a surefire way to guarantee she wasn't going to make Izzy Atwood's spring camp roster. Her last chance to redeem herself before the World Cup.

Her body deflated, slumping back against the IKEA couch.

"Now, Alex…" He morphed into his big brother pitch, an endearing habit the players loved him for, but which only made Alex cringe in the moment. "It's like we talked about last weekend—you can't let this get into your head."

Last weekend. The morning after her expulsion and now Twitter famous red card—the social media platform obsessed with her early match profanity garnering the yellow for dissent, followed by the nauseating caught-on-camera/replayed-on-slowmo-loop shattering of Bethany Hayes' right tib-fib, resulting in a call of violent conduct from the ref. To Alex's slim fortune, the straight red was widely judged as an erroneous call from a disgruntled official—there had been no clear and obvious foul on Alex's part in the box —just a misfortunate aerial collision.

When Rodney had called Alex into his office the following morning she'd expected to be sacked. At twenty-eight years old, in her seventh season as a professional in the NWSL, she was almost certain she was getting cut. As much for her behavior off the pitch as on it.

"About last night," she'd started, unable to look the slender, quiet-natured former premier league champion in the eye, "I know I shouldn't have—"

"Walker told me she sent you home. That she thought you needed to cool off."

Alex looked up, catching his steady gaze, before returning her attention to his cluttered desk.

"I let her know that's not how we do things here—maybe the coaching staff has different protocols back at Arsenal—but that's not how I run my team. If a player's sent off, I expect them to be waiting for me in the dressing room at the end of the game. She assured me she wouldn't make the mistake of undermining my authority again." He said it in such a way that Alex knew he hadn't believed Amelia, but was willing to let her take the fall.

Her unprofessional dereliction of duty addressed, he'd then launched into a story of his own. A situation almost two decades earlier when he'd been playing for the English national team and badly fractured a German player's femur in a friendly match—an injury that had ultimately ended the other man's career.

"A bad slide tackle, poor timing on my part—I let it get to me, Alex. It plagued me for years. I was never able to play with the same heart; the same verve again. It dampened my entire game." He pulled off his glasses and tapped the frame on his desk absentmindedly, his fingers running over a file folder that read *Grey* on the cover. "You've had a rough couple months— there's no denying it. The start of this year has been polar to the promise you showed last season. But," he looked up, resolute, "I believe you've got a lot of game left in you, Alex. I think you're still coming into the peak of your career. I've spoken with ownership and assured HEG you still have a lot to offer, and—if you can get your act together, and get your head back on straight—I think Izzy Atwood will feel the same." Pulling open the bottom drawer of his filing cabinet, he stuffed the folder back in place, sliding it closed. "I've filed an appeal for the length of the suspension—I'd really like you back on the pitch for opening day. But for right now, take the downtime, roll up your sleeves, pull up your socks, and get yourself set right. I'll be counting on you the next time you lace up your boots."

When he'd said *set straight* he probably hadn't meant down a half a fifth of vodka while streaming footage of her teammates playing the Panthers in Utah, as she held herself a pity party on her living room floor.

Feeling guilty, Alex tried to clear the dryness from her throat, forcing herself to sit up as the room did a nebulous oscillation around her.

"I know it's not the result we wanted—but don't let it get you down. Two more weeks, an unfair bit of cash, and everything will be back on track— am I right, Grey?"

"Yeah," Alex managed, nodding her affirmation into the darkness of her living room. "Back on track."

Because how could she tell him *back on track* for her wasn't just a matter of getting her game right? That for more than two months now she'd been second guessing every action of her personal life since the moment Carlton Cleveland had darkened her door. That her thoughts ranged from the self-admonishment she dealt out in heavy doses for her handling of his threats— telling herself she was a fool for having not immediately gone to the police —or at the very least, having trusted Catharine with the situation. To chastising herself for even considering turning him in—knowing the senator would make good on his word if she even dreamed of involving the law. Men like him didn't pay the consequences of their actions. It was the whistleblowers who met their downfall.

But either way, right or wrong, her choice had been made—and yet she still hadn't been able to find a way forward. To accept that it was over. In the imbecilic delusions of her dreams she'd wake, temporarily forgetting everything that had happened, and try to restart her day on the crux of that Christmas Eve morning. And then reality would dawn and the shitshow of her life would come back into focus.

Back on track didn't feel like it was getting any closer. Not on the field or off it. The only thing that seemed to help were finding various ways to dull away her hurting.

She rolled the Grey Goose bottle to the side and forced herself to her feet, her phone pinched between shoulder and ear as she tugged off her running shoe and turned toward the shower.

"One last thing, Alex—I talked to Walker on the flight home this morning. I know it's outside club protocol, given you're on suspension, but she suggested it would be good for team morale to have you travel with us to the opener next weekend. I'm not sure HEG will spring for the cost, given the certainty you will not be playing, but I'm in accordance with her all the same. So please plan on making the trip to Florida on Thursday. We can talk about it more at training in the morning."

Alex shuffled around a noncommittal agreement, thanked Rodney for the call, and stepped into the lukewarm drizzle of her shower that badly needed cleaning.

She pressed her forehead against the tile wall. Of course Amelia had suggested she travel with the team. It was part of her white knight crusade to save Alex from herself. She hadn't even wanted to let her stay home for last night's final preseason game in Utah—a fair enough assessment, given the state Alex had woken up in. But the fact that she was right was beside the point. It was the insistent meddling in her affairs that irked her. Alex had only reserved a table for one at her pity party. She made show of wanting to be left alone—to the detriment of her own devices.

A truth her friend chose wholeheartedly to ignore.

Both to Alex's annoyance… and covert relief.

The entire flight to Miami Monica Ashby bemoaned her exhausting schedule leading into the summer, taking every opportunity to gloat in front of Alex about the arduous months leading to the World Cup. Whining about the previous month's SheBelieves Cup, the handful of remaining friendlies, the six weeks the team would spend in London during the competition. And when that subject had been exhausted, she gleefully announced how her boyfriend was flying in for the season opener.

"I can't believe you made me come here," Alex complained to Amelia, stretching out on a lounge chair by the hotel pool. They'd arrived mid-morning and been left to their own leisure until they were due for a team dinner in late afternoon. The warm Florida sunshine was a welcome change from the late winter cold front that had accosted California's northern coast.

"Yeah," Amelia languidly rolled on her side to face Alex, half a bottle of sunscreen covering her fair cheeks, making her eyes more emerald than jade. "Terrible punishment, this." She gestured toward the canopy of palm trees and sparkling saltwater pool. "Imagine, you could be home drinking yourself to death instead of soaking up the rays."

Alex ignored the dig and flopped onto her back, her eyes closed. "At least then I wouldn't have been forced to listen to Monica brag on about her oh-so-strenuous life for six hours on a plane. You know she sat behind me just to get my goat."

"Quit whinging," Amelia smeared her fingers through the coating of white lotion, trying in vain to rub it in. "The US lost to Canada. You wouldn't have wanted to be there anyhow."

"Might have won if I was there," Alex smarted, and out of the corner of her eye saw Amelia smile.

"Ah, there she is," she remained on her side, watching Alex, "I was wondering when the Alex I know would finally make an appearance. Perhaps she's coming back from the Self-Doubt Express cruise she's been on?"

Alex searched for something snarky to say, but ended up laughing instead. "Come on," she rolled back on her side, "I've not been that bad. It's not like I started shooting up between my toes or anything."

"I don't know, mate—you scare me a bit when you're in the doldrums."

Not caring for the heavier turn of the conversation, Alex brushed her off. "I'd feel a lot better if I was dressing out tomorrow night."

"Two more games, Grey. A hundred and eighty minutes. It'll be over before you know it."

"Says the girl who's played every minute of every match since she set foot on US soil."

"Eh," Amelia mused, closing her eyes and turning her face to the sun, "I was subbed out on the Matildas in the last seven minutes of the Olympic quarterfinals three years ago. Score was level and went to extra time and we ended up losing in the shootout. Worst view I've ever had from the bench. So I get it."

"The last seven minutes," Alex reached for one of the pool towels pretzeled into the shape of an animal—a seal or walrus, she wasn't sure which—and shook it out, twisting it into a tight spiral. "I'm supposed to feel sympathy for that?"

"Bloody right! We'd have been on to the semis if I'd still been in the match. I haven't missed a penalty since my first year with Arsenal."

Alex sat up and positioned her aim at Amelia's unsuspecting thigh. "I see you ditched Humility 101 at the University of Sydney."

"Fair dinkum," Amelia shrugged just as the snap of Alex's towel landed its mark, sending her bolting upright on the lounge. "Bugger me, that hurt!" She lunged for Alex, but overshot her reach and tipped the chair, landing chin first on the ground. "Damn you, Alex Grey!"

But Alex could hear her laughing behind her as she sprinted for the safety of the pool.

The game was a total domination by the Sirens, to the disappointment of the sold-out Miami Hurricanes home crowd. Beginning with a diving header by Amelia in the fourth minute of the match, things only got worse for the Hurricanes when Jill Thompson and Bree Decker—the rookie holding Alex's position—scored back to back early in the second half.

Alex stared at the screen of the TV in the hotel bar as the clock ticked down the final minutes. Rules of suspension prohibited players from sitting with their team in the technical area, and she hadn't wanted to watch from the stands. Not with eighteen thousand fans cheering on the Hurricanes. The last thing she needed was for someone to recognize her, beginning the onslaught of cell phone photos posted to social media with captions she wouldn't appreciate.

When Even the Bench Won't Have You.
Grey—came all this way—can't even play.
Move over, Tonya Harding.

And whatever other crap twelve-year-olds and fickle fair-weather fans could conjure up.

When Bree Decker scored a second goal in stoppage time, Alex mentally kicked herself for feeling anything other than happy for her. It wasn't the girl's fault she was playing in Alex's place. That was on Alex and Alex alone. But even still she couldn't swallow the bitterness of envy. It was the season opener—a textbook win for the Sirens—and they had done it all without her.

Alex tuned out the commentary and turned to her tonic water, wishing it was something stronger.

"I thought I might find you here."

Alex swiveled toward the familiar voice.

"Shouldn't you be out celebrating? That was quite a shut out."

"I am celebrating," Amelia gracefully swung herself onto a stool as if it were a pommel horse.

"With the girls, I mean."

"You're still one of the girls, aren't you?" She planted her elbows on the table, her tousled hair still dripping from her shower, and motioned at the bartender. "Couple of lagers, please."

Alex contemplated telling her to make it a single—she was out in public and didn't want to risk any further debacles with HEG—but it seemed a little silly, all things considered. How much trouble could one beer get her into?

Footage from the post-match press conference rolled up on TV and Alex saw Rodney had brought Bree Decker to join him. The rookie looked nervous, fidgeting behind the microphones, and Alex was reminded of how young she was. Young and talented and on target to a stellar career.

Rodney brushed through a few questions about his roster, how he felt the team would do when the summer grew closer and the World Cup call-ups thinned his starting XI, and heaped praise on Decker for her two goals and bang-up start to the season. A reporter asked if Alex Grey would return to play in the coming game against South Carolina and he calmly responded that she'd miss one more match but would be back to her regular starting position for their home opener rivalry in two weeks against Portland. Then another reporter chimed in to inquire if he had any comment on the news that Bethany Hayes was officially out for the season.

Alex turned her attention from the TV and swiped up the bottle the bartender had placed in front of her.

"Little salt for that wound?" Amelia flicked a sugar packet at her, kicking her foot under the barstool. "Ignore the yabber, Grey. There's always going to be yabber."

"Where's the celebration tonight?"

Amelia took a sip of her beer. "Don't know. I showered and split. Local club, my guess. The game was a beaut. Girls have right to piss-up a bit. Just not my scene."

"And this is?" Alex looked around at the empty bar in the luxurious hotel lobby. It had a 1950's mint-julep-fur-coats-and-cigars vibe written all over it. Not exactly a happening spot in downtown Miami.

"I thought swanky was your thing," Amelia goaded, downing her beer and dropping a twenty on the counter. "Let's get out of here. I want to check out the beach before we fly out tomorrow."

"Right now?"

"Unless you can think of a better time?"

Alex tipped her bottle back and hopped off the stool. She had loved running in the sand late at night when she lived in South Carolina and the idea sounded appealing. Northern California was beautiful, but the beaches were nothing like the coast along this part of the Atlantic.

The pool gate was locked, closing at nine due to winter hours, but Amelia didn't give it a second thought as she hopped the fence and strolled through the empty cabanas, making her way toward the exit leading to the private beach running down to the water. Alex followed less gracefully in her wake, nearly catching her t-shirt on a Silk-Floss tree along the path as she hurried after Amelia.

Two steps onto the finely combed sand and Amelia took off in a sprint. "Last one to the water has to sit beside Ashby on the flight home!" She shouted, unfurling herself into the darkness.

Caught unprepared and several paces behind, Alex raced after her shadow, laughing and stumbling her way toward the water as fast as her legs would carry her. She caught up to Amelia a few strides before the ground turned damp and managed to get a hold of her arm, jerking her back and propelling herself forward, nearly landing them both on their asses.

"That's holding, ya damn yobbo," Amelia cussed, struggling to catch her breath between gasps of laughter. The two grappled in the sand, vying to make a break away effort to the water, but when Alex finally got a stride ahead Amelia flung her foot out and hooked Alex's ankle, sending them both sprawling in a heap of laughter.

"You're a bastard," Amelia flipped onto her back, staring up at the night sky glowing with the light of the city. "I had you."

"Not a chance," Alex followed suit, crawling to lay beside her, wiping sand from her cheeks and chin. "You may be able to take me on the pitch—but the beach is my home turf."

"You know we have beaches in Australia, right, mate?" Alex didn't have to look at her to know she was smiling one of her crooked smiles.

"Filled with nothing more than sharks and crocodiles, according to *Animal Planet.*"

"How do you think I learned to run so fast?"

"Meh," Alex discounted, "I'll ante you a croc over being chased down by an Evangelical missionary in the Bible Belt any day of the week."

Amelia laughed. "Fair enough."

"And regardless—I had you on this one. The grass might be yours, but the sand is mine—we can rematch, if you'd like. I'll best you any day of the week."

Beside her Amelia pushed up onto an elbow, looking down at her, her face half covered in sand, a blonde eyebrow raised in query. "Is that so?"

"Entirely so," Alex taunted with mock bravado, folding her hands behind her head, trying to appear far more casual than she felt. Amelia was regarding her so intently—a subtle amusement behind her smile—Alex almost looked away. But she didn't. She knew that look. She knew what it meant. And with the whirl of thoughts spinning around her head, she couldn't read her own mind fast enough to decide whether she was okay with it or not.

A few seconds passed, the steady eyes never leaving hers, before Amelia shrugged. "I'm going to kiss you, Grey." She wasn't seeking permission. It was just a statement; a warning. And then she calmly leaned down and kissed Alex on her mouth.

Her lips were chapped—dry from endless hours in the sunshine—but softer than Alex had imagined. Warmer than she'd anticipated.

Anticipated. The thought gave her pause. Had she anticipated it? Had she not wondered, somewhere in the back of her mind, while they were sitting at the bar, what it would be like to kiss Amelia Walker?

She didn't know. She wasn't sure. She wasn't sure of anything at all.

And then Amelia was pulling away and Alex opened her eyes—uncertain when she had closed them—the two of them remaining just a breath apart.

It had been a chaste kiss, a fleeting kiss, but one that left Alex immobile all the same.

"Tell me what you are thinking, Alex." Amelia stared down at her, still propped on her elbow, analyzing her with her imperturbable gaze.

She never called her Alex. That was the first thing she was thinking. And she was thinking Amelia's hair smelled like Pantene Pro V, which meant she'd forgotten to pack her toiletry bag, because she usually smelled like Paul Mitchell. And she was thinking, for all of Amelia's dauntlessness, her straight-forward certainty, there was a sudden element of softness to her she'd never imagined possible from the headstrong Australian.

She was as confident as she was cocky, always knowing what she wanted and how to get it—on and off the pitch. She knew exactly who she was and seemed satisfied with the answer. Alex envied the complete control she exhibited over her emotions. Her conviction without regret or question. Unlike Alex, who overthought everything. Who second-guessed her every decision.

That was some of what she was thinking.

But she was also thinking Amelia had a girlfriend somewhere in Australia. One she never talked about, that never called or visited or existed in any part of Amelia's day-to-day life. One Amelia spoke of so seldom Alex didn't even know her name. They had an *understanding* relationship, Amelia had said, the night of the gala. Whatever that meant.

She was thinking she was already treading on thin ice with HEG. That she and Amelia were both endorsed *Kickstar* athletes—but only one of them was bound by a "moral clause" written into their contract that became terminable if violated.

And more than anything she was thinking she was still in love with Catharine. She didn't know how to let that go. To accept the reality whatever they'd had was over. They may as well have lived in a parallel universe —their lives separated by too many obstacles; too many impossibilities.

But beneath all that she was also thinking Amelia's mouth felt good against hers. That she'd never really studied the subtle lines that creased the corners of her green eyes, or the perfect straightness of her teeth. Or appreciated her androgynous beauty sculpted by the chiseled angle of her strong jaw and high set of her cheeks.

And lastly, she was thinking she was lonely. It was an isolated climb to the top. Wanting to be the best, grappling to find every foothold to get a little bit ahead. Giving your entire life to a single goal. It was something Amelia understood. A common objective they shared. They pushed each other forward. A burden no one outside their world could truly understand.

"You have sand in your hair." Alex reached up to brush the thick shock of short hair away from Amelia's brow.

"That's what you're thinking?" Her mouth twisted into her lopsided, close-lipped grin. She had a rakish sort of charm. A brusqueness always teetering on the ledge of impudence. "That's deep, Grey."

Alex couldn't help but laugh. For a second she stayed as she was, an arm folded behind her, her hand cradling her head off the sand, the other still at Amelia's brow, her fingers toying with a wayward wisp falling in front of her ear. The sway of the ocean and murmur of water lapping the shoreline was the only sound rising above the steady cadence of her heartbeat.

"I'm thinking that we're playing with fire." She sat up, letting her hands fall to her sides, and met Amelia's unblinking eyes.

"Perhaps." A blonde eyebrow arched, Amelia's gaze indifferent. "But I never pegged you to be one to back down from a challenge."

"It's a challenge, then, is it?" Alex rallied her own nonchalance, welcoming the swing in lightness to the banter. This, perhaps, she could do. Light. Fun. Nothing more. If it was a challenge Amelia wanted, a challenge she just might be up for.

Shucking off her tennis shoes, Alex sprung to her feet and grabbed Amelia's hand.

"Let's go for a swim!"

"Yeah, nah," Amelia resisted, firmly planted in the sand. "I'm not into the whole Florida-coast-sharks thing."

"You're from *Austraya,*" Alex mocked, snagging hold of Amelia's other hand and luring her to her feet, backing them several steps into the water. The Miami coastline was warm, even this early in the year, and a welcome change from the frigid temperatures of the Oakland estuary. Still fully dressed, her jeans clinging to her legs, Alex moved out further. "Isn't everything bigger in the land down under?"

"Bigger doesn't always mean more dangerous."

"Now who's the one afraid of a challenge?" Alex taunted, ceasing her wading progress.

"If you think you're getting me to swim in the Shark Bite Capital of the World, there'd better be something good in it for me." They'd stopped, both chest deep in the water, their faces close together.

"Oh yeah?" Alex tipped her chin, baiting Amelia to kiss her, but as soon as she leaned forward she raised her feet from the shallow surf and stroked backward in the water. "I guess you'll have to be brave enough to find out. Besides," Alex looked over her shoulder as she started a long, deliberate stroke parallel the shoreline, "I guarantee I'm a better swimmer than you."

The further out she swam, the more the city fell away, the glow of the skyline growing dimmer. The private strip of beach was on a sandbar, never deep enough for the ground to disappear, but when Alex pulled up to wait for Amelia she didn't put her feet down, instead continuing to tread the buoyant water.

She'd needed the minutes to collect her thoughts, to decide what she wanted. Amelia was her best friend. Grown to immeasurable importance to her over the year, as close to her as Sawyer. She knew her in-and-out. Her quick temper. Her single-mindedness. Her unapologetic demands for perfectionism. They had the perfect relationship, accepting of each other's faults, comfortable in their friendship.

Alex didn't want to ruin that. Didn't want to risk it. Better to be safe than sorry. Even if it was all in fun. Nothing more than casual.

"You're bloody crazy, Grey." Amelia swam up beside her. "What the hell are we doing out here?"

"You wanted to see the beach."

"View was stunning from the shoreline. Dry. Shark-free."

"But where's the fun in that?" Alex asked, aware immediately of Amelia's nearness, of the hands that settled on her waist, sending her fleeting conviction to play it safe sailing swiftly across the Atlantic.

Allowing herself no opportunity to change her mind, Alex slipped her arms around Amelia's back, drawing their bodies together, finding her mouth with hers. She didn't leave the option for slow. For hesitant. For sensual. She didn't want to be seduced, didn't want the prolonged progression of lovemaking. This wasn't that, and to her relief, Amelia appeared to understand—to share the same conception. The same sense of wanting.

Dropping her feet to the sandbar, Amelia supported them both in the buoyancy of the water, and Alex welcomed the abruptness of the hands that found their way beneath her shirt, mapping out a hurried exploration, before sliding to work at the button of her jeans.

"These come off better dry, you know?" Amelia chastised into her mouth as Alex focused on the unfamiliar taste of her tongue, diluted by the tang of saltwater splashing up from the backwash of the receding tide.

A snarky retort surfaced, but was as quickly extinguished as Amelia succeeded in her efforts of unfastening, running her hands lower, slowing down only to tease, to force a catch of breath, before brushing up inside her.

And then there was nothing leisurely about it. No uncertainty. No questioning. Alex laced her hands together, her fingertips digging into Amelia's back as she wrapped her legs around the slender hips suspending their weightlessness in the water. It was impossible to breathe. To think. To do anything beyond bury her face in the space between Amelia's neck and shoulder.

Her mind remaining mercifully blank, her body found its liberation of all the months of stress, of heartache, of anger. Insulating itself in her release. Repairing itself in the ragged gasp as her hands moved to Amelia's head, her fingers threading fistfuls of hair as she once again drew her mouth to her.

When at last she could breathe again, she slowly unwrapped herself and floated back a body's width of space, maintaining a light hold on Amelia's forearms.

"I'm going to say it again," Amelia broke the silence, not entirely managing to hide her hoarseness. "Grey—you're bloody crazy." She smiled when Alex laughed, pulling her closer, but when their lips brushed she shook her head, her eyes alight with the city lights behind her. "No—we're taking this to shore. I'm not sitting out here like shark bait any longer."

"Coward," Alex teased, following her out of the water.

They'd not made it to dry land before their hands were back on each other, smothering laughter between the stripping of clothing and cursing of sand. There was a heightened sense of fervor. An urgency to it all, knowing the risk of exposure—laying on the empty beach, kissing every line and angle, curve and axis of one another's bodies.

Alex didn't dare to think beyond the immediate moment. Beyond the ways she found to steal Amelia's breath, to make her muscles tense, to persuade her to lose control.

There would be time to think later. About how this wasn't lasting. How it wasn't smart. But at present, she refused to dwell on it at all.

It was after midnight when Alex managed to slide over the pool gate, catching the belt loop of her jeans and nearly falling flat on her face.

"Jesus, Grey," Amelia hissed through suppressed laughter, "you're clumsy as a duck in a plowed paddock."

Alex hopped one-legged in between cabanas, feeling her bare foot down for splinters, one shoe lost to the tide. "You try climbing a six foot fence in soaked jeans." A feat not quite as difficult as getting back into them had been.

Amelia shot her a grin, casually stretching in her already-dry joggers. "Not my fault you didn't dress for the occasion."

"Oh yeah?" Alex side-eyed her as they lowered their voices and headed toward the elevator just inside the rear-entry door. "You have all this on your agenda?"

"If I'd known the u-turn my night would take I'd have gone out with the girls. Not been forced to spend such a miserable evening with you."

Alex flipped her the bird as the elevator door was shutting and Amelia caught her finger, pausing with her keycard in her hand. "Ah, is that an offer?"

"Not after that remark." She tried to pull away with no real effort and Amelia didn't let go.

"I'm calling your bluff." Her lips were at her neck as she reached over her shoulder, pressing the button for the eleventh floor. "Your room?" It wasn't actually a question, given she'd elected to skip coding in her own floor.

The one benefit of having been suspended from the team. Alex didn't have a roommate. She'd had to book the room on her own dime.

"What's Halsey going to say if you don't show up tonight?" She closed her eyes as Amelia's hand released her from her hold, her fingers slipping beneath her shirt to the small of her back.

"She sleeps like the dead. She'll never know I wasn't there."

A ding at the fifth floor sent them scattering apart as the doors opened to admit a couple waiting in the hall.

Alex had turned her gaze to the floor, trying not to laugh, feeling her cheeks flaming. She was wearing one shoe, her jeans still dripping, sand covering the both of them from head to toe.

"Nice night for a swim?"

The voice seeped with sarcasm as Alex's head snapped up, her gaze promptly returning to the puddle at her feet as every fiber in her being tensed with current.

It was Monica. With Caleb.

"That's right." Out of the corner of her eye she could see Amelia meet Monica's stare with her unremitting boldness, leaning casually against the wall. "Can't beat Miami Beach at night."

Habitually never lost for words, Caleb said nothing as the doors creaked closed. Alex could feel his eyes on her, feel him taking in every detail, filing away ever intimation. Judging her. Disparaging her. Finding every fault.

Horde of carpet munchers, he'd said.

She looked up and met his eye. *Fuck him.* He no longer got to have this kind of control over her. She no longer cared what he thought.

"Didn't see you at the afterparty. Find something better to do?" Monica was still in her standoff with Amelia.

For what Alex assumed was her sake, Amelia didn't bite. "Knackered after the game." She motioned at the opening door, the light blinking *seven*. "Isn't this you?"

Monica raised a pencil thin eyebrow. "Aren't you rooming with Erin?" The entire team was on the seventh floor.

"Reviewing game tape with Grey. Care to come? Sorry," she added, as an afterthought, "I'm afraid curfew won't permit your boyfriend to join us."

Ashby slipped an indignant arm through Caleb's and dragged him through the door. "I do not wish to be around this depravedness," she hissed, even as Caleb looked back at Alex, holding her gaze as the doors closed.

She'd just opened Pandora's Box. She was certain of it. He would never let this go.

But before her thoughts could shift, before her mind could take over, Amelia's lips were back on hers, her fingers tangled in her damp hair, and Alex forgot about her troubles for the night.

Alex startled awake, blinking into darkness. The room was silent, the blackout curtains drawn, and the digital clock on the dresser flashed 12:00, having been unplugged and never reset. Throwing an arm toward the nightstand, she fumbled for her phone, and came up empty handed. She couldn't actually remember the last time she'd had it.

The flight left at noon. Meaning they had to be at the bus by nine-thirty. But it was impossible to gauge the time with only a thin sliver of sunlight slipping through the outline of the window frame.

Panic setting in, she started to climb out of bed, but a hand on her hip stayed her.

"Simmer down, Grey." Amelia's voice was groggy, her accent thicker than ever. "It's not even six yet."

"Are you sure?"

"Do I seem like the type that would find myself naked in bed with my best mate, oversleep and miss the plane the next morning?"

Alex couldn't see her face beyond the slope of her silhouette, but knew she was smiling.

The hand on her hip dipped to the small of her back, pulling her closer, into the warmth of her body.

"Do you want me to answer that honestly?" Alex let her head fall to Amelia's pillow, slipping her arms around her waist. For whatever her misgivings of the night before, it felt good to wake beside her. To hear her unfailing sarcasm and know, whatever they had done, things hadn't changed between them.

"No. Stick with telling me what I want to hear. Protect my fragile ego." She pressed her forehead to Alex's. "I checked the time a few minutes ago."

"I don't know where my phone is."

"Probably on the beach somewhere with one half of your only pair of shoes. Keeping company with your modesty."

Alex groaned and Amelia taunted her with a kiss, tugging at her lower lip. "I'm kidding. I think it's on the floor by the shower."

"My modesty or my phone?"

"The latter. Based on last night, I don't think you'll ever find the former again."

Alex could feel her cheeks heat, even in the dark, memories of their night piecing together in the wide-angle of a blockbuster trailer. The beach. The elevator. The shower. Her stomach muscles hurt from laughing as the two of them had struggled out of soaked saltwater clothing, spraying each other with cold water, scrubbing sand out of places it never should have been. She couldn't remember the last time she had laughed that much. The last time she'd felt that comfortable in her own skin. It had been a balm to wounds that hadn't stopped hurting. A reprieve to the heartache she'd been lost in.

Yet, she knew it wouldn't last, and despite the mouth that grew more insistent, the hand that traced a line from her hip to the ticklish skin of her inner thigh, Alex's mind threatened to wander. It wanted to chart out all the dangers, remind Alex of all the reasons this was wrong. She could pen an unabridged dissertation on how their decisions from last night had lit the fuse to a ticking time bomb.

"You know when we leave this room we have to forget this ever happened."

Amelia's hands stilled in their progression as she drew back to look at her through the hazy light. "Are you always this much of a killjoy in the morning, Grey?"

"You know what I mean. You've got a girlfriend. I've got HEG. I'm still…" She left that thought unaddressed. "It's just—it's not smart. We play on the same team."

Amelia brushed her seriousness away, rolling to sit astride her and catching hold of both her wrists, pinning them above her head. "Any other addendums you need to get off your chest?"

"Amelia, come on—"

"Yes, Grey. I heard you. Yes, it's understood. Are we good?" There was a terseness to her Alex had not expected. Amelia was the one who lived her life no-strings-attached. She'd expected her to brush the night off with a shrug of her shoulders, the same way she did everything else. The way she had with Nathalie Comtois. What was it she'd said that night? *It's just sex.*

Amelia's grip on her wrists softened, the edginess in her tone fading. "We're on the same page, okay? I'm sorry." She smiled, though it appeared a touch forced. "I'm not a morning person. There aren't many activities I find worthy of waking up for at the crack of dawn."

Alex took her cue, returning a sly smile, allowing the friction to fade between them. "I can think of one."

On the flight home to Oakland, Amelia sat beside her, same as she'd done on the way to Miami. But this time, as Amelia dozed behind her sunglasses, tuning out the world with her AirPods, Alex found herself aware of every glance, every laugh, every whisper on the plane.

She could feel Monica's glare from half a dozen rows down, hear her furtive murmurs to Valerie Sims, her bosom buddy and fellow cohort on the team.

Alex envied Amelia. Her ability to tune out the noise. Turn a blind eye. Care nothing for the opinion of those around her. Alex couldn't stop worrying about what Caleb had seen. What he would do. If everyone on the team knew? And if they did, what would they think?

"You look guilty as a whore in church," Amelia whispered over her shoulder as they stood at the turnstile, the luggage making a slow revolution on the carousel. "No wonder goalkeepers psyche you out on PKs. You have no game face."

"Not everyone can be as perfect as Amelia Walker," Alex bristled, but she couldn't help but smile when Amelia shouldered her bag to carry it to the bus. "So chivalrous."

"Wouldn't want you to hurt that wrist again. It's proven to have a few hidden talents."

"Shh. You promised." Alex hushed her and drew her hoody up to combat the briskness of the Oakland evening, hoping to cover her blush. They'd agreed to forget it ever happened. Not mention it again. But unlike Vegas, what happens in Miami... follows you home to Oakland, and by that night, when Amelia stopped by on her way back from a run, Alex found herself waking up the next morning in bed with her again.

They didn't make any more promises after that. What was the point? Alex was lonely.

And Amelia was looking for a pastime until she eventually headed home to her life in Australia. What was done was done. They couldn't walk it back. May as well enjoy it while it lasted. It filled a void. Gave them both something more than they had.

They didn't talk about the consequences. The challenges that might arise. There was no mention of Amelia's longtime girlfriend, eighty-six hundred miles away. Or the fact that Alex was still in love with someone else. Their secrets were their own. And none of it seemed to matter anyway.

Chapter Twelve

"I can hear you following me."

Catharine didn't bother to turn around, her focus split between the newspaper she was reading and the curving path encircling the Bridgeview Garden. She'd taken an early lunch and opted to get some air, the warm spring morning a refreshing change from the cold snap of the past few weeks.

Jogged footsteps caught up as Malcolm fell into step beside her. "Ma'am."

She didn't take her eyes from the paper. "It's an enclosed rooftop garden, Malcolm. I don't think I need to be babysat."

"Just stretching my legs, ma'am." The lanky Scotsman took one languid step for every two of hers. She'd tried to slip from her office without him taking notice, but as usual, he was too efficient. "I pay you too much to enjoy a walk in the park on my dime." From the corner of her eye she could see him smile, unfazed by the riposte. She continued, sticking to her apathetic tone. "Perhaps you could make yourself more useful and fetch us a tea instead."

His gaze swept the surrounding area—the urban nature trail winding along the imported foliage, manmade streams, exotic trees that were somehow coaxed to survive outside their indigenous habitat. It was a civic park, built atop the transit center and open to the public, but frequented mainly by those holding office space in the adjacent Bridgeview Tower. Today there were a few dozen people milling around, lured from their desks to enjoy the clear skies and pleasant weather.

"Malcolm, really." She stopped, giving up on the paper. "I'm fine. I just want a few moments of peace before I head back to the tower. If it makes you feel better, I'll text you when I get upstairs."

He was reluctant to leave. With Carlton's popularity increasing and the press constantly lurking, he didn't like to leave her on her own. He'd convinced her to allow him to drive her to-and-from her office and accompany her whenever she left her home alone. An invasion she found tedious, yet comforting all the same. A buffer from the neo-fascist wackos who worshipped Carlton like a shrine.

"Twenty minutes. Now leave me alone, I mean it. I don't want to see you up here again."

"Ma'am." He waved his discontented consent and she resumed her walk.

The front page of the *Arts and Entertainment* section of the *San Francisco Chronicle* featured a photo of the recently acquired property in the Theater District, with the caption *Twentieth Century Brewery Gets a Facelift: New playhouse on the horizon—Le Classique.* The article went on to detail the plans for the building, and gave an overview of the highlights of Nathalie Comtois' career, hailing her endeavor as the new owner of *Le Classique* as *innovative* and *paramount* and projected a welcome reception by the arts community.

Weaving around the trunk of a towering sycamore, Catharine called Nathalie.

She answered breathless, and a touch curt. "Allô!" In the background was the sound of hammering, followed by the unpleasant whirring of a drill and shout of a man's voice. She was at the theatre, overseeing the construction. "Cate?"

"Yes—can you hear me?"

"Barely. Is everything all right?"

"Yes." Catharine slipped onto a bench beside the glass railing surrounding the park and looked out over Fremont Street a dozen stories below. "I saw the article."

"Flattering, wasn't it? They compared my vision to the *Globe!*" One of the most famous Shakespearean houses of all time.

"Rightfully so." Catharine couldn't recall the last time she'd heard her friend so happy. So motivated. So passionate about her work.

"Are you still in Iowa?"

"No. I got home last night."

"The lion released you early from his jaws? To what do we owe that generosity?"

Released her was not accurate. Carlton had released her from nothing. She'd spent four days with him on his midwestern campaign trail and abruptly left. Walked out in the middle of a rally. He'd come unglued during a private luncheon earlier in the afternoon when she'd told him she was gridlocked trying to reach an agreement with the Russians over Port Kaliningrad, and would need to leave a day earlier than planned. In his fit he'd swiped his lunch plate onto the floor and overturned a chair. He'd called her a bitch. A selfish twit. Unfolding into a full blown tantrum in front of his entire traveling campaign staff.

As they'd left the restaurant an hour later, the cook had pulled her aside. He'd asked if she needed him to call anyone—if she might need help? His kindness had been humiliating. She was Catharine Cleveland—owner of one of the most powerful shipping companies in the world—and a gentle line cook from a diner in Templeton, Iowa had feared for her safety. She'd thanked him, assured him all was fine, and that evening walked out of her husband's town hall and flown back to San Francisco in the middle of the night. She would suffer no more of Carlton's degrading outbursts, no matter their agreement. It had taken the kind concern from a stranger to remind her of who she was.

Nineteen voicemails from Carlton still sat in her inbox. She'd yet to listen to a single one.

"I had to deal with Kaliningrad. Carlton had no choice." Nathalie didn't need to know. It would only add one more stressor to her already overburdened plate. Malcolm was plenty capable of worrying enough for the three of them.

What sounded like a jackhammer went off in the background, followed by more shouts and curses from the construction crew.

"Cate, I'm sorry, I—"

"Yes, yes—you go. I just wanted to congratulate you on the article."

"We'll get together this week?"

"Of course."

More hammering and the grinding of a saw.

"À bientôt!"

Taking one of the less trafficked paths back to the bridge connecting the park to Bridgeview Tower, Catharine heard the quick steps of Malcolm again.

"Unless you've brought me a cup of tea, I—" she scolded, turning around, but was surprised to find a man who was certainly not Malcolm on her tail. "Oh." She took a step backward. "I'm sorry."

"Mrs. Cleveland." It was not a question. He was certain who she was. "There is something I'd like to discuss."

She recognized him at once. He was the man from the theatre. The weekend she and Alex had gone to see Nathalie's play in New York. He'd worn a red Braves ball cap. At the time he'd been clean shaven. Today his cheeks looked more hollow, stubble grown across his face—but she'd have recognized him anywhere. He was Carlton's man.

An unbidden current of fear coursed up her spine. They were alone on the path, concealed by the foliage, muted by the trains running underground. Had Carlton sent him to harm her? To teach her a lesson for walking out on him?

He must have read her face. "Relax, Mrs. Cleveland. I'm not here to hurt you. Physical aggression is not my thing."

"You should know, Mr.—?"

"*Jones*. Mr. Jones." He provided the pseudonym through the wink of a watery blue eye.

"You should know, Mr. Jones, my security detail is only a shout away. You would not wish me to call for him."

"We both know that is not the case." He offered a tight-lipped smile. "I am not in the tendency of making mistakes, Mrs. Cleveland."

Despite his unkempt appearance, she did not doubt him. Carlton would not risk his endeavors to anything less than a professional. But she was also inclined to believe him that he meant her no bodily harm. It was not the ideal setting for such a situation.

"May I assume you are here on behalf of my husband?" She considered resuming her walk—a pair of businessmen had come into sight along the path up ahead, briefcases in hand, engrossed in conversation—but her interest was piqued and she wanted to hear him out without disturbance.

"On his behalf, no. In respect to him, yes."

"I am not in the habit of participating in word games, Mr. Jones."

"He owes me money."

She laughed. Of course he did. Leave it to Carlton Cleveland to hire a man to follow his wife and then expect her to foot the bill. "I am afraid you have come laboring under a misapprehension if you think I will remedy that situation."

"No," he mused, "I imagined you would say as much. I've written off the senator's debt as a loss. I am, however, in possession of something I thought you might find of value. A means, perhaps, to regain my financial investment."

She waited as he produced his cell phone, swiping open the lockscreen.

"I'd like to say, before I shortly change your opinion of me, that I admire you, Mrs. Cleveland. You have a far larger set of balls than your husband has ever swung on his best day."

"Charming," said Catharine, unsmiling.

He shrugged and handed her his phone.

For all her years of schooled impassivity, of a poker face developed essential to her career, Catharine knew her reaction was anything but indifferent. She'd expected some manner of scandal regarding her husband. Unethical campaign funding. Promiscuous photos of Carlton and one of his liaisons. When the man had spoken of *value* she'd anticipated it to be something intended to blackmail the senator—not the other way around.

She managed to keep her fingers steady as she swiped from one image to the next. Photo after photo of her and Alex. Tennessee. New York. Colorado. On and on. As she came to the last photos—the only photos damning in nature, intimate photos from her own sitting room of her home —she lost the battle with a quiver in her fingertips, and pressed the phone back into the man's hand.

"I see my husband has kept you busy." Her heart felt like it was chiseling its way through her chest. She needed to get a grip on herself. Understand his angle. "This, I suppose, is the contract for which you have not been paid?"

"No, I was paid generously for those. It was the following contract where the breach arose."

"And how do you propose these be of value to me, Mr. Jones?"

"I imagine it would be worth something to you, Mrs. Cleveland, to keep them between us?"

Her throat constricted but her voice remained blessedly level. "That is my husband's intent, then? To blackmail me with these photos?"

His sparse eyebrows elevated. "Oh, no, to the contrary. Senator Cleveland demanded all trace of these be eliminated. He did not want to risk them being leaked. He felt they'd be damaging to his campaign." He quirked an amused smile. "I thought they might actually give him a little boost. People like to root for the underdog. What could attract more pity than a man losing his wife to another woman? There's not a man alive that wouldn't sympathize."

A hundred feet down the path Malcolm materialized, two styrofoam cups in hand. He caught Catharine's eye, the man's back to him, and she managed an imperturbable shake of her head. Whatever this was, she needed to finish it.

"If Carlton wanted these destroyed, what was the point of ever taking them? If he does not intend to blackmail me, why are you here?"

"I'm here because I want to recuperate lost profits. I am giving you the chance to buy these from me, Mrs. Cleveland, before I make them available to someone else."

"To someone else?" Now her voice was cold, edging into territory with which she was familiar. Negotiation. Threats. Pressure. Her entire life had been spent in these waters. Extortion. Steamrolling. Strong-arming in attempt to reach a deal. She was comfortable on both sides of this table. "By *someone else* I assume you mean the media?"

He shrugged. "The media. Your husband's political adversaries. Your business rivalries. Whoever will pay the most."

"I see. And what is that sum?"

"Because I like you, Mrs. Cleveland, with you I'm willing to make a deal. I will place these in your possession for the money owed to me by your husband. Nothing more."

"And how am I to be certain no other copies exist? You've already told me you were ordered to destroy all evidence of these—what guarantee am I to have that you will not do the same thing again?"

The diluted blue eyes held her own, easy, unperturbed. "None. You're entirely at the mercy of my word. And the hope that I do indeed respect you more than I do your husband."

Catharine took a step forward, intent to return to her walk. "I do not make deals around words such as *hope* and *mercy*, Mr. Jones. Our time here is over."

He slid to block her path. "Would you not rather gamble on my ethics than leave it to certainty that I will act? When we part this afternoon, there will only be one conclusion. I am either heading straight to approach the highest bidder or I am disappearing from your life with a substantial amount of cash. The choice is yours. If not for your sake, Mrs. Cleveland, then for your... *friend*—I hope you consider my offer."

Catharine paused. He wasn't wrong. He gave her little choice in the matter. One way or another, the photos were going to be released. To her or another party. And if it was the latter, it was not just her they would hurt.

"What kind of figure are we talking about, Mr. Jones?"

"One million one hundred thousand—cash."

Her face remained impassive. "You're telling me my husband owes you one point one million dollars?"

"One million. And a ten percent late fee."

"For what?"

The man worked the material of his sleeve. He was less comfortable than he wanted her to believe. "He hired me to dig up information on one of his opponents. The matter turned out to be something sensitive to the man's fifteen year old daughter. I am not opposed to exposing secrets for money, Mrs. Cleveland. But I am not in the business of ruining children's lives."

Catharine filed this to the weighted side of ethics. Still, she kept to her hard line. "I take it you did not deliver this information to the senator?"

"No, ma'am."

"Why, then, should payment be made?"

"My time was still spent, Mrs. Cleveland. My efforts and skills put to use. I will be compensated."

She didn't point out the inanity of his statement. With no results delivered, he was owed nothing for his time. They both knew that. It wasn't about Carlton. It was about her. And those photos. And the profit he could gain.

"One million dollars, Mr. Jones. Nothing more. And those photos disappear." She knew he would have settled for half. He'd come knowing the media would give him nothing close to his demand. Another high profile scandal, an affair exposed—another day, another headline. Carlton's political contenders would have paid more, but it was no guarantee. But it didn't matter. She didn't care about the money. She would have to take him on his word. He was a clever enough man to know blackmailing her a second time would not go as smoothly. And she had retaliating resources at her hand.

He cracked his knuckles, making show of deliberating, before nodding his head. "Deal."

She took a step and he paused her again. "You're remiss in your curiosity, Mrs. Cleveland."

She waited.

"Do you no longer wonder why your husband had them taken in the first place?"

"I assume he meant to use them against me if I did not comply to his demands."

"Not you, Mrs. Cleveland. Your friend."

It took a moment to sink in. To understand. To comprehend the implication of what he'd said.

"You—you mean," her voice shook and she didn't care. She felt sick. The park was nothing but a whirl of hues of green—emerald, moss, forest, lime. She didn't deny the hand he offered to steady herself. "These were shown to her?"

"Yes."

"You are certain?"

"I was there."

She dropped his arm, forcing herself to breathe. In the back of her mind it registered to her that Malcolm was coming toward them. She couldn't focus enough to motion for him to stay away.

"When?"

"The morning of Christmas Eve."

"Ma'am?" Malcolm stopped a half dozen yards away and a flicker of fear shifted across Mr. Jones' face. He'd grown flighty as a deer.

"I'm fine, Malcolm." She swallowed a dryness in her throat that wouldn't go away and continued to stare at the man. A strange mix of euphoria seeped into her revulsion—the dawning of understanding. Alex hadn't left her because she wanted to. She'd left her because she had to. She'd been the one threatened. Blackmailed. "Mr. Jones and I are just finalizing an agreement." She caught the Scotsman's eye and he obediently backed away.

"I have your word, Mr. Jones? All copies of those photos disappear? No loopholes."

"Like I said, I like you, Mrs. Cleveland. I'd rather not cut off my nose to spite my face. I'm hoping we can do continued business in the future."

"I'll make arrangements for the transaction."

He nodded and started to walk away, then paused a final time. "Because you've been so agreeable, Mrs. Cleveland. Have your man look into Susan Lyndon—Senator Lyndon's wife. A Christmas party on the Keys. Might come in handy to you one day."

And then he was gone and Malcolm was at her side.

Chapter Thirteen

Alex paused in the terminal of the Phoenix airport to snap a few photos with a pair of young fans.

"That hat trick was siiiick." A girl, not more than fourteen, flipped her Astros baseball cap on backward and threw peace signs while her friend wrapped an arm around Alex and flashed a hang loose. The mom behind the camera thanked Alex profusely while the teenagers loped ahead, arguing who got to post the photo first.

"My daughter's not going to talk about anything else for weeks, I swear. She's your biggest fan. She screamed when she saw your name on the roster. She's been begging us to fly to England for the World Cup." Alex thanked her and shouldered her bag, heading to settle in at the gate that read OAK.

There were a dozen text messages waiting for her when she switched on her phone. Halsey confirming she'd landed safely in Mississippi, where she'd stopped to visit her aunt. Sawyer with a series of GIFs of women in skintight blue and red lycra, continuing to razz Alex about being called *Captain Marvel* during their final match in New Jersey. Alex had opened the game against Brazil with a diving header, prompting the commentators to dub her as the Marvel comic hero, claiming she could fly. There was a text from Rodney Collins, confirming the Sirens schedule beginning after the international break. And three texts from Amelia, all an hour apart.

> aw—*will u pick up BioFreeze on ur way home?*
> aw—*u make it safely to OAK?*
> aw—*Grey...?*

Alex started to type out a response that her plane had been delayed for over three hours on the tarmac and she was running late—the truth—but deleted the text and started again.

ag—*Sorry! Weather was lousy in NJ and they cancelled my flight.*

The response was immediate.

aw—*Ur still in NJ???*

ag—*<sad face>*

aw—*tomorrow's my bday <broken heart>*

ag—*is it??????*

aw—*ur fucking with me...*

ag—*You should have said something!*

aw—*now i know ur fucking w/me*

ag—*You just want birthday sex <shrugging emoji>*

aw—*I actually just want BioFreeze, but if ur offering...*

Alex's phone rang and she knew she failed to hide her smile. "Hey."

"Where are you, really?"

"Jersey."

"You're lying."

"I'd rather call it being economical with the truth."

Amelia laughed. "So you are getting in tonight, right?"

"Yeah. Just late."

"You're a dick."

"Paybacks a bitch."

"Hey!" Amelia humphed. "I had nothing to do with that."

Two and a half weeks earlier Alex had received a phone call at the crack of dawn. She'd been disoriented with sleep when she answered, blinking through her daze, not registering the restricted caller ID. The voice of Isabelle Atwood had greeted her on the other end of the line. She'd sounded like she had a cold.

"Alex, I'm sorry if I woke you. It's Izzy. I wanted to call and let you know, before you saw the roster, that I had to make a tough decision and I wasn't able to include you in the camp. I know you've worked really hard to elevate your game, and your performance with the Sirens has been remarkable since you returned from your expulsion, but I just don't feel you're ready yet. So I'm afraid the answer is no."

Alex had been stunned and only managed a *thank you for letting me know* before hanging up the phone. She'd spoken to Izzy the week before at a Sirens home game and the coach had given her all the indications she felt she was ready to rejoin the team. The omission from the second-to-last roster before the World Cup had caught her entirely by surprise.

Amelia had been awake beside her side and asked what was wrong. It had been all Alex could do not to cry.

A moment later her phone rang once more, this time with the caller ID displaying US Soccer. Confused, Alex answered and again, Isabelle Atwood apologized for ringing so early.

"I've got a long list of calls to make, but I wanted to reach out to you first. Like we talked about last week—I'm impressed with your turnaround. Whatever demons were weighing you down you seem to have handled. And I look forward to seeing you in camp in a few days."

"I'm sorry?" Did the woman have amnesia? Fully awake, Alex pulled her phone away to look at the caller ID, and noticed the date on her screen. It was April 1st. *April Fool's.* Beside her Amelia was trying to hide a grin into the crook of her elbow. "What's going on?"

"Is there some kind of static on the line?" Atwood questioned. "I think I've made myself clear?"

Amelia was laughing into her pillow.

"Who is this?" Alex had grown frustrated, swatting at Amelia's head before turning her attention back to the call. "Halsey? Are you screwing with me?" The goalkeeper was known for her perfect imitation of the Welshwoman's accent. "I swear, I'm going to kick your ass! It's not funny —"

A notification came through at the same time, a text message from Halsey:

—April Fool's!! Atwood's calling you next!

Mortified, Alex had apologized over and over, and still been apologizing when she set foot in her first US camp a week later after four months of being cut from the team.

The gate agent came over the loudspeaker announcing boarding for Oakland.

"You knew Halsey was going to do it. You let me tell Isabelle Atwood I was going to kick her ass—"

"Not my fault you went polar, mate—that was all just icing on the cake."

"I still don't forgive you." Alex headed for the counter.

"You will."

"We'll see."

"Pick up BioFreeze."

The next morning Alex woke to find Amelia dressed and sitting on the edge of the bed. The clock on her dresser read a quarter past seven.

"Why are you watching me sleep?" She covered her face with her hands. Between all the flights, all the airports, the training camp, three friendly matches, and suffering an Oakland Walmart at eleven pm to bring Amelia her damned muscle gel, she wanted nothing more than to sleep until noon.

She opened one eye and peaked between her splayed fingers. Amelia was smiling.

"Quit looking at me like that!" Giving up on sleep, she dropped her hands from her face and sat up against the headboard. "What?"

"What?" Amelia feigned innocence.

"Why are you staring at me?"

Amelia shrugged. "I don't know. I guess I missed you."

It wasn't an Amelia thing to say. They didn't say things like that to each other. Aside from the sex, nothing in their friendship had really changed. It was easy. Casual. They didn't talk about the future. They didn't delve too deeply into one another's lives. Amelia still talked about returning to the Women's Super League when her contract was up. Alex still found it impossible to look across the bay without staring at Bridgeview Tower and counting to the sixty-third floor. Whatever they had didn't have a name. It wasn't what she'd had with Catharine. Amelia never made her heart skip or her breath catch beyond a mere physical reaction. It wasn't like that between them. It was fun. Uncomplicated. But it wasn't Catharine. It never would be.

"You just missed having someone to help you fold your laundry."

"Nah, you suck at that. You crease my tees in the wrong places. You're good for a few things, though."

Alex rolled her eyes and Amelia assumed an air of indignation.

"You've got a dirty mind, Grey. I only meant we're scheduled for a scrimmage match at training tomorrow—and I'll need someone to captain the losing team. You'll be aces."

Alex snaked an arm out to rough up her already tousled hair, but Amelia was faster, and before Alex could retreat, she found herself in a wrestling match she quickly lost. Flat on her back on the bed, Amelia straddled on top of her, her knees pinning Alex's arms down to her sides. Despite being several inches shorter, Amelia was unquestionably stronger, and when it came to grappling, always had the upper hand.

"Not fast enough, Grey."

"I only let you win because it's your birthday. For breakfast I thought I might take you out to the senior center. Sign you up for water aerobics to help protect your joints."

"For someone completely at my mercy, you've got a smart mouth." She drew the hem of the t-shirt Alex had slept in up over her belly, trailing her fingers in its wake. "As you might recall, I know all your ticklish spots."

Alex tried not to flinch when Amelia drew a fingernail along her ribs, raising the shirt up higher. She'd always been wildly ticklish and even more so when held captive, knowing she couldn't pull away.

"Tell me again about how old I am..." Amelia dragged the shirt over her head, but instead of pulling it off, left the permeable cotton covering her face. The only thing that made her more sensitive—as Amelia already knew —was if she couldn't see.

"If you hurry up," Alex challenged through the thin material, unable to stop herself from squirming as Amelia traced the outline of her breasts, following the trail of her fingers with the brush of her tongue, "we can use your senior discount to get the early bird special down at the Denny's." The last words came out rushed, her body twisting beneath Amelia's touch.

"Was that before or after we stopped at the assisted living for a riveting round of bingo?"

Amelia moved south and Alex clawed at the mattress, trying to convince herself to relax. To breathe. Pinned down, unable to see, every caress and kiss was magnified. And then without warning, stopping just short of her destination, Amelia sat up, releasing Alex from her hold, and swung her legs to the side of the bed. "Sorry, don't want to risk a crick in my neck. Not at this age."

Breath shuddered, Alex yanked her t-shirt down over her face, her eyes still shut. "I hate you."

"Yeah... it shows..." Amelia grazed her thumb across her inner thigh, making Alex jump, before getting to her feet. "Come on, get dressed. I want to go hiking. It's my birthday. You don't get to tell me no."

The California Coastal Trail was empty as they made their way toward the Golden Gate from Baker Beach. Alex hadn't wanted to come to this side of the city. Why not Angel Island or Tiburon? There were beautiful trails over there. But Amelia'd had her heart set on the Presidio's western shoreline— and like she'd said, it was her birthday—Alex couldn't tell her no.

She'd spent most of the hike trudging after Amelia, jet lagged and sore from the whirlwind of the last two weeks. Her mind was on the summer to come. As she studied the tail of the serpent tattoo curling around Amelia's ribcage and disappearing beneath her sports bra, she wondered what it would be like if the US got matched against Australia. Her against Amelia. *If* she was lucky enough to make the team.

But she knew she'd make the team. It no longer felt like a question. Even after being cut and the turbulent start to her year, she knew she deserved a spot on the roster. This last call up she'd scored a hat trick against Brazil. Two assists against Japan. Earned a PK against Mexico. Izzy Atwood had told her to block out her summer calendar; she wouldn't be home. An apocalypse not withstanding, she would be in England come July.

The thought brought her full circle back to Amelia, who'd paused on a ledge overlooking the coastline. While Alex was preparing for her first World Cup, Amelia was prepping for her fifth. Her international career spanning nearly twenty years. The number of players with five World Cups on their resume could be counted on two hands—men and women combined. The woman was a machine. A legend. Earning her first international cap at fifteen, Amelia still held the record for the youngest player—two months after her seventeenth birthday—to compete for Australia on the world stage. And at thirty-three, there was a chance this summer would be her last. There was no telling in sports where she might be in another four years.

Their careers couldn't be more polar. Yet it was all aimed for the same destination. And Alex knew, without Amelia, she never would have been wearing the Stars and Stripes in the first place. Amelia had pushed her. Encouraged her. Made her better in every way.

"Earth to Grey."

Alex stepped onto the ledge beside her. She hadn't heard what she said.

"Look." Amelia nudged her.

Alex followed her gaze to the water just beneath the Golden Gate. The sea was flat, the weather mild. There was little wind sweeping into the bay. Nothing was happening. Then what looked like an oblong boulder shot out of the water, twisting toward the sky, before arching its descent and flopping against the glassy surface, showering a white wash of spray.

"A humpback." Amelia grinned and caught her eye. "Bonzer."

"I didn't even know we had whales in the bay."

They watched, side by side, before the whale breached again, then disappeared with a fluke, settling in for a long dive.

"I wonder if—" Alex was cut off as Amelia leaned over and kissed her. On the middle of the California Coastal Trail. In the middle of the day. Overlooking San Francisco Bay.

When she stepped away, she didn't look at Alex, just set off up the trail.

Alex stood, catching her breath from more than just the hike. She'd never kissed her in public before. Never like that. A kiss that suddenly didn't feel like just-sex. It sent a shockwave of thrill through her. And scared her in equal measure.

"Hurry up, Grey! You're lagging."

It was midafternoon when they stepped onto the sidewalk of the Golden Gate viewpoint south of the bridge. The sun was high over the water, the air remarkably clear, offering a panoramic view of the city.

Amelia paused at the tourist overlook and pulled her heel to her butt, wincing at the stretch. "You might be right, Grey. Maybe I am getting old." The quad had been giving her trouble for the past several weeks, but nothing, she insisted, to warrant any downtime.

Feeling a little guilty about razzing her earlier, Alex hooked a finger in the pocket of Amelia's joggers and looked over her shoulder at the bridge, but still couldn't pass up the opportunity to rib her. "Don't worry," she smiled, "you'd still leave Erin in the dust." Erin Halsey was notoriously the slowest runner on the team, despite her catlike reflexes between the posts.

"Get stuffed," Amelia shot back, pulling away to stretch her opposite quad. "You weren't within a cooee of me coming up the backside." She did a couple calf raises, testing her muscles, and turned her attention to the running track traversing the cliffside to the waterfront. "Ready?"

Alex hesitated, her eyes drifting along the coast toward Crissy Field. Past the beaches and marsh. Little Marina Green. Marina Yacht Harbor. Catharine's home just feet across from the water. She hadn't been to this part of the city since she'd last seen Catharine in January. She didn't want to go down there.

"We got six miles in. Why don't we go out for an early dinner?"

"Calling it quits already, Grey? And you tell me *I'm* the one getting old?"

Alex couldn't think of a snarky reply fast enough. Instead she went with practical. "You said we were doing full scrimmages tomorrow."

"And?"

"I don't know—seemed like it might be good to take it easy today."

"Not like you to be a dole bludger—it's not even three more miles. All flat and downhill." Amelia scrutinized her. She had a built in lie detector like no one Alex had ever met.

"Catharine lives down there." She didn't know why she said it. As soon as the words were out of her mouth Alex knew she'd made a mistake. She should have said she had a sore hamstring or was developing a blister or had been bitten by a rare mosquito that was going to turn her into a yam. Anything other than bring up Catharine.

"Where?" Amelia's lips turned into something that was almost a smile—but not quite.

"Down there. It doesn't matter. If you want to continue, let's go."

"Nah—you don't get off that easy." She used the height of the curb to drape her arm over Alex's shoulders, her chin beside her ear. "Where?"

"No." Alex clenched her jaw. "It doesn't matter."

"Tell you what," Amelia stepped off the curb, "if you can beat me to that building, I won't mention it again. If you can't, you'll show me the house."

Alex followed her gaze to the building. It was the Yacht Club adjacent Marina Green. Not a stone's throw from Catharine's front door. "I'm not playing this game with you. Give it a rest."

"I wouldn't rest long," Amelia baited, taking off at a jog down the winding descent leading to the shorefront trail, "you know I'm faster than you."

Alex watched her retreating figure, the tattooed serpent shifting over the muscles on her back, before cussing to herself and picking her way down the slope a half dozen yards behind her.

It was less than two miles to Crissy Field and the track was flat and tightly packed, allowing the pair to open up, flying past the other joggers and cyclists on the trail.

Amelia *was* faster than Alex. There was no doubt about it. As a striker, Alex was explosive on the pitch, but when it came to holding her own against the midfielder's endurance, she didn't stand a chance. By the time she reached the Yacht Club Amelia was perched on the low wall separating the beach from the parking lot, her knees drawn to her chest.

"What was all that yabber about the senior center?"

Alex threw herself onto the wall, too winded for words. If she'd wanted the excuse of a blister earlier, the universe had manifested her wishes. Hiking tennis shoes were not meant for sprinting. She managed to drag herself up, loosening her laces.

"I hate you."

"So you said this morning." Amelia shook her sweat drenched hair out and Alex shielded her face and shoved her away in disgust.

"Gross! I double that statement."

"You have a funny way of showing it." Amelia grinned at her, threatening to wipe her face on Alex's shoulder. "Okay—I won. Pay up."

"I didn't agree to the terms."

"Your acceptance was non-verbally implied by your desperate actions to try and beat me here." Amelia dropped to her feet and offered a hand to Alex. "Come on, Grey. It's not like we're going to drop in for a cuppa. I just want to see the place."

Alex brushed aside her outstretched hand and jumped to her feet, her calves pulsing from exertion. "If I point it out, you promise we can just go? No bullshit?"

"Scout's honor."

Amelia fell into stride beside her as they crossed the parking lot onto the grass of Marina Green. Reaching the sidewalk, Alex stopped short, lifting her eyes to the corner adjacent where Catharine's magnificent home looked out over the bay.

"Wow." Amelia followed her gaze across the street. "I guess I don't have to ask which one it is."

Seeing the house through fresh eyes, Alex knew Amelia was right. There were opulent homes lining the boulevard, packed in tight succession. This wasn't the world of the working class—but Catharine's home stood out in a league above the rest. No different than its owner.

She'd been so ready to walk away that day, when Jules Sweeney had called to her from the balcony. Uncertain of the grandeur, the intimidation of the place—when Catharine had been such a mystery.

Standing on the corner, looking up at it from an outsider's perspective, Alex almost wished she had. Whoever said it was better to have loved and lost than never loved at all had not fallen in love with Catharine Cleveland.

"That's something." Amelia stood quietly beside her, no longer teasing.

"Are you good? Can we go now?" She was impatient to get away. As far from this place as possible. With the marina beside them all she could think about was that last day. Catharine had said she loved her. *Loved her.* And Alex had said nothing, just watched her fall apart, Catharine never knowing she, too, had been crumbling.

Amelia's green eyes reflected the water off the bay, turning their usual emerald a darker shade of jade. Her attention was still on the townhouse.

"How does one compete with that?"

Alex turned to her sharply. It was an uncharacteristic thing for her to say. Amelia's thoughts were veiled behind the glare of the sun, her lips in a thin line. Alex set her hand on the small of her back. "There's no competition here."

"Oh, please," the wry smile was back as quickly as it had faded, "*every-thing* is a competition. You know that better than anyone, mate." Amelia took one last look at the marina house before turning toward the water. "Uber? Or you want to grab dinner down here?"

"It's your birthday. My treat. I'll take you wherever you want." *Anywhere but here.* Alex resisted the urge to steal a last glance at the house.

"Jack London Square, then." Alex knew Amelia'd chosen Oakland for her sake, not her own.

They flicked their phones off airplane mode as they turned toward the parking lot.

Alex's phone chimed a dozen or more times as service was reconnected, her screen full of notifications. Fourteen texts. Six voicemails. It had only been off for a few hours.

"Someone's popular." Amelia glanced up. "What's cracking?"

Alex didn't hear her. She was too busy scrolling through the texts.

Sawyer.

Halsey.

Molly.

She quit scrolling—there were too many—and selected the most recent one from Sawyer.

> —*call me*
> —*hello??*
> —*have you seen this shit?*

Her stomach muscles cramped as she swiped to Halsey's texts.

> —*that bitch! I'm calling Rod and Izzy.*

And Molly's.

> —*wtf! She's just jealous AF.*

She could feel the color draining from her face as she looked up at Amelia and handed her her phone. Skimming through the texts, she turned her attention to Sawyer's voicemail.

"Something about an interview with Ashby." Amelia pulled up Twitter while Alex stared at the water. Whatever it was—whatever had happened—she knew her briefly acquired peace was coming to an end.

"I don't see it. Call Abby back," she handed Alex her phone and ordered them an Uber. "Let's get home."

118

Chapter Fourteen

Catharine waited as Nathalie looked over the printed photos spread across her dining room table, each accompanied with a spreadsheet of its own. Times. Dates. Names. Locations. Last known whereabouts. Immediate family members. Each color-coordinated in a system intended to prioritize their importance. Red: vital. Orange: critical. Yellow: substantive. Green: menial.

A matrix of information. Compiled evidence that would either set her free or get her killed.

"Well?" Catharine rose, her arms folded across her chest, hugging herself to keep her fingers from tapping out an anxious rhythm.

Nathalie picked up one of the photos, misplacing it from its order, and Catharine had to resist the urge to snatch it from her hand and put it back where it belonged.

"I can't tell, Cate, if you're trying to convince *me* of this plan, or you're hoping to convince yourself?"

"You think I would have gone to all this effort if I wasn't convinced?" She dropped her arms and waved a hand over the surplus of data, pacing the room. Nathalie was right. She wasn't convinced. She was terrified. Now even more so, since she'd gotten Nathalie involved.

The Frenchwoman gave her no immediate answer, instead returning to the browsing of the details. Nineteen photos. Nineteen women. Secretaries. Lobbyists. Interns. House aides. Staffers. Housekeepers. Wives of her husband's friends. The list went on and on. A dovetail of information—minor incidents, an inappropriate remark with sexual undertones, to full blown affairs, some lasting months and even years. The only things she'd uncovered appeared to be consensual. Women, she imagined, who'd hoped to gain advancement in their careers. But there were others of which she was uncertain. Those were the ones she was most interested in. Had any of them told him no? Had he forced them anyway?

The thought left her spinning. Married for a quarter of a century, she'd known he'd had his flings, but never guessed it was anything to this extent. Nineteen women—aged twenty-one to fifty-five. And those were only the ones she'd managed to uncover. There were others, she was sure.

"You did all this in the last five days?" Nathalie dropped the photo to the table, too far from its report, and Catharine quickly adjusted it into place.

"Yes."

"By yourself?"

"Obviously not. I enlisted Malcolm."

"But no one else?"

Catharine resumed her loop around the room, unable to stand still. "No one else. I cannot risk it."

Nathalie sighed, relieved.

She'd told her about her conversation with Mr. Jones. About the blackmail. The photos. Alex. And the name the man had given her—Susan Lyndon—the wife of a six-term senator from Florida. A man who had been one of Carlton's closest friends. A man he'd had a falling out with in recent history.

The name had led to the dovetail of information covering her dining room table, infiltrating her dreams.

"And here I've felt so sorry for you, thinking you were holed up in your office over Russia. Instead you've been starring in your own real-life episode of *Law & Order*." Despite her attempt at humor, Nathalie slumped into a chair, her elbows on the table. "So what do we do with all this, Catharine? Release it to the media?"

"No." It wasn't that simple. "Not yet. I need more information."

"The National Convention is around the corner. It's not like you have the luxury of time."

"I don't want any names released without permission. They aren't my story to tell."

"So what do you propose? You can't mean to go and talk to all of them. If Carlton found out you were sniffing around..."

Catharine paused at the head of the table, placing her palms flat on the surface. "*I* can't, no." She stared at Nathalie. She couldn't bring herself to ask. To even make the suggestion. Fortunately, her friend's fast dawning discernment was a step ahead of her.

"Oh." Nathalie's dark eyes returned to the photographs. Beneath her cool exterior, Catharine could see her try and hide her swallow.

"Nat, look, I can find someone else—"

"Who?" Her head shot up, her laugh short and abrasive. "Who else, beside Malcolm, are you going to trust with this information? And we both know these women won't talk to him…"

No, they wouldn't. Women weren't prone to divulging their affairs to a stranger, especially a man. Even if the encounters had been consensual.

She wanted to expose her husband for the lying, cheating, philandering, hypocritical lecher he was, but she didn't want to out any women who weren't willing to tell their own story. Many of these women had husbands, boyfriends, children to think of. It wasn't for Catharine to smear their names across international news just to unearth the decades of misdeeds her husband had committed while in office. It was a sensitive subject—one she hoped would force his followers to reassess his character and prove him unfit for the presidency.

Nathalie continued in her silence, her eyes still glued to the photos and spreadsheets. "Who would you want me to be? A reporter? Disgruntled former lover pretending to be one of them?"

"No!" This last proposal was out of the question. "I do not want any of them led on under false pretenses. They must come out on their own. I just…" She didn't have it all figured out. That was the problem. "I just need them pointed in the right direction. Given the suggestion. They'd be doing the country a favor. No one needs morals like Carlton's sitting behind that much power."

"An anonymous whistleblower, then?"

"Something like that." She leaned over the table. "I just don't know where to start. There isn't enough time to track down all of them."

Nathalie tapped three photos. "The secretary. The intern. The housekeeper." She paused, deciding on a final photo. "And Susan Lyndon. The first three because people will sympathize with them. An unbalance of power. Even when consensual, it leaves a bad taste behind. And the senator's wife because it will turn his friends against him. Split his allies. Dilute his support."

"Are you sure acting was your calling?"

Nathalie tsked. "Don't you regret all these years of grief you've given me for my addiction to political crime novels?" They shared a laugh, but the strain in the room remained. This wasn't a game and they both knew it.

"I'm sure you know," Nathalie said quietly, watching Catharine's nervous hands as she worried the edge of one of the photos, "there's a chance this won't cripple his campaign. This country's moral standards have been lowered to a nonexistent level. Sometimes the voters don't care what a candidate has done, just so long as he continues to preach to their own personal agenda. It's a big risk to take for an outcome of uncertainty."

"It's a small risk to take compared to what I'm asking you to do."

Nathalie waved her off with an unconvincing laugh. "Bêtises. I'm not the one he'll kill if this all goes sideways."

A spell of silence passed as Catharine reweighed all her options. Reassessed her motivation. She wanted revenge against her husband. She didn't deny the original instigation for her inspiration. What he had done to her... done to Alex... She wanted him to pay. She wanted him to suffer as much as she had suffered. To take from him the one thing that mattered above everything else—just as he had done to her.

But it was more than that. After looking into Susan Lyndon, falling down the rabbit hole of his affairs and indiscretions, she couldn't hold onto the knowledge without making an effort to expose him. The world needed to see him for who he was. *What* he was. He didn't deserve the support he'd been given. The trust of the people. Not while he was gaslighting his followers into believing he held sacred his proclaimed Christian values.

"What about Alex?"

The question snapped her from her deliberating. "What about her?"

"There's a chance she could be dragged into all of this."

Catherine withdrew her hand from the edge of the photo she'd been tapping. "She has nothing to do with it."

"If he got suspicious—"

"He *won't!*" She quieted. "He can't. He can never know it came from me. If he did, like you said..." She shook her head, clearing away the thought. She was too committed to be scared out of it now. "Besides, exposing my affair with Alex would hurt him as much as it hurt me. If he wanted to retaliate, he'd take it directly to my father. Keep it all in the family, so to speak."

Nathalie went to the liquor cart and helped herself to a finger of Hennessy as Catharine stared at the faces on her table, wondering if any of them would speak. And if they did, would people even listen?

"Are you going to tell her?" Nathalie set down a tumbler beside her, resting her hand on her shoulder.

"That I know?"

"Yes."

"I don't know." Catherine picked up the drink. "I imagine we've both probably suffered all the heartache we can take."

"If I were her I'd want to know. Even if it didn't change things, it would offer some closure, I would think."

Catharine sighed and set the cognac to her lips. Perhaps Nathalie was right. She had a right to know. Especially on the off chance her name was dragged into any of this. And if she was honest with herself, she knew she hoped there was a chance… a possibility it could change things.

But for the moment her focus needed to remain elsewhere.

She reached up and set her hand atop Nathalie's, giving it a squeeze. There weren't words to thank her for what she was asking her to do. The risks she was asking her to take.

Chapter Fifteen

"Are you sure about this?"

Amelia sat in the row behind Alex in the nosebleed seats of the empty Sirens stadium, leaning over her shoulder to preview the words typed on her phone. It was early on a Sunday morning and the pitch was quiet, the only signs of life the groundkeepers tending the field after the home game played against the Salt Lake Panthers the previous evening.

Rodney had subbed Alex out at the half, which had come as a relief. For the first time in her career she'd been grateful to pull on a pinny and leave the game, watching the remainder of the match from the bench.

Eight days on an emotional rollercoaster had taken its toll. She'd tried to tune out the noise and just play her game, but it had been challenging to deal with in front of thousands of speculative fans. Knowing she was being watched, not for her talents, but instead held under a microscope for the disparaging remarks based off the social media shitshow that had gone down the week before. She'd just wanted to melt away, blend into the crowd, and bury her head in the sand.

"No." Alex said simply. "I'm not sure about this at all." She stared at the letters on her phone that had become nothing more than a blur. For a week she'd struggled to come up with the right thing to say, uncertain if it was better to say nothing at all. Her agent had recommended the latter. "It'll blow over," he'd said, through a scratchy line in the Bahamas, vacationing with his latest fling. But it didn't, and as the days went by, her silence became deafening.

Sawyer, Halsey and Amelia were of one mind. She needed to address it head on.

"Run it by US Soccer before you post—just to cover your ass—but let the statement be your own." Ever the voice of reason, Sawyer had spent hours helping her draft her thoughts over multiple long distant calls. "Keep your chin up, sugar. Maybe it'll turn out a blessing in disguise."

It hadn't felt like a blessing, however. Ever since Alex had returned from her hike with Amelia the previous week and found an interview with Monica Ashby making its social media rounds, her life had felt like a living hell.

How a thirty second sound bite from a jealous, jaundiced shit stirrer could cause such a nightmarish viral witch-hunt was beyond Alex.

In a virtual interview with a reporter from an online publication, *Tackle For Him*, Ashby had been asked how she upheld her Christian values while maintaining a career in sports. As if the two couldn't go together hand-in-hand. Instead of keeping to the unspoken professional standard of sticking to high ground, Ashby had sunk low, and made a cutting remark that it was difficult to play in an environment that didn't hold its athletes to the highest of moral standards, and how her love of Christ felt frequently overshadowed by being forced to share the pitch with players who did not live up to the core Christian values, instead seeping in immorality and questionable ethical turpitude.

Questionable. Ethical. Fucking. Turpitude.

The ambiguity of the accusation caught the immediate interest of its viewers, and within twelve hours the interview had expanded from the narrow reach of the niche publication to the widespread audience of the online sports community. The clip was shared thousands of times, with varying speculation on what, and more importantly, *who*, Ashby was talking about.

Instead of lying low, or attempting to put out the fire she had ignited, the Sirens holier-than-thou outside back made matters worse the following morning. While Alex had been hiking with Amelia, Monica Ashby had taken to Twitter in an attempt to end the confusion on her statement from the previous evening. Deciding it would be better to name the subject of her accusations outright, instead of leaving things to the imagination.

In a series of Tweets stating she'd not intended to create an uproar amongst the sports community, she'd gone on to say that, while she did not ethically agree with teammate Alex Grey's personal behavioral choices, she believed it was only for God to judge, and God to forgive, and regretted any distress or disorder she'd caused her soccer family.

"I knew she'd been too fucking quiet!" Amelia had raged on the way home to Oakland in the backseat of an Uber. She'd found the initial interview and Halsey had texted the screenshots from Ashby's Twitter account, since both Alex and Amelia were blocked from the woman's social media. "It's all over the place. *The Eighteen. The Athletic. Gist. Even ESPN.*"

Initially, Alex's only concern had been about being outed. Not because coming out as gay in present-day society was shocking or dangerous—these weren't the times of Billie Jean King or Ellen—but because of the image she'd allowed *Kickstar* to paint of her. The contracts she had signed. The lifestyle from which she'd been raised. She'd been living as a fraud and was worried how her authentic self would be received. Both by the gay community, which she'd unintentionally deluded, and her Southern Baptist roots, from where she'd come.

But very quickly it became clear getting dragged out of the closet was the least of her worries. It hadn't initially occurred to her that the media and fans would not link Ashby's accusation of "questionable ethical turpitude" and "immorality" with being gay. Had that been the case, Alex would have simply been the latest on the short list of athletes being unprofessionally outed by their teammates. A week or two of chatter would commence, the LGBTQ+ community would weigh in, her aunt and uncle would simultaneously combust, and life would have moved forward all the same.

But the twenty-first century didn't lunge at *ethics* with *homosexuality.* Being gay was old news. Instead it jumped to the conclusion of drugs, alcohol, poor sportsmanship, being a locker room diva, cheating, and all sorts of other accusations Alex found far more difficult to bear.

So with advice from her friends, and the support of Rodney Collins, Alex decided to address the matter head on. The best defense was a good offense —the number one rule in sports.

There had been a few nights where she'd wanted to call Catharine. To seek her advice. To simply hear her voice. But she couldn't. Not after all that had happened. The months that had passed. Not while Amelia Walker was sharing her bed every night.

This mess was hers to deal with alone.

But she wasn't alone, she had to remind herself. Her friends were there. Her coach was there. Amelia was there. They had her back.

Sitting in the quiet stadium, her fingers quivering with nerves, she re-read her statement and handed her phone over her shoulder to Amelia. "Is there anything else I should say? Change?" Amelia carefully pressed the phone back into her hands. There was no reason for her to look it over again. They had gone over it a hundred times. All that was left was to release it.

"It may cost you *Kickstar*." Amelia rested strong hands on Alex's shoulders. "I know you already know that."

"I think it's going to cost me a lot more than that." Alex's voice broke as she fought through the whisper, her eyes stinging with tears for what felt like the millionth time. She swallowed and forced them away. She didn't want to cry anymore. All she wanted was to move forward. She was so tired. Tired of hiding. Tired of being afraid.

Amelia squeezed her shoulders. "No, Grey. You're wrong. A few sleepless nights. Some Bible-thumping-hate-rhetoric. She's-too-pretty-to-be-gay speculation. In exchange, a world of weight off your shoulders. You'll still have the Sirens—you're protected by the NWSL there, and if HEG cuts you out of *Kickstar*, so what? Their shoes suck anyway." She smiled. "Sometimes I think you forget you're Alex Grey. Or you just don't realize how good she is. One of the two. There will be companies knocking down doors to sign your name." Amelia smoothed a flyaway strand of hair behind her ear. "There are endless people who support you. Most of all, me."

Alex leaned her cheek against the fingers lingering beside her temple.

"I guess it's just..." Her voice trailed off.

"It's scary," Amelia finished. "It's scary, and it's wrong. No one should be forced into this position. But it was bound to happen sometime. Better now than in the middle of the World Cup. May as well get it out of the way so you can focus on the game."

"My aunt and uncle are going to disown me." She stared at the field below, small and unimpressive from the height of the cheap seats. "I doubt they'll ever speak to me again."

"That's on them. If they aren't proud of the amazing, talented, beautiful woman they raised because she loves outside their comfort zone, that's their loss, Alex. Not yours."

"They're the only family I have left."

"That's rubbish, mate, and you know it. You've got plenty of family. You just have to look around."

Alex leaned back so she could catch Amelia's eye. "And what about you?"

"What about me?"

"You know everyone is going to—you know, they all suspect... what will this do to you?"

"You don't have to worry about me, Grey. I've dealt with this nonsense since I was a teen. This isn't uncharted territory for me."

That wasn't what Alex meant.

"What about—back home?" *Her girlfriend*, she wanted to ask. But the subject was off limits. No talk of family. Future. Feelings. No definitions of what they were doing. Nothing too personal—nothing too real.

"I've got me covered." She squeezed her shoulders in finality. "Let's just worry about you right now. She'll be apples."

There was a sense of comfort in the familiar saying, and Alex felt her throat tighten when Amelia leaned forward and kissed the back of her neck, resting her forehead against her ponytail. "I'll get you through this. I promise."

Chapter Sixteen

A piercing ring jolted Catharine from a dream. Her heart was still racing by the time she'd oriented herself to her surroundings, but the recollection of the dream had faded. Addled with sleep, she fumbled across the surface of her desk until she located her mobile.

"Nat?" she blinked, trying to bring her eyes into focus. "Did you arrive safely?"

"I don't imagine I'd be calling if the plane had crashed." Nathalie tsked. "Not one of those things you tend to walk away from."

Catharine flipped on her desk lamp, curbing a retort. Her notes were scattered, disrupted from her sleep. She swept them together. "What time are you going to see her?"

Today was Susan Lyndon. The Florida senator's wife. Their last chance at getting anything worth while. No one had been willing to talk. Not with Carlton running for president. Not with the threat of retaliation.

Nathalie had visited the intern and the secretary, along with two other staffers, and all had been reticent on their encounters with the senator. The housekeeper, no longer working on The Hill, had been the most forthcoming.

"There's an unofficial *creep list*," she'd told Nathalie, "passed by word of mouth. It's whispered to you in the break rooms and the hallways when you first get started. They tell you what politicians to avoid. What closed doors not to get caught behind." But she'd been unwilling to say anything further, other than acknowledging Senator Cleveland held a permanent position amongst the top offenders.

It was clear the sex trade on Capitol Hill ran a mile deep and had existed throughout history, but no one was ready to stand up against it. Not if they wanted to keep their jobs. Or in the most extreme cases, their lives. For some, it was tit for tat in hopes of career advancement. For others, like the housekeeper, it was just one of the detriments to working behind the veneer of the U.S. Congress. Nothing anyone wanted to tackle on their own. A fear Catharine readily understood. One she could not fault them for. But one that also doubled down her determination to see that her husband never held the power of the presidency.

Nathalie was muffled on the other line, telling a cab driver the name of her hotel. Beneath her sarcasm and nonchalance, she sounded exhausted.

"I don't have an exact plan." She returned to the conversation with Catharine. "She has a tennis lesson at the country club this afternoon."

Stressed, downhearted, anxious for her friend, Catharine tried to find a glint of humor. "You're terrible at tennis."

"I excel at country club cocktails, however. And I look good as a blonde, in case you were wondering." A horn honked in the background. "It's not why I called, however—I take it you haven't been on Twitter?"

A feeling Catharine had grown accustomed to settled in her stomach. A tightening of dread. The unpleasant tingling of apprehension. What had been said about her now? What idiotic thing had Carlton painted their lives with this time? She avoided social media as much as reasonably possible. Nathalie knew that.

"Nicole hasn't brought anything to my attention."

"I wouldn't imagine she would, in this case."

"What is it? Susan Lyndon?" Catharine looked at her pile of notes. She'd hardly left her desk in the four days Nathalie had been gone. Checking references. Cross-references. Scheduling flights. Confirming details. Worried none of it would be enough. That nothing would pan out.

"It's Alex."

The uncomfortable sensation heightened. "Has she said something?"

"Just log on. It's something you should see—"

"Nat—"

"Humor me. You owe me. Big time. Like—for the rest of your life—"

"Nathalie—"

"I've got to run. I have a tennis lesson to prepare for. À plus!"

The line went dead.

Catharine rubbed her pounding temples and checked her watch. It was three in the morning. Carlton had a rally in Michigan in the evening. Volkov was meeting with Gordon Liebermann in Novorossiysk in a couple of hours. Nathalie was skirting around an allegorical powder keg while Catharine continued to keep herself too far from the risk of the peril. It wasn't right. She was expecting too much of everyone else.

If Susan Lyndon wouldn't talk—she would have to take another route. One she'd wanted to avoid, more hazardous to herself. But one she should have started with in the first place, before asking anything of anyone else.

She tipped a finger of brandy into an unwashed glass and raised it to her lips. Nathalie and her obsession with social media... her insistence at dragging Alex's name back into her life. It was never-ending. But on one thing, Nathalie was correct—Catharine owed her a billion times over. It was the least she could do to humor her requests.

Swiping through her phone she keyed in Alex's name.

A dozen headlines popped up, but the one at the top caught her eye. A headline read *Unethical Behavior or Bigoted Beliefs? NWSL star Alex Grey Speaks Out About Being Called Out.*

Catharine clicked the link.

On a page dedicated to women's sports, she found an article about a postgame interview with Monica Ashby—she recognized the girl as the date Caleb Anderson had been with at the House of Salt—and a series of screenshots of tweets she'd posted in the aftermath of the interview specifically singling out Alex Grey.

The author went through the course of events over the past week and the viral sensation Ashby's accusations had stemmed in speculation as to what behavior she had been referring to. It then referenced a link to a public statement Alex Grey had put out the previous morning in response to the allegations of immoral and unethical behavior.

Catharine opened the hyperlink and poured herself another glass of scotch.

As many are well aware, one of my teammates made remarks in an interview and public tweet this past week blatantly challenging my morals, personal life, and "ethical turpitude." After much consideration I felt it best that I address these accusations forthright and head on so that the speculation as to the meaning behind her words could meet with a timely end—both for me and for the poor light it has cast on the NWSL and the Federation.

As those who know me well are aware, I have always put great value on my privacy and kept my personal life my own.

As a professional athlete, I leave everything I have to offer on the pitch. I hold back nothing and have always given my all, no matter the cost: be it mental, physical or emotional.

I give everything.

However, when I step into that locker room and pull off my jersey after a game, I have always been grateful to set aside my public image and become nothing more than Alex Grey—an admittedly shy, quiet, introverted individual that has always placed significant merit on privacy outside the public scrutiny that becomes inevitable in a frequently publicized professional career. I am not one who has ever felt the need to broadcast my life off the field, and were it not for the recent insinuations this past week, I would keep it that way.

With that being said, the speculation over the past week as to the intent behind my teammate's words has proliferated a vast number of false rumors that need to be addressed. The truth is, the 'moral' and 'ethical' standards in my life that do not meet Miss Ashby's 'core Christian Values' revolve around the fact that she does not approve of the gay community of which I am part. She does not condone or agree with my lifestyle, and in her desire to publicly question my ethics has forced me to come out of the proverbial closet in which I have felt most secure.

The only 'questionable unethical turpitude' in this matter is the undesired desecration of my privacy on a subject that should never have been brought to public light. As a member of a professional athletics organization it goes without saying we hold ourselves to a code of honor in protecting our fellow teammates, maintaining their privacy, guarding their secrets and treating them as we would our own flesh and blood. Miss Ashby has gravely violated that unspoken code and level of trust our squad has placed in one another by making accusations that cannot be recalled.

Who I fall in love with off the field has no bearing on my ethics. It has no bearing on my morals. It has no bearing on my ability as an elite athlete to compete and play a game which I love; a game that has been my entire life's commitment and journey, and a dream that has finally been realized in being honored to wear our nations colors and represent this country to the very best of my ability.

I would remind Miss Ashby that I, too, have been raised with core Christian values, and that though her thoughtless words have caused an overwhelming heartache and hardship in my life, I will pray that she never finds herself facing the magnitude of public speculation and criticism that I have experienced over the last seven days. It is something I would wish on no one.

And to my teammates, coaches, friends, family and fans that have stuck by me over the course of the last week and helped me navigate the best way to handle this unexpected spotlight: I truly cannot thank you enough; for your support, your love, and your guidance.

There is nothing in this world I love more than being a footballer and I hope to continuously make you proud.

Always,

Alex Grey

The author closed the story with the mention that this was not the first time Miss Grey had unintentionally made national news outside of her career as an athlete. A year and a half earlier she had been the subject of a viral video of her then boyfriend, Caleb Anderson, proposing to her on her birthday—clearly catching the Sirens forward off-guard—and the aftermath of her declination of his proposal had become an internet sensation. The irony was not lost on the author that Mr. Anderson's new girlfriend was none other than Monica Ashby—and that the readers could draw their own conclusion from there.

There were dozens of follow up articles and hundreds of replies. Speculations on who Alex Grey was referring to when she mentioned 'falling in love off the field,' what had happened between her and Caleb Anderson, which of the USWNT and NWSL superstars were out and which were still speculatively closeted, etc.

Catharine did not click any additional links.

Removing her glasses, she folded her arms across her desk and laid her head against the cool oak surface.

What a mess she'd made of all of their lives. If she'd had any part in exposing Alex... if any of this had come about because of her... She closed her eyes. None of this was ever what she'd wanted. What she'd meant to happen.

She would need to go and see Alex. With the hornet's nest she was preparing to kick, Nathalie had been correct—Alex had the right to know. Even if it never touched her, she should be made aware. Just in case.

Listening to the pendulum of the clock on her wall, she allowed herself to drift into a restless sleep. So much was left up in the air. So much to the unknown.

Chapter Seventeen

"Hanging in there?"

"Hanging in there." Alex slid over a foot to make room for Amelia on the top step of the aluminum stadium bleacher facing their practice field.

It was early, still an hour before training was due to start, but she hadn't been able to sit home in her apartment any longer. Today would be the first time she had to face her teammates since her Twitter post had gone viral two days before, and though most were supportive, there were a couple that were on *Team Monica*, so-to-speak, and she worried that the drama amongst the squad would fall on her shoulders. No matter the fact that she had done nothing to start this furor. If Ashby had just left well enough alone...

"You sure you want to be seen with me today?" Alex only half joked, staring at the grass stained toes of her tennis shoes.

She had also come early with the hopes that she could speak to Rodney and the assistant coach, Lynn Armstrong, before the rest of the team arrived. Rod had been nothing but supportive, outraged at the locker room turmoil Ashby had instigated, and promised Monica would be dealt with accordingly. Lynn was a different vibe. A staunch supporter of Monica Ashby, the defender had played for Lynn at Florida State before the collegiate coach transitioned to the NWSL. When she was hired as the assistant coach for the Sirens, she'd been the driving force behind Monica's trade from the Texas Bluebells.

Mercurial in temper, Alex wasn't sure where she stood with Rod's second-in-command. Ever since her expulsion during preseason, Alex had sensed a hint of disapproval from Armstrong, and was worried this last debacle would only add fuel to the fire if she meant to campaign against her.

She already figured her time with the Sirens would be limited. Her two-year contract was up at the end of the season, and she doubted HEG—as a majority owner—would be content to keep her around. They'd yet to respond to the tumultuous week Alex had encountered in the media, but she didn't imagine it would be long before she was relieved of her endorsement with *Kickstar*. No doubt Monica had already submitted her application to take her place—her ethics and morals included.

Yet no matter what happened with *Kickstar*, Alex didn't want to find herself released from the Sirens in the middle of the season. Heading into the summer teamless hadn't been how she envisioned the start to her first World Cup.

Amelia bumped her with her shoulder. "I guess I've been seen with girls with less *ethical turpitude* in the past. I mean, I can't think of anyone who tops you right now, but—"

Alex pinched the sensitive skin behind Amelia's knee, unable to curb a smile. "You're such an ass." An ass that had gotten her through the worst months of her life. The one person who had been there for her since the day she arrived in California. Supporting her through Caleb. Through injuries. Through self-doubt. Through getting cut from the US roster. And getting called back up. Through her expulsion. And most importantly of all, through Catharine—a loss she would have had to suffer solitary, without anyone even knowing she was hurting—but a loss Amelia never let her feel alone. Even if it wasn't discussed directly, Amelia'd never discounted the emotional turmoil she was going through, and had been her silent pillar of support all along.

She was the one constant in Alex's life. The one thing unwavering.

"I'll own it," the Australian cocked her head, "but you wouldn't have me any other way."

"I wouldn't," Alex laughed, slipping her arm through Amelia's and leaning against her. "I never could have gotten through all this without you."

Alex waited for Amelia to rebuke her for her sappiness, donning her contemptuous disregard for all things sentimental. But she remained uncharacteristically quiet, her standard sarcasm absent from her tongue. Casting a side-eyed glance at her, Alex found her introspective, the keenness of her emerald gaze soft as she stared out at the field.

"You know, I've been thinking... about, well..." Amelia broke the silence, halting through her words. "That maybe we should talk." She didn't look at Alex. She didn't seem to be looking at anything at all.

Alex said nothing, waiting for her to go on. She'd never been one to mince words, or dally in indecisiveness, yet everything about her seemed irresolute and faltering. Immediately Alex worried she was going to tell her she was returning to play in Europe. That she'd been offered a better opportunity somewhere else. That she was leaving—and wouldn't be back.

But whatever direction her mind had taken her was quickly diverted by the sound of a car door slamming and a trio of figures making their way across the field.

"Well," she shook off her discomfiture as quickly as it had been donned, "looks like you can get the hard part over early." Her eyes followed the advancement of the arrivals. Even from two hundred yards it was impossible not to recognize the outline of Monica and Caleb, the pair crossing the grass hand-in-hand. Behind them was Valerie Sims, Monica's sidekick from Florida U. The two were inseparable, and admittedly shared a formidable chemistry on the backline—but the bookends were just as vile off the pitch. And held equal equity in the power of their whispers in Lynn Armstrong's ear.

Not far behind them Erin Halsey's lumbering gait strolled in from the street, with Molly Rodrigues on her tail. A handful of other women behind them.

"C'mon, you newly minted queer," Amelia stood and offered Alex her hand. "Let's get this over with." She trotted down the bleachers. "We're up for 1v1s and I want to draw Ashby. She doesn't need both those knees, does she?" She stopped at the bottom and waited for Alex.

"Should I say something to her, do you think?" Alex jumped to the polyurethane track encircling the training field. Monica and Caleb were stopped at the center circle, talking with Valerie. Monica risked a glance over her shoulder toward the bleachers, but quickly looked away, hiding in the shadow of Caleb.

"Nah. You said your piece yesterday. We all know she read it. Don't give her anything else."

Halsey and Molly approached, gear bags slung over their shoulders.

"Sup', you headline-topping-son-of-a-bitch." At almost six feet tall, Molly's densely inked arms and broad shoulders had given more than a few opposing forwards cause to hesitate in a challenge. She was not a woman Alex would want to cross, and though she shared the backline with Ashby and Sims, Alex was grateful her loyalty lay with their keeper. Teammates of over a decade, she and Halsey had come up through the ranks of the youth National team together, which meant her alliance fell to Alex by default of Halsey's friendship.

"Can't say we don't call her *Hollywood* for nothing," Erin tapped Alex's cheek with her open palm. "How you doing, Grey? Ready to kick some ass today?"

"On the pitch, of course," Rodney interjected, coming up behind them. He was sans his usual button up shirt, his peppered brown hair askew, and looked abnormally tired. "We good here?" he asked no one in particular, but his eyes landed on Alex.

Amelia answered. "Bonzer. Never better."

"As captain, I expect you to keep things in check, Walker. There's no place for all this external noise on the pitch."

"There's no place for a lot of things on the pitch," Halsey challenged, her eyes flicking to where Ashby had migrated to the touchline." Secure in her clout as one of the best goalkeepers in the world, the habitually amiable Mississippian enjoyed the luxury of saying pretty much whatever crossed her mind. "A particular right back included."

"Pull your head in, mate." Amelia patted her back, a warning in her tone. "We're all professionals here."

"A few of us even have *morals*." Halsey smacked Alex's hip before jogging toward the goal line.

Training kicked off as usual. Other than Alex and Monica avoiding direct eye contact, nothing felt like it had changed. No one looked at Alex differently. She was treated the same as she'd always been. If she'd thought coming out as gay would alter her dynamic on the team, her teammates were there to prove her wrong. She was still just Alex. A little shy. A keen left cross. The current butt of Captain Marvel jokes. Even Caleb, glowering at her from the bleachers, didn't have the effect on her she'd thought he would. The only thing she felt was relief. A freedom she hadn't known. She hadn't even realized how much extra baggage she'd been carrying around.

The weight of deception. Of willing everyone to believe you were someone you weren't. For the first time in her life, she could just be herself. Whoever that turned out to be.

Training ran long, closing out with conditioning drills that were met with grumbles and curses throughout the squad. The final exercise, known as *pain shuttle*s, brought more than one player sprawling to the grass when the drill was complete. The united misery of the workout had served its purpose —keeping everyone's mind on their burning lungs and cramping legs, instead of the rift at the core of the team.

"I'd like to remind you all we have a beep test coming at the end of the week." Rodney's announcement was met with universal groans as the women dragged off cleats and stretched sore muscles, lounging around the track. It was midafternoon, already hot for early May. A mugginess had descended on the city, with no breeze coming up from the estuary.

With training officially over, the women turned their conversation to evening activities and plans throughout the week. Come the weekend they would be back on the road, playing a series of away games starting with Rage in South Carolina. Alex was looking forward to seeing Sawyer—and picking up a win against her former team.

A pair of shadows crossed the track where Alex was tying the laces of her Vans, chatting with Halsey and Molly. Glancing into the sun, Alex half expected to find Monica come to say her piece, but instead found two of her younger teammates, Kylie Young and Jess Combs, dropping down to join them.

"So..." Kylie singsonged, eyeing Alex with a mischievous smile, her warm eyes glistening. "Now that you've clapped back at Ass-by, we want to know when you and Walker are going to officially make #*Amex* a thing?"

Amex. The so-called *shipping* currently trending from fans of women's soccer. The habit of merging two names together in hopes or anticipation that the two objects of their interest might become an item.

Alex opened her mouth to object, but the two younger girls giggled, brushing away her protest. "Come on, Alex," Jess chimed in, "it's not like everyone can't see. It's cute! And think of the publicity you'll get this summer as rivals in the World Cup."

"Oh!" Kylie shimmied. "They could make a docu about you! Enemies on the field, lovers off... You, gazing off the camera... '*Prodigious birth of love is it to me.'* Camera pans back and you look directly into the lens. *'That I must love a loathed enemy.'* Can you imagine?"

"Tell us you flunked out of drama school without telling us you flunked out of drama school," Molly rolled her eyes, winking at Alex.

Shaking her head, only partially amused, Alex looked to recruit Halsey's help in warding off the two young busybodies, but found the keeper's attention focused toward the parking lot.

"Grey." Halsey didn't look her way. "Isn't that Portland?"

A fast-spreading course of apprehension flowed from Alex's fingertips to the rush of blood in her head as Halsey's words took meaning. *Portland.* The nickname the keeper had dubbed Catharine the one and only time they'd met—the night Catharine had shown up, unexpected, at her game.

She forced herself to follow her friend's gaze across the field. Two-parts hoping she was wrong. One-part unable to curb the desire she might be right.

Two hundred feet away, standing behind a bench on the opposite side of the track, was Catharine. Dressed down in jeans and a black t-shirt, her hair pulled back in a low ponytail, she was still unmistakable. The tilt of her head. The posture of her shoulders. The elegant way her hands rested atop the back of the bench. At once, Alex could feel her return gaze, the easy confidence, the subtle smile. Everything that made her who she was. Everything that made Alex's pulse quicken.

"The snack's with you?" Kylie broke her train of thought, looking toward the sideline approvingly. "We've been stanning her all afternoon. Thought she was a suit with HEG."

All afternoon? Alex's focus was briefly derailed. How long had Catharine been there? She tried to find something to say to Kylie, but mechanically her attention diverted back to Catharine.

There had been no communication between them since that day at the marina. All the hurt. All the heartache. All the unresolved anguish of a wound left festering had slowly felt like it had begun to heal. Her life taking on some resemblance of normalcy.

But all at once that fragile armor was separating. The seams were coming apart, allowing feelings she'd tried to drown to swim back toward the surface.

"Grey?" Halsey touched her knee, but Alex was already rising. She felt lightheaded, her stomach doing cartwheels. It wasn't a welcoming feeling. Self-consciously she glanced around to locate Amelia. Her back was to them, her attention on an animated conversation with Lynn Armstrong.

"Give me a minute," she said to no one in particular, forcing her feet across the field.

Stopping in the middle of the track, Alex left a handful of yards between them, her heart continuing to strum a chaotic cadence inside her chest.

"Hello, Alex." The words were a salve, a soothing balm, to a wound that felt self-inflicted.

"What are you doing here?" The quiver in her voice contradicted the coldness of her tone.

"I needed to see you. To speak to you about something that's happened. That will be happening."

"It's, uh," Alex toed a tuft of grass that had been uprooted during training, "it's not a great time. I've had something of a week." She looked up and found the cerulean blue eyes watching her. Studying her. Decoding her. She'd forgotten, almost, how stunning she was. How everything paled in her presence.

"I know." Catharine's gaze did not waver, "I saw the articles. I'm sorry that happened, Alex."

It was the simple compassion in her voice, the sincerity that stung. Alex inspected her hands, the heels of her palms streaked with grass stains, dirt beneath her fingernails. She wanted to ask her to leave. And wanted to beg her to stay. Both in equal measure. Behind her she could hear the voices of her teammates. Laughter. The promise that their privacy would soon be invaded. "It's okay," she took a deep breath and looked up again. "It's all for the best."

An illusive smile toyed across Catharine's exquisite lips, the action never touching her eyes.

A silence commenced, evolving into awkwardness, the affliction of two people who had so much to say, but didn't know where to start, or if they should begin at all. Catharine exhaled and drummed her fingers along the back of the bench, battling nerves she'd done well to hide, but losing the contest with her slipping composure with each passing breath.

"I know he came to see you," she said at last, not elaborating who. They both knew what she meant. What the words implied. "I know what he did. With the photos. All his threats." She spoke slowly, haltingly, each word softer than the one before it. "The choice he made you make."

Alex felt the weight of their exposure, her inability to react with eyes she knew were on her. Her teammates. Her coaches. Ashby. Caleb.

Amelia.

Behind her balls were being tossed into bags and zippers were tugged closed on duffles while for the hundredth time her life felt like it was spiraling out of control. She wanted to feel relief. That at last, Catharine knew—knew she'd not chosen to walk away. But the only emotion that pushed through her collapsing defenses was a short-fused anger. Anger at the timing. Anger at herself. Anger at Catharine for treading across the fragile framework of happiness she'd found.

It was unfair, this all happening now. When it was too late. When the time for going back had past.

"I should have just told you." A deflating sensation sucked the strength from her anger, leaving her hollow. Her senses dulled. "At the time I didn't know what to do. I wanted to protect you."

"I know, Alex."

Beneath Catharine's composed exterior there was something more she hadn't said. Her eyes swept over Alex's shoulder, taking in their surroundings, before returning to her face.

"There's something you need to know, Alex. In the very near future there is bound to be a three-ring circus in the media—about Carlton—and in return, an inevitable backlash against me. I have done everything in my power to see your name does not appear in any of it. But I felt it only fair to warn you all the same." For the first time that Alex could recall, Catharine struggled to hold her eye, dropping her gaze to the grass. "And I guess, through some selfish level of vanity, I hope that when you see it, it will not change your opinion of me."

Alex wanted to tell her there was nothing she could do that would ever alter how she felt. How she loved her. Even now. Instead, she asked, "what kind of things?"

Catharine's gaze was steady when it returned to her, all signs of her insecurities vanished. "His indiscretions, mainly. Affairs while he's been in office. Illegal campaign funding. False financial disclosures. Racketeering. Those kinds of things."

Alex nodded stupidly. "And you think they'll drag you into it?"

"I know they will."

"Why?"

"Because the information they'll be receiving is going to come from me."

Alex stared at her, uncomprehending. "You supplied them with it? Won't he… When he finds out, won't he…?"

Catharine waved her off, changing topics. "It shouldn't affect you, Alex. I just wanted you to be aware. There's a chance, if anyone probed too deeply, they could come up with our affair."

Their affair. That was what it had been reduced to?

Hurt, Alex snapped at her, her voice rising. "You think I'm worried about me? Don't be ridiculous, Catharine! I didn't go through everything I went through just for concern for myself."

"Alex." Catharine stepped around the bench but stopped before she got to the track. Her voice was quiet, her eyes resurveying. She was anxious about their surroundings.

"I'm sorry." Alex quieted. "I just—what will he do to you when he finds out?"

"He won't. If everything goes as planned, he won't." She sighed.

They were close enough Alex could have reached out to touch her. Yet still a world apart.

Instead it was Catharine who reached forward, resting her fingers on Alex's grime covered arm. Covered in sweat, stained and disheveled, Alex couldn't help but be struck by the pristineness of her appearance, her manicured nails, her tailored clothing—all a blatant reminder of the dissimilarities of their lives.

"I've missed you, Alex." Her fingers closed lightly around her arm. "I would have chosen you over everything."

"I didn't want you to have to make that choice."

"But it is my choice—my right to decide."

Behind them the chatter of voices grew nearer. An unintended intrusion into one more private moment in her life.

Some imbecile cat called and Alex took an involuntary step away from Catharine, breaking their touch.

"I wouldn't let ol' captain see you hanging around like that. I bet she's got a possessive streak beneath that Australian temper."

Valerie Sims flashed a saccharin simper at Alex as she strode to her car. Monica and Caleb were no where in sight.

Not far behind, Halsey, Molly and Amelia were crossing the field. Amelia's eyes landed on Alex, her expression unreadable, and she'd almost passed by before she turned and approached them.

"Hello, Mrs. Cleveland," Amelia's smile was cynical. "You come to see if you can buy your way onto the team?"

"Amelia," Alex whispered, thrown by the uncharacteristic jab. Despite her constant sarcasm, she had never been spiteful.

Amelia raised a blonde brow, feigning indignation. "What? Am I wrong?" She surveyed Catharine. "Is that not what you do, Mrs. Cleveland? Buy your way into places you don't belong?"

"*Amelia!*"

Her eyes snapped back to Alex as she raised her hands in compliance. "Don't worry, Grey—I'm leaving." She laughed and the brittleness of it cut straight through Alex. The unexpected hurt behind it.

"Don't," Alex breathed, holding her eye. "Please don't." She didn't know what to do. How to salvage the unraveling situation.

"It's okay, Alex," Catharine said softly. "I need to be going. I'm late to catch a flight."

"Don't let me interrupt your tête-à-tête," Amelia waved a flippant hand, walking backward toward where Molly and Erin had continued for the parking lot. "I've got that interview with *Good Day Sacramento* in the morning, so I won't be home tonight. Don't forget we invited Halsey and Rodrigues to dinner tomorrow. Unless you've been offered better company and need me to change that?"

Alex began to respond, but thought better of it, knowing nothing she said would take the edge out of Amelia's mood. She'd been bummed to know Amelia would be gone to Sacramento for the night, but now the break was something of a relief. It would give Amelia time to cool off. Give Alex time to think.

The training grounds had cleared, leaving only Alex's gear bag on the far side of the track, the last cars pulling out of the parking lot.

"I'm sorry," she started, turning back to Catharine.

"Don't be." The impassivity she'd arrived with had returned, despite the fact that they were alone. Laced with an indiscernible degree of hurt beneath it.

"It's not—" She stopped, unable to continue. It wasn't what? What it looked like? Because wasn't it exactly what it looked like?

"It was presumptuous of me to show up uninvited at your place of work. I'm sorry. I just didn't want you to be caught unaware if someone linked your name with mine. I hope it's not the case. The last thing I want is to cause you any more undue suffering."

"Catharine…"

"Life moves on, Alex." Catharine said, not unkindly. "I know that better than anyone." She rallied a close-lipped smile. "I'm happy for you. For all of your accomplishments. For all that you've got going. I mean it, most sincerely."

She turned to go, but reconsidered, leaning over to kiss Alex on her cheek. "Be well, Alex," she whispered, before turning to walk quickly toward her waiting car.

Malcolm came to open her door, where Catharine stepped inside without looking back, and offered Alex a half wave before returning to the driver's side. And then they were gone, and Alex turned mechanically across the field to grab her gear.

Chapter Eighteen

"*THIS IS AN ABSOLUTE FUCKING SHIT STORM!*"

Carlton pummeled the tile counter of the mini bar inside the luxury hotel suite. He was deranged, his veins bulging, the whites of his eyes bloodshot with rage. Catharine watched the knob of his Adam's apple work up and down in a frenzied motion and wondered if he was on the verge of having a stroke. Not that the universe would have granted her that sort of luck. Fortune wasn't in a habit of falling in her lap. She'd always had to work for it.

Swiping an arm across the bar top, he toppled a floral centerpiece with a red, white, and blue flower arrangement of fresh camellias to the floor. His pitch had grown to such a frenzy it was difficult to distinguish his words. In the room adjacent, his assistant, Matthew Stellar, was frantically making phone calls. *CNN. The New York Times. Fox News. The Los Angeles Times. The Washington Post. MSNBC. Chicago Tribune.* Even the *BBC.* Anyone who would listen. But none of them were interested in what threats the peon lackey of Carlton Cleveland had to say. Even with Carlton screaming in the background, the furthest Matthew got up the chain of command was to the secretary of the CEO's coffee boy.

"You tell them I'll close them down! I'll have their jobs! I'll sue them for every lying word!" He kicked the fallen camellias, sending petals across the ivory carpet.

Malcolm, standing stationary beside the balcony window, his gaze turned toward the street, stiffened. Catharine knew he was aware of Carlton's every move, his eyes following the senator in the glass reflection. He'd flown into Alabama with her late the night before, Catharine's visit strategically orchestrated to put herself in the presence of her husband when the first bomb dropped. She couldn't distance herself this time. She had to be front and center. Taking as much fire as he was. It was the only way to keep herself safe.

Heart galloping, she returned her attention to her Macbook, trying not to wince every time Carlton's foot connected with another piece of furniture. A half dozen browsers were open on her screen. The papers had run with the breaking news that morning, the news channels following in their wake. She'd arrived to discuss the convention schedule shortly before his team discovered the first accusatory leak.

Wife of Florida Senator, Wayne Lyndon, Accuses Presidential Candidate of Sexual Misconduct

Support Wavering for Candidate Cleveland Amidst Accusations of Foul Play

Presidential Frontrunner Caught Red-Handed in Myriad of Racketeering

Interspersed amidst the stories, there were smaller captions with fewer views:

WorldCargo Whistleblower Exposes Financial Crimes

Wife of Candidate Cleveland a Leader Amongst Reported Price Fixing Fiasco

Transportation Giant Sailing in Hot Water Over Internal Drug Smuggling Scandal

And on and on it went.

Most of it harmless. Carlton would skate through unscathed by the allegations of profiteering and extortion. The illegal campaign funding would fall by the wayside. Even Susan Lyndon's narration of sexual assault would likely be forgiven by the voters—written off as a drunken pass at a woman who'd been wearing too short a mini skirt. The people were vile that way. There was so little they wouldn't forgive if a politician continued making promises through their teeth.

For her part in it, she'd receive some bad publicity. A slap on the hand for breaking antitrust laws by the FTC. WorldCargo would be hit hardest by the coverage of the drug smuggling operation a former captain of a cargo ship had run for six years before his illegal side hustle was detected by an internal investigation. Brooks Corp had paid to have the story buried, and the media wouldn't take kindly to big business flaunting their ability to sink bad press by means of payoff.

But it was recoverable. Repairable. Ultimately non-detrimental. Most importantly, it set her up for what she needed to do next. It would offer her a safeguard against suspicion from Carlton that she'd had any part in the anonymous evidence compiled against him. Against *them*. For why would she incriminate herself? Drag her own name through the mud?

Matthew slunk into the dining room, cell phone abandoned.

"I'm sorry, sir—they refuse to pull the story."

"Who?"

"All of them, sir. They are claiming irrefutable proof."

A bottle of whiskey shattered against the dining room wall. "Irrefutable proof?! From who?!" Carlton wheeled around, challenging no one in particular. He turned his attention to Catharine. "This is an inside job, God damnit! Those campaign financials are confidential information."

That he was more upset about being accused of campaign fund fraud than sexually assaulting his former friend's wife spoke volumes to his character. He'd hardly remembered the woman's name.

"Lyndon's piece of ass?" he'd called her when the first headline hit the news. Twenty-five years younger than the Florida senator, Wayne Lyndon's wife had proven to be more than forthcoming with Nathalie. She despised Carlton and despised her husband in equal measure for never addressing the situation. She'd been at a Christmas party in the Keys. Tipsy. Celebratory. Dancing with her husband's colleagues and staff, she'd never thought twice about sharing a cigar with Carlton on the balcony of the private hotel. Only the cigar hadn't been all he'd wanted to share. Drunk, the South Carolina senator had tried to kiss her, and when she'd attempted to duck away he'd grabbed her around her waist, groped her inappropriately, and stuck his tongue down her throat. Where it would have led if they hadn't been interrupted by her husband, she would never know.

Lyndon had never taken her side in the matter. Though his friendship with Carlton had ended that night, he'd blamed her for the interaction. A resentment that had festered over time. A resentment that made her willing to talk—when the opportunity presented itself.

But it wouldn't be enough.

"Are you hearing me, Catharine? An inside job!" He took a step toward her and she could feel Malcolm angle himself across the room. The Scotsman had been aching to get his hands on Carlton ever since the night at The

Fairmont. But today was not the day and now was not the time. Besides, there were a half dozen personnel in the rooms adjacent, and Matthew standing ten feet away. Carlton was a behemoth fool, but even he wasn't so reckless.

"I need to get back to my office. Assess the damage. I have the board breathing down my neck. I need to stop the hemorrhaging."

"*Hemorrhaging*? All you can think about is yourself and your fucking company! Do you have any idea what this is doing to my polls! What it could do to my race?"

Catharine was careful to keep her tone midway between belligerent and pragmatic. "Have you reached out to your contacts at *The Wall Street Journal*? Asked them to run a counterstory?"

"They were the first paper to run the exposé, God damnit! A thirty year relationship with the editor-in-chief and they spout off due to an anonymous whistleblower! I'll fucking destroy them, I swear!"

Catharine snapped her computer closed and shoved it in her bag. The *WSJ* had been the first paper she'd hit. An anonymous package delivered by an overnight courier with the evidence condemning Carlton. She'd wanted him to feel the prick of their betrayal.

"You need to make a statement this morning—refuting that you've ever so much as looked at another woman, Carlton. Your base doesn't care about campaign funding. It's Susan Lyndon you're up against."

Matthew stepped gingerly around the shattered vase on the carpet. "Perhaps it is best to wait on that. To maybe allow the uproar to die down. We could run a couple surveys and see where the polls fall."

The little bastard knew it was better for Carlton to own his mistakes and move on. An option he would never take. So the next best course of action was to do nothing at all. Elsewise he'd come out swinging blindly, getting caught in another lie, and end up punching himself in the face. Exactly what Catharine was counting on.

"Sexual assault is nothing to lie low over," Catharine countered carefully. "One accusation uncontested turns quickly into a dozen. You do not want to sit on that." She kept her eyes only on her husband.

"Sir—if there might be others—"

"What are you insinuating, Stellar?" Carlton was off again, wound up like a top. His chest strained at the buttons of his dress shirt, his tie tightening to a noose around his neck. Clawing to loosen the knot, he wheeled on his assistant. "Catharine's right—I need to put this bitch in her place. I won't have the media painting me as a Clinton. Family values! *Traditional* family values! It's what we've built this campaign on. Dig up anything you can on Lyndon's wife—affairs, parking tickets, showing up late to the PTA for all I care. Find me something! We'll put out a statement—prove her a liar, disgruntled by my lack of support for her husband's last campaign."

"Sir—"

"*Now*, Stellar! Send in Ben. And tell Miller to start working on a press release—denying every accusation."

Catharine waited a beat. "Perhaps, Carlton, you should listen to Matthew. If there's any chance—"

"Have I hired you as my campaign manager?" Carlton snapped, yanking at the top button of his shirt. Sweat was pouring from his brow, his labored breathing evident. "Stick to your numbers and your ships and your little sea ports and leave the politicking to me, damn you." The top button broke free, disappearing into the wilting petals on the carpet.

Catharine gave only an acquiescing nod. It was the one thing she could count on. Give him enough rope, and he was bound to hang himself.

Chapter Nineteen

Alex walked the long way home from training, attempting to delay the inevitable. Amelia would be back from Sacramento and they'd be forced to talk. She hadn't responded to Alex's text the night before—wishing her goodnight, or her text that morning, telling her to break a leg on the television interview with *ABC10*. But she knew she'd gotten home earlier, based off Halsey's oblivious commentary throughout their afternoon weightlifting session—relaying to Alex via back and forth texts with Amelia, what they'd decided to barbecue. Unaware Alex was being given the silent treatment from their mutual friend.

Arriving on the third story landing, she found her door open and a variance of laughter drowning out the commentary of pundits weighing in on an international football match. Part of her had wondered if Amelia would change the dinner venue to her own apartment, one floor down. A clear slap in the face to Alex, given they hadn't spent a single night apart since Miami two months earlier. It was always Alex's apartment where they congregated, with or without company. But she was there, and the noisy hollering at the TV came as a relief. Maybe Amelia's vexation had blown over. Maybe they could talk.

"Bloody Kiwis!" Amelia was perched on the bar separating the living room and kitchen, a longneck bottle in hand. Two more empty bottles sat beside her. Halsey was on the couch, and Molly standing in the center of the floor, fist pumping a beer through the air. The New Zealand men's side was playing a friendly against Portugal. Molly, whose father was Portuguese, was celebrating a recent goal. Amelia, by default, was rooting for New Zealand.

"Hey," Amelia greeted her with a tilt of her chin. "You're late. Beer?"

"No." It was the middle of a training week. They never drank outside the weekends. Unless Molly came over. But even then, they were strict to only having one.

"Portugal is kicking ass!" Molly slung herself onto the sofa, kicking her legs up into Halsey's lap, before the keeper immediately dislodged them.

"Pig! Feet off the furniture."

The two engaged in a slew of insults as Alex met Amelia's eyes over the top of her bottle.

"Could I see you for a minute?" Alex didn't want to wait to settle things between them. She needed it off her chest.

"Can it wait?"

"No."

"Well, okay, then." If their friends were aware of the hostility electrifying the room, they didn't show it. A couple beers deep, football, the promise of free food, neither Halsey nor Molly seemed to care.

"Well?" Alex shut the door behind them in her bedroom.

"Well what? We're having a few coldies—it's been a shit week and it's only Wednesday. I think they've been earned."

"I'm not talking about the beers."

"What, then?"

"What was that yesterday?"

Amelia rested her shoulder against the door. "I don't know, mate. You tell me."

"Quit the crap. '*You come to see if you can buy your way onto the team?*' Are you kidding me?"

"Fair dinkum question. She was there to buy something. Just depends on what's selling."

"Jesus, Amelia," Alex rubbed at her brow, feeling the pressure of a headache brewing. "What is that supposed to mean?"

"Then why was she there, Alex? Just happened to be in the area and popped in for a quick hello? You want me to believe that?"

"What does it even matter to you?"

Amelia's face shifted, her eyes flashing as a pulse appeared at the hinge of her jaw. She was on the verge of being drunk. Angrier than Alex had seen her before.

"What does it matter to me? Are you being serious?" Her voice was low, slow, deliberate.

"Entirely! We don't talk! Just, football—training—day-to-day nonsense. Nothing specific—nothing consequential—"

"Not everything is words, Alex! *Watch what they do, more than what they say.* My father raised me on that. Can you really stand there and tell me I have done anything less than stand by your side? That I have not championed you? Pushed you? Kept you afloat? And what has that toff done for you? Beyond leaving you feeling worthless. Brokenhearted. Throwing your whole career away!"

"She didn't leave me," Alex said quietly, not knowing what else to say.

"What do you mean?"

"I left her." It was nothing they'd ever discussed. Nothing that had come up between them. It hadn't mattered at the time. But it felt like it mattered now. Felt like it had probably mattered all along. "I was blackmailed— threatened by her husband. He gave me an ultimatum to call it off." She closed her eyes. She didn't want to see the anger leaving Amelia's face. The hurt washing over her expression. So much had been left unsaid between them, but lately so much more had been implied. It was like Amelia said— words weren't everything. What had started out as fun—as casual—had changed over time. In simple ways: Alex packing combined lunches, Amelia footing the grocery bill since Alex paid the electric, the two of them splitting the drawers in Alex's dresser. Or subtle changes—a kiss on the back of Alex's neck when Amelia returned from the gym, laying together on the sofa with no intentions of taking it further after a long day of training. The unspoken language they'd learned to share between them. It hadn't mattered what they said—things *had* changed between them.

"And you tell me I'm the one with all the secrets." Amelia crossed from the door and slumped onto the bed, her elbows on her knees. She didn't look at Alex.

"It wasn't my intent to keep anything from you. I couldn't tell anyone. It wasn't just me he threatened." She thought about Amelia's father. His debt. The mental illness he had battled. She couldn't tell her any of that. Couldn't explain the millstone she'd been carrying.

Alex reached out and ran her fingers through Amelia's hair, bidding her to lift her downcast face. "I don't know where we stand. I don't know where we've ever stood." She dropped to her knees when Amelia wouldn't look at her, forcing their faces level. "I've always thought this was just temporary —a void filled for both of us. I thought that was what you wanted."

Amelia tried to pull away, but Alex caught her hands, unwilling to be put off the conversation. "It's gotten more serious than that—I don't think either of us can deny it. But I don't know what it means. You have a life thousands of miles from here. A house. A girlfriend. You talk about your waiting roster position on the WSL—how you can't wait to return to play in England. Every time one of your friends calls you from Arsenal, I expect you to tell me you're leaving. And when you retire—however long that is from now— I know your heart is in Australia. Please. Talk to me."

"I wanted to talk to you yesterday morning." If it was a smile Amelia tried to summon, the effort failed miserably. "But then Ashby arrived."

"So talk to me now."

"It's a little late for that."

"Why? Because I spoke to a woman I once knew for all of five minutes yesterday? And we both left, no different than before?"

"No. Five minutes. Five seconds. Five hours. It doesn't matter. I saw how you looked at her. How you forgot the rest of the world existed. I can't compete with that. There's no fair suck of the sav here, Alex. I won't even try."

"I already told you—it isn't a competition. There is nothing for you to compete against."

Amelia's smile was cold. Distant. Closed. "And like I told you—everything is a competition." She looked down at their entwined hands before meeting her eye again. "Could you honestly tell me you're not still in love with her?"

"No," Alex said without pause. "I couldn't. But it's no different than it was yesterday, or the day before. We are no different than we have been. Could you tell me when your contract is up and it's time for you to go you wouldn't jump on that plane without ever looking back?"

"I guess we'll never know now, will we?"

Angry, Alex shoved herself to her feet and turned toward the door. "You're impossible when you're drunk, you know that?"

"I'm honest when I'm drunk."

"That doesn't make you less impossible." With her back to her, Alex paused. She didn't know what she wanted. What Amelia wanted. The conversation had cleared up nothing, leaving her even more uncertain than before. But the one thing she was sure of was that she couldn't lose Amelia. Couldn't lose her friendship. Everything she meant to her. She just didn't know how to say it.

"Well," leveled Amelia at last, her own frustration evident. "Good talk. Let's do it again sometime." She started to pass for the door, but Alex grabbed her arm, spinning her around, reaching to frame her face with her palms. "It's not a competition, okay?" She stared at her, faces so close their noses were nearly brushing. She wanted to shake sense into her. To snap the underlying presence of hurt out of her sea green eyes.

But Amelia had already donned her mask of sarcasm and mock bravado, her vulnerability buried once more. "C'mon Grey—you know what they're going to accuse us of if we stay in here much longer." And kissing her nose, she walked out the door.

An hour later the wind had whipped up and ruled out the plan to barbecue in the picnic area. In true Amelia fashion, she'd abandoned Alex to rummage through the fridge in search of something to feed their friends while she bolted for the shower.

Having unearthed ingredients to put together a spaghetti dinner—sans actual marinara—Alex was bringing the water to a boil when Molly called for her over the din of a *CNN* news report.

"Holy shit, Grey! Isn't that the woman you were talking to yesterday afternoon?"

Alex glanced over the partition to see a photo of Catharine and Carlton smiling at a recent townhall. Below the image was a red *breaking news* banner highlighting the caption: *Following denial of sexual abuse allegations, Cleveland R-SC faces new accusation of domestic violence.*

Alex lost her hold on the can of tomato soup she'd been opening, splattering scarlet pulp across the counter and floor. She'd grown accustomed to seeing Catharine's face in the headlines, but something about this was different.

"Wait, that's… Portland." Erin stared slack-jawed at the TV, before looking over her shoulder to Alex. Shaking herself loose of her temporary paralysis, Alex slowly made her way to the couch to listen to the report.

"Following a whirlwind of allegations ranging from campaign fraud to the more heinous accusation involving sexual assault, Presidential candidate Carlton Cleveland released a statement earlier this afternoon staunchly denying the validity of all accounts. While a follow-up testimony has not yet been made available for Susan Lyndon, the woman accusing the senator of sexual misconduct, new evidence has been released indicating an established behavior of domestic violence.

"After more than two hundred documents pertaining to Cleveland's three-decade-long political career were provided to various news outlets by an anonymous source, the following photo came to light after the senator's strongly worded disavowal of the allegations raised against him over the past twelve hours. We must caution our viewers that the following image contains graphic content and viewer discretion is advised."

At once Alex felt like she'd been sucker punched in the gut. Magnified on the screen on the six o'clock news was a photo of Catharine. Sitting alone at the end of a hallway in front of a vanity mirror, she was dressed in the gown she'd worn the night of the HOPE Gala. Her face nearly beyond recognition, partially concealed by blonde matted hair, one eye was swollen entirely shut while her split lips and hemorrhaging nose streamed blood down her chin and neck. The ivory satin was drenched in scarlet, the delicate lace of the décolletage wholly saturated. She'd turned slightly away from the camera, but not enough to hide the violent bruising and taut swelling covering the entirety of the left side of her face. The violence of it was appalling, but more than that, to Alex, was the immeasurable degradation of her expression. The humiliation. The defeat. It was something she'd never imagined possible of the proud Englishwoman. With all her self-assertion and dignity.

It was the night Nathalie had met her in the bar and sent her and Amelia home without explanation. Alex thought about how she'd given Catharine the silent treatment for over a week. How angry she had been. How jealous of Nathalie. The headlines she'd seen in the weeks following—Catharine with her oversized sunglasses and billowing scarves, unsuitable for the

California weather. The freshly healing scar on her lip she'd asked her about in Colorado.

He'd hit her. They'd left it at that. But Alex had never known, had never realized it had been anything like this. This was not a short-tempered backhand. A slap in a heated conversation.

She'd been so self-absorbed and sorry for herself, Alex had never seen the writing scrawled across the walls.

Wrapped up in the footage on TV, Alex hadn't heard Amelia come up behind her.

"The night of the gala." She set her hands on her hips, looking over her shoulder, and Alex leaned back against her. "Did you know?"

"No." Alex shook her head. "Not that it had been like this."

Molly craned around on the couch. "Wait, what? How do you know this woman?"

Alex held up a hand, trying to catch the rest of the news report.

"...the CEO and private shareholder of the global transportation giant, WorldCargo, and its parent company, Brooks Corporation. Mrs. Cleveland, a true magnate in the shipping industry, has been married to Senator Cleveland for twenty-five years, born to the English business tycoon, Colonel Benjamin Brooks, who turned over the management of the family dynasty to his only daughter in the early 2000s.

The photo we are showing you is from last year after the HOPE Charity Gala, hosted annually by WorldCargo in San Francisco—a fundraiser for the education of underprivileged youth and adults around the globe."

Beside the photo of her bruised and battered face they posted an image of Catharine earlier in the evening, standing on the grand staircase of the San Francisco City Hall, looking as regal and self-composed as royalty.

"The photo on the right is allegedly the state the presidential nominee left his wife in after departing her hotel room the night of the gala. Among the documents released earlier this afternoon are allegations directed toward WorldCargo for tax evasion, price fixing and drug smuggling. This is a developing story and we will continue to update our viewers with the most reliable, neutral, nonpartisan details of this breaking case as it continues to unfold."

The newscaster shook her blonde bob gravely, looking toward her partner. *"Really, Russ, this is almost too much to take in all at once. In the span of the last hour, three more women have come forward, accusing Senator Cleveland of charges similar to that of Susan Lyndon. Let's go back for a minute to the laundry list of allegations the senator faces in respect to the documents released by an undisclosed source earlier today."*

Alex reached over the top of the couch and snatched the remote out of Erin's hand, flicking the TV off. There was an unanimous protest from the couch, but Alex tossed the clicker onto the kitchen bar.

"You guys can watch the news in your own apartment."

Erin unfolded her tangle of limbs and propped herself up so she could see Alex. "Hold up. I'm confused. You're telling me the woman from the pub in Portland is the wife of the unibrow running for president?"

"Probably not running anymore," Molly smirked.

Alex couldn't think of anything beyond the image on the TV. "She—it doesn't matter. It's a long story."

Molly stretched her tatted arms over her head and gave show of stifling a yawn before folding her legs underneath her. "Good thing the night is young."

"It's not something I want to talk about."

"I'm gonna bet you're outvoted, three to one," Molly ribbed. "Am I right?" She glanced between Amelia and Halsey for their verdict.

"Hundred percent," Halsey confirmed.

Amelia remained silent.

"Okay, so, one abstention and two yeas." Molly shrugged. "Still a majority. So spill the tea. Beginning with how you're acquainted with the wife of a US senator and ending with what she was doing at our training yesterday."

Alex just wanted them to go. To leave her alone with her thoughts for a while. Between her conversation with Amelia and the photo of Catharine, her nerves felt exposed, her emotions raw. But she didn't want their speculation. Their waxing interest to run amuck. Better to deal with it here and now.

"I met her on Daufuskie Island when I was still playing for Rage." Without significant detail, she recounted their first encounter, how it had led to the slow growing friendship over the following months. She emphasized Catharine's help with her contracts and the amiable rapport they'd developed over the past two years. "I hadn't seen her in a few months so yesterday when she was in the area she opted to stop by. There's nothing more to tell."

"Bullshit," Molly scoffed through a cough, draping herself over the back of the couch. "I may have only gotten into USC on athletics, but I wasn't born yesterday. You looked like you'd seen the ghost of Tony DiCicco when you saw her on the field. Let's have the deets—we want something sordid. Were you shaking the sheets with that looney tune's wife?"

"Put a sock in it, Rodrigues," Amelia broke her silence, vexed. "She's just seen a photo of her mate beat to shit and you want to turn it into a daytime soap. Why don't you both pack it up for the night? We'll do dinner another time."

"Easy, killer," Molly slung a long leg over the top of the couch and slid to her feet. "Inquiring minds, is all." She flicked the back of Halsey's head. "Come on, Erin—pizza at my place. Let's leave these buzzkills to themselves. They either need to fight or fuck—for neither of which do I want to be present."

"I'm sorry," Alex offered lamely, walking them to the door. "It's been a weird couple days."

"No big," Molly, already unruffled, snagged two beers off the counter before waltzing to the landing. "You got some crazy shit in your life, Grey —I'll never accuse you of being boring." She winked. "But don't worry, bro —you're part of the fam now. We've got your back." She chucked her chin at Amelia. "Night, Cap."

When they'd gone Alex dragged herself to the couch and curled into the corner. Half of her battled with wanting to turn the TV on and fixate on the story, while the other part demanded she bury her head in the sand.

Her eyes closed, she felt Amelia's weight settle beside her, not quite close enough to touch.

"Hey."

Alex opened her eyes and stared at the popcorn ceiling.

"Are you okay?"

"Yeah. I guess." She wrapped her arms across her chest, feeling like she needed to hold herself together. It was too many things all at once. Catharine finding out about Carlton's threats. Seeing her for the first time in months. That appalling photo on the news. The thought her name might be dragged into all of it.

As if Ashby's drama hadn't been enough.

And then, the undercurrent beneath it all—Amelia. Who she didn't know how to talk to. Who she didn't want to lose.

"Is that what she came to talk to you about?" The drunken hostility was vanished. Despite the invisible rift between them, Amelia was offering to fill the roll in Alex's life she'd held from day one. The supportive friend. The patient ear. The shoulder to cry on. Alex knew she didn't deserve it, but she also didn't know how to navigate this on her own.

"No. Not exactly. She said Carlton was going to be facing some backlash —and wanted me to be aware that with the scrutiny from the media, my name might be dug up. She just didn't want me to be caught unprepared."

"Is it something you need to worry about?"

Alex almost laughed. A week ago her greatest concern was being outed by Monica Ashby as a small-time sport's celebrity—*that girl from Kickstar*. Unknown outside the little-recognized world of women's sports. A disclosure that was ultimately proving to have little effect in her life. She still had her friends. Her job. The National Team. Whereas Catharine was having the entirety of her life torn inside out. Her privacy demolished. Her company attacked. Being scrutinized at a level of global impact.

Alex's problems paled in comparison.

"No. At this point I guess having an affair with the wife of the man running for president decreases in significance compared to it being internationally broadcast that you use your wife's face as a punching bag."

From the corner of her eye she could see Amelia turn a hint of a smile. "I don't know—it still kind of gives you status as a celesbian."

"A what?"

"Come on, Grey—a dykon?" Amelia's smile grew earnest and Alex laughed, dropping the arms still clenched across her chest and sliding over to make room for Amelia beside her.

Accepting the offer, Amelia pressed in along side of her, drawing their bodies close and alleviating some of the heaviness between them. "Is there anything I can do for you?"

It was wrong to seek her solace with so much up in the air. The future left unclear. She'd hurt her—she knew that now, even if it had been unintentional. This was her chance to do the right thing. To let her go. But knowing what was right, and being able to do what was right, were two very different things. And so Alex took the easy road, the one that led them no where, but offered a sense of comfort with its familiar scenery.

"Please stay with me tonight." She closed her eyes, absorbing Amelia's warmth behind her, afraid the response she got would be the one she deserved. Yet almost hoping Amelia's self-preservation would be stronger than her need.

But the arms that slipped around her gave no sign of leaving, and Alex breathed out her relief as Amelia pressed her lips against her ear.

"I'm here, Grey. I'm not going anywhere."

Chapter Twenty

"Was I just too stupid to know?"

Nathalie glanced over the frame of the borrowed reading glasses and planted her elbows on the kitchen bar. It was the longest she'd looked away from her laptop since she'd arrived early in the morning, her full attention on the magnitude of the escalating snowball effect of their shared conspiring.

"What?" Disinterested in the conversation, she returned her focus to the computer screen. "Have you seen this, Catharine? *The New York Times* ran an editorial suggesting that along with Carlton withdrawing from the race, you ought to resign your position as CEO from Brooks Corp."

"Well, fortunately Arthur Sulzberger doesn't sit on my board." What did she care what the media tyrant's chairman felt she should do? It wasn't his name that signed her checks or submitted her payroll. "Do you think it started before Carlton ever went to her? Was that why she just acquiesced and disappeared?"

"I'm going to pretend we aren't even having this conversation." Nathalie uncrossed her legs and jabbed a nettled finger onto the counter. "Have you been paying attention to what is happening, Cate? You're getting chewed up and spit out by the media nearly as much as Carlton. One half sees you as the self-inflicted abuse victim sticking by her man while the other views you as the enemy of their chosen Messiah, come to topple the GOP. Neither are good and there's not much of an in-between."

"You think I care how the American political parties view me? Until yesterday there wasn't a soul alive this side of the Atlantic that had ever heard of Brooks Corp. Transportation isn't exactly a headlining industry. All these people calling for my head wouldn't even know what I'd be resigning from. It'll blow over." She shoved her phone aside. "Do you know football

---

fans have been using the hashtag *AmEx* since early last year? It's some name blending thing they do when they suspect someone is in a relationship —"

"Or when they *want* someone to be in a relationship. Meshing isn't exclusive to sports, you know? Hollywood's been at it for decades. It doesn't mean anything. Besides, what does it matter? Alex is gone, you're in hot water, and there are far more pressing matters you need to concern yourself with right now."

"Are there?" Catharine did nothing to mask the sarcasm from her tone. "It's like I'd almost forgotten. Please, remind me."

"Stop. I'm not the enemy here, and you know it, Cate. I'm sorry things didn't go as you'd hoped they would with Alex the other day, but there are other things that require your full focus. However," she folded her hands in front of her, steepling her fingers, "if it will get you off the subject: *no*, I do not believe anything started with Alex and that Australian at any time during your relationship. I think you are being petty, insecure, and looking for someone to blame for the disastrous monstrosity that bastard you call your husband has made of your current situation. I think he threatened her, scared her, and forced her to do the only thing a person could in her position, under the circumstances—run as far away from you as possible. It's what any sane person would do. And it's exactly as I have told you all along: the world you live in is overwhelming. It's intense. It's frightening. You know I'm right. And I know, whether you'll admit it or not, that you must understand why sometimes it would be easier—and safer—to just move on with your life in the world with which you are familiar, instead of trying to survive this alternate reality where people like you exist."

Catharine's head snapped up. "People like me?" She was so tired of hearing that phrase.

"Yes, Cate." Nathalie didn't back down. "People like you. Don't pretend you don't know what I'm talking about. We've been over this."

"So you're saying it is just simpler to walk away—because my life is intimidating?"

"Sometimes it is the better option, yes."

"You mean like you did?"

It wasn't what she'd meant to say. They were just five stupid words uttered in anger. She was hurt. Frustrated. Disappointed. And though she wouldn't admit it to Nathalie, she was scared about the uproar in the media. It hadn't been what she'd expected. She hadn't anticipated the backlash against Brooks Corp to be as violent as it had been. She'd only meant to sully her name to a minor degree to protect herself from Carlton's suspicions. She'd thought, after releasing the photo of her battered face, the media would redirect their attention to her husband. But it seemed once blood had been spilt, the masses simply enjoyed watching the downfall of a giant. The burning of a kingdom. No matter who the fire consumed in the process. And in her defeat, she was taking out her resentment on the one person who deserved it the least.

But she'd said it. And the words hung in the air like a guillotine between them.

"Like I did?" The whisper permeated the silence of the room as Nathalie slowly closed her laptop and slid from the high top stool, her bare feet making a muted thud against the tile as she stared at Catharine, incredulous. "*Like I did?* You mean after your father yanked me from your bed and flung me to the floor as if I were less than a dog? When he called me an abomination—a slag—and threw me from your room, naked in the hall, while all your servants looked on? Like *that*, you mean?" Her lips were quivering in fury, her eyes dangerously dry. "Or did you mean after I was imbecilic enough to return to London—despite his threats—and bang on your door, refusing to leave until he let me see you? Where I pleaded—*begged*—for you to come with me! You were my entire life! And I was cast to the wind like a worthless scrap of rubbish so you could reign on as the esteemed heiress of the Brooks Family throne! Forgive me if I didn't languish the remainder of my life away waiting on something I could never have! You live in your own delusional world, Catharine—impervious and unaffected by what goes on around you, never noticing who or what gets destroyed along the way!" She slammed Catharine's glasses onto the counter and yanked her laptop into her arms. "You're right about one thing—this *will* all blow over. That's how it always goes for *people like you*! But don't you dare blame the rest of us for trying to seek shelter from your storm! We're just trying to survive your wake!"

"Nat—"

"Don't! I have better things that I can do today. I'm sure you'll have this neatly handled with all the loose ends tied up before the week is over. You're good at putting things in their allocated place."

Catharine didn't turn from her place at the counter as Nathalie headed for the stairwell. There wasn't anything she could say to stop her. Maybe what she said was true—she was out of touch and out of reach. Perhaps it was her penance for putting Brooks Corp first, above all else, all those years ago? Even if all of her scheming panned out and she was able to pry her life apart from Carlton's—maybe this was her lot? And it would all turn out for nothing in the end.

Her phone rang as Nathalie's footsteps disappeared down the flight of stairs. It was Nathan Lundy from ALT, the PR manager who handled Brooks Corps' public relations and communications.

She answered as the front door slammed. "Mr. Lundy."

"Mrs. Cleveland." His greeting was subdued, far from his usual animation she'd grown accustomed to over the past twenty years.

"I take it this is not a social call, Nate."

"I wish it were." Delaying, he cleared his throat. Nicole had been working with ALT, devising statements for both Catharine as an individual and from the corporation's official standpoint, but Catharine had yet to see the finished result. All she knew was her father had not yet weighed in, and she wanted to release something from Brooks Corp before he had time to demand his individual opinion be heard.

"I wanted to reach out to you directly, given time is of the essence. I know things are, um," the rich baritone faltered, abnormal for a man never lost for words, "*complicated* with Senator Cleveland's current situation. But I feel it is my duty to advise you, Mrs. Cleveland, that if we do not take measures to separate Brooks Corp from the present media outrage, there is a chance the consequences may become unrecoverable. I have spent the morning on the phone with Mr. Liebermann and we are in agreement, ma'am, that a statement must be made—both literal and figurative in nature —separating you from the senator's allegations."

"Yes, of course, Mr. Lundy."

"Of course?" It was not the answer he'd been expecting. Why should it have been? More often than was acceptable, women in her position stood staunchly beside their husbands, martyring themselves to uphold their vows.

For better and for worse, and all the rest of that rubbish that chained women to their fate. They were expected to be loyal. Unwavering. Committed. No matter the sins of the husband. Split lips and bloodied faces were meant to be dealt with in private, at home—at least that was the trending opinion of many of the comments on the more conservative news outlets, appallingly not only from men. State-to-state, neither reduced to just one demographic or generation, the comments had poured in, belittling Catharine as a wife, as a business owner, as a woman.

She'd known it wouldn't be peaceable—things like this never were—but she hadn't expected to find herself as much part of the controversy as Carlton was.

He was the story, after all. Not her. Not Brooks Corp.

Carlton.

"Yes, Mr. Lundy. It's the only feasible option." She rose from her kitchen table and crossed through the dining room to step onto the lower balcony overlooking the bay. The time had come. It was now or never.

She hadn't gone into this thinking she would bow out gracefully, fading into the sunset to keep her hands clean. Susan Lyndon wasn't having her life turned upside down for Catharine to stand beside her husband and tell the world it was okay... what he'd done to her... to Susan... to these other woman... it didn't matter, she'd support him anyway.

No.

She'd come to set the bridge on fire. To blow up the whole fucking town.

"I'll have a statement over to you shortly regarding my impending divorce."

"Divorce?" His voice rose an octave. She knew what he was thinking. They were eight weeks away from the National Conventions. "We needn't take such drastic measures, Mrs. Cleveland. I was only implying that it was perhaps wise to—"

"Have you ever hit your wife, Mr. Lundy?"

He fell silent, before answering quietly. "No, Mrs. Cleveland. Never."

"And have you ever assaulted your colleagues' wives? Made passes at their teenage daughters? And still thought you were a suitable candidate to hold one of the most powerful, prestigious elected offices in the world?"

"No, Mrs. Cleveland. I understand your position. And I imagine you have not come to this decision without weighted consideration. It is just my job to inform you on the possible backlash—"

"—*certain* backlash," Catharine corrected.

"*Certain* backlash," he conceded, "you and your corporation will receive. With the high publicity and your husband's supporters, it is sometimes better to make smaller adjustments over a longer period of time—"

"In my position I am damned if I do and damned if I don't, am I not?" The country was divided. If she stayed with him she was a coward—a woman without a backbone. If she left him she was a Judas—abandoning her husband during his time of need.

Nathan did not answer, so she continued. "I'm filing for divorce, Nate. Now I need you to do your job and handle the press. I have complete faith in you."

There was a brief pause before Catharine heard him release his breath, resigned. "Send me the statement. I'll work with Mr. Liebermann and we will go from there."

"Thank you, Nate."

"Off the record, Mrs. Cleveland," he added, before she hung up. "I do think you are one of the bravest women I know."

Chapter Twenty-One

"You know some people celebrate after a win? It's a wild thought, I know." Sawyer leaned her cheek over Alex's shoulder, hugging her from behind, her magnolia perfume overtaking the aroma of fried food. "Especially," she slipped beside her, her arm still around her waist, "when they bag a goal *and* an assist with Izzy Atwood in attendance—knowing the summer roster is being dropped in the next few days."

Alex smiled, welcoming the warmth of her old friend. She'd stepped out of the bar where her teammates were waiting for their private reservation and taken a moment for herself in the quiet of the outdoor patio. She was still processing the evening. Reflecting on her conversation with Izzy in the tunnel after the game.

"You ready to add a UK stamp to your passport?" The Welshwoman had fallen in step beside her as she headed to the lockers. Uncertain if the statement was in jest, or an official invitation to the roster, Alex had stopped short, unable to manage the shock in her expression.

"I mean it, kid." She'd squeezed her arm with weathered fingers. "You can pack your bags."

And that had been it. A lifelong dream, realized. She was going to the World Cup. After all the setbacks, the uncertainty, the underdog probability —her chance had finally materialized. What kind of minutes she would get —if she would ever even see the pitch—was yet to be determined. But her name would be on that roster, and this time next month she'd be in England.

"Shouldn't you be salty?" Alex teased, leaning against the railing of the patio. "I mean, we did just knock Rage out of first place."

"Lotta season left, plum," Sawyer tapped her cheek with a turquoise nail, a slow smile on her lips. "Don't get too comfortable with those rankings."

She flicked her eyes toward the bustling bar room. "Why are you out here all alone? That boy and his dingleberry still giving you grief?"

Alex laughed. It was exactly what Monica was—a cling-on. "No, thank God."

Surprisingly, ever since Alex's rebuttal to Monica's tweets, the pair had remained remarkably quiet. No drama in training. On the road. Even when Caleb had shown up after their team dinner the night before, there hadn't been any theatrics. Which made for a welcome relief. Alex was beginning to think he may have come to grips with the reality they would never be together. That their story was old news.

"I just needed a moment to take it all in. Tonight, playing in the old stadium—it just kind of felt full circle. I'd been so scared to leave here two years ago. I hadn't known what the future would hold." She laughed. "And I still don't—but it feels right, you know? No matter where I end up next season."

"Still no word from HEG?"

"Amelia thinks they'll wait until after the Cup. They'll want to leverage all the publicity they can out of me."

"Mmm." Sawyer smoothed back a black spiraled tendril of hair behind her ear. "I hope they do drop you, personally. Not from Sirens—Rod Collins is a gem to play for, and you've found a home there—but you're better than *Kickstar*. You deserve more than HEG."

The pair turned toward the frenzied laughter flowing through the open doors. Through the wide windows they could see the mechanical bull sitting on the elevated stage in the center of the bar, footballer-after-footballer swinging onto its cowhide-covered barrel before getting flung to the airbag on the floor.

"Oh, don't you roll your eyes at them," Sawyer smirked when she caught Alex's expression. "I have a lot of fond memories of you on that damned monstrosity, a couple beers deep. Don't forget—I know where you came from, little miss celebrity." She prodded her fingers into Alex's side, eliciting a yelp.

"Touché." She squirmed away, laughing.

"Those were the good ol' days." Sawyer sighed, reflective, before fixing her eyes on Alex. "So… sip tea. What's the status?"

They hadn't talked much since the release of Alex's statement. Between training, traveling games, and the general chaos of their lives, there hadn't been much time for catching up.

"Ironically non-eventful," Alex said, mostly honest. She'd stepped away from social media, not wishing to come across disparaging homophobic comments, and kept the TV off in her apartment. Whatever went down in the so-called Cleveland Kingdom no longer had anything to do with her, and she was tired of seeing the image of Catharine's bloody face pop up on her screen. She knew Catharine had announced her impending divorce—it had been on every station, every TV in the gym, the cover of every newspaper in the market. The story had garnered more attention than the entirety of the senator's run for the presidency. But Alex had stuck her head in the sand, wanting to know nothing of the all out war waging in a very public battle of accusations and hostility.

The last she'd heard was a talking head segment on the TV at the local taco bar. A woman being interviewed who'd worked in some capacity for WorldCargo in the past. It was her opinion the Clevelands were merely trying to divert attention from the election, giving the government the opportunity to cover up the real scheme in jeopardy: the truth about who had killed JFK.

Alex had tuned out after that, and gone to extremes to see nothing since. She didn't want to know.

But that wasn't what Sawyer was asking about. Her problems had become inconsequential in comparison.

"It's been good, actually. I guess, in some weird way, I'm glad it happened."

"Still, fuck Monica." Sawyer raised an imaginary glass to which Alex clinked her knuckles.

"Amen."

"I mean, I had you pegged that first day of training—you had the vibe, you know?" She winked. "Not like you were a hundred-footer, but still. We know our own." She segued into the real question she was skirting around. "So, are the rumors true?"

Though Alex imagined she knew what she was getting at, at this point in her life she didn't want to leave it to a chance misunderstanding. "Depends on what you're asking."

"You and Walker. Is that a thing?"

Alex watched Molly Rodrigues somersault through the air off the mechanical bull.

"You don't have to answer that, sugar. It's none of my business."

It wasn't that. She had no desire to hide anything from Sawyer. She just didn't know. Everything had defaulted back to the status quo, no different than before. Football. Summer. Sex. The World Cup. Amelia asked her nothing more about Catharine. And Alex didn't ask Amelia to open up.

"Yeah," she said, after a second, even if it wasn't as simple as it sounded. She found a smile that felt almost genuine. "Is it that obvious?"

Sawyer gave her a good-natured poke in her ribs. "Well, let's just say, if you were hoping to keep Amex nothing more than a credit card with an astronomically high interest rate, you failed Down-Low 101." Her dark eyes crinkled at the corners, her smile warm. "I'm glad for you, Alex. You guys are good for each other. There's no question she's smitten with you—you can see that, even on the field. I was a little worried for Parsons tonight after she fouled you from behind. I'm sure the whole stadium could see the daggers shooting from Walker's eyes."

Alex said nothing. That was just Amelia. Protective. A proponent of fair play. She was like that for everyone on the team. At least, that's how it seemed.

"And, I mean, at least she's not plastered all over the news at the heart of a money laundering scheme."

The reply that flew to Alex's mouth was cut short by Halsey's tenor bellow, summoning their party to the private bar. An expedient interruption, given the lack of thought preceding the rebuttal Alex intended to make. Catharine didn't need her defense. Didn't need her arguing the difference between tax evasion and money laundering. It was neither here nor there.

"I miss that bossy voice cussing at me from the box," Sawyer said as they made their way into the bar.

"You'll get your fill of it this summer."

Sawyer grinned. "I'm counting on it. It'll be good to have our trio back together again."

They joined the cattle call through the double doors toward the private barroom where several banquet-style tables had been set to accommodate their large party. TVs were blaring on all four walls, showing various games and commentary, while young servers took drink orders from the group of mingling athletes.

"Reserved for someone?"

Alex grabbed her purse off the seat beside her, making room for Amelia. "Depends on who's asking?"

On the opposite side of her Sawyer laughed. "You let her get away with that smart mouth, Walker?"

Amelia shrugged, nonchalant. "I just let her think so." Beneath the table she found Alex's hand, giving it a squeeze. A gesture so unlike her it made Alex give her a double take. She'd been gone for a half hour, on a phone call she'd received when they first arrived at the bar.

"Everything okay?" She looked flushed from more than the heat of the South Carolina spring.

"Aces."

But there was something lingering.

As the tables filled around them, Amelia leaned over, close to Alex's ear. "Instead of flying back tomorrow, why don't we stay an extra night? We could drive down to Carlisle."

"Trust me—there's nothing to see in Union County."

"Except it's where you grew up. That's something."

Before Alex could digest the implications of her request, they were interrupted by the scraping of chairs across the table, and the unmistakable pierce of Monica Ashby's laugh.

"I still can't believe Izzy kept her on the roster," Sawyer hissed between the three of them, annoyed at the arrival of Monica and Caleb. They'd waited too long to sit and a quick inventory of the room showed no other seats available, leaving no option beyond the forced proximity. "So much for disciplinary action."

"Unfortunately she's a capable right back," Amelia responded, curbing the conversation. She knew Alex was tired of talking about it. Tired of it being debated. They were about to spend six solid weeks together—if the US progressed through the tournament—and the feud between them needed to end.

"Is this where the party's at?" Dragging up a chair to the end of the table, Molly squeezed herself between Sawyer and Halsey, spilling her beer as she settled. "Shit," she wiped at Sawyer's thigh, "my bad, amigão," she apologized, but Sawyer didn't notice. Her attention was locked onto something over Alex's shoulder on the back wall.

"Alex."

There was something in her tone that raised what was becoming a familiar feeling of dread in Alex's stomach, the suspended notion of waiting for the axe to fall.

Slowly, she followed the trail of Sawyer's focus, unconsciously gripping Amelia's hand so hard the woman tried to pull away.

"Hey—!" Her chastisement cut short as her gaze fell on the TV. "Fuck."

"I need to go," Alex whispered, panicked, "I don't want to be here for this."

"It's okay, just—let me get it shut off. No one's seen it." Amelia started to rise, but stopped as they both caught sight of Caleb, his interest keenly piqued in their direction.

"Please." Alex wasn't sure if her throat made any sound, her eyes locking on his gray stare. *Don't*, she pleaded silently, praying just this one time he would remember that they were the best of friends, once upon a time. *Please don't.*

His eyes flicked back to the TV where the nightly news report was muted, its captioned letters running across the bottom of the screen. A series of changes crossed his face—surprise, disbelief, and slow understanding, followed by the cruelty of a smile Alex knew far too well. A smile he'd reserved all his life for those moments when he knew he had the upper hand. A killshot in volleyball. A home run at the plate. A slam dunk sailing through the net. A smile that promised the crippling of an opponent. The drawing of first blood.

"Caleb," her voice grew louder, pleading. "Don't. *Please.*" All he had to do was turn away, pretend he hadn't noticed, give her enough time to make her exit, where she could at least be granted privacy as she prepared for the next bombshell to detonate her life—but that would have been far too gracious. Far too compassionate. Neither traits that her once-friend appeared to harbor any longer.

"*Wow*," he exclaimed, making certain his voice would carry, cutting through the clamor of the room. His eyes shifted back to the TV. "You are just full of endless wonders, aren't you, Alex Grey?"

The announcement fulfilled its purpose, quieting the room. Alex froze, Amelia half risen beside her, but now she slowly sat back down, strung tight as a violin.

"Leave it, mate." Amelia warned him, but he paid her no mind, his lips drawn back in a vile sneer. He gestured toward the TV.

"Whoa! Alex, you're on TV," Rachel Parsons drawled, sitting on the opposite side of Ashby.

"It makes so much more sense now," Caleb continued, looking back at Alex. "Running into her in the strangest places. All chalked up to coincidence. I guess DC should have been my sign."

"She's my friend, Caleb," Alex tried, her voice faltering as one by one the conversations quieted, eyes turning their direction.

"You've sure got a lot of *friends,* Grey. I mean, it seems to have been a busy year for you—"

"Enough," Amelia's jaw and temple were ticking, the veins on the back of her hands beginning to show.

In the back of her mind Alex was aware she should probably intervene. Amelia's tone had shifted, promising more than bluster, but her mind had rendered itself impossible to think. To act. She only possessed the self-preserving urge to run. To save herself from any more humiliation and misery.

In the reflection of Sawyer's wine glass she could see the image on screen. A promotional photo of her from US Soccer, dressed in the Nation's home colors, smiling with her arms folded across her chest. She remembered the photoshoot, the goofy photographer, the industrial leaf blower they'd used to emulate the wind. But instead of headlining a match, or announcing a starting XI, the headshot was being used for yet another *breaking news* caption on national TV.

Once, there would have been few who knew who the Clevelands were. Especially amongst the younger generations of the professional soccer league. But Alex knew there wouldn't be a soul in the room who weren't aware of them now. If not from Carlton's campaign, they'd have been introduced to them from the upheaval of one of the most powerful marriages in the United States. The story was receiving more airtime than the Clinton-Lewinsky drama of the nineties. Camelot was going down in flames.

But even with all the coverage, all the prime time publicity, Alex hadn't actually expected anything to lead back to her. With everything going on she seemed so insignificant, so far removed from whatever small roll she had ever played, it didn't seem realistic her name would ever surface. No one cared about the Clemson Architectural Engineering major from Carlisle, South Carolina. The soccer player who'd yet to play in her first global tournament. The girl from the athletic shoe ads who'd recently been outed as gay. She was irrelevant in the grand scheme of things.

At least she'd hoped that was the case.

But now, from the brief seconds she'd glanced at the captions on the barroom TV, she'd seen the block lettered headline beneath her smiling photo in red, white and blue that read "South Carolina senator accuses wife of affair with athlete on US women's soccer team." It was as far as she'd gotten before her mind turned into the panicked necessity for flight.

"Who knew we were honored to have such a celebrity in the house," Caleb crowed, holding the attention of the room. In the background the animated commentary poured through the speakers of the play-by-play actions of the Knicks V. Lakers game broadcasting on the main screen, but no one was paying attention to LeBron shooting downtown.

"Were you really dating Catharine Cleveland?" One of the young midfielders from the Rage piped up, impressed, oblivious to the tension in the air. "Like, the billionaire?"

"I..." Alex breathed, unfunctioning. This couldn't be happening.

"I mean, it says—"

"Shut up, Kacie," Sawyer hissed, silencing her teammate. She stood, her hand on Alex's shoulder, trying to defuse the situation. "Come on, girl, let's grab a drink."

"Oh, come on, Abby," the derision in Caleb's laugh sent a jolt of ice through Alex's veins. Her heart felt like it had stopped, unable to find a regular rhythm again.

"Don't be such a killjoy. I think the girls would love to hear how she met the charming Mrs. Cleveland. Storytime, Alex—regale us with how you became her Knight in Shining Armor." He paused. "Is that politically correct? Do they make Princesses in Shining Armor? I'm not sure how that works when you're, you know—when it's two women involved."

Alex turned away, her cheeks flaming between humiliation and fury. She was vaguely aware of her phone vibrating on the table in front of her. Glancing at the screen she saw, true to the comedy of errors, that it was Catharine's photo lighting up her screen. No doubt she had just seen the news.

"It's okay—I can tell it, A. I remember the day well." Caleb cleared his throat in a grandiose gesture of preparation. "A couple years ago, while we were vacationing on little Daufuskie Island—"

Alex shoved her chair back, the metal dragging across the concrete in a high-pitched scrape, before she launched to her feet, ready to make a break for the door.

This wasn't happening.

This couldn't be happening.

Not here, in front of everyone.

"Don't go now, Grey—come on, you like this story! Such dashing bravery, a damsel in distress—apparently your selfless efforts brought you a lot more than a thank you card and bottle of turn-of-the-century scotch. I should have known I was the one who got cheated."

"You're such an insecure son of a bitch," Amelia said, rising to her feet, her hands planted against the surface of the table. "One day your little girlfriend there is going to realize all you've ever used her for is to stay close to Alex. Because she's your one obsession—the one thing you can't have. And it drives you crazy."

"Sounds like you're speaking from experience," Caleb sneered, though the accusation had clearly knocked him off balance. He leaned forward, his theatrics forgotten, and leveled his face with Amelia. "Are you not quite man enough for her, Walker?" He made a lewd gesture with his hand before switching tact to mockery. "No, that can't be it. You appear to have that part covered. Maybe not rich enough? Not—" Before the next word was out of his mouth Amelia was lunging across the table, her hand finding the collar of his shirt, dragging him forward as she smashed her elbow into the center of his face, a resounding crack following it.

"You fucking dyke," Caleb spat, reeling from the blow as he pressed his palm to his nose to slow the flow of blood spurting down his chin. "I swear I'll—"

Amelia, still halfway across the table, grabbed his glass of Scotch and tossed the remainder of the contents in his face.

"Get stuffed," she spat, shrugging off Halsey and Sawyer. "I'm done. I'll walk myself out."

Alex, temporarily forgotten in the commotion, wove her way to the back of the bar and slipped through the patio door. Without pausing she hopped over the waist high booze fence and hit the sidewalk at a jog.

She knew she should go to Amelia. Stay and try to smooth out the aftermath. Amelia had been protecting her and she was abandoning her to bear the consequence. But Alex only picked up speed. Amelia had Sawyer and Halsey and Molly. Alex didn't want to see any of them right now. She wanted to disappear somewhere where no one knew her name. Whatever planet that might be, she thought, her mind stuck on her headshot on TV.

Jaywalking across the boulevard, she turned her steps toward the Carolina beach and the unfolding expanse of sand.

Chapter Twenty-Two

Catharine pushed aside the stack of mail and laid the plain white envelope in the center of her desk. Unlike the rest of the pile that had been previously opened—screened for the barrage of hate letters and death threats flowing in daily—its seal remained intact. There had been no reason for Nicole to sensor it; it was Catharine's own handwriting on the address.

Return to Sender had been stamped across the front, and hastily scrawled beneath it was a note from the mail carrier. "Occupant deceased."

Catharine had posted the envelope herself, several weeks prior, same as she'd done every month for the past twenty-five years. Inside there would be a check, handwritten from her personal account, paid to the order of Mrs. Alice Ainsley, residing in Tottenham, North London.

She ran her thumb across the word *deceased* and closed her eyes. She could still picture the woman on the day she'd last seen her. Blonde hair neatly plaited to hide the streaks of gray at her temples. Smart white blouse tucked into her knee length skirt, stockinged legs settled in sensible shoes. The same as she'd worn every day since Catharine was a child. It had been the night before Colonel Brooks walked in on her and Nathalie. The evening had been warm, tea in the garden. Mrs. Ainsley had winked at Catharine as she collected their plates, and as she was heading to the kitchen she'd brushed a loving hand across Catharine's cheek.

It was a gesture Catharine thought much of over the last twenty-five years. The simple way the woman had loved her. The way she had raised her as her own. Taught her to tie her shoes. Read her bedtime stories. Made her laugh with butterfly kisses and games of hide-and-seek in the lonely manor. She'd kept her secrets. Kept her confidence. And in the end, what had it gotten her?

An hour.

An hour to pack her belongings and uproot the life she'd lived for more than thirty years in service to the Brooks household. No letters of recommendation. No severance package. Not even a chance to say goodbye to the girl she'd cared for since the day she was born. Colonel Brooks had fired the entire staff in retaliation for his daughter's indiscretions.

After moving to the States, Catharine had begun sending Mrs. Ainsley a monthly salary to her new London address. A woman in her late fifties, displaced from everything in her life she had known, she couldn't bear the thought of her seeking new employment in what should have been her retirement years. For six months the postings were returned, unopened. Then word reached Catharine Mrs. Ainsley had suffered a stroke. After, the checks were cashed and no further mail was returned.

Tucking the letter into her purse she left her tasks unfinished and headed for the door. It was late, the office quiet, with only Malcolm waiting in the lobby. She didn't have to ask him the status of the foyer. The press would be waiting, scabs intent on snapping photos as they shoved microphones into her face, demanding a statement. As had been for the past two weeks, they exited the private parking garage and Malcolm drove through the waiting media in the direction of the Marina District to safely see her home.

Tonight, she redirected him east, and a half an hour later found herself walking along the empty peninsula of Heron's Head Park.

"Do you ever miss home, Malcolm?" She'd asked him to walk with her, preferring his company to being alone.

He considered the question. "Aye. I suppose."

They'd stopped at the only bench at the end of the narrow finger of land, the lights of a ferry floating through the dark toward Alameda, leaving its wake to wash onto the grainy sand. She sat, inviting him to join her.

Her mind was on Mrs. Ainsley. On Henley-on-Thames. On the manor she hadn't laid eyes on in more than a quarter of a century.

Her father had yet to break his silence of the last two weeks. Nothing about her divorce. The bombardment of critical press against Brooks Corp. The accusations of her infidelity.

It was coming. She knew he was simply biding his time. Waiting to see where the shattered pieces of her life fell before striking her while she was down.

A flock of pelicans dipped through the dusk, sailing close to the water, the tips of their wings brushing the surface of the bay.

"Do you ever think of going back?"

"Depends, I guess, on if a certain boss of mine is thinking of relocating." His smile turned sly as he stretched his long legs out in front of him, crossing his ankles. "I'll warn you though, ma'am—if you're thinking of running off with me, the north country isn't as mild as the bay. I'll have you chopping wood and chucking corn to the chickens come winter."

She rolled her eyes but laughed all the same. "Oh, please. You were born in Aberdeen, not the Grampian Mountains."

He laughed and after a minute she sighed, feeling the weight of the evening descending.

She'd tried calling Alex. Seeing her name in the headlines had caught her as unaware as anyone. There'd been no tip off. No warning. Just Nathan Lundy back on the line, informing her about the allegations from Carlton. And then Alex's name and photo broadcast on every station.

She doubted she'd ever speak to her again. Not after this. Not after the reoccurring tailspin she'd once again set in motion.

And this time, she couldn't even call Nathalie. Not to be sent to voicemail for the fifth day in a row. To have her messages left unread and emails unreturned.

Through the dark, in an unexpected gesture, Malcolm reached out and draped an arm around her shoulder, offering her the solace of a hug. "If my mam were here, she'd tell you: *it's a lang road that's no goat a turnin'.*" He squeezed her shoulders and she allowed herself to relax against him. Grateful for the comfort. For his kindness. "It'll be right, ma'am. Just keep your head. And if it's not, well—as me da would say: fuck 'em."

In the middle of the night Catharine woke to the clamor of bells. She'd been back in Henley-on-Thames, standing on the bridge, the cathedral on the corner practicing the tintinnabulation for the following Sunday morning. She blinked in the dark and discovered the screen of her mobile illuminated, ringing.

It was a 510 area code. Oakland.

Pushing up on an elbow, she answered, trying to disguise the sleep from her voice.

"Mrs. Cleveland?" It was not a voice she immediately recognized. Not the one she'd expected. Sitting up, she flipped on her light and glanced back at the phone. It was one in the morning.

"Yes?" She was tentative. It would have been better to leave it to voice-mail. There were reporters who'd sleuthed out her number and she wouldn't put it past them to call in the middle of the night.

"I'm sorry to wake you, but I can't find Alex. I was hoping she may have contacted you tonight?"

Slowly the Australian accent and mutual subject merged into a vague comprehension. It was Amelia Walker.

"What do you mean you can't find her?" Catharine was awake now, her mind racing.

"No doubt you've seen the news, Mrs. Cleveland." The woman had an edge to her voice. An accusation she wasn't clearly voicing. "It took Alex by surprise—she didn't receive it well and took off earlier this evening."

"Where are you?"

"South Carolina."

That meant it was four am. "I—" Catharine pulled her phone from her ear to check her call log. No calls. No texts. "What about her aunt and uncle? Have you tried them?"

"If you think she went there, you're even more out of touch than you seem."

Unnerved by the insult, Catharine tried to think. "Her friend Sawyer—"

"I've tried everyone, Mrs. Cleveland. Trust me when I say you were my last resort. If you haven't heard from her, I'll not keep you—"

"Please," interrupted Catharine, "wait." But she didn't know what she was asking her to wait for. She had nothing to offer. Nothing to suggest. She just didn't want her to hang up. She needed to know Alex was okay.

"Is there something else?"

"No, I..." Catharine smoothed her hair out of her eyes. "Please, just tell me how I can help?"

There was a brief pause. "Help?" The word was followed by a callous laugh. "Don't you think you've helped enough, Mrs. Cleveland?"

"Miss Walker, please, if—"

"Let's cut the bullshit, shall we? You're ruining her life. Every time she gets her head on straight, every time things settle down—just when I think she's over the worst of it—you reappear with your three-ring circus in your wake, dragging Alex down. The best thing you could do to help is bloody disappear."

Stunned, Catharine said nothing. What defense could she give? Was what she said not true?

"Now, I'm sorry to have woken you. Trust me when I say I regret the call."

"Will you let me know when you find her safely?" Catharine couldn't stop herself from asking.

Amelia exhaled a sigh. "If Alex wants to contact you, I'm sure she will. Good night."

After a long time of staring at her ceiling, Catharine flipped off the light.

Chapter Twenty-Three

Shortly before six a.m. Alex stepped off the elevator on the twelfth floor of the downtown Charleston hotel. The hallway was empty, the rooms quiet as she shoved her keycard into the lock on her door. Before the magnetic bolt released, she was surprised by a voice approaching from behind.

"You know, a simple text that you were all right would have been nice."

She turned to look at Sawyer, hand paused on the handle. "Hey." She glanced down, noticing her friend was still wearing the same clothes from the bar the night before. "I'm sorry. I turned off my phone."

"Yeah." Sawyer's eyeshadow was smudged, her makeup worn thin. "We got that." She leaned back against the opposite wall of the hall. "But not a word from you. Not a single acknowledgement you were okay. Ten hours—and you just thought... what? No one would notice?"

"Can you cut me some slack? I just—I couldn't deal with everything at once. I needed some time alone."

"You didn't think anyone would worry?" She gave a disgruntled laugh that never touched her dark eyes. "You didn't think we'd begin to panic when you didn't show back up?"

Alex stared at the spiraled circles on the carpet leading down the hall. She hadn't, in truth, given thought to what anyone might think. She'd only known she couldn't face a single soul she knew. Not her teammates. Not her friends. Not even Amelia. She'd just needed to be alone. To gather herself. To find the next step forward. To convince herself this wasn't the end of the road. That Izzy Atwood wouldn't throw her off the team for the drama that followed her everywhere she went. That her friends wouldn't abandon her. That this, too, would blow over.

"I should have called—you're right. I'm sorry."

Sawyer's full lips thinned, disappearing in a straight line. "I'm not the one you owe the biggest apology to. I'm not the one who covered at least twenty miles on foot searching for you through the night. You don't just disappear on someone who loves you, Alex. It's not fair. And it's not right."

Down the hall a door clicked open, the sound of muffled voices carrying along the wainscot walls. The other women would be waking, getting ready for the long flight home.

"Where is she?" Alex asked, studying the decorative baseboard on the floor. Anything was better than feeling the weight of Sawyer's disappointment.

"In there," Sawyer nodded toward Alex's door. "She swapped rooms with Halsey to wait for you to come back."

"Is she mad?"

"I think you scared her. You scared us all." Another pair of voices came from the elevators. "Look—I'm tired. Now that I know you're okay, I'm heading home." She reached an arm out, her fingers at Alex's elbow. "Don't make this harder on yourself than it has to be. It's not something you have to carry alone. You just have to remember to share the ball." She squeezed her arm. "I'll see you in a couple weeks. Send off games in Jersey and then England, here we come." But her words didn't carry the excitement they usually would have as Alex watched her disappear down the hall. Instead there was only an overshadowing disappointment in herself for letting down her friends once more.

Careful to close the door silently behind her, she stepped into the room. The lights were on, the bed still made, Amelia's sweatshirt and ball cap thrown over a dining room chair. Amelia was sitting on the couch, her phone dangling precariously from one hand, her shoulders rising and falling in a steady rhythm that confirmed she was asleep.

Beside her sat a hotel notepad, a dozen numbers scratched in her illegible scrawl, crossed off one by one.

Alex watched her from the middle of the room, thinking about what Sawyer had said. How Amelia'd been out all night looking for her. *You don't just disappear on someone who loves you.* Loves you, she'd said.

She moved the notepad and sat down beside her, setting a tentative hand on her knee. "Hey."

Amelia's eyes fluttered open, blinking her into focus, filtering through a pinwheel of emotions—surprise, relief, anger.

She threw a glance at the window, registering the rising sun. "You've been out all bloody night."

"I know."

"I looked everywhere for you." Her voice was raw. Tired. Dark circles bagged under her eyes.

"I know. I saw Sawyer in the hall." She gripped the knee Amelia tried to pull away. "I'm sorry. I really am."

"Do you know what I thought, Alex?" Amelia shook herself free and stood, moving halfway across the room. Her back was to her, her shoulders taut, her fists clenched at her side.

Alex took a deep breath. "I didn't mean to scare you."

"Well, you did."

Rising, Alex moved to stand behind her, laying her hands above her hips, registering the tension building at her touch. "I promise, the thought never crossed my mind."

Amelia didn't move. Didn't say anything. The sun cleared the window frame, pouring into the hotel room, unwelcome with its cheery light.

"I have to go shower and change," she said at last, stepping away. "I'll see you at the bus in a couple hours."

Arriving late in the lobby, Alex expected to find herself alone. A quiet trip to the airport, sitting at the back of the bus as her teammates avoided her, whispering behind her back. A middle school nightmare come true.

Instead, Amelia was sitting on the tile of the hotel entrance, her feet kicked up on her bag, with Halsey, Rodrigues, and Jill Thompson intense at a game of cards on a neighboring patch of floor.

"Atta girl," said Halsey, dragging herself to her full height. "Fashionably late—good to see you're taking your celebrity status seriously."

"Give the girl a break." Jill stretched before lithely springing to her feet. "She's already got more coverage than the Ninety-Niners on their best week. It's a win for women's soccer, especially heading into the World Cup." She winked at Alex. "Thanks for taking one for the team, Grey. What's that saying—any publicity is good publicity?"

"Yeah! I mean, look at Miley Cyrus!" Halsey bent the cards in her hand to demonstrate a stylish shuffle, and instead dumped them all over the foyer.

"Are we really trusting those hands with the success of our summer?" Molly ribbed, bending down to help gather the casualty of her clumsiness.

"You're gonna catch these hands if you keep that up," Halsey chaffed back, bumping her with her hip.

"Think I'll take my chances with you over Walker. You see that cabrão leave early this morning? She wiped that shit-eating grin right off his face. Dude looked like he'd pissed off the wrong bruno in the back alley of a Compton Walmart."

"Doubt he's going to want to tell his friends he had his ass kicked by a chick he outweighs by a hundred pounds," Jill added, toeing Amelia's foot where she hadn't yet moved from the floor.

"On the contrary. He's pressing charges."

They all turned to look at Amelia, but she was only looking at Alex. The mood sobered quickly.

"I'm sorry. I didn't know." Alex said quietly as they made their way to the bus, falling back a few paces behind the others.

"How could you have?" Amelia looked over her shoulder as she stepped through the narrow door. "You weren't here."

The mood was somber on the way to the airport and Alex had a sense everyone was walking on egg shells around her. Nothing more was said about the night before, not even in jest, but as the morning wore on some of the usual banter resumed, and by the time they were settled on the plane at cruising altitude, the atmosphere felt bearable.

Despite her steadfast ire, Amelia sat beside her, and didn't jerk her arm away when Alex slid her fingers beneath the tray tables to touch her hand.

"Do you want me to try to talk to him?" She hated to bring up the subject, but was afraid it would be worse if she simply let it go. Charges of assault were serious. They could impact Amelia's status in the NWSL. Affect her entire career.

"Just leave it. I'll deal with it." Amelia waved off the flight attendant who offered a soda and pinned up her tray. "Get some sleep, Grey. It's been a long night for all of us." Instead of using Alex's shoulder as a headrest, she balled her club jacket into a pillow and turned toward the aisle.

When they arrived in Jack London Square that evening, Amelia disappeared to her own apartment for the first time in months. She told Alex she needed to make a couple calls. Her attorney, likely. And given the hour, a call to her family back home.

Alex waited, ate nothing, and tried to watch recorded games from the other club matches that had taken place over the weekend. But her mind wasn't on soccer. It wasn't even on the headline she'd seen when she opened her internet browser: *Affair with the Senator's Wife: What We Know About Alex Grey.* It was on the empty nightstand where Amelia dumped her pockets. The hoodie missing off her dining room chair. The loneliness of the muted TV without her running commentary—her quick eye that annoyingly saw every play before it was made.

When eleven pm came and went, Alex left her apartment barefoot and took the stairs to the floor below. A light glowed behind Amelia's drawn curtain and the sound of English football play-by-play filtered through the gap of her front door.

"What are you doing, Grey?" Amelia stood in her tank and boxers, unmoving from her doorway, after Alex tapped on her window long enough to rouse her from her couch.

She'd come with the intent to apologize. To say whatever it took to make things right. But every thought that came to mind seemed futile. There were only so many words to say you were sorry.

In her silence, Amelia turned from the threshold, but Alex caught her arm, stepping through the half closed door.

"Don't walk away from me."

"Why?" Amelia spun, the word charged with electricity. "You don't like how it feels? You do it to everyone else."

Galled by the well-aimed arrow, Alex pressed her against the wall, covering her mouth with hers. Determined to prove she wasn't running away. That she didn't want to disappear. For a moment Amelia was still, unresponsive, before abruptly reacting in turn. Her kiss hard. Unyielding. Overridden with pent up anger.

Alex's hands were at her face, her hair, digging into the small of her back. Pulling at her clothes. Finding her way beneath. There was nothing delicate about it. Nothing considerate or fair. She took no care in the command over the most sensitive places, and welcomed the harshness that met it in return. A thigh pinned between hers, forcing hers apart. The hint of iron on her tongue, the consequence of a kiss too rough, as frustrated as her own.

Powder from cheap paint caught beneath her fingernails as they dragged against the whitewashed wall, the two of them pressed between the doorframe and the hall. When their breathing grew erratic, when there was no where else to go, Alex curtly slowed, taunting an insufferable withdrawal until Amelia grew intolerant and pulled her to the floor. Covered in sweat and anger and the desperation of holding something together that felt like it may have already fractured. A thin layer of glue applied to a crack running a mile deep.

Yet at the apex of the moment, when their bodies broke, Alex could feel the fury melting, dissipating from them as they lay gasping on the floor.

Later, when they'd moved to the unfamiliarity of Amelia's bedroom, Alex lay in the tangle of sheets with the comforter hanging off the side of the bed. Her lips felt sore, bruised, congruent with her thoughts. Amelia was awake beside her, her breath steady in the dark.

"I called her."

It was the first they'd broken their silence.

Alex wanted to play dumb. To pretend she didn't understand. But there was only one *her* in this equation. One ostrich with its body sticking out of the sand.

"Okay." Alex said nothing else for a long time. She willed herself to fall asleep. To not give the satisfaction of a further reply. Instead, she finally gave in. Allowed Amelia to prove her point. "What did she say?"

"She asked me to let her know when you were found safely."

Another long silence ensued as they lay stiffly side by side.

"Did you?"

"No." Amelia sat up and swung her legs over the side of the bed, rising to find a t-shirt. She stood in the doorway, looking back through the dark, the leanness of her body silhouetted by the light from the hall. "I thought I'd leave that to you," she said, before disappearing into the hall. A moment later the TV flicked back on, and this time Alex didn't follow her.

Chapter Twenty-Four

"Are you never going to talk to me again? Is that the plan?"

Nathalie eyed Catharine from an over-upholstered chair in the corner of her theatre green room. "I'm talking to you now, am I not?"

"The woman in your box office who finally took my call made me make an appointment." Catharine stood, bristled, in the center of the room, with no seat having been offered.

"And you were on time. I appreciate that."

"Oh, don't you...!" Catherine flexed her fingers, pressing her palms against her thighs, and exhaled a slow breath. The room was too cluttered. Playbills and abandoned dessert trays, mismatched chairs tucked along a mirrored wall. Catharine had never cared for the backstage of a theatre. The chaos. The organized mess. The hurry-up-and-wait atmosphere. "I don't know how you can think in here."

She crossed the room, uninvited, and dropped herself into a canary yellow plastic chair. "I'm going insane, Nat." The mirror beside her revealed her hollowed cheeks, the deepening lines at the corner of her eyes. She looked dreadful. Felt it, too. She couldn't remember the last time she'd slept through the night. The last full meal she'd eaten. "The bloody media... Carlton... it hasn't stopped. I don't know what to do."

"You tossed him to the wolves. What were you expecting to happen?"

"I don't know! I just—!" She took a breath, forcing herself to a level tone. "I just didn't expect it to be like this."

Behind the closed door a cart lumbered down the hallway, the theatre in full swing in preparation for its approaching opening night. Nathalie had not extended an invitation and Catharine did not ask. She didn't want her presence taking anything away from the success of her friend's premiere.

She wouldn't have been able to sit through a show, anyhow. She wasn't able to sit anywhere for long.

"I haven't been paying much attention, but... news of the intention to divorce came as something of a surprise." Nathalie pulled at a loose thread on the needlework of the chair. "Had you planned that all along?"

Catharine was honest. "No. I wish I were that brave. I didn't decide on it until I heard Limbaugh call Susan Lyndon a bottom-feeding-parasite for speaking out. And berated her for not standing behind her party. I didn't want her to bear the brunt of it on her own."

"I wish you would have said something to me."

"I didn't want to be talked out of it."

"And you think I would have tried?"

Catharine stood and paced the room, turning her back to her reflection. She didn't want to see the stranger staring back at her. The vacuity in her eyes. She felt like someone she no longer knew. Someone growing too tired to fight.

She looked at Nathalie. "Yes. You would have had more sense than me. Told me to take it slow."

Nathalie arched an eyebrow. "It's like you read my mind." The thread on the chair snapped. "Last year I would have been all for it. After the night of the gala, after he laid his hands on you—there's nothing I wanted more than to wake up and see that headline. But you let him get away scot-free, and in doing so gave him another full year to steamroll everything in his path. He's gotten too powerful, Catharine. He's built his base and even with the accusations piling against him, his foundation doesn't appear to be on shaky ground. This morning there was a three point upswing in the polls."

"I thought you said you hadn't been paying much attention?" Catharine tried for a smile and failed, returning to her abandoned chair. "But really, Nat, tell me something I don't already know."

It was true. Despite the media backlash. Despite nine women coming forward, accusing him of unwanted sexual advances. Despite a former secretary calling him *Humbert Humbert* on The Oprah Winfrey Show. Despite her bloodied, battered face plastered on centerfolds. He was still hanging in there. He was still in the race.

The people had believed his lies. Had believed his two bodyguards who stoically testified they'd been with the senator the entire time he was with his wife in the Fairmont Hotel—swearing he'd never laid a hand on her. They'd believed the jittery hotel maid who claimed she'd overheard Mrs. Cleveland on the phone that weekend, telling a friend she'd come up with a plan to 'get even' with Senator Cleveland.

He'd given the people enough rope to hang themselves with benefit of the doubt. And as the days went by, as he endured, the tide of his political alliances began to sway back under his control.

"You really want to hear something you don't already know?" Nathalie uncrossed her legs, her air of disconnected disdain fading. Catharine braced herself, regretting her choice of words.

"I was going more for the idiom sense of the phrase… but I imagine you'll tell me anyhow."

"I will. Because it's important." She leaned forward, resting her elbows on her knees, and fixed her with a stare. "I'm really proud of you, Cate. It took a lot of guts to do what you did. And I know you're scared. You'd be out of your mind not to be. But you did the right thing. For the right reasons."

Catharine swallowed something in her throat she didn't want to allow. Not here. She'd yet to permit herself to get emotional, and she wasn't about to start now." So I take it you're not as mad at me as you wanted me to think?"

"Wrong. I am entirely mad at you. What you said was out of line. You really hurt my feelings, Cate. And I'll need another week or two before I feel like letting it go."

Catharine nodded, rising from the chair. "Fair enough."

She'd wanted to tell her about Amelia's call. About the things she'd said. How she should *bloody disappear*. But Nathalie's ear wasn't hers to burden. This was one albatross she'd need to carry alone.

Nathalie walked her to the door. "But me being mad doesn't change the fact that I love you. And that my heart hurts for everything you're going through." She touched Catharine's arm. "This, too, will pass, Cate. Remember: À vaillant coeur rien d'impossible." *For a brave heart, nothing is impossible.*

"Thank you, Nat. For seeing me."

Chapter Twenty-Five

"Before you guys head to the recovery room, I have a quick announcement."

Rodney Collins stood on the edge of the track, tapping his iPad against his thigh. He'd looked ill-at-ease all afternoon and Alex had begun to develop an uncomfortable sense of apprehension. Amelia had called out of training. With no explanation, no notice—she simply wasn't there.

Alex had seen her briefly the morning before, after waking alone in Amelia's bed, Amelia having slept on the couch. She'd found her in the kitchen, burning eggs, distracted on the phone. Someone from England, Alex had assumed, given Amelia's heavy Melbourne dialect morphing into a diluted blend of UK slang. They'd shared an awkward *hey* and Amelia returned to her call while Alex gathered her clothes, still piled on the hallway floor. It was their rest day after the previous day of travel and Alex needed to catch up on laundry, anyhow. That night, when Amelia didn't come by, Alex left it alone. With the discomfort between them, a night apart seemed wise.

But she hadn't expected to find her absent from training the following day. Not without mentioning it to her. Or Halsey. Or any of their friends. It was so unlike Amelia, and Alex's unease had tripled by the second time Rodney cleared his throat. She felt like he was staring straight at her. That the announcement, whatever it was, would impact her more than anyone else.

"PR will put out a statement this afternoon, but I wanted everyone to hear it from me first." A third clearing of his throat. This time Alex looked away when he caught her eye. "In an unexpected move from management, Amelia Walker's been placed on loan."

Alex could feel several pairs of eyes turn her direction. She didn't look around, the best she could manage was to stare at Rodney's iPad still tapping against his leg.

"To where?" Her voice sounded so foreign she wasn't even sure if she was the one who spoke.

"Arsenal. Back to the WSL."

There were a few mutters. And then a long silence.

She was leaving. Back to England. Back to her life. And she hadn't said a thing.

"Why?" Halsey dropped her goalkeeping gloves to the ground and dried her hands onto her shorts. "It's the last few weeks of Arsenal's season. We're only at the start of ours. It doesn't make any sense."

And it didn't. Loans were made for younger players to get minutes when they weren't playing on their home club's first team. Or to reduce dead-weight on a roster stacked with talent in one position. Or to free up spending during a trade window. They weren't made for a star player mid-season. For a box-to-box midfielder who carried the squad. For an experienced captain whose leadership had been integral to a young team's success in the league.

"I wasn't made privy to the arrangements with HEG, but I imagine, with the World Cup this summer, management was looking to share some of the expense of her contract when she was already going to be absent from the team. Arsenal will benefit from having her for playoffs and we—"

"Oh, please." Monica Ashby glared at Alex. "We all know why she left."

"Maybe it was your boyfriend's showboating mouth that did it," Molly Rodrigues challenged. "You ever consider that?"

"Listen, ladies," Rodney held up a hand in an attempt to keep the peace, "I know Walker's departure is unexpected, and we've had a few tense weeks on the team, but right now we need to steer away from speculation, and just focus on the game this weekend."

Valerie Sims gave a snort of derision. "Yeah, let's all pretend we didn't know Grey was fucking the captain—and there was trouble in paradise when Alex's love life got flung all over international TV."

"Shut your face, Valerie!" Rodrigues towered over the five-foot-nothing defender, looking like she was ready to bust open her skull.

The girl swung her black hair over her shoulder, meeting her teammate's challenge unfazed. "What, you got the hots for Grey, too, Molly? Better get in line—she's had a busy year."

"You want to fucking go, Sims?" Rodrigues was in her face, her temper steaming, as Halsey shoved her way between them, trying to keep them from getting at each other's throats.

It was Amelia who usually kept the peace. Amelia who the girls looked up to. Amelia...

Who was gone.

How could she have left without saying anything? How could she let Alex find out like this—in front of everyone. Caught unaware. She felt so betrayed.

"Knock this shit off, both of you!" At the threat of a physical altercation, Rodney had dropped his diplomatic demeanor and joined Halsey in dragging the pair apart. "I swear to God the next person who opens their mouth will be benched for Saturday's game!" He was disheveled, panting, his iPad abandoned on the grass a few feet away. "I've had enough of the discord on this team. In all my years of coaching, I've never seen such elementary behavior as I have in the past few weeks! You're supposed to be professionals—"

"Honest question, then," Monica chipped in, encouraged by her support from Sims. Her eyes were fixed on Alex. "Is it professional to enter a romantic relationship with another member of your team? Knowing what can happen when the relationship goes south? Or is it only acceptable because it's two women and everyone's too afraid of being called a bigot if they say anything?"

"I'm so sick of you making everything about your homophobic agenda," Molly snapped over Halsey's shoulder, Rodney's warning forgotten.

"Maybe you should just keep your shit in the closet, where it belongs," Sims was back at her, more than ready to champion Monica's defense. There was another scuffle, threats from Rodney, and then a blaring whistle from Lynn Armstrong, who'd arrived from the other end of the field to review the disorder of the scene.

"What in the hell is this!"

Rodney Collins may have been full of idle threats, but Lynn Armstrong was not. A woman with a volatile temper, who had spent six years as the head coach of the Brazilian national team, she was unafraid to throw her weight around. The players loved Rodney for his compassion—almost as much as they feared Lynn for her disposition. If she threatened someone with the bench, they'd see no minutes the following game—of that there was no doubt.

Alex knew she should stay to weather the woman's dressing down. She was the cause of the altercation. The reason for the rift in the team. Whatever Sims and Ashby had to say against her, she needed to be there to defend herself. After all, she no longer had her champion—the one person who always had her back.

But defending herself was the least of her concerns. What they said no longer mattered. The only thing she wanted was to get back to her apartment. To see for herself. To see if she'd really left without saying goodbye.

Still in her training gear, Alex walked off the field. They weren't excused, but she didn't care. Bench her. Fine her. Whatever they wanted. Armstrong barked at her to stop; to turn around. But she kept walking, the studs of her cleats clicking a slow cadence as she made her way along Embarcadero, dreading her arrival at Jack London Square. Because she already knew the answer. She knew she wouldn't be there.

Chapter Twenty-Six

The figure weaved in and out of traffic with an athletic agility that drew Catharine's eye. The boulevard was busy, amidst the chaos of rush hour, but the pedestrian skirted the street with ease. Face concealed beneath a ball cap and dark sunglasses, an oversized hoodie tugged over jeans, Catharine could only assume it was a woman from the slenderness of the physique.

Sitting on her third story balcony, she was surprised when the passerby stopped directly in front of her townhouse, looking up from the street. It hadn't been unusual to get gawkers lately. Her days of peace as an unheralded businesswoman in an industry of little interest had come to an end. Now she was one of two things: Catharine Cleveland, purveyor of income inequality, enemy of the people, a one-percenter who lorded over the working class to live in her castle in the sky—or Catharine Cleveland, Judas to the conservative Messiah, a traitor to her kind. As Nathalie had pointed out, rather dourly, it took measurable talent to establish yourself an enemy to both sides.

But the onlooker didn't pull out her mobile to snap photos—which meant a caption of: *Standing in front of the House of Satan* (most often spelled *satin*), followed by the tags #CarltonClevelandIsMYpresident #RotInHellCatharine, signed, Deborah, Sunday School Teacher from Alabama—was unlikely. Nor were any vulgar gestures or crude expletives thrown her way.

Instead, the figure disappeared out of sight, crossing onto the sidewalk below her balcony, and Catharine assumed she'd continued on her way. But a moment later the doorbell chimed and by the time Catharine reached the hallway, she could hear Grace, her housekeeper, adamantly sending someone away.

"You are disturbing the peace at a private residence—"

"My name is—"

"I don't care if you're Pope Francis, if you don't get off this property, I'll be forced to call the police!"

"Look, lady—I'm racking up misdemeanors this week faster than you can root a two pot screamer, so do me a favor and just give your boss my name. I think she'll see me."

"Grace." Catharine stepped onto the stairway, her interest piqued at the familiar voice. "It's all right. Please show Miss Walker to my study and set on the kettle. I'll receive her shortly."

Ten minutes later, when she felt she'd delayed her entry long enough, Catharine stepped into her study to find Amelia Walker sitting on the edge of her desk, regarding the only photo she kept on the empty surface. A framed print of her and Alex standing cheek to cheek in Times Square. A selfie Alex had pulled her into the weekend they'd gone to see Nathalie's show. A lifetime ago. One of the few photos they had together, she hadn't been able to bring herself to put the picture away—but now she wished she had.

"Please sit, Miss Walker." Catharine calmly approached the woman, gently lifting the frame from her hands and setting it facedown. It wasn't hers to observe. "Tea?"

Amelia considered, then shrugged. "Cuppa'd be great."

Pouring from the tray Grace had left on her cabinet, Catharine watched the younger woman from beneath the veil of her lashes. She had an easy confidence about her, a self-assurance that verged on brashness. But contrary to her professional media and TV adverts, a carefulness lay behind her cockiness. A solemnness her photos didn't show. Catharine hated that she knew absolutely nothing about her. This woman who felt like a rival in an uncontested battle where the outcome was already known.

Milk and sugar added, she set the cup before her.

"Ta." Amelia took up the tea. "I have to admit, I'm a little disappointed it wasn't served with a silver spoon."

Catharine ignored the dig. "What can I do for you, Miss Walker?"

Amelia sipped the brew, her eyes taking another sweep of the study. "Stunning place you have here, Mrs. Cleveland. I doubt my father would believe me if I told him where I was sitting right now. He works for you, you know?"

"Does he?" Catharine couldn't decide whether to sit or stand and settled for leaning against the back of her chair. She tried to remember everything Alex had ever mentioned about Amelia. Born in Melbourne. Played most of her career in England. One of the top-rated footballers in the world. Well-loved as captain. A good friend.

Very good friend, apparently.

"Well, for WorldCargo, I should say."

"What's his name?"

"You wouldn't know him."

"You might be surprised. I've spent a lot of time on the docks in Melbourne."

"He left the docks in the nineties," Amelia said flatly, "but I can see why you'd think someone like me would come from a battler."

"It's not what I meant."

"Isn't it?" Amelia raised her gaze over the rim of her cup, holding Catharine's stare. Her eyes were almost alarmingly green. The color of the Amundsen Sea.

"It was a poor assumption," Catharine allotted, unaccustomed to being reprobated in her own home. "What does he do?"

"Manages the stevedoring firm for the Port of Melbourne."

"Dave Walker, then." Catharine nodded, the name filing to the forefront of her mind. They'd never met in person, but she'd seen his name signed to memos before she handed off the Victoria account. If the Australian was impressed, she didn't show it. In the silence, Catharine took up her tea, marveling at the woman's ability to make her self-conscious. It was, perhaps, in her unfaltering stare. The way she carried herself, unintimidated by her surroundings. Her certainty they were equals. A confidence that made it true. It was refreshing. Almost. "I don't imagine we're here to talk about your father, Miss Walker."

"No." Amelia tipped back her tea and set the cup down with finality. "I'm not here to fuck spiders, so I'll get right to it." She stood, a hint of discomfort revealing itself as she reached the essence of her visit. Crossing to the glass doors leading to the bay-facing balcony, she stared out over the water. "Do you know Alex's favorite color?"

Of all the questions Catharine anticipated, this was not at the forefront of considerations. "No." Her defenses were reconstructing. "I do not believe the subject of preferential palette was ever a discussion."

"Teal." Amelia didn't turn from the window. "Not the dark turquoise of fake jewelry and not the blue hue of aquamarine. But mint—the color of seafoam."

"I see," said Catharine. Though she did not.

"We've never talked about it, either. Never had a reason to. But I'd gladly bet your fortune on it." She pivoted to face Catharine, the scrutiny of her gaze pinned on her once more. "It's the color dice she picks when we play Yahtzee. The color of her laces on her favorite boots. The color of the sharpie she carries to sign jerseys after our games."

"It sounds like a safe bet, then," Catharine allowed, still trying to determine her angle.

"And her favorite bands?" This time she didn't wait for Catharine to acknowledge she didn't know. "*Green Day. Matchbox Twenty. Counting Crows.* She has their soundtracks on repeat, listening to endless renditions of *American Idiot* before every match. It's also not been a topic of conversation." She strode across the room and took a half seat in the chair, unwilling to commit to settle. "I've spent a year and a half trying to understand Alex Grey. Not through conversation—I'm not gifted with the eloquence of speech that no doubt comes natural to you, Mrs. Cleveland. Raised in a lifestyle rich with culture—art, music, philosophy. As you pointed out, my father was a dockman, born to break his back for toffs like you." She subconsciously drew down the cuff of her sweatshirt where one of her tattooed forearms had slipped into view. "The only things we talk about are things that don't matter. Games. Training. Why *Ted Lasso* is the world's funniest show. Nothing personal. Nothing about the future—what we want to do with our lives when football comes to a close. What makes us tick." She stretched her legs out in front of her, running her palms to her knees and continued her monologue. "When I first arrived in Oakland I told everyone I had a girlfriend back home. A long-term, committed type of thing. I had only come here for one reason—and that was to play football. To make certain management got what they were paying for. It's where I wanted my focus, and things have a tendency to get complicated playing in such a high-tension setting with a bunch of women. So I made up a simple mistruth to help keep my head in the game." Pausing, she pulled her hat off and ran her fingers through her sun-bleached hair, gathering her thoughts. "It was perfect for a time. I liked Alex—she was a great baller, but an even better friend. But when things fell apart between the two of you, she hit an all-time low. She wasn't in a good place and she needed someone—needed *something* more than a friend. I filled a void. And I knew that was all it ever was. So I kept up my deceit—never told her the life I talked about back home was nothing more than a lie. I didn't want her to feel obligated that whatever was between us needed to be anything more. But overtime, as things went on, it started to feel like more than it was."

Catharine listened without interruption, despite her aversion to the subject. She didn't want to know about their relationship. What it was and what it wasn't.

But she asked the question she felt Amelia was seeking. If for no reason other than the inability to curb her curiosity.

"Why not just tell her what you just told me? Certainly it would change things between you."

"Because a non-existent girlfriend is the least of our problems. The truth is," she continued, matter-of-fact, "I'm in love with her. And she's in love with you. And there is nothing I will ever do or say to change that."

The disclosure took Catharine aback. It wasn't what she'd been expecting. Not from the implacable gaze and pragmatic narrative. The set of her jaw didn't slacken, her unblinking eyes still holding Catharine's with that same categorical certainty, but she at last allowed herself to sit back in the chair, her head dropping back against the headrest. "So I've survived our ill-fated affair under the guise of us both knowing it was never destined to go anywhere serious to begin with. Nothing more than temporary and superficial. Unfortunately for me, for one of the first times in my life, my head and heart weren't of one agenda—and I started to hope there might be a chance this could work." Her fingers played with the cuffs of her sleeves; a habit Catharine suspected was unnatural to her. "But then you turned up at the training center, and I saw how the two of you were together—and I knew. I knew what I had always known. But it's easy to try and ignore a truth when it goes against your grain—when it interferes with your hopes. I thought about telling her how I felt—I'm certain if I had, it would have changed things. She's so bloody loyal. But that's not how I wanted to hold onto her longer. I don't want to be her obligation. We've been good for each other in a lot of ways, but I don't want to get down the line and be a choice that she regrets."

Lost to her thoughts, she picked up the framed photo on Catharine's desk and reexamined it.

"You might give her the choice, instead of deciding for her." Why she felt the need to offer advice, Catharine didn't know. But there was something in the stolid face that resonated. She knew the hurt behind the mask of indifference. She'd been there. She still was.

"Oh, please, Mrs. Cleveland," Amelia rallied from her introspective state, looking up with an ironic smile. "Look around. You think I can compete with this? With you?" She laughed, humorless. "I'm thirty-three years old in the twilight of my career. If the Gods of Football are kind, I'll have a few more years left in me. But after that, then what? A yabbering pundit? A coaching gig? I'll never amount to more than I am right now. The best of what I've got to offer is behind me." She set the photo down, upright and facing Catharine. "I don't like to lose, Mrs. Cleveland—I'd rather walk away before anyone can claim a victory. So I'm going back to the life that I know best—the one where I belong." She stuffed her hands in the pockets of her sweatshirt, finished with her soliloquy.

"And you came here to tell me this, why?" Catharine asked, coolly. "I believe in our previous conversation you informed me I was ruining Alex's life. And the best thing I could do to help was 'bloody disappear.'"

"I was upset," Amelia conceded. "It should have been one of the best nights of her life. She'd just been told she was a shoe-in for the World Cup roster. Do you know what that means to her? And do you know how it felt, watching her surrounded by her friends and teammates, when her headshot popped up on the telly? Knowing she'd just been through the week from hell and come out the other side? It was like witnessing a never-ending nightmare. When she went missing for the entire night, I was terrified—my thoughts went to the worst places, so by the time I talked to you—yeah, I was angry. And you seemed like the right person to blame. But I've had a few days to think on it now, and I was wrong. Fair dinkum, you may be the only person who is right for her. The only one who can keep her on track."

"I am more inclined to agree with your original sentiment. I seem to have a gift for hurting those I care about, and Alex has clearly been no exception."

"I don't know your story, Mrs. Cleveland—and I won't pretend that I care to. I'm not here as your friend. But I am here for Alex—with her best interest in mind. So I hope you'll think on what I've said. After everything, you owe that much to Alex."

Amelia stood, finished with the conversation. Despite everything, Catharine admired the woman's willingness to show her cards, hiding nothing in her hand. She had come to say her piece, and was there for no other purpose than she implied. She wasn't looking for Catharine to tell her she was wrong—to convince her to stay. She was simply there to tell her the truth as she knew it, and then walk away.

Amelia's mobile rang as Catharine rose to walk her to the door. Fishing it from her pocket she declined the call, but not before Catharine saw Alex's face—a closeup selfie with her impossibly captivating smile—flash across the caller ID. She looked entirely happy, carefree—the laughing woman she was meant to be. Nothing of how she'd seen her a week prior.

"How did she feel about you leaving?" Catharine asked, nodding at the mobile.

"I guess I'll find out in her message." Amelia flipped the phone to silent and returned it to her pocket.

"You haven't told her?"

"No." She met Catharine's eyes without apology. "I never would have followed through if I had been the one to have to tell her."

Catharine suppressed her criticism. She was the last person granted the privilege to fault her.

Amelia glanced at her watch. "Thank you for your time, Mrs. Cleveland. I have a plane to catch." In the doorway she paused. "We all need someone in our life who knows our *preferential palette*," she said, handing Catharine's words back to her. "Please be that for her."

Chapter Twenty-Seven

The drive on the bus from Manchester was rowdy, the women keyed up from a win in the World Cup quarterfinals the previous day. The 3-1 victory over Japan was sending the US on to the semifinals, a match that would take place a week later in the famed Wembley Stadium in London—pitting them against the host nation: the Lionesses.

Alex sprawled at the back of the bus, her headphones on and music blaring, trying not to constantly look over Halsey's shoulder to check the score of the Canada vs. Australia match the goalkeeper was watching on her iPad.

"Cheese and rice!" Rodrigues broke Alex away from the chorus of *Boulevard of Broken Dreams*, leaning over her lap to grab the tablet from Halsey's lap. "She sent that from the center circle!"

Alex couldn't help but pull an AirPod out of one ear and watch the replay on the screen. It was Amelia, of course—receiving the ball in the middle of the field, trapping it on the half-turn, and driving a one-touch rocket directly to the waiting head of her teammate, Sarah Bellamy, who managed to stay on-sides to sink the ball into the back of the net. Canada's goalkeeper never had a chance to go to ground. Her dusted defense had left her entirely unprotected.

The score on the screen said 1-0. Australia in the lead. Eleven minutes on the clock.

"Get it together, Canada," Molly voiced Alex's thoughts, not too PC to say it. She'd yet to forgive Amelia for abandoning them midseason and was therefore rooting for every team that played against Australia.

Alex was, too, but for entirely different reasons. She couldn't imagine facing Amelia on the pitch. In fact, she hoped not to run into her at all. The hurt was still fresh from six weeks earlier and it wasn't something she wanted to deal with in front of ninety thousand screaming fans. Or deal with at all. Ever.

So she needed Australia to lose.

Instead, they beat Canada 2-0 and moved on to the semifinal the following week against Germany.

"The damned Matildas are on fire," Rodrigues lamented as they stepped out of the bus into the sweltering heat of the late June afternoon. London was bustling, alive with World Cup Fever, and the US team was hopped up on caffeine, a five-game winning streak, three-hour bus ride, and the promise of some R&R granted them for the evening.

"They have no chance against Germany," Shelly Altman asserted, which brought a slap to the back of her head from Halsey. She was the second string keeper and the only person that ever seemed to get on Halsey's nerves.

"Don't forecast future games—it's bad juju."

"You and all your irrationalities," Shelly rolled her eyes, but got no support from her surrounding teammates. The deeper into the tournament the US got, the greater the superstitions. Legs unshaven. Underwear inside out. Eggs eaten only scrambled. Talismans clutched. Lucky socks folded half down. You name it, someone did it. And the number one rule—don't predict coming matches. Or—mention the finals.

"It's hotter than a billy goat's ass in a habanero patch!" Jill Thompson slung her travel bag over her shoulder and started for the front entrance of the lobby. They'd lucked out with FIFA on location and amenities, landing in the heart of London, only a few blocks from Wembley, in a dazzling metropolitan hotel.

"But it's not as hot as Grey's left foot!" Sawyer crooned, coming up behind Alex and wrapping her in a headlock, performing an undesired noogie with her knuckles. Alex broke free and fussed at fixing her hair as Halsey gave her a hip check.

"She's not wrong—maybe we should all start kissing your boot before we take the field."

"Oh, shut up," Alex swatted the two of them away from her, laughing. It was true—she'd had an unbelievable start to the tournament. Playing every minute of the three-game group stage, she'd earned an assist in her very first World Cup game—a match versus Sweden—then bagged a brace against the young team from Vietnam and two additional goals four days later when they played Nigeria. Atwood had rested her for the round of sixteen, before sending her for another full ninety in the quarterfinals, in which she'd pocketed another goal and assist against Japan. Five goals and two assists in four games played was the stuff fairytales were made of. It didn't feel real. Every morning Alex woke in a hotel expecting to find the last five weeks spent on the road were a dream. From the send off games in New Jersey to the coming semifinal in Wembley. The journey felt ethereal. On the field she felt invincible. Like nothing could take her down. And off the pitch she did everything to keep her mind busy, careful not to allow her thoughts to drift onto shaky ground.

In their new hotel room, Halsey flung her duffle on the bed nearest the door and flopped onto her back. They'd been assigned roommates throughout the tournament and reached an easy compatibility from years of experience. Alex knew Halsey would want first dibs in the shower, the suitcase stand instead of the dresser, and a light left on in the hall. And Alex's only requirement was that Halsey didn't cook anything in the microwave that left a lingering smell. Or—for more recent purposes—turn on the news. An acceptable arrangement from both. And on the plus side—Halsey didn't snore. Unlike Sawyer, who could rival a freight train as soon as her eyes were closed.

"Are you going out tonight?" Halsey rolled on her side and stretched a long arm over her head, grimacing at the strain. She'd taken a hard knock to the ribcage during the match against Nigeria and was still feeling the repercussions, validated by the forehead sized bruise.

"Yeah." Alex settled on the end of the bed by the window. "I think I will. Rodrigues is meeting up with some of her former teammates from OL, and I doubt I'll have another chance to see the city before—"

"Don't say it! You'll jinx us!"

"—*before*," Alex continued pointedly, "the weekend. Calm down, I can't believe you thought I was going to mention the—"

"Alex!"

"—team dinner tomorrow night." Alex stuck out her tongue, teasing the keeper for her paranoia that she was going to breathe the word *championship*. It was taboo to even think about it—yet they all knew it was the only thing on their minds.

They couldn't say the word until they got there. And first, they had to beat the Lionesses.

"Be careful going out with Molly," Halsey warned later, as Alex was applying a thin layer of lipstick to hide her chapped lips. "You know how she can get."

Alex knew. Rodrigues wasn't the exemplary citizen when it came to curfew and responsibility. But Alex had never been to London, and it sounded fun to see something more than the inside of a stadium and the hotel gym and jacuzzi.

"Salty and Shelly are coming, too." Alex brushed on a trace of rouge. Salty—Kristin Salter—was their team co-captain who shared the title with Jill Thompson. A year younger than Alex, she was a longtime veteran of the team, and the women looked up to her. She was the main reason Alex felt comfortable going out. If the captain determined a night on the town was fair game, who was she to judge? Atwood had given them an evening of leave. With a lot of rules and restrictions.

Halsey gave a discontented grunt and stretched her hamstring.

"Why don't you come with us?" Alex pulled her hair back over her shoulders, deciding to leave it loose, and glanced at Halsey in the mirror. "Grab some dinner, see the bridges, then—"

"I played two years for Chelsea straight out of college, if you'll recall. The city's overrated and the food sucks."

Aware of her abnormal crankiness, Alex let the subject go. Halsey had allowed two goals in six games—statistics most keepers would have been thrilled with in a high stakes competition—but not her. She wanted a shutout every game. Every tournament. Every match of her career. An impossible feat, but one she aspired for all the same. She wasn't happy with her performance and wanted to stew.

"Be back before curfew," Halsey called as Alex stepped into the hall. "And bring me a pastry."

Crammed in the backseat of an Uber sedan only intended for three, Alex sat wedged between Rodrigues and Shelly, with Salty —the lightest of the four —perched across their laps.

"You're crushing my leg," Rodrigues griped, trying to shift the length of her legs out from under the driver's seat. "How can someone five feet tall weigh as much as a horse?"

There was a yowl as Salty found the skin of the defender's thigh, giving it a well-deserved pinch. "I'm five-three, thank you."

"You took offense to her shaving three inches off your height, but not to being compared to a horse?" Shelly asked, her voice muted behind Salty's back.

The captain flicked her copper hair deliberately into Rodrigues' face. "Horses are fast, smart, and get shit done. I'll take it as a compliment."

A few minutes later the four women piled out of the car in front of a pub pumping Dua Lipa, a sign painted above the awning indicating they'd arrived at *The Golden Crow*.

"I thought you said *dinner*, Molly?" Kristin Salter lectured, taking on her captain's roll. But the admonishment lasted less than a second before she grinned and followed the towering form of the defender toward the crowded front door.

Alex followed in the trail of the others, waiting as they were stopped by a bouncer who gave them a disapproving once over.

"Americans?" His broad chest was covered in a skintight muscle shirt bearing the logo of the Three Lions—England's football crest. "Come for one last pint before we send you packing for home?"

"Don't fire 'em up, Wes," a thickly-accented voice drawled from inside the threshold. A woman in an untucked tuxedo shirt and checkered tie appeared in the doorway, shouldering the bouncer aside. "Don't mind him, he's a proper cross gadgie," she smiled as Rodrigues swooped her into her arms and swung her around.

"Huntley! You handsome son of a bitch! It's been a minute!" Rodrigues dropped her to her feet, ruffling her tightly coiled, short-shorn hair. "You haven't changed a bit!"

"Eh, lost a leg, gained a few minutes on my mile," the woman shrugged, motioning toward what Alex realized was a prosthetic right leg. "But otherwise, still the same."

Alex recognized her. Anyone with half an interest in football would. She was Sam Huntley, the famed Geordie from Newcastle, a three-time World Cup veteran, the first Black woman to win the Ballon d'Or, one of the greatest stars England had ever produced. Two years earlier, in the middle of her club season with OL in Lyon, France, she'd been hit by a truck on her motorcycle and lost her leg in the aftermath. At twenty-nine years old, in the prime of her career, her life had been shattered by a drunk driver on a Tuesday night. The tragedy had topped all the sports headlines.

"I'm sorry, man," Rodrigues gripped her boxy shoulders, "I really am."

"All good, marra—took me a year to stop wishing the truck had finished the job, but I'm good now. Good as can be, at least." She downplayed the event with a crooked smile and waved away the subject. "I can't believe the semis are coming down to my girls and you yanks. We're going to snuff you, of course—but I'll be sorry to see you go." Her attention swayed from Rodrigues as she stuck out her hand to Salter and then Altman. "I've seen you all on the telly, of course, but it's good to officially meet you." She then turned toward Alex, her smile broadening. "And you, no doubt, are the infamous Alex Grey. Can't say there'll be many who won't know your pretty mug around here. You're something of a legend—the lass who snared a London heiress and put that revolting doylem in his place." She grinned, amused at Alex's discomfort. "Oh, don't take that the wrong way, marra! You did your country a service."

"I'd rather be known as the lass that took England out of the finals," Alex snapped, before she had time to think. It was so unexpected—the hostility and rudeness so unlike her—she didn't know where to begin to apologize, so instead shouldered through the door into the crowded pub.

No one had mentioned Catharine to her since before they left the States. It was a taboo subject, and Atwood had made it clear the first day of camp that anyone causing drama within the squad would find themselves on a one-way ticket back home, no questions asked. So to have it brought up by a stranger, in such a flagrant manner, had knocked her off balance.

"She's harmless, Grey," Molly caught her before she was enveloped in the crowd as it swayed to a Lizzo remix, "c'mon, Salty said the first round's on her."

Half an hour later and two whiskeys deep, Alex pulled herself onto a stool at the furthest end of the bar. A live band had taken over, the speakers blaring through the airless pub, and she desperately needed a water. The alcohol had caught up with her faster than she expected, and she realized she hadn't eaten since before they left Manchester that morning. Alex waved at the bartender but he looked straight past her, serving up a couple girls with flashier cleavage.

Waiting for him to make a second loop, Alex turned her attention to a discarded paper on the countertop. *The Daily Telegraph*, flipped open to the sports section. At the top was a photo from Australia's blowout match against Scotland. Amelia Walker suspended by her teammates, her cocky smile flashed across her face, hair plastered to her forehead, her signature strong arm pose toward the audience. She'd scored a hat-trick, sending her team on four to nothing to play the quarters against Canada.

Alex reached to pick up the paper, but a hand caught her wrist, surprising her, and she spun to see Sam Huntley at her side.

"You all right, lass?" The woman's skin was glistening from her time on the dance floor, her shirt damp with perspiration. Through the white cotton Alex could see the faint outline of tattoos covering her arms and shoulders. Even with the loss of her leg, she was still outrageously fit, and looked every inch a footballer. "You been pied off by your mates?"

"Sorry," Alex pushed the paper aside, her head buzzing. She shouldn't have had the whiskey. She hadn't had a drink since before Amelia left. She hadn't wanted to find herself on that road again. "You just surprised me."

"My bad," Sam leaned against the bar and wiped the sweat from her brow with an inked forearm, her cuffs rolled to her elbows. She took another moment to loosen her tie, before hopping onto the barstool next to Alex, making herself at home.

"Look, I hope I didn't offend you earlier. It wasn't how I meant it."

"No, that's on me—I'm sorry, it's just been a sore subject."

"No apologies needed," she offered a lazy smile, "I wouldn't consider it a good night until I've pissed off at least one canny lass." She winked, before turning more serious. "That was some real dodgy shit your teammate did to you. And the cock-up with Cleveland right after— I'll give you some huge props for weathering through and still making it here. Lot of people would have caved in for much less."

"It is what it is." Alex's defensiveness creeped back. She didn't want to talk about it. "I wasn't going to let it affect my game."

"And that you haven't. Sitting in second place for the most goals scored —couple more and you might just bag yourself the Golden Boot before you head home."

"Unlikely," Alex said, below the din of the room. She knew the former superstar knew exactly who was most likely to take home the Golden Boot. There wasn't a person connected to the tournament who didn't know Amelia had tied the record for most goals scored in a single World Cup— with at least one, if not two, games left for her to play.

"It's looking pretty good for Australia, wouldn't you say?" Huntley said, as if reading her thoughts, before turning to snag the barman. "Hey man, can I get a double of your single malt?" She glanced at Alex. "What are you drinking?"

Alex shook her head. "I'm good. Water, please."

"Nonsense! Your one and only night off. The evening's still young. You aren't doing this cup right if you don't share a drink with a has-been. It's tradition." Her teeth flashed in the dim light of the pub. "So humor me and name your poison."

"Whatever you're having." Alex looked around again for her teammates, who had upped and disappeared. One more drink and then she was out. No matter who she offended.

Sam collected their two doubles and pressed one into Alex's hand, clinking the glasses together as she did so. "Cheers! To good football! May the best team win!" Again her wry smile appeared. "In this case, the Lionesses."

Alex didn't bother with a retort as the smoothness of the brown liquor warmed her throat, offering the calmness of a numbing sensation.

"So," Sam was back to business, "Australia took Canada this afternoon 2-0. Next weekend they play Germany. Who's your money on for the final?"

"Germany," Alex took a longer swallow of her drink.

"Is that spite or theory?"

"I'm sorry?"

"Please. The whole Amelia Walker thing. You two were pretty good mates, weren't you?"

Another sweep of the room came up fruitless. It was just a sea of strangers on the dance floor. If her friends had left her there, they'd better prepare to get an earful.

Alex looked back at Sam, resigned to answer her question.

"Um, I mean, yeah, she was my club captain for the last year and a half, so, I guess you could say that."

"Ah." Huntley's eyes flickered. "Rumor had it it was a little more. But we all know how rumors go."

Alex said nothing. The woman wasn't even in the mix of the sport anymore. Her intrusiveness was nothing more than meddling.

"Pretty gutless move leaving your club in the lurch like that. I've known Walker for years. It seemed so out of character."

"Arsenal wanted her back," Alex tried to disguise her irritation with another sip of whiskey. "It's not like she hadn't always planned to return to England. She just left a few months early. With the World Cup here, her girlfriend here, her life here... you can't really blame her."

"Girlfriend?" Sam's eyebrows shot up, displaying a ripple of wrinkles across her forehead.

"Yeah?" Alex didn't understand what was so intriguing.

Abruptly, the woman laughed, the high-pitched tone entirely contradictory with the tatted, muscular figure. "I can't believe she's still singing that song-and-dance all these years later. I swear, that girl is never going to settle down. She's used that story for every club she's played for. When we were young, I got it—it left her unavailable—no strings attached. Ol' girl was something of a playboy. But man—we're ten years later. Surely she's given up the game by now." Again she laughed before becoming aware that Alex failed to see her humor. "Oh," the wrinkles appeared on her brow once more, "you really didn't know?"

Sam was so certain. So adamant.

But she had to be wrong.

Alex drained her glass.

Amelia would have told her. She repeated it to herself. *Amelia wouldn't lie to her*.

And this woman knew nothing. She hadn't pulled on a jersey in over two years. Things changed. People changed. Time moved on.

"Sorry, marra," Sam's amusement had drained along with Alex's whiskey. "Didn't mean to lay that on you. "

"Well, it's here nor there," Alex heard herself say, satisfied with the nonchalance her voice carried. She felt warm. A little woozy. And reminded herself this woman's opinion didn't matter.

"Speaking of girlfriends," Sam looked eager to segue onto a different subject, "do you think Catharine Cleveland is going to come to the match?"

The brief interlude of tranquility vanished at Catharine's name on this stranger's lips.

"To the match?"

"Yeah, man. This weekend? Not sure if you know, but there is a big football tournament going on and the yanks are squaring up with the limeys for an old time showdown of redcoats versus continentals—football style."

Alex was too focused on the question of Catharine attending the semifinals to find enough motivation to acknowledge the overblown sarcasm.

"I somehow doubt she plans on flying five thousand miles to see a football match."

The last contact Alex had had with Catharine was the night before she left for training camp, two days after Amelia had flown back to the UK without so much as a goodbye. She'd finished a workout at the gym and gotten to her locker to find a voicemail from Catharine, asking her to call.

Still reeling from Amelia's unexpected departure, and from the barrage of media inquiries swarming Alex's privacy and personal life, and the altercation the week before with Monica Ashby, Alex hadn't been in the right headspace to return the phone call. Instead, determined to put the last two years behind her before she set foot on the plane to begin her World Cup summer, she sat in the empty locker room and sent Catharine a text message that simply said: *please, whatever it is, don't call me again. I can't do this anymore.* And hit send before she could change her mind.

And she'd regretted it every day since. But Catharine had heeded her request, and Alex had promised herself they were both moving on with their lives.

"Oh, you don't even know," Sam leaned back from the counter and motioned at the barkeeper to bring them two more. This time Alex didn't say anything. She was too focused on the half amused smile, the glint of humor she imagined was preparing to kick her in the teeth in the next breath. "You live in an oyster shell?"

"Know what?"

"Your old flame is here in town. It's been a big deal. Topping all the headlines. She was sacked as the CEO of her own company. Given the old heave-ho by her own father! He's been all over the telly calling her vile and a disgrace. An 'embarrassment to the family name.' Been a real rigamarole. Word is she's here now with her legal team in tow."

Fired. It was the only information Alex could absorb.

She *had* been living in an oyster shell. She had deleted all her social media and refused to be anywhere near a television turned to the news. She went out of her way not to look at papers or read headlines. Nothing about the election. Catharine. Herself. She hadn't wanted to know anymore. If she didn't know about it, it couldn't affect her.

The fresh round arrived and she beat Sam to the nearest glass.

"Easy, tiger," a strong hand steadied her as the stool shifted beneath her. The room swayed, but Sam Huntley's face remained clear. She was smiling, amused by Alex's reaction. "Didn't mean to dump all that on you. I thought you must have known. Apparently not." Taking up the lowball, she toasted Alex once more. "To my big mouth and an overload of information."

"There you are!" A woman with short blonde hair and lopsided smile draped her arms over Alex and Sam, drawing their three faces close together, as if they were old friends. "If you're Alex Grey—your mates are looking for you on the patio."

"Sinc, you smell like you've been hitting the hash," Sam grinned at her friend, speaking in a stage whisper. "Apparently the party's started without us, Grey."

Alex recoiled at the stench coming off the stranger's clothes. She'd never been a smoker, especially not weed, and found the smell revolting.

"Ohhh, methinks our girl Grey here doesn't have her sea legs" Sam gave an exaggerated wink, before turning her eyes back to Alex. "What were you, kid: the preacher's daughter?"

Alex couldn't help but laugh at the irony of the question. *Niece, actually.* But not even that anymore.

"I was no one's daughter," she mumbled, her tongue thick and uncoordinated as a vignette closed around her vision.

"Howay man, now's no time to be morose," Sam chided, catching Alex's hand and pulling her along behind the newcomer through the throng of people on the dance floor.

Pushing out the back door, Alex found Altman, Salter and Rodrigues standing around in a circle, chatting with a few girls Alex didn't know. A blunt was being shared amongst the strangers, which Sam snatched from the mouth of an almond-eyed beauty who flipped her the bird.

"Save a little, will ya, pet?" she chastised, taking a hit from the spliff. Exhaling deeply, she smiled, and held the joint toward Alex. "Here, rook—inauguration time."

Before Alex could decline, the woman who'd led them to the patio swiped the joint from Huntley's hand. "She's got a match next week, you bloody lembo." She took a hit herself and passed it further down the line.

"You take all the fun out of things, Sinc," Sam complained, but the woman ignored her.

"Here, preacher's kid," Sinc winked, producing a green bottle of Absinthe from a table behind the group, "we got you yanks covered. When in Rome…"

"Drink up!" It was Molly's voice, sounding far away. "You got some catching up to do."

Salty laughed, swiping the bottle and taking a swig, before pressing it back in Alex's hands. The smell of black licorice was nauseating, but Alex took a sip anyway.

Catharine had been fired.

"There's a lass." Sam tipped the bottle back further until Alex coughed. She laughed, clapping her hard on the back. "Best way to make all your troubles go away."

Around her, the faces of her teammates and strangers all swum together, and Tower Bridge swayed in the distance as the London city skyline tipped on its axis.

Chapter Twenty-Eight

"It's more complicated than that." Gordon Liebermann tried to sound diplomatic, but there was a sigh in his voice that edged through his professional barrier. A rhythmic rat-a-tat was thumping through the line, a sound Catharine knew was coming from the flick of his thumbnail against the receiver. It was a bad habit he'd developed over the twenty years she'd known him, and one he did exclusively when he thought they were on the losing side of a legal battle. It wasn't a sound she wanted to hear. "Private corporations are held to different standards. Especially in the UK."

"Find me something, Gordon. A loophole. A prehistoric clause. Something. It's what you do best!"

"I'm not even supposed to be talking to you, Catharine!" The uncharacteristic use of her first name was jarring. It was a familiarity he never used, even after decades of working together. "To be clear—any of our conversations from here on out are as friends, not as counsel. This would be a significant breech of client confidentiality—"

"Oh, for the love of God, Gordon—"

"It's the law, damnit! You know it as well as I. It's what makes me good at what I do."

"Not good, Gordon. The *best.* And the best is exactly what I need right now."

"I'll keep looking, Catharine. In the meantime, you have to trust the Wrightman firm. They aren't incompetent—"

"They aren't *you!*" She snatched the throw pillow from her couch and flung it at the wall of glass providing a panorama of Tower Bridge and the Thames, lit in a silhouette of darkness. She wanted to smash the window, watch the web of fractures splinter, distorting the cityscape into a mosaic.

Instead she settled for hurling a second pillow, which landed with an insignificant thud beside the first.

Across the globe he was quiet. They both knew she was right. The odds were stacked against her and she needed a cutthroat in her corner—to fight against him.

"This isn't about me," she resumed at last, regaining something of her composure. "If it were I'd just tell him to burn it to the ground for all I care —do whatever the bloody hell he pleased! I've got plenty to keep me occupied beyond Brooks Corp. But there are people that count on me— count on *us*, Gordon—for their livelihood. You know what he'll do to punish me if this all falls apart. Tens of thousands of jobs eliminated, just like that—and all for what? So two out-of-touch plutocrats can have a row at each other in their blood feud? No," she stood and strode across the hardwood floor to retrieve the pillows, unable to tolerate them on the floor. "I won't let him get away with it. If he learned nothing else from this three-ring circus with Carlton, you'd think he'd at least come to realize I won't go down without a fight."

"We'll figure it out, Catharine—we've managed worse over the years."

Catharine couldn't think of anything even teetering on the line of how bad this was, but she tried to appreciate his optimism.

"For now, follow the Wrightmans' advice, trust their guidance, and I'll keep feeding them what I find—off the record. All right?"

Catharine leaned her forehead against the cool glass and closed her eyes to the view before her. It was a view she'd seen more of in the last fortnight than she had over the last two decades combined.

"Okay."

"If all else fails, you could just kill the bastard."

"Don't think I haven't thought it." Catharine didn't smile. Gordon was silent for longer than was appropriate, so she added, "it was a joke, Lieber-mann. Don't take it to heart."

"I'm Jewish. We take everything to heart." He sighed on the other end of the line. "Get some rest. What is it, after eleven there?"

Catharine glanced at the Dalvey crystal globe on the coffee table, the hands ticking mindlessly toward midnight.

"You'll keep in touch?" She wanted to hear him say it. She didn't want his lip service. She wanted his promise. Legal or not.

"You have my word. Hang in there, my friend."

When they hung up she sat on the sofa and watched the silver minute hand wind toward the hour. How could it have possibly come to this? Her own legal team working against her. This was *her* company, God damnit. Nothing of it resembled the cornerstone foundation her father had dropped on her decades earlier. She had worked her whole life for this. It had become hers. A reflection of her. *Her* employees. *Her* decisions. *Her* time, money, sweat and tears had built it to what it was today.

And in a single email he had shut her out. Cut her off from everything. Her own corporation was fighting against her at the orders of a man who hadn't so much as glanced at a quarterly in over fifteen years. Forty-nine percent. Fifty-one percent. The difference of everything.

It was implausible.

Yet entirely her reality. For the first time in her life she'd entered a legal battle that was stratospherically out of her league. Lost in unfamiliar territory, she was slowly being forced to face the fact that there was a chance she wouldn't win. That she could, in truth, lose everything.

Still, she wasn't willing to quit. Whatever it cost, whatever it took, she wasn't going to give in.

But every day that went by, every hour she was separated from the job that had become her life, a pebble of fear lodged itself deeper that a reconciliation was not in sight. That it had become insurmountable. A little less attainable. The corporation was riding a topsy-turvy wave of turmoil, floundering at the tailspin her dismissal had brought with it, and the financial strain was capsizing. If it continued the way it was, the corporation would implode, unable to sustain itself.

It was exactly what her father wanted. And all because of his desire to exact his revenge over a decades old vendetta he was unwilling to let go.

And now, in short time, she would be forced to meet him face-to-face. A punishment she found worse than her very public fall from grace.

Frustrated with her plunge into self-pity, Catharine dragged herself to the kitchen and reviewed the contents of her fridge, before settling on a cup of tea. Too worked up to sleep, she stepped onto her master suite terrace and embraced the humidity. The Thames snaked out beneath her, glistening with city lights, disappearing around Canary Wharf in the distance. It was a view she hadn't realized she missed while living in the States. She'd been so long gone from London she forgot how much she loved the history of the city—the architecture. The culture. The diversity.

When this was all over—whichever way it went—she thought she might stay in the UK for a while. There was nothing to hold her in San Francisco, and the further she could distance herself from Carlton, the safer she would feel. In a month he would be going into the National Convention, and she wanted to remove herself as far from that fiasco as she could.

For a few minutes longer she watched the liveliness of the city unfold below her as it hung on to the last calls of a summer Saturday night. Of one thing she was certain: no matter whose world was coming crashing down, the rest of the universe just forged on around them, oblivious and unforgiving.

For the second time in as many months, Catharine was woken by a phone call in the middle of the night. It was darker outside than when she'd last closed her eyes and the traffic on the bridge was sparse. It had to be the early hours of the morning.

She waited for her phone to ring again where it sat atop her dresser across the room, but it remained silent. Someone from the States, no doubt, forgetting there was any other time zone. After a minute when no beep came to indicate a voicemail, she closed her eyes. If it was important they would have left a message.

Another few minutes passed and she sat upright, swinging out of bed. What if it was Gordon? What if he'd had an epiphany about the impending mediation.

Swiping the screen open on her way back to bed, she paused midstride when she saw the name on her missed calls log.

1:17AM: Alex Grey

Dialed in error, most likely. She hadn't heard from Alex in over six weeks, and the last time they'd communicated Alex had made her feelings clear. She wanted Catharine to let her go. To stay out of her life. A wish Catharine had honored. Amelia Walker may have felt she was the right person for Alex, but Alex had decided otherwise. And who could blame her? The muck of Catharine's life had dragged Alex down with her, and it had been too much. Too much to ask of anyone.

Catharine climbed into bed and set the phone beside her. If she called again, she would answer.

But several minutes went by and there were no calls.

What if she was too afraid to call again? Too embarrassed? What if she *had* meant to call but lost her nerve.

Jesus, Catharine scolded herself, sitting up. It was just a damn phone call. She wasn't a child. Call her back or go to sleep—but make a choice one way or the other.

She opted to call her back.

The phone rang through its cycle before going to voicemail.

So the call had been accidental.

As Catharine was reorganizing her duvet, the ringer toned again, causing her to jump. Her fingers were jittery as she answered.

"Alex?" There was no voice on the other end, just a scuffling sound and a muffled noise that sounded like crying. Or staggered breathing. Or a mixture of the two. "Alex, can you hear me?"

"I'm sorry." The words were strangled with a sob, but the voice was clearly Alex. Catharine's heart made an erratic shudder, her limbs going weak. Bolting up, her feet landed firmly on the hardwood floor.

"Alex, what's happened?"

"I didn't know who else to call." The words were slurred and barely coherent, lost in an unintelligible mumble.

Catharine was halfway to her dresser. "Where are you?" She knew she was in England. All of Europe knew when the American soccer team had arrived. The World Cup was practically a month-long holiday in the UK, and with England acting as the host nation for the first time in the women's cup history, the entire country was abuzz.

"I don't—I don't know." There was another sob and the sound of traffic in the background.

"What city, Alex?"

"London."

"Tell me what you're near right now." In the long silence Catharine pulled on a pair of jeans and trainers, trying to calm her mind. Alex should have been with her team. Sleeping. Preparing for their next game. Whatever had happened, she had to find her.

"The river." Helpful, but not. The Thames was over two hundred miles long.

"What buildings? What bridge can you see?"

Alex said something about a bird statue. At least that was what Catharine could make out of the garbled sentence.

"Look at the river and tell me what bridge you can see." She was on her way down the lift, stopping on the lower penthouse floor and rapping on the wall to wake Malcolm. He appeared, hair awry, unshaven, pants unbuttoned, shoes in hand, but asked no questions, just stepped into the lift, completing his dressing as they descended to the street level.

Alex identified towers, which meant she was within sight of Tower Bridge. Minutes from Catharine in any direction.

"Is the statue in a park?" Catharine motioned for Malcolm to search his mobile for parks within range.

"I don't—God, I don't know." She went into a gagging fit and by the time she caught her breath Catharine was already in her car, Malcolm behind the wheel, waiting for her directions.

"There's got to be a sign, Alex. Or a plaque."

"Heritage Gardens."

Fumbling through the navigation of the unfamiliar car, Catharine searched for parks near the Towers connected to the name Heritage. The results came back empty.

"A statue of a bird," she said out loud, looking to Malcolm, trying to think of anything nearby that fit the description. But she wasn't familiar with the area any longer. A great deal had changed since she'd last spent time afoot in London.

Malcolm flipped quickly through the navigation system and tapped the screen with his index finger to gain Catharine's attention. Hermitage Riverside Memorial Gardens. *Hermitage.* Not Heritage. It was less than a mile away.

"I'm going to come get you. Just stay where you are. Don't hang up."

Five minutes later Catharine ran down a dirt path in a small grass park surrounded by hedges and shrubs with the Thames running along the south side. Closest to the river was a plain memorial with a steel block sculpture centered with the cutout of a dove. And beside it she found Alex, still on the phone with her, sitting on the brick walkway, her head buried between her knees.

Malcolm had exited the car, but now hung back as Catharine dropped to the ground beside the crying girl, her hand at her back, worried what she would find.

"Alex?" She touched her fingers to her chin, urging her to look up. "Are you hurt?"

"I'm so sorry," Alex was overcome by another sob, looking up only long enough for Catharine to realize she was positively soused, reeking of smoke and whiskey. "I didn't know who else to call."

"It's okay." Catharine let out a breath, relaxing. She appeared unharmed, unhurt. "It's okay," she repeated, more for her own self-assurance. Her heart rate declined and sensibility took over. Wasted in a wayside park in Tower Hamlets wasn't what she'd been expecting—but it was the better of the alternatives. She took ahold of the sweat-drenched arm and looked toward Malcolm for help. "Do you think you need a hospital?" she asked as Malcolm hoisted the unbalanced girl to her feet, slinging her arm around his shoulders.

"No!" It was more a plea than anything else. Her eyes found Catharine's, glazed and unfocused, but her adamancy remained. "Please. No hospitals. They'll never let me play."

Catharine shot a silent inquiry to Malcolm. She wasn't versed in things like this. She wasn't sure what to do—if a trip to the hospital could even be spared.

"Some sleep, water, and aspirin, ma'am," the Scot nodded appraisingly. "I think she'll sort out."

Catharine nodded, willing to trust his judgment. "Come on—let's get you out of the chill and cleaned up."

Without protest from Alex, Malcolm lifted her into his arms and carried her to the car.

Catharine dimmed the lamps in her master suite, leaving just enough light so she could see Alex's face through the darkness. She'd left her propped on her side in the middle of the bed in the event she was sick again, though it seemed the worst was over.

The previous hour had been spent sitting on the bathroom floor, holding Alex's hair back as she cried over the toilet, her words unintelligible beyond the thousand times she'd said she was sorry. And stupid. The two words interchangeable.

When the sickness had passed and she'd gotten her cleaned up in the shower, Catharine had taken Malcolm's advice and managed to get her to drink some water, followed by a couple aspirin.

"I'll wager a hundred quid the culprit is absinthe," Malcolm had said on the drive over. It was an alcohol unfamiliar to Catharine, and though he'd jovially gone on about the effects of wormwood and high levels of ethanol providing a perfect chemistry as a pseudo-hallucinogen, she hadn't followed much of his assessment. Even less had been gained from Alex, beyond the broken explanation that she'd been out with a few teammates in a pub not far from where Catharine found her.

With her finally sleeping, Catharine picked up Alex's mobile that had been buzzing with nonstop notifications. She'd no doubt missed her curfew and the consequences of her actions were about to catch up with her. Catharine knew from Alex's previous summer on the USWNT that the nightly curfew was not a suggestion. Women were dropped from the roster for breaking the rules—though she imagined at this point the curfew was the least of Alex's worries.

If her coach found out about her current condition…

Catharine scrolled through the texts to see if she could best determine who to speak with to prevent things from getting out of hand.

There were two dozen messages from four different numbers.

Halsey.

Rodrigues.

Sawyer.

Salty.

Catharine clicked on the one with the most notifications.

Rodrigues:

> *—where the hell r u?*
> *—i dont know where we lost u?????*
> *—call me!!!*
> *—tell me u didnt get picked up by those cops!*
> *—CALL ME FOR FUCKS SAKE!!*

—were back at the hotel!!! Grey! Where r u!?!!?!

Uncertain who Rodrigues was, and unconvinced she could help her, Catharine clicked on the messages from Halsey.

—Rod just came back with Salty and Altman and said they lost you in the city when cops came???

—WTF, Alex! Call me!

—Hello!??

—If you don't text me back I'm going to have to wake up Atwood!

Catharine checked the time on the last message. It had been sent just a few minutes earlier. She quickly typed out a reply:

—Alex is okay. She's safe for the night. She'll be back to the hotel first thing in the morning.

There was an immediate response.

—Who is this? I swear to God, if this is you, Sam Huntley, I'll break your God damned neck. You started all this shit. Where is Alex?

Before Catharine could respond, the phone rang. Uncertain of a better plan, she answered it.

"Who the hell is this?!" the voice demanded, before she'd even said hello.

"My name is Catharine Cleveland. We met before, in Portland."

The admission took some of the wind out of the goalkeeper's sails. "Wait, what? Um—sorry. I mean, yeah. You've seen Gre—Alex? She missed her curfew."

"She called me after she got separated from your friends. She lost her wallet. She's sleeping now—I'll have her back to the hotel in the morning. Where are you staying?"

Still out of sorts, Halsey finally came up with the name of the hotel. "She —uh, tell her I told nightcheck she was sleeping. No one knows. But she has to be back before bye ends tomorrow evening or—well, she knows."

"She'll be there. Will you tell Abby Sawyer and—" Catharine glanced at the phone to catch the other name, "Rodrigues?"

"Yes. Yes, ma'am." She hesitated. "She's—she's okay though, right?"

Catharine rubbed at her temple. The last thing Alex was was okay. "Yes. She's all right. She'll call you first thing in the morning."

"Right." The young woman cleared her throat. "Good night, then, Mrs. Cleveland."

Catharine flipped the phone to silent and slipped back into the room, padding across the floor to set the phone on the dresser beside her own. If Alex had any fortune at all, her teammate could keep her out of trouble. At least until morning. She stopped beside the bed and permitted herself a sigh, running a finger across Alex's cheek to slip a strand of damp hair back behind her ear. She was fast asleep now, her breath no longer labored, her chest rising and falling in slow succession. Catharine moved the glass of water on the nightstand within reaching distance, took one last look at the flushed face, slack in slumber, and slipped onto the enclosed terrace where she settled on the couch. She would be able to hear Alex if she needed anything, which gave her reassurance.

Watching over the top of the couch for a few seconds more, she finally laid back and stared at the glass ceiling.

The stupid, stupid girl. It was sheer imbecility, and nothing she expected from the responsible, determined, dedicated young woman that she knew. This wasn't like her at all.

Catharine closed her eyes. Whatever had happened, she was glad Alex had called. Glad she had trusted her enough to help.

Chapter Twenty-Nine

Alex was certain if she opened her eyes, her skull was going to explode. She lay entirely still, the very thought of moving amplifying the bass drum reverberating in her head. Cognizant thoughts came slowly.

The rudimentary knowledge she was lying down.

Her throat felt like she'd gargled with crushed marble.

Her body ached from head to toe.

She remembered being at the bar. Sam Huntley and her checkered tie. A wall of smoke on the patio. And then walking along the river, the water seeming to rise up off the shore, the ground a tilt-a-whirl. Faces swirling into a kaleidoscope of motion. Laughter. Shouting. *Bobbies*. A word she hadn't been familiar with, but the repeated instruction she was meant to run. Falling. Skinned knees on a dirt path. And the suddenness of being alone.

Slowly, but more alarmingly, her whereabouts came to mind. Not current location, but more circuitous—London. Soccer. *The World Cup!*

She tried to bolt upright, but was hit with such a surge of vertigo she immediately collapsed back down. From the brief glimpse of her surroundings, she knew she hadn't made it to the hotel. Walls of windows, a wooden floor, light filtering in from every angle. Whites, creams, a gradient of colors that flowed together like the under feathers of a bird's wing.

A voice grew distinctive through the division of muffled walls. A voice she knew in a place it didn't belong.

"—if I refuse, what happens then? A panel of overweening suits nod their way through my narrative and write up a decree to withdraw my lawsuit and accept whatever they recommend? With no recourse? No appeal? This is my bloody company, do you understand? Your recommendation to accept arbitration puts me under great concern regarding your commitment to actually winning this fight!" There was a brief pause, before the voice grew louder, clearer, angrier. "I am not concerned with the costs of going to trial!" And then, silence.

Catharine.

Alex sank deeper into the cocoon of sheets surrounding her, squeezing her eyes shut even tighter. She'd called her. She remembered that now. She'd called her because she didn't dare call anyone on her team. If Izzy Atwood saw her...

Her eyes flew open again, focusing on the high-beamed ceiling. *Izzy Atwood.*

It was daylight, the sounds of the city funneling through an open window, the sun leaving late-morning shadows across the polished floor.

Holy Mother of All That was Holy... shit. Alex forced herself upright, ignoring the threat of nausea. She had to get ahold of Halsey—find out how dead she was.

"You're awake."

The voice gave validity to the knowledge this wasn't the continuation of an uncomfortable dream. Catharine was standing in the doorway, her expression neutral, though her eyes held a measure of disappointment and dubiety.

Alex didn't afford herself the luxury of humiliation. There would be time for that later. The only thing she could focus on was finding her phone—calling Halsey.

"I—I need to make a call. I need to—" she looked wildly about her, trying to locate her phone, the contents of her head sloshing like a listing ship at sea.

"It's okay, Alex." Catharine crossed the room to retrieve something off the top of a sleek oak dresser, before taking a seat on the opposite side of the bed. "I spoke with one of your teammates last night. They were panicked and I didn't want them searching all night for you." She held out her phone.

"Who?" was all Alex could think to say.

"Your goalkeeper. She seemed the most levelheaded at the time."

"Did she—am I—?"

"She said your coach didn't know and you'd better be back by the end of the day."

With fingers not wholly functioning, Alex swiped into her texts. Twenty-seven unread messages, but it was the one from Halsey at 07:11 this morning she selected.

—Checking in. Hope your rendezvous was worth it. I've now lied to six different people for you. You owe me huge. If your ass isn't here at team meeting, I'll find you and throttle you myself. Did I mention you owe me? Goals. Gold medals. Trophies. A plaque with my name on it. A blocked ball to the face. All of it. I hate you. I also hope you are okay.

With the fragile relief of not being on a one-way-ticket home waylaid, Alex dropped her phone and felt the tentacles of embarrassment root to the surface. Catharine had a coolness to her, a judgment in her gaze that spoke volumes over the misfortune of her last twelve hours. The outright fool she'd made of herself, the imbecilic predicament she was in.

Alex cast her gaze to her lap. Even the pounding of her head and ache of her body was secondary to the immensity of her shame.

"Catharine, I…" What could she even say? She was in the middle of the most important event of her career, the pinnacle achievement of her life, and she'd almost thrown it all away. Like a freshman sorority girl lured by the vices of spring break. The reasons didn't matter. The excuses were invalid. She had fucked up, and that was all there was to it.

An apology seemed like the right place to start.

"There aren't enough ways to say I'm sorry."

Catharine stood and went to the glass doors leading to a terrace, drawing them open to the morning. "You owe only two apologies, Alex. One to your teammates. And one to yourself." She stood in the doorway, her back to the room. "Because you are better than this, and you know it."

Alex closed her eyes and leaned against the headboard, the thrumming in her head keeping time with her heart. It was a deserved rebuke, piercing all the deeper by the disappointment in her voice.

Fragments of the night came back to her. Her nonsensical phone call. The park. Laying in the backseat of Catharine's car, crying into her lap. Heaving, shivering, curling into a fetal position on the cold marble of a bathroom floor. Catharine holding her hair back while she was sick.

"To you, I think, also."

"No." Catharine turned from the doorway and returned to the bed, sitting down beside her. "Not to me. You saved me from a bad way once, if you'll recall. It was the least I could do to return the favor."

Alex opened her eyes to find her holding out a glass of water. A peace offering from the tepidity of the scolding. "Different circumstances, I think." She lowered her gaze, taking the water and holding it to her lips. The last thing she wanted was to put something in her tumultuous stomach, but judging by the path of the sun in the sky, she had limited hours to convince her body it wanted to live.

"Different circumstances. Same conclusion." Catharine stood, holding her hand out for the empty glass.

She looked tired, Alex realized. Thinner than she'd ever seen her. Her natural grace burdened with a spectral weight invisible to the eye. Sam told her she'd been fired. Dismissed from her own company. Displaced from her life. Her passion. She'd been going through hell—and Alex hadn't even known.

"Do you think you could eat something?" Catharine asked, starting for the door.

The room was still precarious, and the thought of food abhorrent, but Alex nodded anyway. "Could I start with tea, do you think?" She labored for a smile. "A wise woman once told me her mother lived by the code that there was nothing in the world a cup of tea couldn't fix."

"As it turned out," said Catharine, pausing in the threshold, "that woman wasn't very wise. But I'm happy to oblige all the same."

When Catharine had gone, Alex took some time getting to her feet. Her body felt shaky, her limbs weak, but the raging hammering in her head had tapered to a mild roar. On the chair next to the nightstand she found her clothing from the night before, laundered and folded, and beside it a more comfortable pair of joggers and a black t-shirt, identical to the one she currently wore.

It was such a Catharine gesture. A thoughtful consideration. Meticulous and foresightful, the same as everything else about her.

Alex picked up the t-shirt and held it to her face, breathing in the familiar scent of Catharine's clothes. Even hungover and reeling, she couldn't separate herself from the headiness of being near her. The intoxication of her presence. The undeniable desire she had to kick in closed doors. To revisit the past and inquire about a future—but she didn't dare even hope.

Forcing herself to a lukewarm shower, she dressed—the pants too long, the t-shirt snug—and came out of the ensuite bathroom feeling almost half alive.

For the first time since she'd woken, she paid mind to her surroundings. The bedroom was similarly decorated to the San Francisco townhouse, with its muted colors, chic furniture, and a subtle austerity that felt somehow lonely. Luxurious as it was, it lacked a lived-in warmth, with nothing out of place, which Alex would have attributed to Catharine's rare trips to London had it not felt little different than when she'd first visited her home on the bay.

The view, however, was equally majestic, with Tower Bridge a stone's throw from the terrace balcony. The Thames running a half dozen stories beneath.

It was on the terrace that Catharine rejoined her, tea and a paper grocery sack in hand.

"Compliments of Malcolm," she said, sorting out the contents of the bag. Two bottles of coconut water. A pack of saltines. A tube of antacids. A bottle of aspirin. And a shooter of B-vitamins. "He wanted to make you a Bloody Mary, but I told him while you were under my roof you'd need to settle for green tea." She shot Alex a pointed look. "A principle you might consider adopting for the remainder of your tournament."

"Touché," Alex laughed to hide the embarrassment broadcasted by the flushing of her cheeks. But this time she was glad to see Catharine smile in return.

"You know," said Catharine, as Alex tested the tea, and began with the bottle of aspirin, "if you'd wanted to see me, you could have just called. You didn't have to put on such a show."

Again, Alex could feel the color of her cheeks crimson, heated by the warmth in her voice, the musicality turned teasingly seductive.

"Go big or go home, right?" She shook out a handful of crackers. *Nut up or shut up* was what Amelia had liked to yell at them on the pitch, but it seemed inappropriate for the setting. "I'm starting to feel like you have a thing for bridges," Alex steered the conversation away from dangerous waters, her eyes drifting to the beauty of the majestic bridge. It was spectacularly close, the famous Tower of London highlighted in the distance, the grandeur of the city skyline rising up behind it.

"I learned to sail on this stretch of the Thames, just over there at St. Katharine Docks." She indicated a place immediately across the water. "When Butler's Wharf was converted to flats and this corner came on the market, I was young—only a few years moved to the States—and had a chip on my shoulder, feeling like I had something to prove. I loved Shad Thames and at the time there was no more prestigious real estate to own in the city, so I bought this place to rub in my father's face. I thought it might make him respect me—as if the view from your balcony had anything to do with self-worth." She laughed, acidic at the admission. "I honestly doubt he even knows I own a home in the city, so you can see how much it mattered to him." Softening, she smiled, stealing one of Alex's crackers. "In retrospect, I'd buy something more practical—certainly with fewer floors."

A beat of silence passed as Catharine turned her eyes across the water, lost in an introspective gaze.

"I heard about your father," Alex ventured quietly. It felt like a subject needing to be broached. "I'm sorry. I didn't know until last night. I would have…" What? Reached out? Would she have? Or would she have just tucked her head back in the sand?

"It wasn't unexpected," Catharine sipped her tea with an indifference almost passing as genuine. "I knew what I was getting myself into."

Alex wasn't sure if she was talking about her very public battle with Carlton or relationship with Alex. Both had dealt irreparable repercussions.

"What will happen?"

"At present, I'm not certain. I've filed for wrongful termination, amongst other various charges—mostly just meant to muck up the process while I gather my defenses. Things are a bit stickier with a private corporation, but there are still avenues to explore." Taking another cracker, she broke it in four, never raising it to her lips. "Perhaps it will all work out—though, admittedly, I'd expected things to go better than they did." She offered a rueful smile, which Alex didn't share. So much of it felt like her fault. If it hadn't been for her, none of this would be happening. Catharine's life never would have been flung upside down as it was.

"Wherever your mind just drifted, Alex, put it aside."

It amazed her, Catharine's ability to read her so easily. The attention she paid to every detail; the shifting of her thoughts. It was both comforting and a curse.

"I guess it's just difficult to comprehend how one small thing can set so many others in motion." Alex followed the progress of a red double decker tour bus as it crossed the bridge.

"Are you saying you weren't expecting a weekend holiday on Daufuskie Island to turn into one of the larger scandals of the US Presidential election?"

Alex's attention returned to the table to find Catharine smiling at her. A smile she hadn't seen in a while. A smile that acted as a balm to old wounds.

"Something like that." She paused. "Do you regret it?" It wasn't the appropriate question for the moment, but one weighing on her all the same. With the upheaval of Catharine's life. Everything she was battling. Alex had to know.

"The divorce and the business? No. It's been a long time coming. What I do regret is that you were dragged into it. The things it did to you."

Alex didn't brush it off. She couldn't say it didn't matter. She'd hit rock bottom, been turned inside out, felt like she'd been living her life in a beta fish bowl. But through it all she'd found herself. She'd grown. Been knocked down and learned to rise again. She wasn't the person she was two years ago. The girl who'd lived her life according to the rules of everyone else. Never stepping outside the lines established. Never reaching. Never daring. Content in her stagnant career, living her life ninety miles away from the town where she grew up. She hadn't known who she was or what she wanted. Always waiting for someone to tell her what to do, how to act, who she should be.

She wasn't any of that anymore. She was free to be whoever she wanted to be. Her glass house had inadvertently forced her to leave nothing to hide. To run from. And despite the days she'd wished the name Cleveland meant nothing more to her than an Ohio city where she'd occasionally played ball, she knew, sitting there beneath the intensity of Catharine's sapphire gaze, she'd do it all over again. Even knowing what would come to fall.

"It was worth it."

She thought the simple admission would make Catharine smile—or bring levity to a reply. But this time Catharine said nothing, her gaze turned off to the distance, and Alex realized where her thoughts had travelled.

Over and over she had pushed Catharine away. From the very beginning she'd been the one to keep the distance, to set the boundaries, always with one foot out the door. Because she'd been afraid.

But now that it was all out in the open—now that there was no need to run—it was Catharine who'd moved on. Alex had put her off one time too many, and Catharine wasn't willing to be hurt again. The two of them sitting here, the way they were, was only the compassion of obligation. She'd needed Catharine's help—it had been given—and it had changed nothing.

"I understand you have a big game this weekend?" Catharine said as sirens sounded from the bridge, the traffic coming to a halt. A tall sailing ship floated down the river, the massive bascules of the bridge raising to allow her to pass.

Alex knew what the question meant. Catharine was closing the subject. Turning the tide.

"England, yes?"

"Yes," Alex said, hoping to conceal the disappointment in her voice. "Saturday. If I'm still on the team." She took a sip from one of the bottles of coconut water. The pressure in her head had dwindled to an almost tolerant force.

"And after that?"

Alex didn't want to talk about the games. She wanted to apologize for her text message the previous month. To ask Catharine what she could do to help her win her war. But the stolidness of Catharine's expression advised her to say no more.

"Germany plays Australia. Whichever teams win this weekend move on to the finals." She decided to cast one last lifeline. One final attempt. "Would you want to come? I could get you tickets, of course."

Catharine broke another cracker.

"It's this Saturday?"

"Yes," Alex said too quickly, hanging onto a glimmer of hope.

Catharine's lips disappeared in a line. "I will be in mediation. I'm uncertain how long it will run."

"Oh." Alex stumbled. How could she be so stupid to forget Catharine had far greater concerns than a game kicking around a ball. "Of course."

The sirens rang again as traffic resumed on the bridge, the silent progress of the sailboat slowly slipping past.

"Well," Catharine rose, gathering the cups and sweeping up the mess of crackers, "perhaps you'll save me a seat at the final?"

Alex toyed with the wrapper on the vitamin shooter, before looking directly at Catharine. "Would you come if I did?" What did she have to lose?

Catharine's lips never shifted, but Alex was sure she saw the hint of a smile in the way the sun caught her blue eyes. "I guess you'll need to win to find out."

And just like that Alex was left with the breath of hope, the morning of her dismay brushed precariously aside.

"Fine," she said, with a shrug of her shoulders, tipping Malcolm's hangover remedy back in one sip. "We will."

She didn't care that she was breaking every superstition in the history of sporting. Begging the Gods of Football to come crashing through the skies. If it meant Catharine Cleveland would give her another chance—that she might come to her game, sit in the stands—Alex didn't care what traditions she broke. What ancient doctrine of decorum she kicked to the wayside.

And a half an hour later she sat beside Malcolm as he drove her to her hotel.

Chapter Thirty

Ale sloshed onto the bartop as an inebriated hipster crammed his way to the counter. With foam still trapped in his meticulously trimmed beard, he eyed Catharine over the top of his thick-rimmed glasses.

"Say, love—reckon you might move down a stool?" he said, wiping his mouth on the sleeve of his too-snug Tottenham jersey.

Catharine considered telling him to sod off, but Malcolm had disappeared to the toilets and the crowd around the bar was growing denser. If she didn't move she imagined she'd end up wearing more of the man-bun's pint than he managed to get in his mouth.

Sliding to the right, she found herself jostled into a group of obstreperous uni students who were pounding the bar and yipping their armchair captaining in the direction of the television.

This was definitely not her scene.

Her phone buzzed and she elbowed her way into her purse, pulling it out to see Nathalie's name on the caller ID.

"Hang on," she said into the speaker, abandoning her spot at the bar to weave her way out of the main lounge and into the hall, where the sound level came down several decibels. "Can you hear me?" She sat down on a settee along the wall.

"I can now. Where are you?"

"I just left the mediation office."

"It's over already?" Nathalie was surprised. "What happened?"

"It's not over. It's barely even begun. He refused to come into the same room as me."

"He refu—pour l'amour de Dieu! You have to be kidding me? Wasn't he the one who set all of this up?"

"He said he thought they would be dealing directly with my counsel. He claimed he didn't know I'd be there. It's a delay tactic. He knows damn well I would never leave this to someone else's jurisdiction. I think he thinks if he jerks me around long enough I'll give in to his settlement offer."

"And will you?"

"Will I what?" Catharine couldn't hide the hostility in her tone. "Give in?"

"It's a sizable sum of money, Cate. You could start over, build something of your own—"

"Brooks Corp *is* my *own*, Nat! And it's not about the money! I don't need the money! It's the principle of the matter!"

"And if you don't reach an agreement? If he follows through on the threat to dissolve? Then where are you? Maybe it is better to listen to the Wrightmans—"

"Fuck the Wrightmans! They're halfwits!" She smacked her palm against the beer-defiled upholstery, unconcerned about her lack of decorum. She'd spent the last nine hours wearing a forced mask of propriety, listening to a panel of suits tell her what they'd decided was best for her.

"They are the most successful business solicitors in the entirety of the UK—"

"With piss poor advice! I won't take his deal! Don't ask me again."

"So what are you going to do? With no legal ground and no room for negotiation, what is your plan?"

It was a valid question. And Catharine lacked a valid answer. At the moment she didn't have a plan. She'd gone to the mediation in hopes that her father would see some form of reason. That there was no purpose in destroying the thing that made up the whole of both their legacies. The only thing that spoke to their mutual existence on this earth. But that hope had been a pipe dream. And now she could only place her faith in Gordon Liebermann—that he might find her something. A loophole. A foothold to latch onto. Something to slow the demise of the empire for which she'd toiled for the last twenty-five years.

"You'll be the first to know when I know," she admitted, a little more subdued.

"Oh, Cate…"

A roar echoed from the main bar, a cacophony of voices crying out in unison.

"Foul!"

"That's a bloody PK!"

"Get some specs, ref!"

"Sod all!"

Catharine glanced at the small flat screen in the hall, hung for those patrons waiting on the loo. An English player was writhing on the ground inside the box, clutching her ankle while medical jogged across the pitch.

"Where are you?"

"Westminster."

"More specifically."

"A sports pub."

"You went to watch the game? I thought you said you weren't interested."

"Of course I'm interested," Catharine chided, annoyed.

"Just not interested enough to actually go?"

"I was at the mediation all day. I didn't know when it was going to end."

Nathalie made a clicking sound with her tongue on the other end of the line. "Yes, I'm sure that's it."

"Believe it or not, my life is falling apart faster than silt through a pair of pantyhose, so forgive me if attending a football match wasn't at the forefront of my Saturday."

"I'm just saying… you spent the last half a year wallowing in misery over this damn girl, and when she finally comes around, you send her packing—"

"I picked her up mullered out of her mind in a park in the middle of the night! Forgive me if I don't exactly trust her judgment at the moment."

Catharine glanced at the TV. Play had restarted. The Lionesses had the ball at the US end of the pitch. It was easy to pick out Alex, her dark hair pulled up into a high bun, a teal headband at her brow. Number eleven.

"Or yours," Nathalie muttered.

"What?"

"Let's be honest, your own judgment hasn't been on par over the last few months, either, if you want to go that route. Maybe you're more worried about your own decisions than you are about trusting someone else's."

"I'm beginning to think all actors are just failed psychologists who needed to find another gig. I stopped into a pub to watch the game. I want to see her win. That's all."

"And if they do?"

"What?"

"Win."

"If they win, what?"

"Are you going to go to the final?"

"I don't know what I'm doing tomorrow, Nat, let alone a week from now. I have no idea if I will even be able to go."

"Make me a deal: if they win tonight—which is still a big *if*—tell me you'll go to that game next weekend. It'll be the biggest day of Alex's life. She deserves your time and support. If nothing else." She paused. "She doesn't have anyone else, Cate. The year's been a real ringer for her, too, you know."

Catharine flicked a crisp off the settee.

As if she could forget.

Watching the ball change possession several more times, followed by cries of celebration and injustice from the bar, she paused in the conversation as a free kick was awarded to England just outside of the eighteen.

"Why do they get to kick it from there?" Nathalie inquired, but Catharine hushed her—unwilling to admit she wasn't sure. The ins and outs of the fouls were still a mystery.

Two players from the Lionesses stood over the ball, briefly deliberating, before one rushed forward to take the shot, kicking it past the US wall of defense and just out of reach of Erin Halsey. The pub erupted, mugs thudding against the wood and clinking together while a chant of *football's coming home* made its round through the patrons.

"Fine. You're right. If they win, I'll go." It was US zero, England one.

"Promise?"

"Yes! What do you want, Nat, a pinky swear?" The woman was impossible!

"Well, if you were in front of me, I'd extract a blood oath. But I'll settle for your word. Text me when you get home?"

"You'll be in rehearsal."

"Thank you, I know my schedule. Worry about your own. You'll need a free day on Saturday." She blew a kiss into the phone.

A half an hour later Catharine was packed back into the bar with Malcolm at her side. The Scotsman had been uncommonly quiet, his shoulder angled away from her, his attention drifting away from the TV.

"Why aren't you talking to me?" she nudged his ribs, trying to avoid the flailing elbows and offensive breath of the stranger on her opposite side. The atmosphere had taken a turn for the worst with the US team leading 2-1 after a series of back-to-back goals shortly after the half.

"I don't want to look like I'm with you."

"Because I'm rooting for the Americans?"

He shot her a disdainful glance. "Your status as a turncoat has no bearing —remember, as a Scot, I'm obligated to cheer for anyone playing against England." He flicked his eyes toward a table at the back of the pub. "There's a lass back there I'm certain wants to give me her number... and take no offense, ma'am, but sitting with you is something of a hinderance."

Catharine laughed, bumping him away with her shoulder. "Then go sit somewhere else! God knows I don't want the burden of knowing I was the one to foil your sex life."

"Ma'am—"

"I mean it—go on, you're distracting me from the match!"

Without more persuading, he disappeared in the crowd, promising she'd not be out of his sight.

Attention back on the TV, Catharine couldn't hide her cheer when Alex scored a goal with only ten minutes left in the game. The commentators said something about being in the running for a golden boot while the US women swarmed in for a celebration. Alex was swung into the embrace of a towering woman with tattoos covering the entirety of her muscular arms, the name *Rodrigues* across her back. The same Rodrigues, Catharine didn't doubt, that had played part in Alex's previous weekend's adventure.

"What a bunch of todger dodgers."

A man who'd squeezed into Malcolm's vacant stool, still dressed in suit and tie, leaned close to Catharine, his chin chucked toward the television. He'd tried on several occasions to draw her into conversation, twice attempting to buy her a round, but Catharine had paid him no mind. Now, however, he'd finally gained her attention—for all the wrong reasons.

"I beg your pardon?"

"Those munters from the States—bunch of rug munchers if you ask me. It's no wonder they can beat our girls with that much testosterone running through their bodies. We might as well be playing the US men's team."

"Even worse when they're bangable," the man with the repellent breath chimed in, a Chelsea scarf wrapped around his neck, concealing the lower half of his ill-shaven face and bloodshot eyes. He looked like he'd had a pint or ten too many.

"Careful, lad, we've got a lady among us," said the desk jockey beside Catharine.

How noble. Apparently rug muncher was acceptable but bangable was not. She turned her attention back to the flatscreen spanning the wall in front of them. Eighty-four minutes.

The suit beside her was not put off.

"He's not wrong, though, if you ask me," he whispered loudly, his chin beside her cheek. "There is something of a waste when they're hot. That one—number eleven," he gestured with his cleft chin toward where Alex happened to be on the screen, "queer as a three pound pie. Big news in the states, some politician's scrubber—"

"No, ya knobhead," hissed the scarf, determined to stay part of the conversation, "not the politician, it was the poor bloke's wife. Some big wig London businesswoman. Right in the middle of his election. Colossal scandal. Last I read he was refusing to pull out—"

"Already pulled out too often, if you ask me," the suit said with an exaggerated wink, then guffawed at his tasteless ingenuity.

The scarf rapped his knuckles on the bar. "No lie. Chap deserved to lose his wife to the clam smacker if he couldn't get the job done."

"Yeah, well, her lover there is clearly good at going down in the box," the suit cracked again, motioning toward the TV. Alex was down in a tangle on the ground with one of the Lioness defenders. Both women were taking longer than usual to get to their feet. Catharine hadn't seen what had happened, distracted by the tasteless banter of the two gormless fools, but her heart sped up watching Alex clutch her left knee.

"We already know she can't handle balls."

"I don't know," the suit grinned, "I'd still let her dive on me."

"To be fair, she knows how to drive one in," the Chelsea fan quipped.

"Bet she's going to score tonight."

"Think once she gets off the pitch she knows she can use her hands?"

"Or maybe just a little head." The suit gave a repulsive gesture with his wrist.

Alex was back on her feet, the physio spraying an aerosol can at the top of her knee and finishing with a short discussion that ended in a thumbs up.

"I'd be willing to show her how to use that thumb…"

Finished, Catharine turned to her neighbor, having had enough of their revolting routine. "Is this really how you think you're going to pick up women?" She looked between the two of them. "Do neither one of you have a mother? A sister?"

"Both," chimed the imbecilic scarf, "but they're not dykes—"

"Alright, alright," the suit resumed the role of knight in shining armor, "the lady's right. This is no conversation for the ears of the fairer sex."

Rolling his eyes, the scarf opened his putrid mouth to reply, but the pub erupted in wild cheering as glasses were hoisted throughout the crowd. "GOAL" yelled the English commentator, the sound lost to chants and high fiving.

But the enthusiasm was quickly curbed as the clock ticked past the ninety minute mark with only three minutes of stoppage granted from the referee.

Catharine watched as Alex was subbed off the pitch, still favoring her left leg, but she was met with a heroes welcome from her bench, and the ailment didn't appear too detrimental.

There was one last shot by England, denied by an extraordinary save by Halsey, and then the whistle blasted three times and the match was over. The US had beaten England 3-2 in the semifinal at Wembley.

Alex was moving on to the finals of the World Cup.

Catharine kept her celebration internal, disinclined to attract any further attention from the boorish Neanderthals keeping her company. While the crowd around her drowned their sorrows in calls for another round, she pulled out her phone and texted Nathalie.

—*3-2. US. You win.*

The response was immediate.

—in this case, we both win. <a winking face emoji>

Catharine sent back an eyeroll, tucking her phone away, secretly humming with excitement.

With her promise to Nathalie, she had no choice but to go. She wouldn't be able to talk herself out of it. Convince herself otherwise. It no longer left the decision up to her.

And in truth, she was thrilled. She *wanted* to go. Even though it was going to cause a media frenzy. So be it. There was nothing left to hide. Nothing more that could be taken. From either of them.

She started to rise, knowing Malcolm would find her on her way to the door, but the suit stopped her with a hand on her arm.

"Are you leaving us so soon? Come now, it's time to drown our sorrows!" He offered her what she was sure was his best smile. "Stay awhile—tell me a bit about yourself." He gave her a sweeping glance, his eyes lingering on her chest, nodding his approval. When Catharine got home she thought she might shower in bleach. "This doesn't seem like your normal scene—what brings you to the area?"

"A football match on an accessible large screen." She unzipped a pocket on her purse, searching through it quickly.

"You know, I'm sure you hear this a lot, but you're truly gorgeous woman."

Catharine didn't look up from her pursuit. Finally finding what she was looking for, she withdrew a business card and a pen. "Kind of you to say." Out of sight, she drew a thick black line through her contact information while he kicked back on his stool, giddy.

"You're going to give me your number, aren't you?" He offered a sly grin, his eyes rotating a triangle from the card, to her face, to her breasts. "I knew it. I'm a jammy bastard tonight!"

"Of the latter, there's no doubt," she smiled brilliantly, sliding to her feet.

Oblivious to the insult, he pointed to her finger where she still wore her wedding ring. "Is there a mister? Not that I care…" He added, quickly.

"Not anymore." Shouldering her purse, she handed him the card. "There was. Not long ago. An American politician."

"Oh, intriguing." He wagged his brows. "And what do you do, Miss—" he glanced at the front of the card, containing only her name. "Miss Cleveland?"

"You could say I'm a *Big Wig London Businesswoman,*" she affected, referring to his earlier conversation with the muppet beside him. "Look me up." She gestured to the card and gave a wink, before turning on her heels and walking away.

Chapter Thirty-One

"Surreal." It was the only word she could come up with in response to the question of how it felt to win a semifinal match.

Alex leaned closer to the reporter, struggling to hear over the raucous atmosphere, the field deafened by the sonorous chants of *USA! USA! USA*! They may have been in England's house, but the US fans had shown their face.

Wiping sweat from her brow, she caught Sawyer's eye, unable to conceal her grin. The two of them were mic'd up for the *On Pitch* field interview for *ESPN*.

Deftly, Sawyer elaborated Alex's single word answers in her eloquent way. "All the hard work, the dedication of this team—the commitment every single player and staff member has put into getting us here… Simply having the opportunity to compete for your country and wear her colors… it's an honor just to be here. With this squad. This incredible group of people. There's not a woman on this team who hasn't left everything she has to give on the field to get us where we are right now."

The reporter bobbed and smiled, looking to Alex for further comment.

Alex shrugged, trying to sum up the experience—the screaming fans, the pumping adrenaline, the knowledge they were moving on to the final match. "It's a dream come true. Like I said: surreal."

"Now you, Alex, as an individual, came into this competition an underdog. There was a lot of external noise leading up to these games. Injuries. Media attention. A club league suspension. How does it feel to come full circle, knowing you've played a significant role in the United States' advancement? Now scoring six goals and three assists, trailing just one goal behind Australia's captain, Amelia Walker, for the Golden Boot. And all this as a rookie to the tournament."

Alex couldn't remember the question. The stadium was blaring *Born in the USA*, flags, banners, poster boards waving in every direction. Did she think she was on target to win the Golden Boot? Was that what she'd asked?

"I, uh—no, I mean—"

"She's too humble to tell you we're the lucky ones to have her," Sawyer cut in, saving her ass. "There's no one who works harder, with more drive, more talent, and an incredible team mentality, than our girl, Grey. I wouldn't be the only person on the squad to tell you we wouldn't be moving on to the final without her."

Once again, Alex could say nothing—but this time for an entirely different reason. Sawyer meant what she'd said. She could see it in the gleam in her eyes, the squeeze of her arm she gave off frame of the camera. A lot of people had told her how well she was doing—how impressed they were—but it hit a little different coming from her friend. Her friend who knew everything she'd gone through to get here. All the ways she'd messed up.

The interview went on to ask about the knock she'd taken late in the game—Alex assured her she was fine—and congratulated her on her second tournament award of Player of the Match.

By the time she and Sawyer got to the lockers, their teammates were showered, changed, and ready to hit the bus for a low-key celebration. Atwood had banned all alcohol leading up to the finals, but the women were looking forward to permitted downtime before the following afternoon's stretching and low resistance training session.

Last out of the showers, Alex slumped onto a seat near the back of the bus, exhausted from the cyclone of activity leading into the semis, the brutal physical play, and the depletion of adrenaline following the end of the game. On the short ride to the hotel she browsed her messages, rolling her eyes as she listened to Regina Schaff, her *Kickstar* contact, leave another voicemail of gushing support, as if the company hadn't been on the brink of firing her for the last six months, and telling her to 'holler back' if she needed anything. Apparently winning meant money, and money trumped her public outing.

There were texts from her teammates in Oakland, an all caps *YOU ARE KICKING ASS AND I AM SO FUCKING PROUD* from Rodney Collins—which had made her laugh out loud, given the contrariness to his nature—and nothing else.

While it shouldn't have surprised her, given almost everyone who mattered in her life was currently singing a horrifying off key rendition of *Nothing's Gonna Stop Us Now* by *Starship*, the shortlist of acknowledgements while on the road to her life's greatest achievement, stung.

There was nothing from her aunt and uncle, who she was certain hadn't tuned in to a single game, and—at the root of her disappointment—nothing from Catharine. She'd promised herself she wouldn't get hopeful, but as she listened to her teammates make phone calls to home as they piled out of the bus, she couldn't help but fight back a twinge of jealousy. Everyone had someone. Even Monica—whose relationship with Caleb still made her want to gag.

"So…" Halsey fell into step beside her as they dragged their sore bodies down the hall to their room. "In the likely event we end up pitted against Australia next week… how's that going to be?"

Alex ran her fingertips along the textured wallpaper. "You tell me. You're the one who'll be on the receiving end of her boot."

"Yeah, but, I wasn't sleeping with her, so it's a little easier for me to keep my focus on the ball." She shoved the keycard in the lock, shouldering open the door. "You know they'll play her box-to-box against us."

Of course she knew that. Amelia was a chameleon on the field. The Australian national team coach was never afraid to play her out of her natural position as an attacking midfielder. A habit Rodney Collins had utilized on the Sirens as well. With the high press the US would employ against the Matildas, there was no doubt Amelia would be engaged on both ends. Which meant Alex was going to have her work cut out for her in the attacking third.

"Tell me something I don't already know." She tossed her phone onto the bed and flung open the curtain. The streets were still packed with traffic from the match, the muted sounds of voices carrying up from the pedestrians waiting in half mile lines for buses, tempers short from England's loss.

"Sleeping with teammates is never a good idea?" Halsey's languorous smile lit her amber-flecked eyes. She loved pressing Alex's buttons.

Alex rolled her eyes. "Thank you for the insight, Plato."

"Is that like, the yellow dog, from Disneyland? I'm cool with that." Halsey flipped her hair in her best valley girl impersonation.

Unwilling to give her the satisfaction of a response, Alex dropped onto the couch and shook her head. Erin Halsey was goofy, and her savoir-faire wasn't up to snuff, but she'd graduated top of her class at Stanford in Symbolic Systems—a major that basically just meant you were smarter than everyone else in the room and no one was destined to understand you. A feat she loved to play down.

"Slobbering cartoon animals aside; you good?"

Alex untied one shoe and then the other. "I'm good. Whatever," she paused, searching for the right word, "*thing* there was between me and Walker, it's over and done. My only reservations for facing her on the pitch are professionally inclined."

"Like the fact that she knows every single thing about you, where your strengths and weaknesses lie, and is a hundred percent on fire for having the best World Cup of her career?"

"If that was meant to be a pep talk, you failed. You know that, right?"

Halsey was unperturbed. "There's a reason I've never been given the captain's armband. She said to tell you congrats, by the way."

Prying off a shoe, Alex chucked it toward the closet harder than she intended. She knew Amelia had stayed in touch with Halsey. It wasn't the first time a conversation between them had come up. But this one pissed her off.

"If she wanted to congratulate me, she could do it herself." Her second shoe landed on the bathroom vanity, taking a series of lotion bottles with it.

"Remind me again how good you are?" Halsey yawned, bending to collect the fallen toiletries. "I take it your rendezvous with Portland the other night wasn't of the amorous sort. If it was, I imagine you wouldn't be taking out your pent-up aggression on an innocent bottle of *Aveeno*." She righted the face lotion on the sink.

"I told you what happened."

"Yeah... what happened to get you there. You didn't mention what happened *after*, however."

"I swear to God, I never knew how many people could possibly be obsessed with my love life." Alex covered her face with a throw pillow, then peered out from beneath it. "You of all people!"

"Throw a girl a bone—it's been a dry summer."

"That's because you sweet talk almost as well as you pep talk."

"Tell me you didn't get lucky without telling me you didn't get lucky." Halsey stuck out her tongue. "Because if you had, you wouldn't be such a bitch."

Alex flung the pillow at her, which the keeper caught with a reflexive flash of her hand, smiling smugly.

"They don't call me Quicksilver for nothing."

"Oh please. You know we call you Cinderella." She waited the appropriate beat. "Because you always miss the ball."

"Har. Har. Har. So original." Halsey tossed the pillow back. "Okay, back to Portland. Is she coming to the final?"

"Haven't a clue."

"I thought you said you invited her—and she said she'd come if we won?"

"No, I said she said I'd have to win to find out."

"But was it like," she dropped her already low voice an octave and made a come-hither gesture with her index finger, "'win and you'll find out'? Or was it like," she shrugged, her tone dismissive "'win and you'll find out'?"

"I—" Alex shook her head, trying to clear the vision of Halsey's version of seductive from her mind, "please don't ever do that again. No wonder you never make it to a third date. Gross."

"Like you're one to talk. You've got women pining all over the place for you and you still can't hold a relationship down." As soon as the words were out of her mouth, Halsey's head snapped up in the mirror of the vanity, the smile wiped from her face. "Sorry, Alex. That came out way less tactful than I meant it, I swear."

All their teasing and banter aside, Halsey was acutely aware Alex had been hurting over her tumultuous state of affairs.

Alex flashed her the bird, followed by a smile. "Don't worry, a couple months headlining in the media has made my skin thicker than that."

Relieved, Halsey went back to stripping, preparing for her first of three nightly showers. Another of her weird superstitions.

"So why don't you call her up, tell her we won, maybe throw in a flowery 'I scored that goal for you,' and ask her again to come to the game?" She disappeared into the bathroom, leaving the door open to continue the conversation as the water sounded from the shower. "My sister's not coming, so I even have an extra ticket—she can sit with my aunt."

Why did it sound so simple, when she said it like that? A quick phone call. *Hey, what are you doing Saturday night?* Two people, behaving like adults. So what was the problem?

The problem was she'd waited too long—too long allowing the threats of Carlton Cleveland to control her life. And then she hadn't waited long enough. She'd stumbled out of her loneliness straight into Amelia's arms, and managed to hurt everyone—Catharine, Amelia and herself—in the process.

So now, when there was finally nothing in the way—no closet to hide in, no boyfriend to appease, no husband to circumvent, no majority shareholder to tiptoe—when Alex was finally certain of what she wanted, her reticence and reservations abandoned, Catharine had stepped away.

And Alex didn't know if she had the right to ask her back.

"I invited her once already," she said in the general direction of the bathroom. "If she wants to come, I'm sure she'll let me know."

A medley of songs from *The Lion King* belted out from the shower—Halsey's go-to after every winning competition. If they'd lost, she would have crooned out *Victor/Victoria* instead.

Before the chorus of *I Just Can't Wait to be King* started, the water was abruptly shut off and Halsey appeared wrapped in a towel, dripping in the threshold.

"I was just thinking," she leaned against the doorjamb, water pooling at her feet, "tonight—when you received that cross from Thompson and took it wide to shoot for the far post, but it deflected off the cross bar... why'd you circle round for the rebound?"

Alex paused from where she'd been plugging in her headphones, and looked over her shoulder, confused. The question was absurd. She'd missed her shot and gotten lucky on the trajectory of the rebound, finding a second chance to bury it at the near post instead. "What do you mean?"

"Like—you missed the first shot. Why'd you try again?"

"Was the water too cold in the shower? Are you suffering from brain freeze?" Alex plugged in her phone.

"No, really. If you'd already taken the shot once, why'd you give it a second go?"

"Um..." Alex lifted her eyebrows, "I wanted to score?"

"Oh. Okay. So you failed the first time, so you just tried again. Got it. Thanks." Halsey disappeared from the doorway and instead of *Hakuna Matata*, the lyrics of *Try, Try Again* echoed off the bathroom walls as the sound of the shower resumed.

Writing off Halsey's weirdness to simply being Halsey, Alex reorganized her suitcase and settled onto her bed. She knew half her teammates were hanging out in the rooftop jacuzzi, while the other half shot pool in the rec room, but tonight she felt like being an old lady and curling up with a book.

Two pages in, she set the novel down, laughing to herself.

Why'd you try again? It had been such a stupid question. The answer was obvious.

As obvious as Alex was obtuse. Halsey hadn't been talking about football.

She'd missed the first time, so the answer was to try again.

The goalkeeper's way of waxing poetic. Apparently that's what a degree in Symbolic Systems got you.

Try, try again.

Fine.

She unplugged her phone and checked the time. It was late. Just after eleven.

"Hey," she tucked her head into the steaming bathroom, "I'm going to go out for a little bit."

"I didn't mean for you to take "score" literally. I was kind of just thinking a phone call."

Alex laughed. "I'll be back before you've gotten through *Can You Feel the Love Tonight*. Scout's honor!" and pulled the door closed behind her.

Chapter Thirty-Two

Rounding the corner from the parking garage, Catharine's steps faltered. There was the usual Saturday night foot traffic along the quaint Shad Thames neighborhood—comprised of a mixture of luxury flats and chic shops and eateries—but the gathering at the entrance to her flat was unexpected.

Reporters, a dozen or so, were camped out on the corner, lurking beside the centuries-old brick building.

Since arriving in London, her harassment by the press had remained exclusive to her comings and goings from the downtown business office of the Wrightman Firm. She'd yet to be harried at her home.

"Shall I disperse them, ma'am?"

Catharine ignored the glint in Malcolm's eye. There was nothing he'd enjoy more.

"No. Whatever it is, I may as well get it over with." She steeled herself with a breath, resuming her determined steps. She'd not been made aware of any new uproar that would send the media hounds to her door.

"Mrs. Cleveland—" A seersucker suit was the first to notice her.

"Mrs. Cleveland—" A dozen voices followed suit.

Malcolm took a protective step in front of her, shielding her from the various cameras shoved toward her face.

"One at a time, lads."

There was something in the Scot's easy demeanor that was always received with caution. His smile, perhaps, that promised he was anything but posturing.

The seersucker suit opted for the first turn. "Do you have comment, Mrs. Cleveland, on this evening's announcement of the abolishment of the HOPE Foundation?"

Catharine knew her face betrayed the fact that she'd been caught unaware. Nicole, who'd resigned from her twenty-one year employment with Brooks Corp. the day Catharine had been relieved of her position as CEO, had assumed a role as an independent contractor working directly for Catharine. She'd made it part of her daily report to inform on any upcoming actions pending by the corporation, but this time the media had had the jump on the scoop.

The HOPE Foundation provided far more than free education. It provided safe housing, living expenses, medical insurance for those attending school. It wasn't something that could safely have the plug pulled without catastrophic backlash to those counting on its aid.

"I—" Catharine cycled through several responses, deciding the best tactic was honesty, despite breaking the cardinal rule of never allowing the press to know they'd gotten the upper hand. "I was not aware of this development. It goes without saying that I vehemently disapprove of any actions defunding an organization dedicated to providing assistance to those in need of a helping hand."

"The official statement from WorldCargo indicated the charitable cuts were made due to a tightening on funds. Could you perhaps comment, then, on the sizable contribution donated the same day to a political action committee backing Senator Cleveland's presidential campaign?"

Catharine wasn't fast enough to answer. Her brain froze on the implication her father was funding Carlton's campaign. He had seen the photo of what Carlton had done to her. The entire world had. Yet still... It was one thing to go after her through the corporation. Fire her. Try and force her to sell her shares. Hit her where it hurt by ending the charities and nonprofits she had built. But to slap her so personally in such a public manner—to make a public showing of support to the man she'd accused of blatant abuse. To align himself with the man she was divorcing...

"Is it to be assumed, Mrs. Cleveland, as you are still a significant shareholder of Brooks Corporation, that you continue to support your husband's campaign, even through your divorce?"

She felt Malcolm's hand on her back, ushering her forward.

"It's late, lads—"

"I would sooner vote for a gorilla in a three-piece suit than cast my support behind Carlton Cleveland! And you can put *that* on your headlines."

The reporter looked startled, before jotting a word in his notebook.

Behind him a middle-aged woman in khakis held up her hand. "Do you have comment on Senator Cleveland going into the RNC showing a nominal lead?"

Only that his followers would vote for a baboon if it promised them a tax break.

Instead, she applauded herself for saying, "I have faith in the American people to vote for the candidate who will best represent the country without personal agenda."

"Speaking of Americans," another reporter—this time a man in a half-tucked button-up and jeans—leaned forward, his mobile phone recording the interaction, "I'm sure you are aware the US football team beat the Lionesses this evening in the semifinals. It's no secret your name has been linked to the States' breakout star, Alex Grey. Do you have thoughts on the coming match?"

Catharine turned toward the steps leading to the private entrance of her lift. Business was one thing. Personal became another. But before she started up the stairs, she reconsidered. It was a football match, for heaven's sake. There was no reason she couldn't answer.

"Yes," she turned back to face him. "In fact I watched the game tonight. The Lionesses put up an impressive battle, but seemed to have no answer for the high press of the American team." God, she hoped that was the right term. "The United States are ranked number one in the world. It should be no surprise they've shown a dominant performance throughout the tournament."

"Safe to say you are a fan of Alex Grey, Mrs. Cleveland?"

"Myself and millions of others, no doubt. She is tremendously talented, as exhibited."

"And the allegations as to the nature of your relationship?"

Allegations. The implication they had done something wrong. Something illegal. She should have continued into the building when she had the chance. She knew better than to let it get this far.

"I hold Miss Grey in the highest esteem as both a professional and a friend. It goes without saying I wish her the best of luck this coming weekend—though luck plays no part in her talent on the field." She hated herself even as she said it. The canned response. The safe distancing. Even now, when she had nothing left to lose—she carefully stepped away.

"Then you deny the reported nature of your relationship with Alex Grey, Mrs. Cleveland?"

For a man who couldn't properly tuck his own shirt or dust off his trainers, he had some audacity to stand on her doorstep and pry into her personal life with an iPhone shoved in her face.

Her mouth lunged to a defensive response, but her brain convinced her lips into a beguiling smile. "How tactless you must think me if you really think I'd kiss-and-tell?" She reached forward, her manicured fingertip pointing out a misaligned button on his shirt. "Good night, everyone. That's all the questions for now."

A discordant medley of voices called after her, but she didn't turn back around.

"Well," said Malcolm in the lift, leaning against the wall, "you gave them something to haver about this time, ma'am."

"What?" Catharine raised a brow. "As the newly self-appointed head of my PR team, you don't approve of my use of kiss-and-tell?"

"I was actually thinking of 'gorilla in a three-piece suit.'" He stepped backward out of the lift when the door slid open on his floor. "And a man would have to be a masochist to self-appoint himself onto your PR team, ma'am." With a wink and doff of an imaginary hat, he disappeared behind the closing doors.

Settling upstairs, she resisted the urge to pull out her MacBook and search the news on the defunding of the HOPE Foundation. Or the campaign contribution from her father. She didn't doubt Nicole would have an entire spreadsheet on both accounts sitting in her inbox come morning. Instead, she took up residence on the settee in her indoor terrace and thought about texting Alex.

But it was late, and despite her intention to uphold her agreement with Nathalie to attend the match the following weekend, she still held reservations about how she wished to move forward. Attending a game was one thing. Opening the door to further conversation was another.

It was evident Alex had experienced a change of heart since her curt text the month before, but how long would her transformation last? Or had it just been born of the calamity of her misadventure?

Catharine didn't want to find herself hurt again. With everything else falling apart in her life, she didn't think her heart could take it.

In an attempt to shift her focus, she turned her attention to browsing the London Stock Exchange, still wound up from the confrontation with the reporters. *Allegations.* The word soured at the back of her mind. She was so tired of hiding behind doublespeak and evasion.

Amidst a revolving soundtrack of things she wished she'd said—always so much simpler in hindsight—she was lured from her thoughts by the vibrating of her mobile.

It was late. After midnight. The caller ID showed Alex Grey.

She let it vibrate three more times before finally picking up.

"Alex?"

"I'm sorry, I know it's late."

Catharine waited, uncertain the purpose of the phone call.

"I'm not drunk, I swear."

It wasn't the first place her mind had travelled, but after the previous weekend, the disclaimer was fair.

"Is everything all right?"

"Could I see you? Just for a few minutes." Her breath was short, as if she'd been running.

"Where are you?"

"On the street below."

Catharine stood. "In Butler's Wharf?"

"Or we can talk on the phone, if you'd rather—"

"I'll buzz you up."

By the time Catharine had taken the five flights of stairs from her master suite at the top floor of her flat, to the seventh floor sitting room, where her residence began, Alex was stepping off the private lift that ran the distance from street level. Dressed in joggers and Vans, with a tank that looked more like it was meant for sleeping, her cheeks were pink with exertion, her hair falling from a messy bun into her face. She was disheveled, but smiling, albeit self-consciously.

"Hi," she stopped a few feet out of the elevator, wiping a quick arm across her face. "My cab dropped me at the Millennium Bridge by accident." It explained her breathlessness. "I'm sorry if I woke you. I admit the idea sounded a lot better on the drive over than it actually does standing here, now."

Catharine stood in the center of the room, uncertain how to receive the unexpected house call. She couldn't begin to guess what had brought Alex all the way to Bermondsey in the middle of the night. She should have been celebrating with her team. Or locked away on curfew. Anything other than a midnight run.

"Do you want to sit?" She gestured toward the long dining table, meant to seat far more people than Catharine ever intended to entertain.

Alex shook her head. "No, I'm good right here. I won't keep you long, I promise." Her gaze took a momentary tour of the vastness of the open floor plan, seeing it, Catharine realized, for the first time. The previous weekend she'd seen very little of the flat—primarily the floor of her ensuite bathroom; a memory they both undoubtedly wished to put from their minds.

"I know I must seem crazy, showing up here uninvited." Her attention returned to Catharine. "Especially after my snafu last weekend. And I tried to tell myself a hundred different ways this wasn't a very good plan, but honestly, I couldn't sleep without seeing you first. So, good or bad, here I am." She laughed, and Catharine realized she was more anxious than she let on, her weight shifting from foot-to-foot as she tried to maintain her nerve.

"I realized something tonight, after my game. I mean, it wasn't something new, but it was more obvious than ever—and I couldn't ignore it anymore." She spoke quickly, the words all strung together, her breathing short. "Tonight was the biggest night of my career—no, my *life*… my *entire* life. And when I stepped off that field after the final whistle, I realized there was no one else on earth I wanted to share it with more than you. You were the only person I wanted to call. You were the only person I wanted to look for in the stands. And I know I've made a lot of stupid decisions… that I've not gone about things the way I should have. I don't deny any of it. I've pushed you away and kept you at arms length, almost since the day we met. I think I've always been scared—scared that I don't deserve you. That I would never have enough to offer. And if I'm honest, I still don't know if I ever will. But of one thing I am positive—I love you. And I'm in love with you. Madly. Impossibly. Entirely. Whether it's right or wrong."

She took a moment to rally her courage to continue as Catharine said nothing, just watched her from the center of the room.

"I've been in love with you since that first night you came to Portland—since the moment we ran drenched through the parking lot to your car, and spent the rest of the early hours of the morning talking in your suite. I didn't know what it was—I'd never felt like that about anyone before—but I knew I never wanted that night to end. And it's been like that every day and every hour and every second we have spent together since. And it's been intense and wild and sometimes so out of my control, I didn't know what to do with it. And the more in love with you I fell, the more I felt like I had to keep my distance, because I didn't know what I would do if one day you decided I wasn't enough. Because I knew you could have anyone—and I only wanted you.

"So when Carlton came to me that day with his threats and his photos—it was almost a relief. It forced me to give you up. It forced me to say good-bye before you could grow tired of me and let me go. It seemed the less painful option in the long run. So I took it." She inhaled a shaky breath. "And I know you think I just put it all behind me and moved ahead with Amelia. That my life just carried on. But what you don't know is I wasn't able to let you go for a single second. I couldn't move forward at all." Her gaze had shifted to the tile floor, but now she forced it back to meet Catharine's eyes. "I was in a dark place and Amelia knew that. I was drowning and she offered me a lifeline. That's all it was. That's all it ever was. She and I both knew from the beginning that it wouldn't last. Because I was still in love with you."

Somewhere behind them the wall clock opposite the dining room table ticked out the quiet seconds like a metronome. One beat for every two of Catharine's racing heart.

Driving her hands in her pockets to keep from fidgeting, Alex continued. "I've tried every way I could think of to let you go. I've hurt myself, and I've hurt others, and done a lot of things I'm not proud of. And all of it to no avail. None of it mattered. None of it made any difference. And tonight, coming off the greatest high of my life after that match, I knew I couldn't go another night without telling you how I felt. Even if you've moved on—even if you don't have another chance to give me—I had to tell you. Because the weight of leaving it unsaid is more than I want to carry around any longer."

Drawing in a deep, unsteady breath, she let her shoulders sag, her piece said. Whatever courage she'd found had waned, and her eyes shifted to the escape of the city view that filled the sitting room window, the towers lit in sharp contrast to the midnight sky.

Catharine wasn't fast to reply. Her mind was revolving, swimming, filtering through all she had said.

No one had ever directly told her they loved her. Not like this.

Not her mother, though she'd known while growing up the sentiment was there—it was simply never anything they'd said. And though she and Nathalie had shared the three words between them, it was meant in a different way. The closing of a phone call, the parting at an airport, the laughing admission: *I love you, my friend.* But it wasn't having someone look you in the eye and tell you they loved you. Not even when she and Nathalie had been at the depth of their affair had the articulation been put between them.

It wasn't something Catharine found easy to convey.

And perhaps, in her coolness, in her conservation, in her need for control, she'd never been able to give Alex reason enough to see beyond her lack of expression. To believe it meant as much to her as it did to Alex.

"It is on both of us, Alex," she said at last, not knowing where else to start. "I was careless, dragging you into this brutal, unstable life of mine and I didn't do enough to protect you."

"You don't always have to protect me, you know?" Alex made to take a step forward, but changed her mind, rooting herself to the floor. "You didn't drag me into anything. I *wanted* to be part of your life. I *want* to be still, if you'll have me."

"Even now?" The smile that caught Catharine's lips was pinched with derision, her words catching in her throat. "With everything falling apart?"

"Especially now."

She had a choice between a sob and a laugh, and ended with a combination of the two, the back of her hand quickly brushing across her eyes. Why anyone would wish to be part of the nightmare her life had evolved to—when she had nothing to offer—nothing to give—was beyond her. If she continued to fight, which she intended to do, she could lose it all.

"It's probably going to get a lot worse over the next few weeks," she said once she was certain she could trust her voice again. The irony that Alex was at the pinnacle of her career was not lost on her. How the tables had turned.

"So let me love you through it, Catharine." A tranquility had come over Alex with the unburdening of her declaration. Her eyes were bright, pricked with the same threat of tears as Catharine's own, and the sincerity in her voice quivered. "Let me be there for you. Please."

Catharine blew out a slow exhale. "I don't even know where we'd start again."

"All over. From the very beginning. And this time with nothing to hide and no one to hide it from." An unhurried smile crept across her lips, her eyes twinkling. "I think this is where I warn you I'm a footballer. That my career is unstable and unpredictable with an incredibly short shelf life and no where near as glamorous as people think it is. I travel a lot, and you'll almost never see me, and when you do, I'm usually banged up and tired. But I can sometimes get you free tickets to the games, if you're into that sort of thing."

Catharine couldn't help but laugh, feeling the heaviness gathered from the tension of the conversation begin to dissipate, her guard slowly letting down.

"In turn I suppose I'm obligated to tell you I'm unemployed and going through a messy divorce and my father has a tendency to overreact when he finds out about my girlfriends. I've never been much of the sporting type, but I'd be glad to enthusiastically cheer for you when the ball goes your direction." She fiddled with the wedding ring that had worn an indent on her finger.

"Sounds like a pretty good match to me."

Catharine smiled. "A pretty good match indeed."

"I have a game this Saturday. It's kind of a big one. Would you want to come?"

Catharine feigned indifference. "I suppose. First date?"

Alex's dimples deepened. "First date."

For a long moment they looked at each other, neither in a hurry to break the comfortable silence. How good it felt just to stand there, with all of the hurt and uncertainty washed away, with the promise of a clean slate… a fresh start. The real possibility of something lasting.

Catharine looked down to find she was still fiddling with her wedding ring, and pulled it from her finger, examining the golden band soldered to the diamond engagement ring. She'd worn more than half her life. The sight of it was repugnant—memories of everything in her life she wanted to forget. It had no place on her finger now, but had remained simply out of habit.

"Probably time to cast this lot into the Thames." She turned it over and over, reveling in the freedom of having the metal absent from her skin.

"Oh, maybe keep it a little longer." There was a teasing tone in Alex's voice as she looked up to catch her smiling eyes. "We might need to hawk it to get home on the course we're both on."

"I'd imagine there's a bonus if you win the World Cup?"

"Not worth as much as that ring, I assure you," Alex laughed, and finally glanced at her watch, her smile fading. "I probably should get going."

Catharine gave a half nod. "I imagine at this point you've well bypassed your curfew."

"Well, technically I was in my room when curfew came—I left shortly after. So it's a bit of a gray area."

"You could stay? I could drive you back in the morning." She knew it was entirely irresponsible—Alex was already treading on thin ice—but she wasn't able to put aside her desire to keep her there. To share whatever few hours were left before the dawn.

At once the smile was back, her dark eyebrows arched in mock incredulity. "I don't know what kind of girl you take me for, Mrs. Cleveland, but if I've given you the wrong idea…" Despite her teasing she came forward, closing the distance between them, and stopped an arms length from Catharine, reaching to take her hands. "I'm going to go back to the hotel." Her voice was soft, filled with her own longing, her thumbs brushing the skin of Catharine's wrists, before squeezing her fingers. "And not just because Halsey is going to string me up and leave me for the wolves if she has to lie for me again." She brought one of Catharine's palms to her lips, kissing the warmth of her skin. "But because, no matter what happens this weekend, it gives me something to look forward to—knowing you'll be waiting for me. That you'll be there for me. It makes a win all the sweeter. And a loss more bearable."

"A win," Catharine whispered, before gently extracting her hand from Alex's hold. "I have faith in you."

"You promise you'll come?"

"I wouldn't miss it for the world." She leaned forward, their lips brushing, her heart in her throat, before stepping back abruptly. "Go, Alex. I'll see you Saturday."

Chapter Thirty-Three

Lying flat on her back, a pillow covering her face, her arms folded across her chest, Alex counted the beats of her exhalations. She'd spent hours visualizing the day ahead, sleep escaping her. For the past two days a silence had fallen across her teammates, their minds tuned to the match to come. A match now less than four hours from kickoff.

The door opened and someone slipped into the room, but whoever it was had enough sense to remain quiet while Alex and Halsey completed their pre-game rituals.

Finishing her meditation, Alex pulled the pillow from her face to find Sawyer standing in the center of the room. Her eyes were on Halsey, folded into a child's pose beneath the window, her eyes shut and the faint sound of *Metallica* humming from her headphones.

"Sounds like she's on the final track," Alex whispered, glancing at the goalkeeper, before throwing her feet over the side of the bed and stretching her fingers to her toes.

"She's really got a screw loose." Sawyer shook her head, a crease running along her brow. "Who listens to music they hate to psyche themselves up for a game they love?"

"I'm not deaf, you know." Halsey rolled her long frame out of her position and fluidly sprung to her feet, stretching her arms into a mountain pose.

"You will be, after listening to that garbage." Sawyer settled on the foot of Alex's bed.

"It was the track playing on the bus the day we won—"

"—the College Cup Championship your senior year. You've listened to it every game ever since. Yes, I know. You won't let us forget. It's just, you *hate* heavy metal."

Halsey shrugged. "I love winning."

"Fair enough." Sawyer turned to Alex. "You pack your lucky foot today?"

"No, I thought I might leave it in my suitcase."

Sawyer stuck out her tongue. "You ready for this?"

Alex shook her head. "I'm a little torn between puking, skipping out to go sightseeing, or dragging myself down to the bus."

"You know what's scarier than not winning a World Cup? Atwood. When we're late. So pack it up." She hopped to her feet and clapped her hands, heading for the door.

The vibe on the bus was electric, though noticeably quieter than it had been the previous six games. Nerves were strung taut and both players and tech staff were existing in their own private zones. Alex took a seat between Sawyer and Halsey and slipped in her AirPods, staring out the window at the hordes of foot traffic flocking toward the stadium.

By the end of the night, one team would reign the next four years as World Champions. And twenty-three other women would go home broken-hearted.

The USA vs. Australia.

Try as she might, Alex couldn't push thoughts of Amelia from her mind. Ever since Australia had toppled Germany to move on to the final.

She knew what this game meant to her. The final huzzah to her career. A chance the Australian had been waiting for—for almost twenty years. Tonight, when Amelia stepped on the pitch, she'd be making history as the youngest player to compete in her fifth World Cup. But only the first time reaching the finals.

And then there was Alex. Tonight, if all went as planned, she'd pull on the Stars and Stripes for the twenty-seventh game of her international career. Over one hundred fewer caps than Australia's captain. The two of them neck-and-neck to earn the top goal scoring achievement of the tournament, The Golden Boot. Alex with six goals. Amelia with seven.

Coming into this, Alex had expected to be a bench warmer. A seventy-five minute sub to give the starters a breather.

And tonight she felt like her entire team was counting on her.

She tried to refocus as the bus crawled along the main road to the back entrance of the stadium, fans waving and screaming as they rolled along.

It was still uncanny, hearing her name screamed from strangers' lips. Men, women and children wearing her number with her name on their backs. Signs—some funny, some cute, some a little uncomfortable—*Marry Me, Hollywood* she'd found amusing but *I'd Go Gay for Grey* had made her cringe—carried by every age, gender and walk of life she could imagine. It was humbling. It was scary. And a little unnerving. Two years ago she'd had to constantly correct her own admin on the spelling of her last name—Grey with an *e*, please—but that time was long past. Here, people stopped her on the streets—there wasn't an American player on the roster that wasn't identifiable well beyond just the die hard football fans—but with Alex's added—*unwanted*—media attention, her recognizability had been taken to a whole new level. She posed for selfies with grinning teenagers while in line for coffee, the images instantly uploaded to SnapChat and Instagram. Graciously—albeit awkwardly—thanked middle-aged men in restaurants who tried to buy her drinks, signed autographs on her way to and from the busses, and smiled for an endless number of fan photographs with children who told her they couldn't wait to play on the USWNT when they grew up —and be just like her. While all the while she was wishing for a moment of the anonymity she'd enjoyed as an unsponsored, unendorsed striker on Rage FC. Just enough time to breathe without the eyes of the world watching.

But would she give this moment up for that life again? That privacy?

Looking out the window at the throngs of American fans funneling toward the stadium, high on the excitement of the coming match, journeyed thousands of miles to show their support for a team they believed in, Alex knew she would change nothing. In a matter of hours she would pull on her country's colors, listen to her National Anthem, and be given the chance to play the world's most beautiful game in an effort to fight for the right to claim its most prestigious title. And all of that with a squad of the most talented players the world had ever seen.

If this tournament wasn't what dreams were made of, she didn't know what was.

A sign being waved in front of their bus caught her eye, the letters printed in green and gold.

Can't keep us down! Aussie Aussie Aussie, Oi Oi Oi!

While the US was favored to win the match, the Australians had been expected to wash out in the group stage. And every knockout round after. But by the time they'd reached the semifinals, the media was singing a different tune. Maybe it was possible…maybe it was the year of the underdogs? And then they'd decimated Germany, shut them down four to nil, and the world was eyeing the Matildas with a new respect that had come hard earned.

Odds meant nothing. The game belonged to the team that fought the hardest. The team that left the most on the field. The team that was willing to push the furthest beyond their physical and mental barriers and supersede their limits at any cost.

That was the team that would win.

Beside the *Aussie Aussie Aussie* sign, another Matildas' fan held up a second sign. In large block letters it read *AM|EX* with a line drawn through the center of the *M* and *E*. Below it, it said: *EX About To Get Axed*!

"Ohh, that one's clever," Halsey nudged Alex, shooting her a wag of her brow. "Bet it cost her a lot of brain cells to come up with that."

Alex tried to laugh, turning her face away from the crowd. She didn't want her friend to know how much it stung.

Amelia had been her best friend. And the thought of facing her on the pitch in a few short hours prodded at a wound that hadn't had time to heal. Again, Halsey leaned close to her ear. "If I had a marker, I'd write *AM Gonna Get Slammed* on the window." She winked, and patted Alex's leg. "Let it go, Grey. Ninety minutes. Shut it all away."

Ninety minutes. She could do that.

In the locker room Alex listened to *Green Day* while pulling on her gear in the exact same order as she'd done since her first game at Clemson. As always, she left her left sock down around her ankle—something she would pull up after the handshake. Around her, her teammates carried on with their same strange, individual rituals, the room bursting with silent energy.

Two and a half hours later, the twenty-two starting players for the FIFA Women's World Cup Finals walked solemnly out of the tunnels of Wembley Stadium, each lost in their own thoughts of the ninety minutes that lie ahead.

The stadium was sold out. Ninety thousand fans from across the globe packed into the largest venue in the UK, anxiously awaiting the start of what was promising to be a match to remember.

Throughout the singing of both National Anthems, Alex kept her eyes glued to the US flag that was held aloft by two dozen veterans standing at attention, willing her heart to steady and mind to clear. She could feel the pulse of the stadium straight into the core of her bones. The collective breath held as the final notes of *Advance Australia Fair* echoed over the sound system.

As the tidal roar erupted from the crowd, Alex stole a glance toward the sidelines where the majority of the allotted tickets for the US team were grouped. Section one twenty-five, row three, seat sixty-eight. She didn't allow herself the acknowledgement that it was embarrassing to know the number by heart.

There, somewhere just a few rows back from the touchlines, Catharine was sitting with Halsey's aunt. They would make an odd duo, but there was no one in the world who didn't love Clancy Halsey, with her warm Mississippi accent and beaming smile and hugs that smelled like cookie dough.

Alex had only spoken to Catharine once since leaving her apartment. A quick call to let her know where to find her ticket. But Monica Ashby hadn't missed the opportunity at breakfast a few days earlier to point out the *Daily Express* feature, where Catharine was quoted comparing Senator Cleveland to a gorilla, and commenting on the semifinal soccer match.

Over cereal and orange juice, Alex had scanned the fine print, finding her name mentioned yet again. "*In regards to her relationship with Alex Grey, Mrs. Cleveland played coy, stating she was raised better than to kiss-and-tell,*" the article paraphrased. For once, Alex hadn't winced. If Monica had thought the article would embarrass Alex, it'd had the opposite effect.

She'd worried a bit how the press would treat her at the finals, but Sawyer had reminded her she was a 'grown-ass woman' who could handle herself. And after that, Alex had only looked forward to having her at the match.

But the thoughts of Catharine quickly extinguished as the two teams split apart. Around them the stands were a blur of red, white and blue—green and gold. A living, breathing, organism of energy. The signs, the chants, the drums, the flags and banners, all took a backseat accompaniment to Alex's thundering heart. If the American fanbase was larger, the Australians made up for numbers with unquenchable zeal, their wild enthusiasm off the charts. Decades they'd been waiting to see their colors hoisted on the world stage.

Holding with tradition, both sets of starting eleven crossed each other for a good sportsmanship handshake, and for the first time in months, Alex found herself reaching for Amelia's hand.

"Chookas, Grey." The Australian captain met her eye, clasping her fingers in her own, greeting her with the familiar well-wishes she'd said to her before every game back home.

Alex's mouth opened and closed without any sound coming out, but before she could dwell on it, they were off, jogging toward the center circle, where the US would take the kickoff after losing the coin toss.

Chapter Thirty-Four

"We've got company, ma'am."

Catharine had been looking out the passenger side window, having ridden up front with Malcolm. Now, as they pulled into the slow procession of the pedestrian drop zone, she turned to see his focus on the rearview mirror, watching something on the sidewalk.

"Reporters, I think. Dressed too fancy to be the pap."

"Mm." Catharine murmured her acknowledgement. She'd not imagined she'd be left in peace. But reporters she could handle. Paparazzi were relentless.

"Here is fine," she said to him as they crossed the first cone indicating *drop-off.*

"I can get closer." He'd not been keen on the afternoon's arrangement. The match had been sold out and she'd only managed to get him a seat in the nosebleed section opposite the side where she was sitting. Since their seats weren't together, she'd insisted he drop her off up front before he parked so she could meet Erin Halsey's aunt to pick up her ticket.

"My legs do function, Malcolm."

"Aye, but you pay me so you don't have to use them."

"Well, the way things are going, there might be one less zero on your next paycheck."

"In that case," he tapped the brakes harder than necessary, pulling to the curb, "out ya go." But even in his cheekiness, he was sprung from the driver door and holding hers before she had unclipped her seatbelt. A car honked behind them, to which he paid no attention. "I don't love leaving you on your own."

She stepped onto the curb, aware of the handful of waiting reporters standing some hundred feet away who'd trailed her through the parking lot. "Difficult to comprehend, but I'll somehow survive without you."

"Not when the English find out one of their own is a traitor to their people. Sporting tradition demands you root against the team who knocked your country out of the competition."

"And what does tradition demand when the captain of the opposing team is the one who's been sleeping with your girlfriend?"

"In that case, fuck the Australians, ma'am." He gave her a flippant salute, before returning languidly to the driver's side door, amusing himself with the line of angry drivers held up behind him. "Phone call away when you need me."

She waved him off and joined the throng of people heading toward the colossal arch above the Wembley box office, hoping, if she moved quickly enough, she might lose her tail of reporters in the chaos of the crowd.

A woman in her mid-fifties, round in her face and thick through her middle, with a Mississippi accent as smooth as molasses, greeted Catharine at the top of the stairs with an enthusiastic smile. Her cheeks were painted in red, white, and blue—the US soccer crest on one side and "I Believe" on the other.

"Mrs. Cleveland?" She tugged self-consciously at the yellow goalkeeping jersey she wore, a number one ironed across the front, and no doubt her niece's name embroidered along the back. She appeared oblivious to the sea of people parting around her. "Mrs. Cleveland!" she decided without confirmation. "Clancy Halsey!" She offered a hand with nails painted in tiny American flags and shook Catharine's vigorously. "It's really a pleasure, ma'am! When Erin told me you'd be coming, well—I'm tickled pink and a bit twitchy at the same time. But I promised my niece I'd try not to embarrass her, so—" she shimmied her round shoulders in nervous exasperation, "well, I'll do my best."

Catharine smiled and the woman visibly relaxed, still clutching her hand, having forgotten to let go. "You're very gracious to allow me to sit with you, Ms. Halsey."

"Oh, heavens, please, it's just Clancy. We leave Halsey for Erin. And, well, ma'am, I couldn't be happier that it all worked out as it did, having the extra ticket and all. Erin's little sister went and found herself, um, to put it delicately, in the family way, if you catch my drift," she patted her rotund middle, clucking as she shook her head, "so I made the trip solo. I've always wanted to see London, but knew if I waited long enough, Erin would have a big game here to make the trip worthwhile."

"Mrs. Cleveland?" A woman's voice broke into the conversation from behind them. Catharine glanced over her shoulder to find a brunette in a tweed pant suit a few steps below her. She looked familiar, and Catharine thought she may have been part of the group who had waited for her in Shad Thames outside her flat. To her left was a second reporter, half his face hidden behind an ill-trimmed beard, and behind him a photographer deploying the lens of his camera in her direction.

"Have you come to watch the match, Mrs. Cleveland?" the brunette inquired.

"Is there a match today?" asked Catharine, annoyed with the sound of the photographer's shutter. "I hadn't heard."

"I—" the woman opened and closed her mouth, and Catharine almost felt sorry.

The beard inserted himself into the query. "Is it safe to assume you're here to cheer on the American team, Catharine?"

Unaccustomed—and unappreciative—of his familiarity using her first name, she gave him a pointed smile. "As an Englishman, I'm stunned you'd suggest we cheer on the team who knocked us out of the semifinals."

In the pause that ensued while the reporters worked out that they were being played, Clancy Halsey bullied her way down a step, forcing herself between the trio and Catharine. "Have y'all no manners here—bustin' in where you weren't invited? Surely your mamas raised you better than that." She shooed at them, planting her hand in front of the lens of the camera, kissing at them to step along as if they were livestock. "Get on, now. Can't a woman enjoy a soccer game without being accosted?"

The trio of media stared at her, uncertain what to make of the situation, but the southern woman stared straight on back with no sign of backing down.

The brunette conceded. "Enjoy the match, Mrs. Cleveland. And best of luck to Alex Grey tonight—she's been exciting to watch throughout the tournament."

"You don't need luck when you've got skill!" Clancy snapped, tugging at the USWNT scarf around her neck. With a huff she turned to Catharine, placing a hand on her arm to lead her toward the entrance. "Come along, Mrs. Cleveland. Some folks just forget to load their brain before they shoot their mouth off." She shook her head as they filtered through the turnstiles. "Erin mentioned you might have to deal with that. Folks just can't manage to mind their own business, always sticking their noses where they don't belong."

As they came to the staircase leading down toward the pitch, she lowered her voice, close to Catharine's ear. "I know it isn't my place to say, but I'm sure sorry about the rigamarole you and Alex were put through. Being in the news like that—having your personal lives turned inside out by numbskulls that have no right to make judgment on anyone's lives save their own—well, I just can't hardly imagine. Like I've always told Erin: love is love is love. I knew as a toddlin' terror my niece was going to be something special. Her folks—my own brother, God help me—didn't feel the same. They haven't spoke a word to her since Erin found the courage to own her truth in high school. Tossed her out like a bag of rotten apples and still have the audacity to call themselves good Christians. Well, *my* Lord sure doesn't care about a thing like that. I took Erin in, loved her as my own, tried to make sure she never felt the sting of what her parents did to her. I doubt my love ever made up for any of it—nothing can replace that love and respect you hanker for from your folks—but I tell you, that girl has made my life a world of joy. Every time I see her step out onto that field all I can think is how it's her parents who are the ones missing out. They've never seen her in a single game. Comin' into her third World Cup and not a word. I'll never understand it, no ma'am." They'd arrived at their seats, but the rows nearest them were still empty, the patrons getting beer and merchandise before the players took the field. "Listen to me prattle on," she admonished herself, settling with a huff, leaving Catharine the more favorable aisle seat. "Forgive me, Mrs. Cleveland. I guess all I'm trying to say is I love Alex—known her since she was just out of Clemson. She was always a beautiful, smart, talented girl—but she just wasn't blossoming in South Carolina. Like planting a tulip in the mud. And then one day, after she and Erin got moved to California, I came to a game and you could just see she was glowing. There was something different about her. I didn't know it at the time, and, well, you'll have to forgive me for reading into those gossip pieces, but I couldn't help but notice if anything those papers said was true, the timeline fit just about the time that you two found each other. She seemed to find herself. Her stride. Her mojo, if you will. And I just have to say I couldn't be more thrilled knowing she's found someone who makes her happy. She's always been so worried about pleasing everyone else, she never took anything for herself. It's her turn."

The woman finally sat back and took a deep breath, the colorful paint on her face glistening in the hot afternoon sun. She'd chatted on with hardly a pause, but Catharine didn't mind. She found her affable and genuine and loved the obvious affection and adoration she felt for her niece. It was clear Alex's gangly, happy-go-lucky teammate may have lived a very different life with a very different outcome if it weren't for the unconditional love of this woman. If only every family had a Clancy to pick up the pieces where those who were supposed to love you most had failed.

The steady hum of the crowd suddenly notched upward and Catharine followed Clancy's eyes as they flicked toward the grass to see the US squad filtering out of the tunnel, the Australian team right behind them. They were in their warm-up attire, jogging toward their respective sides, preparing to run through drills and exercises to loosen up for the game. There was an eruption of applause and noise makers and horns from both the US and Australian fans as their favorite players came into view, with shouts and screams and whistles for their heroes.

"Jill's always a favorite," hollered Clancy over the cacophony of noise as Jill Thompson raised her hand in acknowledgment to the roar of appreciation from the stands. "She's always known how to work a crowd, that girl. Classy as they come." Clancy's smile widened as her niece appeared, her tall, languid form stretching itself out in a shuffled trot toward the box with her two backup keepers in tow. The woman shot to her feet, screaming and waving her arms overhead, and Catharine rose to stand beside her.

Toward the end of the pack Molly Rodrigues, Abby Sawyer and Alex all came out together. The noise was already ear-piercing, but still it managed to pick up an extra decibel and Clancy jarred Catharine with her elbow, a broad grin across her face. "That's for Alex, Mrs. Cleveland. God help us, we love each and every one of them—but that—" she waved an arm to gesture at the roaring stadium, "that's for her. Six goals, three assists, a Cinderella story to get here—they love her. She's earned every bit of this."

Catharine took in every detail of Alex's face on the giant screen broadcast at the end of the stadium. How strange it was to have someone talk to her about Alex with such familiarity, with such careless abandon. To link them together without the hint of reprimand or castigation. How good it felt. How different than ever before.

Alex offered a fleeting wave and reserved smile in acknowledgment of the crowd, but Catharine could tell from the tightness in her stride that she was overwhelmed. And who wouldn't be? Nearly a hundred thousand people, every eye on you, the expectations overflowing. Most of these women had experience at this level, had traveled this path before, but for Alex it was all new. Her teammates must have felt her hesitance, because Sawyer gave her a playful smack on her hip and Molly said something that brought a laugh, before the three of them jogged to their respective drill stations.

The crowd lulled and Clancy turned to Catharine, saying something about popping up to grab a beer and could she get her anything, but before Catharine could decline, another roar—more deafening than anything that had come before it—shook the stadium, this time from the Australian fans. A booming chant of *Aussie Aussie Aussie, Oi Oi Oi* broke out across all five levels of seating, air horns and drums interspersed, as a thunderclap of approval from the green and gold greeted the Matildas' captain who'd arrived late to the pitch.

Amelia Walker, unfazed and unflappable to the pandemonium, extended both arms in acknowledgment of the colossal welcome, and smiled an easy appreciation as she made her way across the pitch. She was no different here, amidst tens of thousands of voices screaming her name, than she had been standing in Catharine's study. Calm. Indifferent. Sure of herself. Moving into her drills, Catharine could see why her countrymen were so approving. There was a fluidness to her, an athleticism unparalleled by her teammates—by any player on the field, for that matter.

Catharine had seen her play for the Sirens on the televised games for the NWSL, but it was different, here, in person. Alex had told Catharine she thought Amelia was one of the greatest athletes to ever play the game, and it was obvious from the response of the crowd that even the Americans harbored respect for the Australians' unshakable captain.

"Traitor, if you ask me." Clancy said at Catharine's elbow. "Leaving our girls in the lurch like that to go back to the WSL. She had a good thing going with the Sirens. Erin never said much about her leaving, but I know it broke her heart. She really seemed to love Walker. All the girls did. Then she was just up and gone, no rhyme or reason. I'll be curious to see if they call that loan in after the cup. HEG spent a fortune on her. I can't imagine they mean to lend her out for too long. Though I imagine there'll be some bad blood in the locker room if she returns. No one likes a Judas."

"Call in the loan?" Catharine hadn't gotten the impression from Amelia that she had any intention to return to Oakland after the tournament. But it wasn't as if they'd discussed her future. "I thought they bought out her contract?"

"Oh, heaven's, no. Even the WSL wasn't willing to pay what HEG offered that Australian to come and play in America. She's on loan—that's all Erin could say. I doubt any of the players know the terms."

Across the grass Catharine watched the Matildas lunge and side step, same as the Americans were doing at the opposite end. What did it matter if Amelia returned to Oakland? It was ridiculous to dwell on it. She'd been Alex's best friend. It was her tutelage and coaching that had helped Alex get on the National team. It was her name that aided in filling the Sirens' stadium. She was good for the team and good for the league. And Catharine found it maddening her thoughts strayed to worry about any lingering effects of her relationship with Alex.

As the players retired to the tunnel to prepare for the start of the match, Clancy excused herself to get a drink and Catharine settled into her seat, reflecting on how different attending this game was compared to the few she'd been to the previous year.

Then, anonymity had been essential. The success of their fragile relationship had hung in the balance. They'd both had so much to lose. But today, as she sat in the open, so close to the pitch she could smell the grass, see the sun-kissed freckles on tanned faces, hear the voices of the players as they spoke amongst themselves, she knew they'd come full circle. There was nothing the world could take from them anymore.

"Come to celebrate Senator Cleveland's success at the RNC, Mrs. Cleveland?"

Catharine turned from her thoughts toward the familiar voice, somehow unsurprised to find Caleb Anderson staring down at her from the aisle. He held two beers in his hand and a smug smile on his lips, his eyes fixed on her in a manner she'd come to loathe.

"You and I clearly have varying opinions on success, Mr. Anderson. A contested convention is not what I'd deem victorious."

"Contested convention or not, reports have it the good senator will walk out with his party's nomination. No doubt you have some apprehension as to your choice of words last weekend. That gorilla in a suit is about to become the most powerful man in the world."

"November is a long way off, Mr. Anderson. Now, if you don't mind," she gestured toward the field. "Enjoy the match."

"Do you care to know what he Tweeted about you this morning, Mrs. Cleveland?"

Before she could respond, a woman in the row ahead of her turned in her seat, her attention on Caleb. "Shut up, ya dafty—the peanut gallery is that way." She chucked her thumb toward the nosebleeds.

"Excuse me?"

"Quit being a chav and move along." The young woman—from Newcastle—judging by the thickness of her Geordie accent, crossed her tattooed arms, unflinching under his glare.

"I don't know who you think you are—"

"Oh, I know who I am, marra. Half this stadium knows who I am. God knows I've played enough footy in it. But I know who you are, too—can't miss that pan face from your legendary proposal video—only you're even more of a proper doylem in person. Now, I've only got one leg, but I promise I'll still lamp you if you don't shut your cake hole and settle into your seat like a canny lad."

Several others sitting in the row beside her had turned to watch the exchange, amused at their friend's unabashed dressing-down of the boy. More footballers, Catharine imagined, based off their athletic builds.

For a moment Caleb tarried, appearing to consider pushing the matter, but Clancy had arrived in the aisle and was jostling her way past him, bumping into his arm and upsetting his beer. "Excuse me, son," she looked up at him expectantly when she'd settled, annoyed he was blocking her view of the field. "You make a better door than a window."

With a last indignant glance at Catharine, Caleb turned on his heel and stumbled his way through the crowd, taking a seat in the opposite row half a dozen chairs down.

"Sam Huntley," said the Geordie to Catharine, offering her hand. "Not a great admirer of yours, to be honest—but I'm a big fan of your girl, Grey."

Her girl. The acknowledgement came as enough of a jolt to diminish the personal insult. As unsettling as it was to again have a stranger junction her name with Alex, it was also becoming thrilling. That their names could fall into the same sentence—exist in the same world.

"Sam Huntley as in *thee* Sam Huntley?" Clancy gawked beside them. "Three World Cups, FIFA Player of the Year, Golden Ball winner, if I recall correctly?"

"Golden Boot, and two-time Player of the Year, but thank you."

"We're sitting amongst football royalty!" The Mississippian shook her head, bewildered. "Oh, speaking of royalty," she cradled her beer between her knees and held out a bag toward Catharine, "I felt like you might be missing something, Mrs. Cleveland."

Surprised by the offering, Catharine opened the bag and withdrew a white Jersey—the number eleven embroidered in the center and the name *GREY* in block letters across the back.

Smoothing it in her lap, her fingers traced the letters—the identical jersey Alex would wear on the field.

She thought about the reporters. The photographers. The fuel she would add to the fire if she were to put it on.

Do you care to know what he Tweeted about you this morning, Caleb had asked.

It wouldn't just be her she affected if she were to make such a blatant statement. She had Alex to think about.

Alex... who had told her she didn't need her to protect her. Who wanted her love—her support—more than anything else.

Catharine took a short breath, feeling the shift of excitement in the crowd as the stadium lights flashed, the two starting lineups preparing to take the field. Allowing herself no further hesitation, she pulled on the jersey over her blouse.

"Thank you." She looked toward Clancy, meeting the woman's warm gaze. She realized she meant it. She *was* grateful. Grateful for far more than the jersey—it was so much more than that.

The jovial woman laughed, her deep-set eyes twinkling with merriment, giving her a once-over from head to toe. "Now you're part of the team, Mrs. Cleveland."

"Catharine." She whispered as the Star Spangle Banner started, giving the woman's hand a squeeze. "It's just Catharine."

With the anthems sung, the two teams parted, ready to start the match. For just a fleeting moment, Catharine watched as Alex's eyes shifted in her direction, sweeping the stands.

Ninety thousand seats, filled to capacity, and she knew she was the one Alex Grey looked for. The face belonging to the name she proudly wore on her back.

Chapter Thirty-Five

Sprawled out on her stomach, her chin scuffed from her dive through the grass, Alex looked up to find the source of the cry of agony. She'd been clipped by heels she hadn't seen, but the ref wasn't looking in her direction.

Instead, a half dozen yards ahead of her, Kristin Salter lay on the ground, tangled with the Australian striker, Kali Erwin. The ball was trapped between them and Salty was pounding the heel of her palm into her thigh, grimacing in misery.

"Get off me, will you!" The US captain pushed the Australian aside, cradling her ankle.

"Bad?" Alex crawled a few feet toward her.

"Bad." Her voice was quivering.

They were a few minutes out from the half and both teams were exhausted.

The pace of the game had been blistering. Back and forth, pass after pass, a constant battle for possession. As the clock had ticked toward forty-five, the tackles had grown more aggressive, the risky runs doubling. Both teams wanted to spill first blood and go into halftime with the advantage.

Back on her feet, Alex waved to the sidelines for medical.

"I'm out." Salty stared at her in disbelief, her eyes glistening.

"Maybe it just needs to be stretched out? Or maybe they could tape it?" Alex knelt beside her.

"I heard it snap."

A quick look at the already swollen bulge of her ankle above her cleat confirmed the midfielder's fears.

As they waited for medical to trot with their gear bags across the field, Salty twisted her jersey in her hand, trying to combat the pain. Still, ever the captain, she turned her attention back to Alex.

"She's got the jump on you. You have to find space where she won't expect it." Sweat dripped down her brow, stinging her eyes, her cheeks growing paler.

Alex didn't have to ask her who she was referring to.

Amelia had been all over her, foiling her every action. Always one step ahead, she had been reading her like a playbook. Slightly stronger. Slightly faster. Slightly quicker to see space, handily disabling her every push with her indomitable defense. She knew her too well. She could read her too fast.

"You've got this, Alex. Just keep your focus."

It seemed wrong to Alex that she should be the one receiving the pep talk from the player who'd just had her ankle crushed on the field, but she was grateful for her captain's encouragement. Salty was right. Amelia was getting in her head. She had to find a way around her.

On the sideline the board went up for a substitution as Salty limped to the bench. Monica Ashby was taking her place, which meant Atwood was shifting to a heavier defense to get them out of the half.

Ashby had played less than sixty minutes since they'd arrived in England, sustaining a minor injury to her hamstring during the match against Sweden. She'd been medically cleared prior to the final and thrown a fit when she wasn't on the starting lineup.

With Salty out, however, Atwood knew the center back would be useful against Australia's relentless offense.

From the corner of her eye, as Alex waited for the restart, she could see Caleb standing in the stands, thumping his fists against his chest, wearing Monica's name and number on his jersey. "That's my girl," she could almost hear him scream, even though she knew it was no more than a figment of her imagination. It was impossible to hear anything over the blaring of horns and pounding of percussion. But she'd heard him shout the same thing wearing her jersey on countless occasions, and could now only cringe, drawing a linear image between him and a caveman.

The ball was dropped into play and scooped up by a Matilda. Eager to make her mark, Ashby rushed in to strip the ball, and ended up with a poor clearance off the thigh of the forward.

Alex knew, as soon as she saw the loose ball in the box, exactly what was about to happen.

Amelia'd always had an uncanny ability to find space, to capitalize on the smallest of mistakes. It was one of the things that made her so dangerous.

Half the field away, Alex could do little more than watch as Amelia trapped the ball with a single touch of her heel, and flicked it over the head of Rodrigues. With a single glance for Halsey's positioning, she turned her focus to the ball's descent and volleyed it with perfect confidence just beneath the crossbar.

There was nothing Halsey could do. She'd been left one-on-one with no defense, with the Australian uncontested less than a yard from the goal area.

The roar from the Australian fans felt like Alex had had the breath knocked out of her. She came to a walk at the top of the box and watched as Amelia was swooped up in her teammates arms, the stadium going berserk as they chanted the name of their hero.

Walk-er. Walk-er. Walk-er.

It was a strange feeling, watching a player she admired, a person she had loved, an instrumental shareholder in her own success—show off her unequaled skill and not be able to feel happy for her. To feel an overwhelming sense of frustration in its place.

She turned away, begging her mind to focus.

With one minute left in regular time, she jogged toward center with Valerie Sims and Monica Ashby on her heels.

"That bitch needs to be humbled," Ashby snapped to Sims, resetting for kickoff.

Alex wanted to snap back over her shoulder that the goal was a result of her poor clearance, but she held her tongue. It was neither the time nor place.

Shaken by the goal, the US shifted to defense, Atwood wanting them out of the half without any additional damage.

"Okay, okay," Jill Thompson clapped her hands together as the halftime whistle blew and they headed for the lockers. She'd taken over the captain's band from Salty and was trying to keep the team optimistic. "We'll get it back—the next half is ours."

Alex fell into step with Halsey, who was slow to come off the field. It was the second match in a row where they'd been trailing at the half, and she knew the keeper would hold the responsibility solely on her shoulders.

"I thought she was going to bring it to ground." Halsey kicked a dropped water bottle as she pulled off her gloves, ignoring the shouts and waves from the children leaning over the wall, screaming their names. "I should have known better."

"It wouldn't have mattered if she had. She would have just threaded it through another pocket. Ashby left you a sitting duck."

"Yeah," breathed Halsey, more shaken than Alex had ever seen her, "but I read her wrong. And now she knows."

"The only thing she knows," said Alex, her hand on her back, "is that she's up against the best goalkeeper in the world. Now pull the plug on your pity party and help us remind the Australians what we came for."

"Your pep talks are almost as good as mine," Halsey ribbed her, finding half a smile. "It would make my job a lot easier if you'd do yours and get one on the board... just saying."

Alex kicked her heel.

"Ow!" Halsey bumped her with her hip, her gaze sweeping across the sea of faces in the stands. "Looks like they're getting on good," she chucked her chin and Alex followed her gaze.

Three rows back along the center aisle, Alex picked out the profile of Catharine. She was turned toward Clancy, flashing her enigmatic smile, her laughter almost palpable. Alex willed her to turn her way—to catch her eye for just a second—but her focus was on the southern woman. The way Clancy was smiling back at her, the way her face was beaming, Alex knew exactly how she felt. Catharine had that way about her, making you feel like you were the most important person in the world, blossoming under her attention.

"There's not a soul alive who wouldn't love Clancy," Alex said as they got to the mouth of the tunnel.

"She practically had kittens when she found out she was going to be sitting next to Catharine Cleveland." Halsey's brow furrowed. "She's probably up there telling her I deserve a licking for letting that ball through."

Halsey's attention was called away to their goalkeeping coach and Alex paused for just a moment on the edge of the shadow. Looking back toward the stands, she found Catharine turned in her direction, and could feel her eyes on her. From the distance she thought she could see her smile, and offered a smile in return. For only a second she held that warmth—that look—before turning into the tunnel. Her focus needed to be elsewhere. But the weight of being down by one seemed, somehow, to lessen.

She was playing in the World Cup. Catharine Cleveland was in the stands to watch her. And there were still forty-five minutes of game left to right the score. How could life get any better?

Izzy Atwood's fire in the locker room had translated to the second half start on the pitch.

They hadn't come halfway around the world to lose. They had sacrificed their families. Their relationships. Their friendships. Their bodies. They had given thousands upon thousands of hours of time and commitment for this one ninety-minute dream. It was within their grasp, they just had to reach out and take it. They hadn't come here to go home empty-handed. Down by one was nothing. They had forty-five minutes to take it back.

Alex bolted down the field feeling invigorated. Amelia'd had her number, but two could play at that game.

Ceasing possession in an adjusted formation, the US hammered on Australia's defensive line. Within the first fifteen minutes they'd produced more opportunities than they had the entire first half.

In a poor attempt to slow down momentum, the Matildas' left back made a miscalculated slide tackle and tumbled Jill Thompson inches outside the eighteen. Before the ball had left Thompson's foot for the free kick, Alex could see its trajectory. Up, over the Australian wall, and into the corner of the net just out of the goalkeeper's reach.

A clean slate. A breath of life. Now, it was anybody's game.

Ten minutes later, back in their attacking third, Alex struggled to tune out jeering from the front row of Aussie fans. Thompson threaded the ball through a pair of defenders, finding Alex with ample space, but she second-guessed her shot, losing her scoring position, and was forced to chip the ball to Sawyer, who took the shot on goal.

For a triumphant moment Alex was certain Sawyer had put them ahead, but the goalkeeper's fingertips found just enough leather to tip the ball over the crossbar.

"You're not playing like you belong here," a voice whispered over her shoulder as the teams merged to take the corner. "You're better than that, Grey."

There was no chance to reply before the cross was taken and Alex lunged for a header, finding herself propelled to the ground by a Matilda defender as Amelia sprung for the ball and dribbled it toward Halsey.

A series of feints and impressive footwork, and Amelia was in the box before Alex had hardly regained her feet and started down the field. Once more unable to do anything beyond watch the play unfold, Alex saw Monica Ashby step up to challenge Amelia, before the Australian neatly tucked the ball through her splayed legs, rolling it into the net, out of Halsey's reach.

Getting nutmegged was humiliating under any circumstance, but even more so when a goal was involved. Had it been any other occasion, Alex would have enjoyed watching the steam emitting from Ashby's crimson-tipped ears. From the distance, Alex could tell Monica had flung some insult at Amelia, but the Australian only turned around and gave her a mocking round of applause.

The sting of the goal didn't last long before Sawyer lofted a dinker to score. Two-to-two with fifteen minutes on the board.

"Keep it clean, ladies!" The ref issued a second warning as the play grew chippier, neither team wanting to head to penalties.

Around the stadium the fans had shifted into overdrive, a chorus of voices drowning out the ability to hear any coaching instruction from the sidelines. The women were on their own, giving all they had to keep their dreams alive.

You're not playing like you belong here. The comment bounced around and around inside Alex's head.

Six goals. Three assists. She'd earned every second of her playing time. She deserved every minute on this pitch.

Fuck Amelia.

Setting up for an Australian corner kick, Alex kept up the line. If the ball was cleared by her defense, she'd have a jump on taking it down the field. Show her exactly how much she belonged here.

As the ball lofted through the air, Sims and Ashby marked Amelia, knowing she would be the intended target, looking for a hat-trick off her head. But as Alex watched the ball come down, she saw Ashby shift sideways, making a horizontal leap into the Australian captain just as her feet left the grass. There had been no intention of making contact with the ball. No intention beyond slamming Amelia to the ground.

Had Amelia been further off the goal line she probably would have just had the wind knocked out of her in the fall—maybe even maintained the chance of scoring. But instead, in her struggle to regain her balance, her head connected with the goalpost and she abruptly crumpled inside the mouth of the goal.

Frozen to her spot, Alex watched, horrified, as Amelia didn't move. Ashby was at once scrambling to her feet, waving her arms in defense as a yellow card was pulled from the official's pocket.

After what felt like an eternity, Amelia stirred, drawing her knees to her chin, her hands holding her head. Alex had seen her take endless falls, but none had ever kept her down. She wasn't a diver. She didn't believe in faking an injury to let the clock run out.

The ref was waving for the medical team by the time Alex approached the six yard box, slowly realizing the red flowing through Amelia's hands was blood gushing from a cut above her temple.

Halsey was on her knees beside her, along with a handful of players in yellow. Amelia's lips were moving, slowly turning up into her cheeky smile. Alex wanted to go to her—it felt wrong standing there, watching her on the ground—but she couldn't force her feet to move. Halsey was there. The Matildas were there. She didn't need Alex.

"You're a galah," Amelia said to Halsey as the keeper helped her sit up, blood streaming down her lips and teeth and dripping off her chin.

The Matildas' medical personnel arrived with a stretcher, which Amelia firmly waved off. She was reeling and trying not to show it. She wasn't ready to give in.

"Staple it."

The doctor shook his head. "It's not a good location."

"Just do it," she argued, using the hem of her sleeve to clear her vision, before struggling to her feet. She brushed off the hand he offered her, starting for the sideline. She knew she'd need medical clearance and to stop the bleed if she was going to return to the pitch.

"You're likely concussed," the doctor followed a step behind her, and the last thing Alex could hear was her telling him he was as worthless as tits on a bull and to staple the fucking thing.

Monica trotted past Alex, a smirk on her lips. "Oops," she simpered, and it took everything Alex had not to grab her and fling her to the pitch. A yellow card wasn't enough. Alex would have been more than willing to finish the game with a squad of ten for Ashby to have been ejected on a red.

It would have been right.

It was what the Matildas deserved.

A penalty kick was granted to Australia, but Alex had trouble focusing on the set up as she watched the sideline from the corner of her eye. There was an adamant argument between Amelia and the head coach, before the doctor was summoned with the stapler, and Alex forced herself to turn her attention back to the game.

No substitution was called and Australia moved into place to take the PK with only ten players on the pitch.

Sherry Brown was chosen as the kicker and Halsey settled into position to defend her goal.

Brown made a valiant feint and Halsey lunged the wrong direction, but the ball was over struck and sent up into the stands. Australia had missed the game changing goal.

Play continued, but it was immediately clear the Australians were shaken and discouraged. Alex knew Amelia never would have missed that goal.

Waiting for a throw-in, Alex saw Amelia had returned to the field, but her focus turned off her old teammate as she and Sawyer made a run down center, finding themselves with acres of space.

With the ball at her feet, this time Alex did not hesitate. The shot was hers. The game was hers. Izzy Atwood had told them to reach out and take it.

So she took it.

In the eighty-ninth minute of the World Cup final, Alex finally found the back of the net. A long range strike off her laces, a text book goal she knew had won the match. Seven Nation Army blared from the speakers and Rodrigues hoisted her onto her shoulders to present her to the crowd. Her name was chanted by thousands of strident voices as her mind raced a million miles an hour.

Australia was gassed. The US had the momentum. And the pitch shook with the thunderous applause from the stadium.

Alex remembered next to nothing of the stoppage time. Six minutes, a blur of cramping legs and screaming voices, eyes stinging with sweat. Amelia made one last cross to Brown, a final effort to tie the match, but Halsey made an easy save, and by the time she'd taken the goal kick, the three blasts from the whistle sounded. The World Cup in England was over.

The USA had won the match.

Alex had called the semifinal surreal, but in the next minutes of her life, she knew she hadn't yet known the meaning of the word. Emotions she never expected overcame her. Tears. Joy. Relief. Disbelief.

She struggled, even in her jubilation, to see the Matildas broken, collapsed on the field, faces covered, desperately trying to hide tears that fell freely. They still stood and shook hands, still offered congratulations, but her heart hurt for their loss, knowing it easily could have gone the other way.

"Well, I knew you had it in you."

Alex turned to face Amelia standing behind her. She looked exhausted, her left eye swelling shut, six staples along her brow. But she smiled when Alex offered her hand, and brushed it aside, pulling her into a hug. "I'm proud of you, Grey. If anyone was going to take it from me, I'm glad it was you."

"This was your game," Alex said, staring at their grass stained cleats when Amelia released her. "We both know, if—"

"Shut your gob, Grey." Amelia's hand squeezed her forearm, hard. "There's a million ifs in every match—it's part of the game. It's unpredictable. It's what makes it beautiful. And tonight—it was *yours*. Don't sell yourself so short—like I said, you're better than that." She released her arm and gestured around them. Her teammates were still running wildly around the pitch, covered in confetti and draped in American flags. The fans were on their feet, throwing everything from flowers to underwear on the field.

"Own this success, Alex. Listen to your fans. They know who got them here."

She winked, and gave her one last clap on her shoulder. "But don't get complacent—I'll be coming for you next year at the Olympics." And then she walked away, heading for the tunnels, where her teammates were slowly filing into the shadows.

Alex watched her retreating back before turning her face to the sky. The confetti was still pouring down from the blowers, the ground vibrating from the commotion in the stands, and all around her her teammates were hugging and laughing and celebrating.

Dazed, and a little overcome, Alex let herself sink to the grass, sitting in the center circle, breathing in a moment of solitude. Stopping to take it all in. Her elbows atop her knees, her chin propped against her steepled hands, she inhaled the enormity of the moment—and with her exhale felt the monumental release of relief. All the weights of her expectations. Her dreams. Her goals. Her self-doubts. They were there, sitting with her on the pitch.

"Grey!" The euphoric laugh of Erin Halsey pulled her from her meditation, but she turned to the goalkeeper with a smile, ready, finally, to join in the celebration. The bounding woman loped toward her with a jersey in her hand, swinging the shirt above her head as she lumbered to a stop. "Come on!" She hauled her to her feet. "Photos! Let's lift that cup!"

Alex pulled the "Champion" Jersey over her head, hanging back a moment more. "I'll be right there," she called over her shoulder, suddenly sprinting toward the sideline. There was something else she had to do.

Reaching the wall in front of section 125, Alex scanned the sea of faces —faces painted in red, white, and blue, kids waving homemade signs, outstretched hands begging for autographs or to exchange her jersey—but she gently waved them off for now. There would be time for all that later.

At last, along the aisle she found the one face she was looking for, the only face she wanted to see. Catching her gaze, she leapt onto the wall and pulled herself up to hang by her elbows. Catharine squeezed past the clamoring fans and met Alex at the rail, dropping to her knees so their faces were on the same level.

"Hey," was all Alex managed, meeting the deep blue eyes with a smile.

"You did it." Catharine clutched her hands, her face close to Alex.

"I could kiss you right now," Alex whispered, more in jest than anything else, still smiling so hard her cheeks ached.

"So kiss me, Alex." Catharine's eyes never left her own.

For a second Alex was certain she was teasing. They were surrounded by people. By media. By cell phone cameras and professional sport photographers and ninety thousand pairs of eyes following their every move.

But then it finally hit her—what did it matter? This was their moment. This was everything Alex had ever dreamed of and Catharine was the only person in the world she wanted to share it with.

This woman—this beautiful, perfect, extraordinary woman—was finally hers, and hers alone, with no one else standing in their way. No one else holding control over their lives. Commanding over their happiness.

Without allowing herself to think about it further, Alex hoisted herself up a little higher, her tired arms clinging over the side of the railing, and brought a hand to Catharine's neck, pulling their faces together. And with the entire world watching, she kissed Catharine Cleveland for the first time without the burdens of their past, and with only their future in mind.

Let the world see.

There was nothing left to hide.

ABOUT THE AUTHOR

Jen Lyon is an avid lover of sports, travel, theatre, and the ocean. When she isn't writing, Jen can be found sailing, browsing the shelves of her local bookstore, cheering ardently at an NWSL soccer match, or training horses at her Southern California horse ranch, where she lives with her wife, Donna, and their dogs and horses.

Follow Jen on IG @jenlyonauthor where she unapologetically spams her page with photos of her corgis, dachshund, horses and obscenely large Maine Coon cats.

COMING SOON BY JEN LYON

The Unfinished Line
Curse of Queens Trilogy
Let Them Burn

OTHER BOOKS BY JEN LYON

The Senator's Wife: Book I
Whistleblower: The Senator's Wife Series Book III

ACKNOWLEDGMENTS

This book would never have been made possible without the unfaltering, unequivocal, indefatigable love and support of my brilliant wife, Donna. My most devoted cheerleader. My tea steeper. My dedicated First Draft Reader. My muse. My rock. My best friend. Thank you for everything you do for us. Thank you for always believing in me. I love you.

To my mom, Melodie, who has read every word I've written since I was four years old. My toughest critic. My champion. The one who read me bedtime stories every night, filled my head full of marvelous tales, and taught me the power of the written word. Thank you for always encouraging me to keep on writing. I love you to the moon and back.

To Jesse, who puts up with all my midnight texts, last minute projects, zero-dark-thirty rants, and is simply an outstanding friend.

To Chelsea, for her patience, insane work ethic, and positively beautiful art. Thank you for taking on this adventure with me!

To my furry best friends, Piper and Josey Wales—who snuggled with me through a dozen rewrites, snoozed beneath my desk while I stared day in, day out at my computer screen, and kept me company in my office without a single woof of protest.

To my "circle." You guys have encouraged me. Loved me. Inspired me. Slapped me around when I have needed it. And held me up through thick and thin. I love you. You all know who you are.

To my dad, Jim—for your endless optimism.

To my sister, Lara—for sharing your passion of art, theatre, and everything that makes this world beautiful. Oh, and thanks for not dying last year!

And lastly, to the incredibly talented, brave, resilient women of the USWNT and NWSL. Thank you for everything you have done, not just for women's sports, but for women as a whole. For using your voices, your platforms, and the eloquence of the Beautiful Game to continue to lift women up and push through those glass ceilings. LFG ladies! LFG!

Printed in Great Britain
by Amazon